THE
CHOCOLATE
HEART

ALSO BY LAURA FLORAND

The Chocolate Thief

The Chocolate Kiss

The Chocolate Touch

THE
CHOCOLATE
HEART

LAURA
FLORAND

KENSINGTON PUBLISHING CORP.
www.kensingtonbooks.com

KENSINGTON BOOKS are published by

Kensington Publishing Corp.
119 West 40th Street
New York, NY 10018

All Kensington titles, imprints, and distributed lines are available at special quantity discounts for bulk purchases for sales promotions, premiums, fund-raising, educational, or institutional use.

Special book excerpts or customized printings can also be created to fit specific needs. For details, write or phone the office of the Kensington special sales manager: Kensington Publishing Corp., 119 West 40th Street, New York, NY 10018, attn: Special Sales Department; phone: 1-800-221-2647.

ISBN-13: 978-0-7582-8634-5
ISBN-10: 0-7582-8634-1

First Kensington Trade Paperback Printing: December 2013

10 9 8 7 6 5 4 3 2 1

Printed in the United States of America

First electronic edition: December 2013

ISBN-13: 978-0-7582-8635-2
ISBN-10: 0-7582-8635-X

CHAPTER 1

She walked in, blond, small, tanned, smelling of monoï, the tiare-infused coconut oil from the islands. Luc recognized the scent because he smelled and tasted everything that passed through his hands, good or bad.

It wasn't a policy he usually applied to people, but . . . she looked like someone a man wouldn't mind tasting, certainly. A sun goddess you might pick up off a beach on a tropical escape, feel the sand sticking to her skin when you made love to her, shake it out of the sheets in the morning with a smile on your face.

Or so he imagined. He had never escaped to a tropical island, not even once, but his ability to imagine—and realize—impossible things was world famous.

She looked tired, around-the-world-in-eighty-days tired, with a pinch around her eyes that went beyond jet lag. But when she looked up and met his eyes, she pulled out a smile so bright it was several minutes before Luc realized she had no idea who he was. She hadn't recognized him. She had just seen the symbol of the hotel under his name on his shirt and thrown him the same bright smile she would have given anyone.

So right from the start there was a problem. A conflict within him, perhaps. Luc knew with certainty that she had arrived on the edge of nerves and exhaustion. That she needed tolerance and compassion.

Yet he couldn't quite forgive her for that split second when he had fallen for that bright smile, and it hadn't been for him.

She probably thought he was the bellboy.

That was one hot bellboy, Summer noticed. Standing near the polished mahogany reception desk, framed by marble columns, light glimmering on his face from a gold chandelier. *Welcome, Madame, to your mausoleum.* Although doubtless *he* thought this place was a gorgeous palace.

Black-haired, probably about thirty, the man curled like a whip around her attention and yanked it to him.

How? She hadn't slept more than ten hours in the past four days, some of which she had spent hanging sick over the side of a cargo ship. How could he wake her up enough to notice him? Even if he was gorgeous, radiating sculpted, precise elegance, with a perfect, coiled tension in him. Tall and lean and lovely—and watching her.

Maybe someone at the hotel had checked out her dating history, figured out her type, and placed him there to keep her distracted and malleable.

How thoughtful of them.

She smiled at him because she was almost never too far gone to smile at someone as if he was special. The gift cost her nothing, certainly not any iota of herself, so why be stingy with it?

The bellboy, or whatever he was, stood perfectly still, a hotel logo embroidered on his stylish white shirt, with an open collar and up-to-the-minute cut. For a moment the power of his presence forced every detail on her: a honed, startlingly handsome face, the copper tone of his skin, the black hair, the black eyes that fixed her as if he had just spotted water in a desert.

"Monsieur." She put a hand on his wrist, smiling up at him, and a little flick ran up that matte skin. Great. She definitely needed a man who was putty in her hands right now; she didn't have the strength for anyone who could resist her. "Could you show me to my room, please?"

Tricky, for a bronze statue to stiffen further, but he managed it. Maybe not such putty after all. Wow, his eyes were so . . . intense. Greed kicked through her, a desire to grab that intensity and wallow in it. *Mine, mine, all mine.* God, she must be out-of-her-mind tired.

"I think you have me mistaken for someone else," Gorgeous said with distinct hauteur. He kept cutting his way through every blurring of her brain, the one clear thing in her fatigue. He looked like a Greek god. A real Greek god, not those heavy-lipped marble things. Born out of Chaos, hardened by fire, ready to go fight some Titans.

"*I'm* Summer Corey," she retorted firmly. Top that, Greek God. "Come on. Here." She dove into her purse and came up with a handful of fifty-euro bills, fresh from the airport distributor, and lowered her voice as she pressed them into his palm. "Just get me to my room before anyone else realizes I'm here, okay? I need a nap."

"A nap."

Preferably in a hammock on the beach, but she wasn't going to get that. She was going to get some opulent bed that gave her hives. "I promise I won't let you get fired for sneaking me in."

Black eyebrows went up. "I promise you I won't be fired."

Oh, for God's sake, couldn't he take extravagant tips for discreet favors to rich clients gracefully? He was working at the top hotel in Paris, for crying out loud. Maybe she was going about this the wrong way. "I *am* Summer Corey." As in, the person who could do the firing, so stop arguing and get moving. Before she just fell over into his arms. She swayed a little at the thought of someone lifting her, carrying her, taking her away from all this.

"Congratulations." He left his hand open so that the bills scattered over his feet. "I'm Luc Leroi."

If she had had one iota more energy, she might have gasped and genuflected, just to subvert his arrogant tone. *Le Roi,* the King. She hadn't forgotten any European princes her mom was trying to set her up with, had she? No one came to mind. "So what are you king of?" she asked him with a little grin, which she was pretty proud of. Not everyone could pull out friendly grins for indiscreet bellboys when she felt ready for her own funeral.

His lips parted as if he had taken one to the gut, and his eyes went obsidian.

"Here," he said finally, with an edge to his voice. "Welcome to my kingdom, Summer Corey."

That couldn't be right. According to her father, this was *her* kingdom now. Her parents had always had trouble telling the difference between what might be their daughter's fairytale kingdom and her own personal hell. She curled her hand around his arm and leaned into him confidingly and then had a hard time not just letting him take all her weight. He took a soft, sudden breath as her body got close to his. Oh, yeah, so maybe he would like having her weight plastered to his body. She swayed just a bit more into him. "Here's some advice. When the owner of 'your kingdom' asks to be discreetly shown to her room, it's probably a good idea to help her out if you want to keep your throne. No matter who you think you are."

His eyes glinted. "That's thoughtful of you. The advice. Can I return the favor?"

Hard arms swept her off her feet and up against his chest, one arm under her legs, the other her back, the iron grip shocking her. He moved so fast it took her brain a few seconds to catch up and realize he had just saved her from this cold marble hall. And longer still to realize that she was probably supposed to be alarmed that he'd caught her, not overwhelmed with relief. Her body wanted to go limp as a rag doll.

"If you think your daddy's buying a hotel makes you queen of it, you might want to do some research on your new subjects before you come sweeping into your queendom. Thierry, mademoiselle's key."

A young man gaping at them from behind the mahogany desk blinked at the crisp command, fumbled, and finally slipped a card into Luc's fingers.

Black eyes glittered down at her. "And you might want to know a little bit more about a man before you ask him to escort you to your room." Her captor strode into the nearest elevator and dipped her enough to press a button without loosening his grip.

Summer stared up into night-black eyes as the doors shut them in. *Never get caught with a strange man by yourself in an elevator.* Especially if that strange man has literally grabbed you off the floor and hauled you into that elevator.

Oh, what the hell. It was better than being clawed to shreds by rage and loneliness and anxiety. She laid her head down on his shoulder and went with it.

His fingers spasmed into her, a tiny, quickly controlled pressure. His chest moved in a long breath under her cheek.

A strong shoulder. She curled her face into it, concentrating on the male strength and delicious scent of him. Such a strange, complex mixture of scents, whispers and promises of the entire world. Her eyes closed, tension draining out of her body.

His fingers flexed into her again, gentler, longer.

Good. He wasn't going to drop her. That was about all she needed to know at this point. She snuggled her face against his muscles, her mouth curving faintly as she drifted toward sleep.

The elevator's stop and his long, smooth stride as he left it nudged her awake again. Why was he walking so fast? Was he really carrying her off?

Her heart beat harder, adrenaline trying to break through her fatigue. She told her adrenaline to shut up. She liked this, plunging into erotic danger just where she had thought to be buried in deadly, merciless elegance. Kidnapped by a gorgeous stranger—you couldn't ask for a better distraction than that.

She wondered what he was planning to do with her, and how much she might like it. The muscles of his chest and abs flexed hard against her as he walked. It had been three years since anyone had held her, and he smelled so good.

Dimly, she grasped that fatigue and emotional stress had sent her right off the deep end, but she had no strength left to haul herself back up into a sane reaction. Besides, the scents in his shirt lured her like a fairy story. There, that vivid freshness, like strawberries growing in a wood, peeking under leaves. There, a crisp, bright, almost stinging scent, like limes gleaming on a tree in the sunlight. There, something rich and opulent she could sink into, curling up and letting its darkness velvet over her.

Her thoughts skated over the lean, hard muscles against which her body rested as he inserted her room card into the lock. She buried her face extra tightly in his shoulder to shut out the room. Goddamnit, but she hated hotels. Hated them with an intense and utter passion that made her want to scream their walls down—scream herself free.

Please don't leave me alone in this hotel. An irrational plea.

He set her down on the bed. For a second his arms caught under her, his body low over hers. Her eyes flickered open to his face, close enough that it was the only thing in the world she needed to see. "What's your name again?" she asked fuzzily. Probably best to know, since she was about to let him do whatever he wanted to her. Later, who knew, she might regain sense and have to track him down and punish him for taking advantage of her collapse. Find out if he had a deadly disease, or if she should acknowledge his paternal rights, or . . . *Shut up, brain. Let me just go with this.*

His mouth compressed so hard she only then realized how much it had softened in transit. "Luc Leroi," he said, like nails into her brain. "It's on my shirt." He picked up her hand and drew her index finger over the first swirl of the L. "Here. Maybe you're a kinetic learner."

The shirt had a thick, tough texture, almost like an apron, not the usual silk-cotton blend. The thick, high-quality embroidery slid under her finger, the looping curve, the smooth fabric of the shirt, the muscles underneath. Down and around the loops of the L, the gentle wave of the U, curl the C, another L. She kept going after he stopped moving her hand, kept tracing the letters.

The hardness melted slowly from his face, his mouth softening, his eyes growing more intense. Maybe it was just her brain blurring.

As her focus faded, his sharpened. The thought of being at the center of that focus lured her like the one bright light deep in a tangled forest. No. Like the possibility of *being* the one bright light in a dark forest, of sinking into its depths and secrets, of being held as its one pure heart.

She took a breath. How did you keep a focus like that on you? Men with focus never focused on her for long. Luc, the king of something. Kings could be bought. Her dad did it all the time. If she bought him, then he would owe her his focus, right? She could pack him and his scents up with her and take him with her to her island. Clearly, he was worth more than a few bills from her purse, though, and he wanted her to know it.

"I could give you a Bugatti," she murmured to the fold of his shirt, because she couldn't keep her eyes open. Wait, what was she talking about? What use would a Bugatti be to him on that island? "Or a yacht."

His hand closed over her shoulder, hard enough to hurt. *"What?"*

She brought a hand to his, pushing at that painful grip, and he released her as if she stung, straightening away.

Well, damn. Her eyes flickered open enough to notice he looked furious. Gorgeous fury framed by the opulence of gray and rose silk draping above the bed.

Fuck. She threw her arm over her eyes—the next best method of shutting out the world she had been thrown back into. Apparently, being hauled off by a Greek god wasn't going to work out for her. The cold loneliness of the hotel room laughed, stretching little evil fingers toward her. *I'm going to get you.*

Maybe it was confusing the Greek god for her to keep trying to bribe him that way. You would have thought a god would be used to being offered tribute, but maybe not. She was slaphappy, wasn't she?

"I'm really tired," she said suddenly from under her arm.

A tiny silence. *"Oui, j'ai vu."* He sounded as if he was in some kind of pain.

A strong sure hand closed over her calf, and deft fingers released her sandal. Those same strong fingers hesitated and then closed briefly around her toes, wrapping them in warmth. "And freezing," he said low.

Maybe he could warm her up. She peeked out from under her arm hopefully. He gave her an incredulous, hard look and released her toes. Damn.

His hands flew. Faster than she could quite follow, he

had her other foot bare and the comforter folded over her so that she was wrapped up in it like a gourmet hot dog.

And would have to warm herself up with her own reflected body heat. Damn it.

"How do you know I'm tired?"

He sighed. "It's obvious, *soleil*. Do you think I carry every beautiful brat who walks in and tries to buy me?"

He turned toward the door. Cold and loneliness rushed toward her, ready to fill all the void left when he abandoned her.

Beautiful. If you dropped the "brat," that sounded promising. "So you'll get back to me on the yacht?" she asked wistfully, just before the door closed on him.

CHAPTER 2

He still felt dizzy from it the next morning. Almost sick with it. Like some sweet little beauty had stroked her hand down his body, curled it around his dick, and then slapped the fucking hell out of him.

He wasn't into that. He liked the stroking, craved its sweetness, but he didn't want anyone beating on him in careless self-absorption.

The beauty of her, like a ray of sunlight breaking through the clouds, falling into a cold dark place he thought no sunlight could touch. And then he reached out and realized he couldn't catch sunlight. It could glide over his hands, blithely, indifferent to him, but he couldn't hold it in his.

He had been so convinced, in that first moment, that she was drawing on all her strength to keep that sunlight bright. That she needed him to sweep her up in his arms, rescue her from a dragon, carry her into his castle and keep her safe.

And all she wanted was to tip him for carrying her bags. Worse than every other woman whose beautiful, golden worlds he had ever longed for from the incredible distance of the other side of an upturned hat held out in the Métro. At least the golden, glossy women who used to flick him raw with their indifference in the Métro were probably working for their money. Back then, when they had seemed at the very top of his world, he couldn't even imagine women like Summer Corey, who had limousines to take her places.

He should have left her in that marble and mahogany lobby. Walked off, with her money swirling in a little eddy on the floor. But tangled with his pride and rage had been, *still,* the ridiculous desire to save her.

Well, he had cracked. He had saved her because he just couldn't leave her there, dripping money, crumpling from exhaustion, and acting as if he was worthless.

For a moment it had seemed to work. Nothing like kidnapping a woman to make her notice you. She had curled into him, pulling his soul out of his middle with each deep breath she drew against his shoulder.

Until he was melted all over again, helpless with it, ready to kneel at her feet to take her shoes off like Prince Charming, stroke her hair back off her face, lull her to sleep.

And she offered him a fucking yacht. Like her next potential gigolo. *Bordel.*

Sketches lay beside him, a pile of ideas that had kept kaleidoscoping through his brain all night, as if his finger had been thrust into some creative electric outlet. His skin hummed with tension, it shivered on the edges of his teeth, and he kept wanting to take one firm bite of her just to soothe it.

He had finally started sketching out the ideas at four a.m., when it became clear he wasn't going to get any sleep. His back teeth clenched at how fragile the ideas were, so full of sunshine in darkness, so utterly lacking a proper layer of tough cynicism.

But now, as he formed a dark, curving shape out of chocolate, reminiscent of a cupped hand, the muscles of his jaw slowly unclenched. He relaxed into his power.

She had never heard of him? And she was coming to

him after years away from civilization, where her only sweets were probably coconut juice? It was almost embarrassing to target her, she was going to fall so easily.

He smiled. So easily. All her sunshine, yielding to him in a generous rush as if he was impossible to resist.

Her eyes were going to grow wide with wonder, her mouth was going to soften helplessly in longing, and she would never again press careless money into his hand without *seeing* him. As if he was a child sent down the seats of the Métro with his hand held out and his head hung low, sullenly waiting to see if he had danced well enough for the polished, lofty commuters to glance at him. No. Nobody dismissed him now.

"Well, somebody couldn't sleep." His senior *adjoint,* or sous-chef, Patrick Chevalier, stopped in front of the bulletin board to pin up a newspaper photo of Luc kidnapping a beautiful blonde, his face wild and feral. *L'Été revient,* read the title. Summer returns. Right above it was the guiding quote Luc had put up for his kitchens: "Everything beautiful comes from control."

Luc clenched his teeth harder.

Patrick tilted his head to study the effect of that photo under that quote, grinned in complete self-satisfaction, and came to nod at the sketches and the chocolate sphere into which Luc was carving holes. "Have I been inspiring you again?" The younger man reached up as he spoke to pull plates off the wall and lay them out for prep.

"Endlessly," Luc said dryly, easing the chocolate from its mold and trying to figure out how he was going to get that photo off his bulletin board without giving Patrick the satisfaction of knowing how much it got to him.

Instead of beginning a subtle Japanese pattern of gold dust and cocoa powder on the plates, Patrick leaned his hands on the marble counter and gave Luc a bright, expectant look. Patrick always looked—and acted—like a surfer, all bronze-haired and half-shaved and goofy, with a lithe, relaxed way of moving, but his work was brilliant, so Luc put up with him. Fine, actually, he liked him, and it was going to be a severe wrench when Patrick abandoned the nest to set up his own place. As he would be doing any day now, probably. Patrick was ready to fly.

The very idea made Luc more brooding, more bitter. He could just sink into this fucking nastiest winter in history and never have any sunshine in his life, anywhere, how about that?

"And here I was thinking you came in on time to get to work," Luc said.

Patrick made a *pffing* gesture with one hand. "I've got more important priorities going on here, *mec. Gossip.*"

"You know I don't gossip, Patrick. Especially about myself."

Of course, Patrick ignored that. Patrick had a real gift for ignoring things and still managing to come out ahead. "I heard you carried off a *princess.* In your foul clutches and everything."

"Foul?"

"Well, your obsessively clean clutches, but admit it doesn't have the same ring. Is she as pretty as they say? Can I come rescue her from your fell dungeons?"

"I'm sure she's comfortable in them." An image flashed through his mind of her wrapped in that heavy silk rose comforter like some princess's sleeping bag, her lashes drifting down over the circles under her eyes. His idiotic heart squeezed. Should he have walked out and left sunlight unguarded that way?

Sunlight didn't need protection, he reminded himself. It was a huge gas ball millions of miles away, and no one could hurt it, or even threaten it. Best practices for dealing with sunlight involved a lot of sunscreen and mini-mizing exposure.

A little shiver ran over his left pectoral in the shape of his name. Traced through a thick shirt by a slim, raw-nailed finger. He didn't want to minimize exposure. He wanted to invade her body and her mind with everything in him and have her close around him in welcome.

"Yes, but *pining*," Patrick said enthusiastically. "Pining for a prince to rescue her from the evil sorcerer king. Or should I think of you more as the Lord of Hell?"

"Patrick." Luc placed one hand flat on the marble, stretching out his fingers. Callused, they held the long, lean elegance one might expect from a pianist, and even more strength. Piano keys didn't weigh very much, and even the best piano players didn't practice sixteen hours a day. "These are not clutches."

Patrick grinned and placed his own hand beside Luc's, inspecting them. Patrick's palm was squarer, the tips of his fingers broader, the hair on the backs of his hands golden. Both men's hands could play cat's cradle with a bit of hot sugar and spin it into a net to toss over a dream.

"Don't kid yourself," Patrick said. "That's an evil sor-cerer hand if I ever saw one. Look at that black hair. I'm pretty sure the golden boy gets to be Prince Charming. Plus, you're mean."

"Making you redo a screwed-up job is not mean, Patrick."

"And you're so *controlled*. That's got to be an evil sor-cerer trait."

"I thought evil sorcerers got to act on insane rages with wild, diabolical laughter." He had always been a little jeal-ous of evil sorcerers, in fact.

"You watch too many Disney films at one in the morn-ing," said the person who was inventing a fairy tale with an outrageous wave of his hand. "I'm quite sure real evil sorcerers are excessively controlled." He gave Luc a pointed look. "Just speaking from my personal experience about how evil that feels to the rest of us. Which makes last night's gossip all the more interesting," he added, exaggerating his manner like a dog enthusiastically salivating over something juicy. "I heard she cracked that control like a raw egg."

Luc gritted his teeth.

Eggs slipped into Patrick's hands as smoothly as a magician's trick and cracked neatly into a pan, deep golden yolks glowing. "I need to get her to tell me her secrets." Patrick smiled smugly down at the whites already starting to cook over the gas burner.

Luc gave the pathetic eggshells lying on top of the nearest trash can a hard look. "There's no secret, Patrick. It has to be all over the hotel. She tried to tip me to carry her bags to her room." It wasn't in his nature to confide in anyone, but there were some things that rankled too much even for him.

Patrick's mouth dropped open. "She did wh—? *Putain!*" He gave his head a stunned shake. *"Merde. Bordel. You?"* As he thought about it some more, a grin slowly rose through his first shocked sympathy, and he started to laugh helplessly. "Sorry, Luc. *Pardon.* But since you think you're God, there's a side to that that's pretty damn hilarious."

Luc gave Patrick a narrow look, then dipped his head to focus on his work and allowed the hidden corner of his mouth to curl. "I do not *think* I am God," he said with deliberate emphasis.

Patrick grinned. "That's why I worship you, *mec*. There's really no question as to your godhood. Now allow one of your humble acolytes to rid you of this rude princess. I'm *sure*, if she's as pretty as everyone is saying, that I could take care of her for you."

The half smile disappeared off Luc's face. "Patrick. Stay

away from Summer Corey, or I'm going to be lord of your own personal little hell."

Patrick's tawny eyebrows flicked up a little. *"Sérieuse-ment?"* He slanted Luc a vivid glance as he set the perfectly fried eggs on a custom-designed fifty-dollar white plate and, with one deft flick of his wrist, slid it ten feet down the marble counters to stop precisely in front of their intern, Sarah, just beneath the cutting board she was about to set there. Sarah Lin, the American who had abandoned her engineering career to train in French pastry in Paris, stiffened, that perpetual self-pressuring crinkle of her eyebrows relaxing just for a second in surprise. Her eyes flew to Patrick's back. Patrick never even glanced over to see her reaction, already prepping plates again. "What an interestingly villainous thing for you to say." He gave Luc a fond pat on the shoulder. "Not that it would change anything: You already are, *mec.* You already are."

A weight lay on Summer's sleep like a heavy, warm body, and whenever stress tried to prickle her awake, she just snuggled into that heavy warmth and sank back into the depths of sleep, oddly cosseted.

When she woke, she couldn't remember where she was. No sound of waves, no smell of tiare, no humid heat.

She opened her eyes and stared straight at the Eiffel Tower. Serene and dark against a gray sky, framed by the foot-wide silver scrollwork of the perfectly placed picture window.

Oh, it's you, Summer realized. *Oh, damn it, you got me again.*

What was it with this city that made parents think it was such a perfect place to get rid of their kids? The trashcan of the rich and famous.

She rolled on her back so she didn't have to look at the

gloating iron bitch through her window anymore and instead got a sumptuous view of the heavy rose and pearl-gray silk drapes over the embroidered headboard. Even though she closed her eyes, her inevitable glimpses of the room seemed to ripple its image around her, as if she was a pebble lost in it: the heavy silk and embroidery of the cushions and art deco chairs, the muted, elegant rose-and-gray tones, the perfect mahogany wood floor.

She threw her arm over her face. Images flooded her mind, shell leis thrown on the water so she would come back, her father's hard determination when he had kicked her out of paradise, her mother's laughing refusal to understand, all her schoolkids. And black eyes looking down at her, a firm sculpted mouth softening.

Her eyes widened under the shelter of her arm, her lashes tickling her skin, as she remembered that mouth. Her own mouth softened helplessly, hungrily. She scrubbed both hands over her face abruptly, dashing the softness away. What had she been thinking?

She wanted to get back to heat and sea and happiness. She did not want to get caught in some Greek god's toils and be stuck here.

It was probably just as well that he was likely to sue her for sexual harassment. It was probably just as well that he had turned on his heel and left her, burning her with his contempt. It was probably just as well that Greek gods had a lousy reputation for cuddles. A woman could get in real trouble with a man who knew how to cuddle when she was stuck in an elegant hotel room in the unhappiest place on earth.

She climbed out of bed and went into the bathroom.

Where 180 degrees of glass displayed her like a sacrificial virgin to Paris, spread out below her. Who thought up these things? Even if you could trust no one to be out there with a telescope, who wanted to take a shower with the Eiffel Tower looking down her nose at you?

She gave the Eiffel a silky, sweet smile. *Fuck you. My water is warm at least, and you're out there getting drenched in forty-degree rain.*

The Eiffel Tower kept glowing as if she didn't give a damn what Summer thought of her, which she never had. Meanwhile, all of Paris condensed itself in Summer's imagination into one black-haired, beautiful, naked man looking down at her own naked body with some hauteur, and she felt her nipples peak.

Great.

Summer turned her back on both the Eiffel and that imagined beautiful man, but then just felt as if both were watching her naked wet ass, with a little critical moue: *Pas mal.*

She had never considered herself an exhibitionist, primarily because she wasn't that introspective. So desire hit her so hard and so fast that she had to curl her hand around the showerhead, stunned by its impact: Desire to have somebody pushing her back against that shower wall, a human shield, blocking the world out of her mind even while she thumbed her nose at it. Protecting her and taking her.

The body that pushed her back was golden, the hair dark, and that shouldn't have scared her, since her fantasy lovers always had matte skin and black hair, gorgeous Polynesian sea-gods.

But this man was a stranger, with a face forged by fire and cool dismissive eyes. She squeezed her eyes shut tight on her own fantasy, blurring his face in her brain, something that forged face resisted adamantly.

Let him just stay a stranger. Okay? Nothing wrong with the sex-with-a-stranger, exhibitionist shower fantasy, was there? She could guarantee she wouldn't be the first woman to indulge in it.

And the nice thing about a fantasy was she could dismiss *him* when she wanted to.

CHAPTER 3

When Summer got out of the shower, a linen-lined basket of golden *financiers* sat on the table like a gift of sunshine. One of the little gestures to welcome guests, no doubt. The buttery fresh scent drew her, heat from them caressing her outstretched palm. She started to touch one, oddly consoled against the vista of cold, rainy Paris misery, when there was a knock on the door.

"Summer!" Her mother flung her arms around her, but peeled almost instantly back to get a good look at her. Scent flowed around Summer, not one she recognized. Once, as a child, Summer had snuck into her mother's bathroom and tested out every perfume in her cabinet so that she would know what her mother might smell like the next time she saw her. It hadn't worked. Too little to use tissue as testers instead of her own skin, she had ended up, toward the end, spraying little bits on each toe, having run out of all her other body parts, trying to keep the different perfumes apart. Her mother still laughed about the cacophony of scents when she told the story to friends. "How I wish I could have taken a picture of *that!* She had such a headache afterward, too, poor sweetie."

Not that Mai Corey had ever realized why her daughter had done it. Summer had gotten this idea she might need to find her mother in a dark maze and was trying to practice.

"A spa." Her mother touched the corners of Summer's eyes. "We've got to get that sand scrubbed off you. Honey, you're going to need more than just exfoliation if you keep this up." She double-checked the corners of her own eyes and smiled with relief. Summer had been told many times that she and her mother could be twins. But today anyone could tell them apart by Summer's too-tanned skin, her ragged, sun-bleached hair, her rough nails. "And *what* are you wearing?" her mother asked incredulously of Summer's cotton, hibiscus-printed blue sundress and bare feet. "Oh, Summer." Her eyebrows crinkled for a moment in pure confusion. "Thank *goodness* your father finally figured out a way to get you off that island."

"I don't want to be off the island," Summer pointed out. "I'm happy there."

"Summer. You told me yourself when we flew out there that you didn't even have a boyfriend. How could you possibly be happy? Now come on, we've got four years of shopping to make up for, honey, before tonight's gala." Her mother spread her arms and waltzed through the room. "Oh, honey, I'm so *happy* to see you back in Paris again. This is going to be *fun!*"

"Maman." American by birth, just as her husband and daughter were, Mai Corey had always asked Summer to call her "maman." *So much more elegant.* Summer took a slow, purposeful breath, the way she had been training herself to do, and tried something she hadn't tried in a long time—honesty with her mother. "You do realize that I feel like I'm dying when I'm in Paris, don't you? I hate it here."

Her mother paused in front of a mirror and gave her daughter a crinkled, worried look in it. Then she laughed. "Oh, Summer, what am I going to do with you? You are so spoiled. How could you possibly not be happy here?" Swooping up the basket of *financiers,* she upended them merrily in the trash. "Although you have to watch out!" she laughed, grabbing Summer's arm and heading her out the door, with a pinch of her waist. "Those chefs here will get you if they can."

"You found them in the trash?"

Frederic winced and tried to look away from the empty basket Luc held in his hands. "You did ask," he muttered.

"All of them," Luc said very evenly. "All of them in the trash."

The little basket of sunshine he had sent for her to discover as—what, exactly? He didn't know how to say it in words, only with *financiers*. Little golden cakes that said things like *I'm sorry for leaving you cold like that, here's some warmth.* Or, *This is golden and warm and real, and is it at all possible that your golden, warm smile is real, too?* Or, *Think of me. I'm thinking of you. Do I taste good?*

See, a basket of *his financiers* was so much more elegant and compelling than all those words. And a hell of a lot safer way to express himself.

The trash. His wrist flicked so that the empty basket landed hard on the room service cart as he turned around.

And straightened immediately at the sight of the man who had just come in through the back door, one hand slipping into his pocket, the other extending. "Monsieur."

His foster father, whose degree of self-containment even Luc had never been able to entirely emulate, gave the basket a look of restrained indignation. "Someone threw *your* financiers in the trash?"

"We get anorexic blondes from time to time." Luc made his voice bored. Although she hadn't felt anorexic in his arms. She had felt lithe and slender, a supple blend of muscles and softness, not bony. And she had felt tired and something else, clinging to him as if he was hauling her out of the depths of hell.

Bernard Durand shook his neatly cut, gray-brown head. "She would have to be very spoiled not to appreciate you." He gave his foster son that look that realigned Luc's reason for being, that made him want to jump through any hoop out there, a look that held a world full of tightly contained pride. "You want to show me that Victoire of yours? I saw you on TV last night, but the camera crew missed the most important steps. How did you do that one?"

Luc contained his surge of pride to a faint curve of his lips. "I'll show you." *Him* showing his foster father. He always loved that. The man who had showed and showed and showed a wild ten-year-old, a twelve-year-old, a hormone-crazy fifteen-year-old, sometimes making him do it one thousand painstaking times in a day, until he got it right.

"You'll come visit my new boys soon?" Bernard asked as Luc demonstrated the Victoire. "Show them what they can accomplish with a little discipline and focus? It's good for them to see you. Realize they can transition. Sometimes they were raised like animals. Well, you know."

Some rebellious streak in Luc's heart still wanted to argue that his biological father had tried to do a bit better than raise him like an *animal,* but he thought of the cats and dogs dragged around with people in the Métro to milk more money. Bernard would compare his father's use of him to that of those animals, and he didn't want to hear that.

"I've been busy," he said guiltily. It was a ninety-minute car trip out to the sprawling *banlieue* edge where his foster home was. An hour via the Métro and RER, if he could force himself to take it. Worse, every time he helped show this next generation of foster brothers what they could become via ruthless control and discipline, he felt . . . odd. Wrong. As if he should be modeling another way. Although what other way existed besides unrelenting control and discipline?

"And tonight I've got this gala. A thousand people to see the hotel handed over to Summer Corey. We'll have a dozen camera crews down here wanting a clip of us to add color to their coverage."

"Of you, you mean." Bernard didn't smile his pride, but Luc could feel it. Could lap it up.

"And with the new owner, things might be crazy for a bit."

A new owner who thought Luc was a bellboy. And was going to pay for that by letting her soul float as soft as a golden snowflake down to rest in his hands.

A delicate operation, to hold a golden snowflake in one's hands. But he knew all about delicate operations. It was just a question of the utmost control.

Cameras flashed as Summer's father squeezed her shoulders and announced the gift of the hotel. Summer yielded with a big smile for everyone, because what else was she supposed to do at this point? The media was going to be full of ghastly photos of her frowning otherwise, and then people would be calling her a spoiled brat.

Again.

No, this way, it made a lovely photo, her father framed by his beautiful wife and daughter. She was still a spoiled brat to all concerned, but at least she looked happy about it. Meanwhile, crisply attired, her father controlled the room as chair of Corey Holdings, one of the great financial movers and shakers of the world. Gray-haired, his face too angular, he didn't have Luc Not-the-Bellboy's beauty, but he held power in him and everyone gravitated to it.

Summer had, too, as a girl, though much good it had done her. Before she fled to a place where people liked her. Everyone had different goals in life and hers, it turned out, were love and affection.

Unfortunately, her father had just dragged her out of that warm place by her hair to try to force-feed her his own ambitions of money and control. Dragged her to the Leucé, one of the world's top hotels, with its Michelin three-star restaurant and its views of the Eiffel Tower. Her old home away from home.

Dad, you bastard. What kind of man forces his daughter to reign in her own personal hell?

She slipped away from him as the camera clicks slowed, dancing through the crowd. So many hands to clasp with delighted enthusiasm, so many people to promise she had not forgotten them, so many times to laugh and say, *Well, who wouldn't want to laze around on a South Pacific island?* So many times to meet a man's eyes with a warm smile as she passed, just warm enough that he thought she was going to approach and didn't react quickly enough to approach *her* before she wove on past.

Each glance calculating what a man could get out of her seemed to take a layer of skin with it, and she breathed deeply, trying to tap down into that golden core of island memories. For God's sake, anyone could get through three months.

The tip of a whip curled around her attention and she drew a quick breath, turning to discover her rescuer king from the night before nearby, watching her thoughtfully, a glass of white wine in his hand. Her breath went out with what felt oddly like relief, which didn't make any sense at all.

She wanted to hide her face in embarrassment, so she gave him her silkiest, sexiest smile. He tilted his head slightly, studying her smile as if he wanted to submit it for chemical analysis. He didn't smile back.

In the deceptively simple black pants and white shirt of a top designer, he exuded concentration and intensity and utter control, watching her approach with easy arrogance, in that whip's semblance of repose. Her breath shortened despite herself. To punish him for it she shifted discreetly, so that the silk of her dress slid over her body and glimmered in the light. Goosebumps rose on her arms as air-chilled silk slid against her skin. Paris was always too cold for her.

Luc Leroi sniffed his wine thoughtfully. The air smelled darker, within his personal space. Like somewhere she could curl up and be safe. "You really like your men tall, dark, and handsome, don't you?"

Yes, she supposed she had been rather obvious about that, when she'd offered him a yacht. "Now you're just being modest. I call you 'Gorgeous' myself."

A black eyebrow lifted slightly. His chin indicated the room. "They're the ones you flirt with the longest."

Did she really? She nodded solemnly. "They provide such a good foil." Desperate to unsettle him, she pulled a lock of hair free from its elegant coiffure and leaned into the wrist so near her head, wrapping the strand around it, a golden contrast to the dark hairs there. "See?" She smiled up at him, her cheek pressed against his forearm.

His eyes went pitch black, and one deep breath moved through his body. Sudden awareness of the strength in that forearm shivered all through her, not from fear but from a delicious knowledge of his control of it.

"It must do them good," he said. "To have worked and climbed all their lives so that some blonde can consider them a good foil."

She had spent five years in boarding school with a pack of other rich, abandoned, insecure girls, and she had defended herself in needling conversations against the best of them. "Well." She gave a rippling shrug that shivered her dress over her body and smiled at him again as she straightened, her lock of hair sliding slowly over his wrist and then dropping to graze her shoulder. The touch of her hair fresh from his skin raised more goose bumps on her arms, but she blended her shiver into the shrug. "Some people dream bigger than others." Implying that being her foil was the biggest dream a man could have.

"They certainly do," he said evenly. Implying something entirely different.

Yes, she always managed to go after the ones who dreamed so big she vanished in those dreams like a little speck of light.

She straightened away from him, saw a man beyond him shift subtly, ready to take advantage of the window if she started to move away, and stayed where she was, in that potential circle of his arm. He didn't seem to be feeling any urge to wrap her up in his darkness again, the way he had the night before. He must be pretty damn fastidious, to get so turned off by the offer of a yacht.

Too fastidious for her, clearly.

"Were you drunk last night?" she asked suddenly.

A long silence. ". . . Yes," Luc said finally.

In the darkness of his eyes, the image of herself in her silky pale slip dress danced like a tiny flame. "How much had you had to drink?" she asked suspiciously. He had smelled of everything but alcohol—chocolate and raspberries and sweat and citrus.

He touched the glass of wine to his lips, barely wetting them. The light from the chandeliers gleamed on the moisture left there. "How tired were you?"

"Four days. No sleep. Very bad seasickness."

He didn't seem to appreciate the fact that she had an excuse. If anything it annoyed him, but it was hard to tell from his controlled expression. "That explains a lot."

"You didn't answer my question."

The twirl of his wineglass in his fingers released a sweet, golden scent. "We opened a bottle of champagne. I had allowed an author to spend the day in the kitchens, for research, and she wanted to thank the team."

How much of the bottle could he have drunk, if it was split among a whole team?

"In the kitchens?" she said blankly. Hadn't he said he ruled this place?

An obsidian glint in an otherwise polite face. "I believe I did introduce myself to you last night." Another twirl of the wineglass. An edge crept into his voice. "I suppose you've forgotten my name."

She grinned at him. "Well, yes, but I never forget a beautiful face."

The glass stopped twirling so suddenly wine sloshed up its sides. Black eyes glittered.

"I'm just teasing you! Luc Leroi, see? I remembered."

His jaw tightened. "You flatter me."

"Do you want me to drop to my knees, your majesty?" She sparkled her smile right into his tense face.

His lashes veiled his eyes. The tiniest smile relaxed the tension in Luc's fine mouth. "Only if you like the position," he murmured.

Wait. Had he just—

"Mademoiselle Corey!" A voice pulled her attention to a tall, lanky man in his thirties with straw-colored hair and a certain geekiness to his face. Alain Roussel, the hotel director. They had met earlier, just hours before her father announced publicly that the hotel was now hers. "I see you've met Luc!"

Luc gave the other man a sardonic look.

"Again," Alain allowed lamely.

"It's like associating with royalty." Summer fanned herself. "It's going to my head to be on a first-name basis. Or am I presuming . . . ?" A teasing up-and-under look at Luc.

Alain nodded relieved approval. "It hits us all that way at first. But you'll get used to it."

What? "He's really king of something?"

Luc's expression remained flawlessly polite. She didn't know why she had the impression he wanted to strangle her. Alain looked appalled, but an older man drifting into the scene eyed Luc with slightly malicious amusement.

Alain Roussel gave Luc an apologetic grimace, which he doubtless thought was over Summer's head. Somehow, she had that effect on men—they dismissed the possibility she could have anything but looks and wealth. Luc was the one who recouped the moment, giving a wry, minute shrug of his shoulders to Alain, his self-possession today unshakeable. "I believe my grandfather might have been making a statement about Gypsies being the kings of the earth when he invented Leroi to fill out some form. No hereditary kingship, no."

Gypsies? As in colorful caravans and dashing black-haired adventurers, or a poor, wandering, much-despised population?

"Luc is our head *chef pâtissier*," Alain Roussel said stiffly.

Summer stiffened. Of course. Oh, yes, didn't that figure. He had been a dessert personified last night—so gorgeous and enticing, snapping himself out of her hands at the last second and leaving her to huddle in cold loneliness because she had said the wrong thing. Maybe he and her father had swapped notes on how to keep her in line. "Congratulations."

One black eyebrow rose minutely.

"Thanks," Alain said, throwing her off.

She glanced between the two men. Luc's mouth curved in a kind of edged amusement, as if underneath that curve he didn't find her ignorance in the least bit funny. "For being able to convince me to work here," he explained gently.

"He's *world famous.*" Alain stressed the words so hard they almost squeaked out of him. "He's the very best."

She tried to switch gears. "Sounds like the work of a great director—recruiting top talent and keeping it happy." She winked at Alain and stage-whispered: "Is he temperamental?"

"Not even remotely," both Alain and the older man who had come up said at the same moment.

"He's a perfectionistic bastard, though," admitted the older man, with considerable empathy.

Alain laughed. "Nothing but the absolute best for him."

Oh. So maybe she just wasn't good enough.

"I should think not!" her father exclaimed, joining the circle with her mother beside him. "He's the jewel in this crown I just gave you. Only two other hotels in Paris can claim a three-star restaurant, and it makes all the difference between the best and the would-be best. And *none* of their chefs draws the media he does. Don't you lose him, Summer. He's the reason I bought you this place."

"Oh, yes, he's wonderful." Her mother squeezed Summer's waist. "You'll have to watch your weight around this one. He'll get you, if you're not careful."

Luc's gaze flickered between Summer and her mother, and she just tried to bear it. *I'm not getting Botox so I can look as young as my mother, damn it. Not even to survive three months in Paris.*

"Hugo Faure, too." Her father nodded appreciatively to the older man. Stouter and shorter, with a more dated sense of fashion, he too had dark hair that was only starting to gray, and emanated a rougher-edged arrogance.

"*Chef cuisinier,*" Alain mouthed to her from out of Hugo's sight, looking anxious.

"Oh, so *you're* responsible for all this delicious food?" Summer squeezed herself to the chef's arm in breathless admiration. "Hugo Faure! What an honor!"

Luc's eyes almost narrowed. He took another minute sip of his glass of wine.

"And to meet you, too, of course!" she gushed at him, because he had seemed just a tad temperamental to *her* the night before. She gave him a warm smile to make up for the belatedness. He gave her a tiny, edged smile in return.

He wasn't even *remotely* temperamental? Like, not known for hauling women off by their hair to their hotel rooms when they annoyed him? She rubbed her cold arms surreptitiously in memory of his warmth closing over her.

Luc turned away to say something to a waiter. Yeah, she just riveted his attention, didn't she?

"You'll have to show me your kitchens sometime." She layered it on a little more, shifting her efforts to Hugo. Starstruck enthusiasm always worked on the older men on the island.

"My kitchens are your kitchens," Luc said courteously, turning back to her.

Well, that was true, but . . .

"I was being polite." His eyes narrowed again.

He made her brain dizzy. As if she was breathing out carbon dioxide but only breathing in him.

"I'll be happy to show you around as long as you can stay out of the way," Hugo told her roughly.

Her father gave both men a sharp look and glanced at Summer to see how she would reinforce her ownership of the hotel. "I'm pretty discreet," she promised Hugo humbly.

Her father frowned in severe disappointment at her lack of backbone, amusement leaped suddenly in Luc's dark eyes like a secret, and Alain Roussel stared at her as if she was insane.

Look, the indiscreet part of last night was his *fault,* she barely stopped herself from saying, then sent Luc a grumpy look. He had gotten her all over the Web again. Her first damn night.

Her breath whooshed out of her as silk and a fine edge of soft wool slid over her bare arms and closed her in warmth and scent. A waiter straightened away from her, his face politely neutral, as she looked straight at Luc.

He smiled at her urbanely, and she must be imagining that hungry, satisfied edge to him like a cat watching a mouse wander well past its safety zone.

She rubbed the edge of the coat between her fingers. Dior, maybe, the texture very fine. It had to be Luc's, she could tell by the labyrinth of scents: chocolate, butter, spice, stinging bright scents, and secret, mysterious warm ones. She wanted to get lost in them and never come out until morning.

"What the hell is that?" her father asked, since apparently that rule about keeping Luc happy didn't apply to him. Her father had ambitions for a son-in-law with a brilliant financial mind.

Luc gave her father a cool look. Her fingers stilled on the coat. The *chef pâtissier* looked at one of *Forbes'* top five hundred, who had just bought the hotel where he worked as a Christmas present for his spoiled daughter, as if he had the potential to be a headache and inconvenience and not much more.

She pulled his coat more snugly around herself, without even realizing she was doing it.

"Better?" Luc asked gently, reaching out to button the jacket near her throat, so that she wore it like a cape. Her heart beat so hard as his fingers grazed her throat that she was sure he would feel her pulse there.

What was wrong with her? What had she started with her stupid exhausted carelessness the night before? "Was I

not up to the dress code?" Her quick grin invited everyone into the joke. "Coat and tie only?"

"You were perfect," Luc said calmly. "But you looked
cold."

Her father's critical look made her want to tuck herself
up against Luc and thumb her nose at him.

"And you're welcome in my kitchens any time you
choose," Luc told her, with exquisite manners that rein-
forced his possession of those kitchens. "You won't get in
my way."

Damn it. She really hated men who didn't let her get in
their way.

"Welcome to the Leucé." And he walked off and left
her. Again. Draped in his coat, his scent twining all around
her.

CHAPTER 4

Sylvain Marquis stared as Luc approached, reflected back on himself in a vast gold-framed mirror that glinted with the lights from the chandeliers. In it Luc saw Summer forget him almost instantly, turning that sweet smile on the first man to take his place. "How did you manage to do *that?*" the chocolatier asked.

"Do what?" Luc pretended to sip his wine again. He was damned if he would get any alcohol into his system tonight. That half glass of champagne the night before had clearly left him far too vulnerable to being . . . cracked like a raw egg.

"Walk out on Summer Corey. She's exactly your type." Dark-haired poet Sylvain, media darling, regularly named the best chocolatier in the world, had a gift for sounding as if he couldn't possibly be wrong, no matter what subject he talked about. He was at the gala because of his wife, Cade, presumably. Billionaires always stuck together.

"No, she is not." How would Sylvain know? Luc rarely gave himself enough time to date. It didn't work out for him. His dates declared him too controlled, too careful, not affectionate or attentive enough. And the couple of times he had let himself go as a teenager had been disastrous, reducing him to a clinging, desperate, love-starved person he could not stand to be again and whom the girl in question hadn't been able to stand, either. It boggled his mind, the degree of touching and warmth and relaxation between someone like Sylvain and Cade. How did they *do* that? And, having attained it, how did they manage to go out in public, and not lock themselves in an apartment for the rest of their lives, wallowing in it?

"Luc, please. She's exactly any man's type."

That set Luc's teeth again. "Aren't you married?"

"No, she is not," Dominique Richard interrupted, sounding annoyed as he joined the conversation. "She's the kind of woman who *thinks* she's any man's type, which isn't the same thing." He sounded as if he held a long-standing grudge against that kind of woman. But then, Dominique often sounded as if he held a grudge. Big, dark, aggressive, the bad boy of Paris's chocolate scene had only recently been caught by a girl-next-door type who left him so softened and fragile whenever she was around that Luc had to look away. It wasn't good for men like him and Dominique to have their raw-egg insides pouring out.

Damn Patrick for that image.

"I'm married, but *you're* not married," Sylvain pointed out. "We were talking about you."

"Then let's stop. I'm sure talking about you would be much more interesting."

Which proved how knocked off-balance he was, to swell Sylvain's head even further. "Inherently," Sylvain agreed, with a gleam in his eye. "But I haven't kidnapped a stranger and carried her off to her hotel room to ravage her recently." He managed to look both pious and regretful.

"It's not my fault your marriage is boring," Luc retorted. Dominique laughed. He and Dom had worked for a while in the same kitchen on their way up, and Luc had always been one of the few people who could get along with Dominique. Possibly because each man had a fundamental hole in him from his childhood that the other sensed. "What do you do, gossip nonstop?"

"There's a viral YouTube video of it, Luc. Some guest caught it, or some hotel employee, but I think you had better go with guest if you don't want someone fired. According to Cade, Summer used to trail paparazzi like a comet before she disappeared for years."

Luc glanced at Summer, currently smiling up at yet another dark-haired man. Had half the men at this party dyed their hair black to play to her type, or what? In that glittering room, she shouldn't have stood out as the most golden thing in it, but she did. The only gold that was real.

Merde, really? Had he been working all his fucking life not to reign over this gold and marble palace around him, but to have *her?*

"Are they related? She and Cade and Jaime?" Cade Corey, the elder of two heirs to the multinational conglomerate of Corey Chocolate, had married Sylvain Marquis in a surreal turn of events the winter before. One of the best chocolatiers in the world and some producer of mass-market milk chocolate. Even Luc's lip had curled in involuntary revulsion at the *mésalliance.* Sylvain had been accused of selling out more than once.

Younger sister Jaime had taken a break from reforming cacao labor practices long enough to get engaged to chocolatier rebel Dominique Richard about six months later, forcing the two archrivals into much closer contact than they could stand. And that had *really* pissed the Paris gourmets off. They had accused Corey Chocolate of trying to breed the quality out of them. So far the two men had managed to avoid killing each other, a restraint that was indubitably to Sylvain's credit. Nobody ever credited Dom with avoiding violence.

"Third cousins," Sylvain said. "I guess they still invite each other to weddings because they don't have that many other cousins and the common last name gives some sense of attachment."

"Her great-grandfather was my great-grandfather's older brother." Heels clicking on the smooth parquet floor, Cade came up to give Luc a kiss on both cheeks. "The one whose barn my great-grandfather burned down when he was inventing a way to make milk chocolate. I guess the two of them were so intent on proving to each other they were right about the way to make a fortune that my great-grandfather managed to start a major chocolate company while her great-grandfather acquired endless acres, and each generation kept building from there. Our side was winning for a little while, until her father became one of the world's investment geniuses and shot their wealth into the stratosphere."

It was hard to believe Cade could be related to Summer, even as third cousins. Although only a centimeter or two taller than Summer, Cade *felt* infinitely taller—as if there was nothing in the world that wouldn't yield to her when she walked straight into it with her chin up. Cade's hair was a straight light brown, and her blue eyes too direct for Summer's lagoon brilliance. If you tried to swim in *Cade's* blue eyes lazily, she'd strip you of all your assets, restructure you, and move in new management within the first few strokes.

Summer, on the other hand . . . would probably disappear like a mermaid into a glint of sun on a wave, dancing away.

"You do realize it's a bit surreal for Luc, Dom, and me," Sylvain told his wife, "when someone hands you a top luxury hotel as a Christmas present." All of them had worked with relentless determination and perfectionism to climb to the pinnacle of their professions.

Cade's expression cooled. "I worked, Sylvain."

Luc and Dom flicked her incredulous looks, Luc's so

subtle that she probably missed it, Dominique's as brusquely open as everything else about him. Cade's lips tightened.

"Not to climb, though." Sylvain grinned. "Not until you had to work so hard for *me,* of course. That was a definite step up."

Cade rolled her eyes, and Sylvain laughed and stretched a hand toward her. A subtle gesture, but it was enough. Cade shifted into that curve of his hold as naturally and easily as breathing.

Dom looked across the room instinctively toward Jaime, who had fallen into conversation with Summer. Luc followed his gaze because it gave him an excuse to look in Summer's direction.

Jaime's passion fruit–caramel hair had reached a sophisticated bob length now, after the violent attack that had made headlines in the chocolate world. The bob didn't suit her. If any adult woman should have her hair in two braids down her back, it was the extraordinarily freckled Jaime. When Luc had first met her, her wrist bones had stuck out, but six months of Dom's chocolate had put the flesh back on her, and she and Dom both had a glow that made Luc want to hang his head and kick something as sullenly as he used to when he was a kid in the Métro. Of all of them, Dom was the last man he would have thought would find such cozy, codependent happiness.

Instead of which, Luc was the last man. He didn't show even an inkling of his jealousy, of course. He was Luc Leroi, damn it. These days, other people could look at *his* life and long for *it.*

"So what's she like?" Sylvain asked Cade. "Luc needs to know."

Luc sent him a dangerous look. Sylvain grinned. The chocolatier had been insufferably smug even before Cade sealed the one chink in his arrogance—women—by set-

tling that straight gaze on him and leaving no doubt as to
her choice. Now there was really no being around the
man at all.

"I'm pretty much her antithesis," Cade said. "So I don't
really know her that well. Besides, I don't want to comment on someone's girlfriend in front of him." She
smirked in an exact imitation of her husband.

"She asked me to show her to her room and then pretty
much passed out in my arms," Luc lied, driven. "Wouldn't
you have picked her up?" he challenged the other two men.

"Before Cade, probably," Sylvain said ruefully. "And
gotten my heart broken." Only an extremely observant,
obsessive-compulsive person would have noticed the little
squeeze he gave Cade's waist in gratitude for the fact that
his heart couldn't get broken anymore. No reason at all for
it to make a man conscious of how empty his own hands
were.

"No," Dom said. "Either she's well enough to stand on
her own two feet and just trying to manipulate me, or I
need to call an ambulance."

Yeah, he talked big when Jaime wasn't around, didn't
he? Luc gave him an annoyed look.

What was wrong with manipulation, anyway? He didn't
mind if Summer wrapped that silky hair around his wrist
to jerk his heartstrings. She could stroke her hair all over
his body if she wanted. Or . . . *merde.* Maybe not. The key
was to keep control, and twenty years of practice at perfect control might not be enough to overcome all the
wildness still lurking from his childhood if she did that.

But he could manipulate, too. He could control things
that were hot and cold and fragile and hard better than
perhaps any other man on the planet, and he had barely
gotten started. In about fifteen more minutes he would set
before her a golden heart held gently in a dark hand, and
her eyes would light like a child's, and her mouth would

melt as she looked from it to him. That would be how he started, training her, until she couldn't even hear his name without melting, without wanting.

"I used to think she was pretty desperate for attention." Cade shrugged. "It takes talent to have the media after her the way she did. Jamie had to be tear-gassed at G8 summits to get her picture all over the Web. But they never could get enough of Summer, and for a while she seemed to lap it up. The first year after she dropped off the face of the earth, I kept expecting to see a reality show turn up about her South Pacific life or something. But no, she stayed in the islands for four years, way past media reach. Jaime spent a week on a cargo boat getting out there once, just in case she needed someone to save her from a mad island chief or a sudden drug habit, and said she was relaxed, happy, and clearly adored by her schoolkids."

"Her *what?*"

Cade grinned. Seriously, far too much of Sylvain was wearing off on her. "You guys didn't even chat a little to get to know each other first? She's been teaching school out on minimally populated islands that don't even have regular electricity. Her dad can hardly stand it. Well, he clearly can't stand it anymore at all. Why else would she be here?"

Because she had gotten fed up with tropical roughing it and wanted to spend a few months being pampered in a top hotel in Paris, luxuriating in every delicacy Luc's hands could create? Although . . . four years was a long time for a spoiled heiress to last before she got fed up. "Isn't she old enough not to do what her father says?"

"Oh, I'm sure Sam found some way to control the situation." Cade looked a little amused, like someone who also usually had the power to control a situation. "Probably promised to invest in something they need out on the islands. I wouldn't put it past him to have some kind of bonus if she marries the man he wants her to while she's here, too. He's clearly marketing his top choices for future Corey Holding chairs."

Anger stabbed through Luc. Across the room, Sam Corey stopped by his daughter and Jaime with a well-dressed man in tow. "Why? He wants her to be miserable?"

Cade's look was arrested. "That . . . might have a grain of truth. I know he's always blamed himself for spoiling her. He talks about it, when he gets frustrated enough."

Luc remembered blame. Sometimes it flashed through him like it was yesterday, that blame. Sometimes he still believed it. "He's a doting father, then," he said neutrally.

Cade looked doubtful. "I guess. In his way. If you ask me, she's probably got abandonment issues."

Luc's and Dom's eyes met, and then both looked away, expressions unchanged. Luc didn't even know where their awareness of each other's shitty childhoods had come from. Neither was exactly the confiding sort.

"Abandonment," Luc repeated, not particularly wanting to hear the sad story of a beautiful billionaire heiress's difficult childhood. Summer pushed his buttons enough already.

Cade shrugged. "Well—I don't know. If Dad had dumped *me* in a boarding school on the other side of the world at age thirteen, I think it would have broken my heart. Of course, my mom had just died, so I might have been a lot more fragile at that age."

"Fragile" wasn't really a word Luc associated with Cade. On the other hand, Summer . . . he looked at her again, moving through the crowd, elusive as sunlight dancing over waves.

Nothing fragile about sunlight, he reminded himself. *Get close enough, and the sun will vaporize iron.*

With a warm smile, she slipped away from her father's

latest candidate and turned. Across the room her eyes met Luc's and she stilled. Then she was gone again, her father in annoyed pursuit.

Luc's brow creased faintly, and then, cursing himself, he followed after her. *She doesn't need help, you idiot. Or if she does, it's with carrying her bags.*

Summer and her father stopped near one of the great floor-to-ceiling windows. Against the white sweep of the curtain pulled back by gold tassels far above her head, she looked exquisite but caged, stolen out of her natural habitat to delight those too lazy to seek her out where she belonged.

"You're leaving tonight," she was saying flatly when Luc got within earshot. "Even though you said you dragged me back here from my island so you could see me more."

"Well, I *will* see you more." Her father sounded exasperated. "Your Manunui isn't exactly an easy place to stop by between meetings. Paris is central. I'll be back through after I finish up in Poland."

Summer's eyes were brilliant. "I'll get Alain to give me a secretary, so yours can call him and set up a time."

"Not a him. I don't trust you with a male secretary. I'll be paying off lawsuits in no time. You'd better get a woman."

For a second Luc was convinced that shimmering glow of hers came from incandescent rage. But she only smiled. "I'll do what I want with my own hotel, Dad. That's one of the points, right? By the way, if you want to know a worse gift to give someone than a puppy, try a luxury hotel. Fortunately, my sense of responsibility is almost nonexistent."

"Your sense of responsibility is misdirected. That's how I got you here, your overdeveloped sense of responsibility for a dozen schoolkids. You need perspective. More people's lives are going to depend on your decisions in this hotel than there."

"That's why it's a shitty gift. You can have it back anytime you want."

Her father's lips pressed together in temper. "You're such a spoiled brat. You've never been able to appreciate all the things you've been given."

Summer closed her eyes briefly. "I appreciate myself," she said, in an odd, steady tone, like a mantra.

Her father flicked an impatient hand. "At least I've gotten you off that island. That's a step."

The light in Summer grew stronger, as if she was drawing on it. "Until April. I told the substitute I would be back by April 15, at the latest. You did say I could use the plane."

April. All the air was sucked out of Luc's space. It was mid-January. That was only three months.

Her father's mouth hardened. "Why the hell did you even major in economics at Harvard? They don't need a summa cum laude in economics on that island."

Luc struggled to imagine her analyzing the ins and outs of money and its movement. How sad. But it wouldn't be the first time a child had tried to change his or her essence in order to please a parent. He had had two radically opposite fathers himself and knew all about that.

"You knew I got summa cum?" Summer raised her eyebrows.

"Not that again!" her father exploded. "Five thousand jobs were on the line. That's five thousand *lives,* Summer, out there in the world you're so protected from. And you wanted me to put a stupid ceremony ahead of them? You are so *spoiled.*"

Summer gazed out at the street. "Yes, so you've said. But you have to stop beating yourself up about it. I hear

I'm not the only kid whose parents ever spoiled her. You did what you could."

Sam Corey looked tempted to beat his head against the glass. But after a second he relaxed with a sudden huff and shook his head. "Now that we've got you back in the real world, do you think you can start dating someone with a brain in his head? I suppose it's up to me to pass your phone number out to the best candidates. Knowing you, you'll fall for the first man who looks at you twice." His voice was filled with affectionate, amused contempt.

Summer's hand curled at her side. "I believe everyone I've dated has succeeded enormously, Dad. Didn't you read the *Penthouse* article?" Her breaths were even and deep, as if she was practicing yoga. "These days, I've given up on dating men who succeed. I insist on being looked at more than twice."

"You would," her father said with such scorn that Luc took a sudden step forward.

Summer turned abruptly. "Actually, Dad, there's not a single person in this city I would allow near me, so it doesn't really matter what you do."

"Oh, so what's that?" her father snapped, gesturing at Luc's coat. "Someone you're not allowing near you?"

Against the white backdrop, his black coat seemed the only thing that protected her from disappearing into the ether. One small hand slipped up to hold its panels around her. "My flings aren't your business, Dad."

Luc's teeth set. *Oh, I'm not going to be your fling, Summer Corey. I'm going to hold you in my hand. And you'll look at me.*

It relaxed muscles he didn't even know he had, the thought of that warm smile all for him.

Her father frowned at her as if he had birthed an ostrich and had no idea what to do with it. "Well, don't mess with him. I didn't buy this hotel for it to become second rate. Three stars, no less."

"I'll try to keep His Majesty's happiness at the forefront of my mind. Which is a very ironic thing for you to ask me to do, but I'll let you figure out why. 'Night, Dad." She blew him a kiss and turned away.

Her gaze locked with Luc's. And all at once, everything hidden in her seemed to coalesce suddenly into a blaze of rage. All focused on him.

Now there, he thought, as their eyes held, the power of that look pulling his body into one tight bow. There was something to work with. He could turn anything into anything, but he did like for his raw ingredients to be the purest.

His palms itched to mold that passionate rage in his hands. *Yes, I can make something out of you.*

The glimpse was gone in an instant as her rage vanished under her shimmering smile. Eyes warm, as if she had spotted her favorite puppy, she blew him his own kiss as she walked past him.

He was still grappling with the idea of being a puppy when he realized what she had just said. Good *night*? She couldn't leave yet! He had plans for her. He caught up with her at the lobby door, shifting so that she nearly ran into him. "Where are you going?"

"To bed." A lazy, lagoon look that left him as hot as her tropics. "Coming?"

So that he could be her fling who didn't get close? He would be damned if he would. She was going to want *him* first. "Your party's barely started."

"I've been living in the opposite time zone."

If he went to bed this early, he would have hours of intense energy to burn up before he could sleep. He stared down at her, his blood beating so thick and hot at the thought of those hours that the sound of his own heart shut out every other noise around them. "I've got something special for you."

She laughed. "That's what they all s——"

"A dessert," he snapped, before she could reduce him to some casual innuendo. "You have to wait for that." Because silky Summer Corey might wrap him around her finger without even trying but *he* could melt her soul. And make her glad of it. Make her forget her damn father and look up at him with a radiant child's delight.

She did look up at him for a moment, revealing a glimpse of something wild that was instantly covered by a smile. "Why, that's so sweet of you, monsieur." Her gaze drifted down his body and then up, a long brush of silk that drove him helpless with arousal. "But you know"— she leaned toward him as her voice lowered, bringing them both into a secret—"I don't eat sweets."

And she turned around and strolled out. As if he was nothing.

CHAPTER 5

The sky hung over the city like a blimp still bearing a grudge from some old war, and the Eiffel Tower dragged her point along its underbelly and drenched the city with its contents. Summer stood at the window, her arms bereft of some soft stuffed animal to hold, and watched her parents' limousine pull away. When she was still teddy bear–clutching age, they had liked to keep her in whatever city they were in. Liz, her longest-lasting nanny, had put her foot down about working twenty-four hours a day, so in the evenings Summer either played by herself in their hotel room or was allowed to sit at a three-hour elegant dinner while her father talked business. Her father hadn't forced her to give up the teddy bear until she was ten, and she had been thirteen before they realized they really didn't need her that close, and she would be better off in a boarding school.

Or somebody would be better off.

The rain drove off all but the most dogged of the paparazzi that had gathered in incredulous hope at her dramatic return—yes, four years out of the limelight and she still had it, the world's spoiled-brat it girl. But nothing tempted her to go out in that winter rain and revisit all the places she had tried to escape herself when she was a teenager. If she saw that damn Victory of Samothrace in the Louvre again, soaring so triumphantly over all its past, she might start beating at the thing with the nearest other chunk of marble, and she was pretty sure even her father couldn't save her from the repercussions of that.

Or the *Mona Lisa*. Summer had always wanted to take a dagger to that supercilious little smile of hers.

No, forget that. God, was she not going there again. This was her hotel now, right? She was probably too old to go play Beauty and the Beast in its corridors, as her mom had occasionally done with her when she was in one of those thrilled-to-be-a-princess moods.

But she had never once been allowed to explore its hidden workings as a child, peek behind the mysterious doors through which all the waiters and uniformed people came and went while she was stuck at tables or in hotel rooms. The one time she had escaped, in this very hotel, her nanny had been fired, and her last memory of the woman still stuck with her, even today: tear-drenched, a security guard hustling her away so she would quit trying to grab Summer in a last hug, staring back at Summer through all those sobs that were Summer's fault. And standing behind Summer, just waiting until nanny and security guard were gone to tell her what he thought of her, her father, looming and giant.

She curled fists slowly by her sides and lifted her chin at the Eiffel Tower. *Fuck you all.* The memories and the Eiffel Tower and that old quagmire of despair and self-hatred she had thought she would never get out of. *I don't care if you think I'm nothing. I'm going exploring.*

Like a defiant, wayward child. But then she had been crappy at defiance and waywardness as an actual child, so maybe it was high time.

Probably typical of her that she could only manage defiance when there was nobody left to defy, but . . . *You weren't going to get sucked into that low self-opinion the first day back here, remember, Summer?*

Probably best then, in her explorations, to stay well away from the kitchens of a certain Greek god who already thought she was worthless.

Luc paused at the entrance to his kitchens, surveying his kingdom. White figures moved in an unchoreographed dance, hands full of creation, boiling, freezing, sharp-edged, fragile. Stainless steel formed the background to everything, the only bones tough enough to hold up this fomenting world. Beauty sprang up on marble everywhere, jewels formed in heat and cold and pressure, brought up out of the bowels of the hotel to delight those who could afford them.

But what if you met someone who had so many jewels she thought they were worthless?

I don't eat sweets. As if he had offered her a piece of cheap candy. Had she ever even had a piece of cheap candy in her life? She would have been one of those sleekly overprecious children who came to the Hotel de Leucé, their every whim catered to, grown men serving them the world's best pastries on silver plates every time they pouted. She would never have known what it was like to stare through a window and *crave.*

Spoiled brat. It made him sick to think about it, the gorgeous golden layers in last night's dessert, the final touch of three ovals of gold sugar, like the orbits of three stars. The way it had been cupped in a half curve of dark chocolate, melting already the first second it was set there, while the chocolate stayed so strong.

He had had it all planned, the way her eyes would light up when she saw it. The way she would smile at him. The way she would take a bite and be his.

The way she would be sorry that she had offered him a yacht. The way she would say, *Why, yes, it's true that you are worth much more of me than that.*

He strode into the great refrigerator and stood in its cold, staring at the walls of butter and cream and fruits and every other chilled thing a man could possibly want.

It felt like the damned Métro again. Where he would dance and shake that damned seed-filled egg, or the tambourine, or whatever instrument his father wanted him to try that day, and walk between the seats with his hand held out, and people would just get up and leave as the doors opened without even looking at him. While his father played the accordion with a little empty smile on his face, hiding his emotions from the judging or indifferent crowd, frustration simmering beneath the surface, building up into a burst of blame with which he would slam Luc as soon as they were alone.

His father had only struck out occasionally, a slap or a bruising grab of his arm, but there had been days when Luc had wanted to curl up and vomit out his day, the groveling before indifferent strangers, the begging for money, his father's rage and rage and *rage* at his failure to amass more. *If only you would try, if only you would smile, if only you would dance properly, like I showed you, put some heart in it.*

Then his father would get over it, usually, and give him a rough hug and say, "Don't worry about it, we'll manage." And maybe take him to do something fun, like play in the park, to make up for his temper. They hadn't typically managed. When social services had found Luc busking in the middle of a school day and picked him straight up out of the Métro, at the age of ten, it had been the first time food and lodging had been secure. Bernard Durand epitomized security, in fact: a small-time *boulanger-pâtissier* who taught his foster children his trade and the paramount importance of control to accomplish anything of worth.

No more warm, rough hugs. Not ever. But no huddling under eaves in the rain, gazing longingly into bakery windows across the street, wishing he had earned more money on the last train so he could have just one éclair.

It might have been a tough choice for a ten-year-old child, between emotions and security. But he hadn't had the choice. His father had disappeared, leaving the false name Leroi on the papers, and had never made contact with him again. Often Luc imagined him appearing in his restaurant, demanding money, perhaps, and his stomach would grip as he wondered how he would react. Given the option, he wasn't sure he would have chosen the security.

Marko had been such a bad father, the adults who took Luc from him had made that clear. But he had loved Luc with intense enthusiasm at least half the time, and it was harder to say whether Bernard Durand had. Luc could only be sure of the older *pâtissier*'s pride in him, a wild boy turned by the *boulanger-pâtissier*'s perfectionist training into a wildly successful man.

Twenty years of unrelenting mercilessness toward himself, never a moment's compassion for his own fatigue, all to be the very best of the best, to produce things that *no one* could resist, that *everyone* had to look at, and long for, and pay a fortune for.

Unless, of course, they didn't eat sweets.

And why the *fuck* was the kitchen out of sugar?

"*Sucre*," he told Olivier, the young man sitting at the desk in the Économat, the hotel pantry. Sugar. Of all the things for one of his *commis* not to put on the whiteboard list when they grabbed the last ten-kilo bag. "Just enough to get us through the next hour. I've sent someone out to get more."

Olivier smirked oddly, which Luc understood as soon as he stepped between the sliding shelves at the far end of the small, packed room's folding-fan-like system.

Hands clasped behind her back like a schoolgirl, Summer gazed up at the extravagant variety on the shelves with wide-eyed delight. From coconut curry potato chips to organic muesli to cucumber-flavored sodas, if some guest far from home might long for it, they had it. That delight in her face just reached a fist into his middle and yanked it over to her to be her personal little possession. God, but if he had met her as an actual schoolgirl, when he was a schoolboy, he would have crushed on her so fast and so hopelessly.

What was he talking about—he already *had* crushed on her hopelessly. That pissed him off. He was supposed to be far too old and too mature and too *self-controlled, damn it* to fall so pathetically anymore.

Summer glanced his way. Just for a second that young girl's radiance was still in her face, reaching out as if it was for him, and then she saw who it was and jumped, the wide-eyed delight disappearing as if he had snuffed it out like a candle. He wanted to force it back somehow, grab her throat and make her look at him as if he was a damned box of cereal.

The wide-eyed delight came back without need for those measures, even brighter than before. But fake now. Like he wasn't worth showing any part of her that mattered. "Isn't this *wonderful?* I never even knew hotels had these. It's like a treasure trove. Aladdin's Cave. The code to the door should be 'open sesame.' "

He wanted to stroke his thumb over her mouth until that smile faded and she really saw him, bend his head, say "open sesame" . . .

"Does it make you . . . hungry?" he asked tautly.

With a glimmering smile she swooped to pick up a

package of some damned miniature Corey bars, ghastly sour-flavored milk chocolate they kept on hand because some of their idiotic American clients were so damned attached to the things. You would think if he could overcome the scars of his own childhood they could get over that one, honestly. "That's all right, I found something," Summer said brightly.

His jaw set. He put a hand on the shelves to either side of them, deliberately, hot joy shooting through him as he caged her with his body. "I thought you didn't eat sweets."

"Well . . . I'm very particular." Her apologetic smile made the words a triple slap.

His grip tightened on the shelves. He pulled them in, squeezing their space, caging her tighter. "Too particular for *me?*"

She patted one of his tense hands as if it was a dying grandmother's. "Surely you, of all people, can understand someone being particular. I wouldn't worry too much about it, though. It was only a dessert. In your case."

Only a dessert. Only. "Is that why you refused?" he asked between his teeth. "Payback because I was too particular to be your gigolo?"

Her eyes flared at the word, just a second when he thought he had wounded her or at least gotten *something* past her smile. She brought one finger up to worry sexily at her lower lip. "Well . . . you're not the only one who can turn offers down thoughtlessly, you know," she said, all silk and sugar and a tiny, rough grain of sand.

The shelves started to cut into his palms. "Oh, were your offer and mine supposed to be even?" He leaned in on her, took all her space. "I'm sorry. I didn't realize having sex with strangers was your life's work."

The smile went entirely out. And then shimmered back into place, like the silk on her body the night before. "Oh, I beg your pardon." She pressed that lower lip down. And then suddenly—he didn't even know how she managed it—she was on the other side of him, free of his cage, waving her bag of chocolates like she had just won a game of capture the flag. "I suppose I should have dedicated my life to making things out of *sugar* instead?"

It slapped him white. While he was still rigid from the shock she slipped away.

So His Majesty had thought she would be that easy? Summer thought as she swam and swam and swam around the hotel pool. That he could reject her out of hand and still expect to yank her back and make her beg for him any time he cared to pull her strings? She frowned as she showered and dried off and discovered the hotel director was waiting to talk to her. He thought he could control her with *desserts*, that bastard? Oh, had he underestimated her. Nobody, nobody controlled her that way anymore.

Summer gave Alain Roussel a tight, pinched smile, then realized it was pinched. She took one long deep breath and let the smile relax into something glimmering, easy. Her hair still clung wet to the nape of her neck, and she realized she had not swum far enough. She was still, after all, stuck in this damn hotel. With two more months and twenty-nine days before she could earn her freedom and get back home, bringing a satellite with her like one of those heroic animals in legends who brought back the sun. Which always left the animal burned to a crisp or blind, didn't it?

"They don't really make good . . . toys," the geeky, elegant director was saying carefully, watching her as if she was a child with a bad temper made emperor of Rome. Seated across from her at the table in his office, he was ostensibly going over some basic figures of the hotel's operations. But that hadn't really been what he wanted to talk about. The newspaper photo that had been lying on top of those figures—her, being swept away in Luc's arms—was now discreetly folded in four, a little matter they all needed to forget. "These top chefs."

Summer nodded understandingly. "Not like me, for example."

That threw him a little. He obviously halfway thought that she did make a good toy, by her own choice, and therefore didn't know how to respond. He pushed on. "They're very . . . emotional."

She raised her eyebrows. "He seems pretty in control of his emotions to me." They were all packed in him until she didn't know how he kept the dam from bursting. She sighed a little, wistful at the thought of that dam bursting on her. Yeah, wouldn't *that* be a way to screw her life up so fast she might not get it back together again. She really did have crappy instincts about men.

"Luc is controlled," Alain agreed. "Exceptionally."

"Except when he hauls strange women off into elevators, of course," Summer mentioned thoughtfully.

Alain's lips tightened. Clearly he blamed her for that elevator. "But I've had to handle top chefs all my career, and underneath that control, there's no way he can be so different from the others. He lives on his emotions. And his emotions are . . . bigger than ours. More passionate. More powerful."

Hunger curled in her, deep and improper. "Of course." She smiled easily. "It's the mark of a great man, isn't it?"

Of course his emotions would be *bigger* than hers. Who was she but a great man's daughter?

"It would be really disastrous for this hotel if he were to quit," Alain mentioned.

Summer curled her fingertips into the tear in her jeans. "I'm sorry. Are you telling me that I should apologize to him for offering him"—*me, offering him me*—"a yacht? Just so I don't hurt his tender feelings?"

"A *yacht?*"

Luc hadn't gossiped?

"Mademoiselle Corey—a yacht? We need him in Paris! He's not only one of the world's greatest pastry chefs, but he has *showmanship.* The cameras just eat him up, with all that restrained, clean passion of his. He's *invaluable* to this place. What are you trying to do, steal him away from your own hotel?"

Summer was silent for a long moment. And then, low, "Obviously that would be a spoiled thing to do, wouldn't it? No. No, I don't know what I could possibly have been thinking. I'll apologize."

After all, obviously when a woman offered a beautiful, exceptional man a yacht to run away with her, and he left her lying on the damn bed and walked out, an apology on her part was in order.

The first step into the kitchens shocked the smile off Summer's face. Hundreds of milling souls, fermenting chaos, lava bubbling, geysers shooting up, cries of "Hot, hot, hot!" *"Chaud, chaud, chaud!"* and the caught souls ducking away, pressing to their counters.

Oh, wow, this was *so* much better than her lonely, elegant hotel room. Or wandering around the echoing vastness of the Louvre, trying to force her mind to dwell on the art, until the museum guards kicked her out at closing and forced her to slink back to her boarding school, the way she used to the last time she lived in Paris.

Fascinated, Summer stepped forward. Metal clanged. Figures in white twisted around each other between open flames and boiling liquids as if they had been doing this for all eternity. Counters and stoves and stainless steel stretched in all directions. Black demons slipped in and out, tuxedoed waiters carrying great trays.

She pushed deeper, staring at flesh being hacked with

great butcher knives, entrails being twisted, blood boiling over a low flame. Blades flew over roots and fruits of the earth she didn't even have a name for. White souls glanced at her occasionally, solidifying into chefs who were wondering what she was doing in hell.

"May I help you?" someone asked when she nearly ran into him as she rounded a corner. One quick hand touched her shoulder to steady her and then dropped politely away.

She looked up at a lazy smile, a sun-gilt, golden-brown Achillean hero who had got caught down here by accident, or maybe a confused surfer who should be hanging out watching for waves on some Hawaiian beach. He wore white chef's attire, as did most of the people around her, but was bareheaded, no toque or white cap. "Just exploring. I'm Summer Corey."

"*Merde*. I was afraid of that. I suppose that means you're looking for him." He stepped back to reveal Luc Leroi.

Luc concentrated completely, not looking at her at all, that black hair clinging damply to his temples. She locked on him and all the chaos coalesced around her. A ferment of dangerous, beautiful creativity, completely controlled by that darkness at its center. A rich, complex dance where everyone knew his role, and those weren't screams, just firm calls of warning as a great bubbling pot was carried from a stove to wherever its contents were needed.

He was working on something beautiful, and it was crazy how powerful need ran through her suddenly, for him to ignore it in her favor. *Put me between you and that beautiful thing you're working on, forget everything but me, make me forget everything but you.*

Yeah, right. Not that *she* would have any trouble forgetting everything else, but she was trying not to be such a damned idiot about what she expected from men like him.

His focus had no room for her. Seeing it explained a lot about how easy he had found it to dismiss her. Amazing how driven men could do that, shut her out like she was nothing. The concentration that let him achieve so many great things was a black hole for her, sucking all her light toward it until she felt she could be pulled through it into something beautiful.

She had *always* wanted to be sucked into the black hole. To see what was so impossibly wonderful that it was more important than anything she could do or be or say.

Being screwed-up doesn't mean you have to yield to your own screwed-upness, Summer.

But still, she drew closer, even as she fought the pull. All her father's complex projects had been in his head, on his computer, things a child could never see. She could only see him not seeing her. Here, the fruit of Luc's concentration formed into incredible fantasy under his hands. She couldn't help looking at it: Something soft and gold nestled safely in a net of darkness, while the black-haired *pâtissier* carved holes in that chocolate darkness so that the gold heart was protected from the world, but not shut away from it.

She took a hard breath and looked away, trying to breathe under a high, crashing wave.

No. Oh, no.

She wasn't going to start letting desserts have power over her again.

Especially not wielded by someone like him. Even right up close, she didn't penetrate his concentration.

What *was* it with her? After three damn years of celibacy, of getting her act together, how had she possibly, on pure instinct alone, looked around a lobby of strangers and picked out the one man who could ignore her as completely and utterly as her father had? How had she let herself be reduced so instantly to that little girl begging for attention again?

Another step.

Look at me. See how pretty I am. At least look.

She needed a therapist.

Luc didn't even glance at her. Long, lean, controlled hands flecked the heart with gold leaf.

Her own heart hurt so much, so suddenly. Her own heart wanted to ask, *Why do you take so much better care of that one than me?*

And then she did a bad thing. The kind of thing she used to do to her father, when she was still little and brave enough, or to boyfriends, in the early days of hope, only then it was usually a computer mouse she jiggled. This time she just reached out and touched his wrist.

The chocolate net shattered, pieces spilling to either side of the golden heart. Summer jerked back and ran into someone who steadied her with a light touch on her shoulder before disappearing in the fluid dance of bodies around her.

I didn't mean to ruin *it.* She almost yielded to the urge to turn tail and run. Instead, she set her shoulders, lifted her chin, and waited for his anger to burst over her. And at last he looked at her.

Luc had known the instant she stepped into the kitchens, from the shift in activity, and his teeth sharpened, a lion for a gazelle. Oh, so she didn't like sweets, did she? *Watch this.*

Because he had figured out that dessert for her. It wasn't something melting and gold held in a palm of darkness. It was something melting and gold entirely surrounded, a sphere of darkness that held it prisoner, that wouldn't let it get away. And the mousse of the melting heart would be— passion fruit. Tropical, delicate, unforgettable. Saying, *Take me, oh, no, sorry, you can't, I'm only his. Held in this embrace of darkness.*

He lured her in step by step. Knowing exactly what was happening to her, the way her mouth was watering, her body melting, the way temptation was rising in her until she was ready to beg for a taste. He would grant that taste with a smile and watch her get lost in him. Unable to find her way back out. *You think I want a pathetic yacht? When I could have you?*

That elusive sunshine gilded over him. His chest tightened in hunger. *I've got her. She's mine.* Maybe no one else could catch sunshine, but these days he could do even that. It was what, after all, he had worked so hard to learn how to do.

Control. It was all about control. The only way he could share his soul and turn it into a form no one could resist. *This is the sublime. This is who I am. Don't you ever drop money carelessly in my hand. But when you drop yourself—see how well my hands will take care of you?*

Rich, feral satisfaction surged through him as she took that last step. As she reached, uncontrollably, for that chocolate sphere.

And then her touch on his wrist ripped his soul right out of its firm seating and lodged it under those two fingers, pulsing madly against them like a caught human heart. The chocolate shattered. She jerked back.

And his whole world swirled dizzily. *No. No, don't go, come back, I think you have my heart stuck to your fingers.*

She rubbed her thumb over the two fingertips that had touched his pulse, as if she felt something unfamiliar there. Something unfamiliar and a little sticky that she needed to wash off.

"I'm sorry." Her eyes flicked from the mess to him. "I didn't mean to—"

"It's all right," he said, cursing himself for that flash of fear in her eyes, and even more for the mess of chocolate. What a wasted chance to utterly subjugate her. *Control, you fool. You have to keep control.*

She relaxed visibly at his quiet tone. Had she been hearing stories about temperamental chefs and imagined him throwing pans at her head? If she thought he was capable of losing control so easily, he had only himself to blame.

"I just—you weren't looking at me," she said and bit her lip too late to catch the words back.

No, you *weren't looking at* me. "I'm looking at you now."

She flushed. His fingertips caressed the marble counter in hunger for the heat of her skin. They stood completely still as chefs and assistants brushed by everywhere. "Is there something I can help you with, Mademoiselle Corey? Did you want to see how we work, perhaps?"

Oh, yes, his whole body shouted fiercely, *watch me. Grow all absorbed in me. Unable to look away.*

Her eyes flickered to his with a flash of pure hunger.

Yes! Triumph licked him, thorough hot licks of her mouth on his skin. *Oh, yes, I can make you hunger for me.*

And then her smile turned her whole beautiful, luminous, delicate face into something so impossibly wonderful that his hands—*his* hands—almost shook with the need to grab it to him, to *crush* it to him, and never let it get away. His hands. Shaking. Crushing.

"Oh, no, I wouldn't want to disturb you." She sent a rueful glance at the utter mess she had made of his—*her* heart. "They always did say I shattered their concentration."

The "they" she used, in French, was masculine, *ils.* Jealousy burned across his palms, pushing their urge to crush her to him. "Who?"

"Oh"—she waved a dismissive, amused hand—"my father. Boyfriends."

He had been controlling insanely temperamental

people—including himself—in kitchens for all his adult life. And he had never realized he had a jaw muscle that could tighten quite that way. "I'm not your father. And I'm most certainly not one of your boyfriends."

Again that little shimmer in her smile, as if it had slid and settled back into place. Did she do it on purpose, the way she made that silk dress shiver over her body, until a man wanted to lock her in some dark closet with him and spend the night just running his hands over and over that silk against her skin? Fighting himself for control, to make her his and his and his again without cracking?

"Oh, dear, of *course* not," she said lightly and reached up to touch his jaw in caressing condescension, right there in front of his whole team. The touch hissed through him. "I forgot we were still working out the details on that. It's *such* a quandary, about that yacht." She tapped her lower lip with the finger of one hand while the other stroked down from his jaw to smooth the shoulder of his chef's jacket, driving him completely insane with the need to strip it off, to feel that stroke against his bare skin. "I can't think what else to . . ." Her eyes lit. "I know. What about a penthouse apartment?"

Their eyes locked. Rage roared up in him like a furnace, and he *clamped*. Locked it down. "I don't think so," he said very precisely. His whole team had just heard her offer him a fucking penthouse apartment as if she was upping her bid on a whore.

"Oh, dear." She looked anxious. "You *are* hard to buy presents for. Well." Her hand patted his jaw again, and he *hated* himself for the arousal that shot through his body. "I'll keep thinking."

And then she turned and was gone, that blond head glimmering like some beautiful deity flitting back to heaven. Luc's jaw was set so hard he thought he might break the bone. He had no other choice. It was either that or lose control. He pivoted. Multiple people gazing at him with shocked, rounded mouths suddenly ducked back to work in all directions.

Except for Patrick, who leaned over and inspected the oozing ruins of the chocolate-gold heart. "Aww. That's so cute, Luc. You've finally let it out of its cage."

CHAPTER 6

He sent it to her, the sphere, on a day when the rain sheeted down like the end of hope: a delicate ephemeral shield of chocolate around a treasure of gold so brilliant and so fragile that it seemed to pulse there, a frozen mousse coated in gold leaf, hiding, according to the waiter, a melting heart, begging someone to eat it up, swallow it whole . . . and crap it out later, she told herself harshly.

It lured her, just like it was supposed to. It taunted her with its efforts to control her. It made her hurt, wanting desperately to curl up inside some better shield than that fragile veil of chocolate threads, so no one could see her heart so easily and eat it, so no one could mock her for it.

She nearly shoved it off the table, the dessert she hadn't ordered, and the waiter turned rather white. When he neared the door back into the kitchens with it, she saw him trying desperately to pass it on to some other waiter to take back instead of him.

"You're hard to please," the man sitting across from her said as if he liked that about her. He would, of course. If her father had given him her new phone number, he had to be ambitious and competitive. Mike Brodzik, one of his investment managers. Handsome and attentive and very,

very interested in her father's power. He was better than being alone.

She opened big eyes at him. "Oh, no," she said with a limpid innocence, just to mess with everybody, especially herself. "I'm actually . . ." A slow, sweet smile straight into his eyes. "Very, very easy."

Which kept his attention on her, all right, but made her kind of sick with disgust at herself. She wanted to go home.

When the fog crushed everything to gray, like the ghost of every misery past, he sent her three golden orbits of a star around a dark, proud mountain, the mountain a chocolate so pure and smooth it was like glass, to slide off, and hidden in amid the golden sugar orbits of the star, at the very peak of the mountain, a tiny delicate apple covered in gold leaf. She didn't know what the tiny apple tasted like inside the gold, or what was in the mountain, or how easily those golden star orbits would shatter at her touch, because she sent it back. Of course. Her throat closing, her hand curling slow and hard against her thigh under the table, as she tried very hard not to cry out her protest, to beg for it back.

When the setting sun sucked the last life out of the day, like a blood-gorged tick, and she was ready to sell her soul not to be alone in the night, he sent her a glowing ball of red sugar in the form of a most perfect apple; its red glistened in the light of the chandeliers, drawing the eyes of all the diners as the waiter carried it to her. Setting it as he had clearly been trained, the waiter turned it precisely one quarter, so that the other side of the gleaming perfect red showed: white. "It's called *Pomme d'Amour*," the waiter said. The French word for caramel apple. Or Apple of

Love. And that was no caramel apple. She wet her lips as she stared at that tempting, tempting red and white and what it might hide. She could just reach out and take it. Unlike when she was a child, no one could stop her. No one could withhold it from her. Except, of course, the man who'd made it, should he gain that power.

"I'll kiss you," the man across from her murmured, an old fling from her wild college days come to look her up. "If it puts you to sleep."

Snow White, right.

"I don't eat sweets," she told the waiter for the fifteenth time and pushed it away. Inside, the child in her panted hard as she fought not to cry.

He sent her hot chocolate. It was waiting for her when she came in from the hotel's little skating rink with a band of little kids. Summer was laughing, deeply relieved to know she was capable of being happy even here. Proud of herself, the girl who had mostly hung out with her own nanny as a kid, finally able to get a few kids to play with her. Maybe that was why she had ended up teaching school, she thought wryly. A hunger to play with other kids. But at any rate, the ability to find a rapport with small children that she had learned teaching in the islands seemed to stand her in good stead with these rich hotel strays. They reminded her so much of herself that it broke her heart a little bit for them, and she played far too long in the iced-over courtyard, all of them coming in frozen.

The children were delighted to see the hot chocolate waiting for them, waiters pouring it from elegant pots into little doll cups.

The cup a waiter offered her was adult-size, smooth, curving warm and perfect against her palm. It almost got her, that sweet. The scent of it was heady, reminding her of how her nanny Liz would sneak her hot chocolate after bouts of skating exactly like this, their little secret from her parents who, as Liz knew, wouldn't let her have dessert later.

It had been years before her mother realized it, and Mai had kept the transgression to herself, not letting her husband know. Summer had sat through the whole conversation with her mother with acid eating inside her tummy, terrified Liz would get fired. But Mai had concentrated on Summer's own responsibilities: "Sweetheart, it's your body. Do you want to be beautiful? Do you want people to love you?"

Summer closed her eyes and set the chocolate down. Because anything—even never tasting another bite of sugar in her life—would be better than letting those tangled memories of her past control her again.

The next day she was in the hotel playroom with the six-and-under crowd, tossing a plush custom-made elephant sporting the hotel logo back and forth with a three-year-old, when a great tumble of candy arrived. Little penny candies spilled artistically across a great tray from a paper bag: chocolate-covered marshmallow teddy bears, strawberries and bananas made of marshmallow dipped in bright red and yellow sugar, little orange and yellow gummy rings flavored with peach. Only they weren't worth mere pennies, she saw as she drew closer, amid all the other delighted, excited children. They were made by hand, and the paper bag was not paper but constructed out of some near-translucent, edible sheets.

Liz used to buy her cheap penny candy from bakeries on their "let's play at Madeline" excursions. No need for her parents to know about the paper sack Summer would clutch in her hand, skipping off to combine a history lesson with a trip to the Père Lachaise Cemetery because Madeline had looked for her dog Genevieve there. Summer always ate it too fast, even though Liz never once yanked the bag back out of her hands and tossed it in the nearest trashcan because Summer skipped wrong.

She scrubbed her hands suddenly over her face as the children fell on the candies, and started to slip out of the room. Her head turned to keep glancing back at those candies like Lot's wife looking back at Sodom, she ran straight into a hard body and bounced away sharply, jerking her head up to see Luc.

Golden skin, a face forged from greater forces than she could even imagine, that elegant black hair, those impossibly black eyes, that sensual mouth so firmly disciplined. He seemed perfectly controlled, so she didn't know why she was so convinced he was pissed off.

"Cute," she said lightly, not quite sure where not to look, between the taunting temptation of him and the taunting temptation of those candies. Why the hell did the world get off on taunting her with things she wasn't supposed to be good enough for? "Who made them?"

"Me."

She looked back at him, and her smile slipped for a second and was almost real. That was kind of cute, too, to imagine impervious deity Luc making little-kid candies. She tilted her head, remembering what he had said about his Gypsy father, wondering if maybe penny candies had been a rare, special delight for him as a kid, too. "You made their day."

"Not yours?" he said. "No hot chocolate after skating? No candy while you're playing with children? I thought you liked cheap candy."

That wasn't cheap candy. Handmade in a three-star kitchen by one of the top chefs in the world. Her heart tightened, old anxiety rising up. "I really can't." *I don't deserve this, you know.*

Summer, stop! You do, too, deserve whatever you want.

But she just couldn't do it. Or maybe she just couldn't yield him that power.

You can't control me with sweets anymore.

Bad enough she had let her father control her with the offer of a satellite, but what was she supposed to do? Keep her island cut off from the world to keep it safe for her, as if its entire population were her personal toys?

"Are you diabetic?" he asked.

She stiffened, lifting her chin in a gesture of dismissal she had had to learn very young. A lot of people wanted a piece of her father through her. "This isn't your business."

"You're worried about your weight, aren't you?" He flicked an incredulous, angry glance over her slender body.

"No." At least . . . she tried not to be. She didn't worry about it on the island. "Excuse me."

He didn't move. No qualms whatsoever about asking her invasive questions about her personal issues, about using his bigger body to control where she could go or what she could do. And all while that flick of his glance over her body, the anger and contempt in it, still burned over her.

She smiled at him and leaned into him confidingly. Her hand came up to toy with his collar, fingers grazing his throat. "You see, I can put my mouth around—almost—anything," she murmured into his ear and dropped back onto her heels so he could catch her own blissful savoring of her lower lip. "But that particular flavor seems better suited to children, don't you think?" She smiled at him, and let her pat of his cheek linger as she strolled on past him and glanced back. "It's really sweet of you, though."

The Aladdin's Cave appeared right in the middle of an attempt to ask her out. Derek Martin, vice-president of the hotel chain whose luxury flagship the Luxe was one of the Leucé's rivals, had joined her for lunch because, of course, her father's heir had a line of men out to the other end of

Paris who wanted to join her for meals, and when it came to that or trying to face her lonely hotel room or cold, lonely Paris, she had an unfortunate tendency to choose the coward's way out. When the dessert arrived, dark, ambitious, attractive Derek had reined all of his aggression in to one gentle, possessive touch of her hand, his thumb caressing her knuckles, as if he *knew* how desperately she needed warmth and gentleness.

But then, maybe she was just transparent. Maybe that was why men always saw right through her, to her father. Not on purpose, even, but that was an awful lot of money and power to not remember when you were flirting with a woman. You would have to have a really weird brain—completely indifferent to numbers—to forget Sam Corey was in the picture. Derek Martin's brain wouldn't be able to shut him out. She knew that. But he did do a good job of pretending, with that focus that driven men had, right at the beginning, that ability to convince her that she could be the most important thing in his world, if only she would let herself be caught by him.

"They would love to have you at the Abbaye perfume launch, you know," Derek said. "And I would be proud to escort you."

Dread clenched in her at the thought of a luxury house affair, all the models and power and women who had to be the most beautiful in the room no matter what. She didn't want to go back to that. Besides, Abbaye had nearly talked her into pairing her name with a perfume back in college: Spoiled Brat, they had wanted to call it. She had never forgiven them for it. It had been during the period when she had tried assuming the title defiantly, flaunting slutty clothes, wild behavior. She had gone through the negotiations right up until it was time to sign the contract—the perfume was going to be her first "real job" after she graduated. And then she had hopped off that yacht in the South Pacific and never looked back. Abbaye had found an actress who seemed to be delighted to carry on the Spoiled Brat publicity, but Summer was pretty sure the Abbaye people were still a little pissed at her. And some part of her still felt a violent hatred for them, that they had tried to stick that label on her stupid twenty-year-old self, a label that a top-selling perfume and twenty-five-million-dollar advertising campaign would have cemented to her forever.

"Or if the Abbaye perfume launch doesn't appeal," Derek said quietly, stroking her knuckles, "why not something more relaxing? I know. We could fly to Nice for the day. It's warm down there."

Escape Paris? That sounded enticing . . .

Summer. Derek Martin couldn't understand why you would teach school on that island in a million years. Don't collapse this easily. You can make it three months.

And then the dessert slid in front of her.

A long, rectangular plate, crossed with a path of edible sand, glinting with specks of color and light, as if jewels had been ground to dust in it. They almost had, she realized, inspecting it. The hint of gleaming colors must come from colored sugars, but the gold was actual flecks of gold dust. Across that sand trailed serpentine footprints, made by someone's fingertip, leading to a rugged cave of chocolate, its door sealed shut.

A cave of wonders. It was a cave of wonders, for only the person with the magic word to explore. Were those Luc's fingerprints?

No, surely he didn't make every single item that came to her from the kitchens himself. It had to be that dark-haired intern she had seen, or . . .

"This is a new one," Derek said. "I've never seen that on Luc's menu before."

"It's for Mademoiselle Corey," the waiter said firmly,

as if he was the dessert's bodyguard and was prepared to defend it against anyone who wasn't supposed to get near it, no matter how wealthy and powerful Derek Martin might be.

"I asked for green tea," she said. Her mother's little trick for suppressing appetite and resisting desserts. Summer's eyes snagged again on the gleaming sand. That was a tiny sesame seed, right there by the seemingly sealed door to the cave of chocolate. "I don't—I'm not much of a dessert person—"

"I'll try it!" Derek said hungrily.

The waiter shifted, bodyguard preparing to lunge. "I'm afraid Monsieur Leroi was very particular."

"He always is," Derek said dryly. "I've tried to hire him away from you any number of times," he added to Summer.

"Monsieur Leroi thought you would like to be the first to try it," the waiter said to Summer. "He calls it Aladdin's Cave."

It's like a treasure trove. Aladdin's Cave. The code to the door should be "open sesame."

Does it make you . . . hungry?

"I'm sorry," she whispered, pushing it away. "I really don't eat sweets."

"Summer, you are out of your mind!" Derek said. "He'll quit. You can't turn a top chef's specially made dessert down that way."

"I can't," she said through a tight throat and looked away. Across all those other tables, filled with beautiful desserts. God, all the times she had stared at tables full of fantasies in this very same room, always withheld from her. *I can't give him that power.* "Please offer my apologies to Monsieur Leroi, but as I've told him, I don't eat sweets."

The waiter flinched visibly. Derek pulled out his phone. "Do you mind if I call him about two minutes after the waiter delivers that message? I've been wanting to find someone who can land us a third star at the Luxe for years."

Summer's gaze was drawn back, irresistibly, to that dark chocolate cave. What would be inside it? What wonders would a man like Luc Leroi hide in there for her to be the first to discover? The magic of it tempted her so desperately. That excruciating longing to just once be good enough to taste one of those things.

And that was exactly what she wasn't going to play into. Desserts had no power over her anymore.

She turned her head away again. "Do as you like," she told Derek.

At least if Luc left the Leucé in a temper, she would be safe from him.

With any luck, her father might get so pissed off he would let her go back to the island.

CHAPTER 7

Luc was in such a bad temper he couldn't even recognize his own insides. They fought with him like a feral child wrenched out of the Métro and away from his father into a place where love was some distant, pale light that would fall into his darkness only if he was absolutely perfect.

And Derek Martin, with his offers to double his salary if Luc came to the Luxe, could go fuck himself. Anyway, Alain had given Luc a raise three times already since Summer got here. It wasn't that Luc didn't care about money, because he had gone hungry quite a lot until he was ten, but now that he had more than enough to cover lodging, very nice clothes, and the world's best food, all the extra just funneled straight to his broker. Since he had more than enough in his accounts to open his own place if he ever wanted and still finance sous-chefs like Patrick when they finally set out on their own, salary increases were more like a polite compliment than anything else at this point.

And every single time Alain sent a note giving him another raise, he added a P.S. mentioning how many days remained until Summer Corey's departure. *Don't worry, she's not planning to stay. Eighty-three days left now.* Luc had ripped the last one into pieces and dropped it on the nearest open burner.

Putain. Aladdin's Cave? She had managed to ignore Aladdin's Cave? The little sesame seed, even? That hadn't charmed her? She, who had been so thrilled at the hotel's Économat, hadn't been completely taken with the desire to see what was hiding under the fragile shell of chocolate?

Go ahead, you like to crack a man just by toying with his collar and breathing into his ear. Here's something you can crack. While I crack you. The sesame seed was his little symbol for the moment when her mouth opened to his taking.

Unable to contain his temper within the kitchen, he stepped into the Coudrerie, the hotel's sewing room.

And discovered a butt sticking out from under one of the long sewing tables, in erotically patterned leggings, a flirty tunic top leaving little covered at that angle. Laughter came from under the table. "Here's another one! It's the little puppy! Genevieve!"

Laughter—*real* laughter—and Summer's upthrust, barely clad butt. Some great hand picked him up and shook him, back and forth, up and down, watching the way his insides fell out for its own amusement.

Jeannine, who had been a seamstress at the hotel for longer than Luc had been alive, was in the Coudrerie laughing too, more buttons spilled in front of her on the table beside her sewing machine. Because after twenty years of focusing on details he had lost the ability to miss anything—either that or, *merde,* because the first ten years of his life had been spent scrabbling for coins fallen among crowds of feet—Luc spotted half a dozen more buttons scattered across the floor.

"Do you remember the little dog button, the little Genevieve?" Summer's bottom wiggled out from under the table and bumped into his legs. Summer sat back on her heels. "Oops." For one second her laughter vanished, so radically erased that he wanted to hit himself in punishment. And he hadn't even done anything to her. Not one damn thing of all the things he wanted to do. Then her blue gaze crawled up his body, lingering thoughtfully at his crotch, just above her face. His whole body tightened, and he fought with everything in him not to let that body give her a visible reaction.

"Why it's Gorgeous himself!" Summer exclaimed happily. "What perfect timing. I was just wondering whether I should brave the rain to go over to the Louvre and look at all those beautiful Greek gods with hearts of stone. But why bother, when I've got you, right here?" Luc's eyes were still narrowing over all the different ways she had just managed to needle him in one sentence, when she turned back on her hands and knees, in a long, slow arch of her tantalizing *fesses* right in front of him. "Jeannine, do you still have the little princess button?"

Still?

"Oh, *pucette!* The maid was supposed to slip it to you before you left. You were such a sweetie, and it just broke my heart the way those tears ran down your face without a sound. You mean you never got it?"

Tears without a sound? It kind of broke his heart to even hear about it. It made him *mad.* Who had made her cry, and why hadn't he been there to stop it?

Oh, for God's sake. He was getting heartily fed up with his sixteen-year-old reactions to her. *Oh, did you break a nail? Let me kill myself so that you don't cry about it.* Sixteen had not been a good age for him.

The wiggling butt paused. Summer lifted herself off her knees enough to look over the table at Jeannine. "No," she said quietly. "But thank you." For a moment, her face was entirely naked and sincere.

She caught Luc's eyes on her, dropped back onto her

heels out of Jeannine's sight—and the sweetie brought her thumb up to her mouth to nibble on the tip, her eyes resting vaguely on his crotch as if she had no idea where she was looking. Arousal washed him helplessly. She flipped back onto her hands and knees, her butt wiggling as that tunic top flared up and showed pretty much everything and then fell back again.

She just hid from me behind her own worse-than-naked butt, he realized suddenly. And it was working. Visions were taking over any possibility of understanding her, leaving only thoughts of grabbing, pulling, stretching her out before him and stripping all her shields away, making her come and come and come for him until she couldn't think of anything else when she looked at him but . . .

"Summer got lost down here once when she was about five," Jeannine explained to him comfortably, and Luc blinked with the shock of her grandmotherly normalcy in the midst of his fantasies. "She ended up playing with my box of buttons until I could get someone to track down her parents. They had the whole hotel shut down in fear of kidnappers by then."

"Got my first nanny fired," came Summer's flippant voice from under the table. "I'm hell on people, really."

It was only Jeannine's odd, compassionate gaze that made Luc wonder how much he was missing that Jeannine saw behind that flippant manner. And now he had a picture in his head of five-year-old Summer with tears streaming down her cheeks. Why silent? Some of his little foster brothers would cry silently like that—as if their pasts had taught them that being discovered in tears might make their troubles worse—but didn't your average, healthy, normal five-year-old girl make noise when she cried? Because, you know, she believed someone would pay attention and try to fix her grief if she made them aware of it?

"What about the beast?" Summer called. "Do you still

have that one? That's my favorite button. There's something about it that makes me think of you, your majesty."

If crying hadn't gotten her the attention she needed, she certainly had learned some other techniques as she grew up, hadn't she?

"What can I do for you, Luc?" Jeannine asked, and he looked up to find her amused eyes on him. He had often wished that Jeannine was his grandmother. How strange to think that Summer might have wished for the same thing.

The butt just below his gaze flexed as Summer stretched to reach a button, moving into a position a woman would only otherwise take if . . . if . . .

He dragged his hand over his face and forced himself to meet those shrewd eyes again. "I wanted to talk to you about my buttons."

"Why?" Blue eyes glinted. "You're not getting enough of yours pushed already?"

Merde, what had he just said? "Cloths." He dropped his sketch on top of the damned buttons. "I want to talk to you about doing a linen square for this." A heart-shaped *coeur au fromage blanc,* soft delicate sweetness nestled in its own little box, wrapped in a linen square, like the artisan work of a small farmer. If that farmer could afford hand-embroidered linen cheesecloths. It would be one of the dessert's three artfully presented elements, pulling in red themes of passion and romance, using the early strawberries that might just be starting to come in from the Garrigue if spring arrived soon enough.

Otherwise he would have to import the strawberries from South Africa or get them greenhouse grown, but sometimes you just had to steal spring into your life any way you could.

"Oh, *look,*" Summer said from under the table. "It's a little cupcake button. I never saw this one before. Your majesty, you should have this one." She poked up to set it on the table in front of him. It was pink.

He really should have known she had an affinity for other people's buttons. "I do not make cupcakes," he said between his teeth. Unless . . . "Do you like them?"

Something flashed through her eyes—what *was* that roar of feeling she hid so quickly?—and then she disappeared under the table again. "I don't know. Are they sweet?" she called back up merrily.

If he ever made a cupcake for her, she might end up wearing the damn thing. On her face, or . . . actually he might rather smash it on her breasts, and . . . *control. Don't let her do this to you.*

"Do you want an unfinished hem?" Jeannine asked of his sketch. "To give it that pseudo-rustic touch? Or something very elegant, like a queen's handkerchief?"

"Unfinished. Give it an element that feels real." Like you could actually reach out and touch it and it wouldn't disappear on you with a smile and a promise of a yacht.

"Like it's not completely removed from life?" Summer murmured below, a little button clinking into the tin she held.

He was the one completely removed from life? He filled lives with wonder, while she swung in a hammock on an island and . . . taught schoolkids, fine, in a place so remote that it apparently frequently lost electricity, but—

"How many do you need?" Jeannine asked. He tried to focus. Not usually something he found hard to do.

"Could you make eight hundred?"

"As long as we can use one of the machines to embroider the logo and your name," Jeannine said sternly. "Don't start with your hand-embroidered spiel."

Luc folded his hands behind his back and fixed dark eyes on her.

Jeannine made a humphing sound. "I don't know where you learned to look at a woman like that, but it should be outlawed. I'll see what we can do about the hand embroidery. Maybe my daughter would like to do some while she's at home with the baby. No promises. But we'll get you eight hundred, *perhaps machine-stitched,* by Valentine's."

"The weekend before, really," Luc said. "Since Valentine's is midweek. You know we book up then."

"Anyone would think you were a very spoiled child," Jeannine said severely. But he had a suspicion she knew he hadn't been, because she laughed and reached out to squeeze his arm. It was funny how hungry he was, to this day, for touches like that—casual, friendly, breaking through his isolation.

"I love you, Jeannine," he said, quite sincerely, and she waved her hand at him and blushed, not buying it for a second.

Summer poked her head out from under the table and studied him.

"So how is it, exactly, that I look at you?" he asked Jeannine curiously to help him ignore Summer while the seamstress drew a copy of the linen he'd sketched, noting measurements. "That you say should be outlawed?"

Jeannine waved her hand. "All that pent-up passion and you being so ruthless with it. We feel sorry for it. Plus, I figure passion is like the universe. You can compress it down into a tiny dot, but eventually it's going to explode again."

Maybe he shouldn't have asked this question with Summer Corey in the room. "Origin of the universe theories? You read too much, Jeannine. Shouldn't you be resting your eyes when you get home?"

"Audio books are a wonder," she retorted, as he turned

away and headed past Summer to the door. "*I've* got a long Métro trip."

"Careful!" Summer snuck her fingers under his foot so fast she had to be trying to make him step on her.

He didn't, of course. Reflexes honed from much greater challenges than her, he didn't even brush against her.

"*There's* the beast," Summer called to Jeannine, holding up a carved black button. He caught a glimpse of a wild, fanged face as he opened the door. "I knew it was around here somewhere. Although myself, I still think it's really supposed to be the Lord of Hell."

CHAPTER 8

A nd another day. Summer finished writing postcards to each of her twenty-one schoolkids, packaged them up with various new toys and mementos from Paris that were going to make their eyes light with joy, and looked at her calendar, counting the eighty more days between her and escape.

Not so bad, right? She had gotten through ten days. She was miserable, but God, she had been far more miserable than this, and with no end in sight to it, either. Five years, her time in that boarding school. She could do three months.

She tried and failed to get through to her schoolkids via a video link. Connections must be out again—they really did need another satellite in that region. Funny how when people talked about what a wonderful philanthropist her father was—because he did give away a huge chunk of change—they mostly remained oblivious to how much that philanthropy worked to other purposes, always getting him something he wanted in exchange. Even from his own daughter.

She thought about pretending to help run the hotel, but for God's sake, Alain had enough to suffer through just having her here. So she added some more photos to the island ones she kept scrolling on her big-screen television, playing with the different options for the slideshow until she really didn't have any excuse to play with them anymore. She loved those photos. They reminded her that sunshine and happiness did exist somewhere, and she had found it for herself, and she would get back to it very soon.

She supposed she could have read a book or something after that, but by then the solitude of the room was eating at her, bringing back all those years of loneliness. On her island, she had finally found a place where she could shower love on people and get loved back, and being separated from it . . . God, it was like this place was sucking her down into an old black quagmire, drowning her in that muck.

She picked up her stack of phone messages. No women, of course. Women never liked her. Well, except for on Manunui, her island, but that was probably because she was such an exotic there she was easier to tolerate. Plus, she lived like a damned nun. Old boyfriends—a lot of those. At least three of them were married. Enough paper slips with journalists' names on them to start her own little bonfire. *Penthouse, Playboy* . . . she crumpled them up hard and tossed them in the trash. Men whose names were only vaguely familiar, meaning they were people working a tenuous connection in the hopes of landing her and through her, her father. Her father might be encouraging some of them. A porn filmmaker. The industry must have some fresh blood in it, ignorant of what had happened to the last person who tried to approach her with a porn film offer, back when she was in college. Her father had destroyed an entire film house. Lashing her viciously all the while for having behaved in a way that would "encourage them to think she would be willing."

Vincent Morin.

She stopped at that, a chill rising all along the back of

her neck, and her stomach knotting into nausea. Oh, God. How *dare* he? Hadn't her father obliterated him? Had he climbed his way back? One word to her father, and the man would be history again, but oh, God . . . nausea threatened to overwhelm her at the thought of what her father might say to her again. The memories.

She shoved herself away from the desk and gave the Eiffel Tower one vicious glare through the curtain of rain. The empty hotel room pressed on her like some fist trying to squeeze every last bit of life out of her heart, but Summer knew exactly how the rain would spatter cold against her legs if she walked the length of the Seine under a big umbrella to get away from that loneliness. She had done it so many times. She had tried all kinds of colors of umbrellas: rainbow, pink with glittering silver sparkles, a jaunty yellow. In the end, the umbrella might as well be black. All the others just made you feel more pitiful, more desperate, that loneliness trailing behind you and curling back around you at every opportunity like a vampire's cloak.

She hauled on the old Harvard sweatshirt she always kept with her. XXL, swamping her. She had bought it once after a breakup, after she had returned yet another boyfriend's sweatshirt, during her college years, and thought that maybe the warmth and reassurance she was seeking needed to come from her. It had been the beginnings of a change, but it had still taken years in the islands to reach . . . well, her current pathetic point. Throwing herself at supposed bellmen and going out with men who wanted her father, just so she wouldn't have to face the loneliness again.

A text from her mother indicated that her parents were postponing their planned swing back through Paris yet again. "Love you, sweetie! Hope you're having fun! Wish I could be in Paris with you!"

She dropped the phone in the trash, but no matter how many times she did that, someone in housekeeping always fished it back out and put it on the little stand near the trashcan.

She could go for a swim, or she could go to the Louvre, yet again. Or she knew one place where it was warm and she wouldn't be alone. Where she would be distracted. She knew she wasn't supposed to let herself go there, but . . .

"So are we working on your captured heart today?" Patrick asked merrily, painting cones of dark chocolate with a rippling pattern of gold. Luc flicked him a quick, narrow glance.

"*Aïe!*" Patrick ducked. "How many times do I have to talk to you about that look? I've got scars from that thing."

"Then don't ask for it." Was *that* why she called him the Lord of Hell? The way he could look at people when they were out of line?

"It's a reasonable question! If we're going to put your heart on the menu, you have to warn me, as it's the last thing I'll ever get to make for the rest of my life. You know it's going to be popular."

"It's not my heart," Luc said between his teeth. "And no. We're not working on it today." The photos of her and Derek Martin at that perfume launch had peppered the Web this morning. Summer's face turned up to Derek's dark one, smiling. Not even Patrick had dared put those on his corkboard.

Patrick nodded thoughtfully. Pursed his lips in a silent whistle while he sprayed gold. Glanced at Luc. "Too sweet?" he asked sympathetically.

"Patrick, you fu—"

He broke off as the door opened and the kitchens went quiet.

Quiet that lasted the length of a glance from Summer to Luc, a second of stillness. She gave them all that bright smile of hers. "Do you mind if I watch?"

Just for his ear alone, Patrick gave an incredulous little huff. "Do you *mind?* You mean she doesn't realize what a narcissist you are? You two need to work on your communication skills."

Luc ignored him, because it would give Patrick far too much pleasure if he reacted. "Not at all," he told Summer, his heart starting to beat too hard. She wanted to *watch* him? Just—stand there and watch?

Was this another manipulative game? Had she realized that weakness of his, how being the center of her focus would reduce him to pure craving? Had she any idea that when she asked to watch him, his whole body flooded with pure, sexual delight? He bet she did. She was bored, and he was an easy toy for her.

She tucked herself up very small just inside the door, pressed back against the wall. Like she was trying to efface herself out of existence, which was *ridiculous* given her beauty. No one was going to forget her existence.

Still, he tried, because what else was he supposed to do? Dance for her? Shake his little tambourine and hold out his upturned palm and hope she would put something in it? After she had dismissed his entire *worth,* over and over and over?

He hated himself for the compulsion, but his body started performing for her anyway.

Watch me. As he dipped the prongs of a whisk into caramel and whipped them through the air, spinning sugar off them like some Fairy King spinning gold into sunlight.

She folded her hands behind her, tucked firmly back against the wall. *No, don't resist. Come here.* Catching the hair-fine sugar in his hands, making a net of it to settle over a tiny, stubborn dark heart.

Coolness emanated off his team toward her, since she kept negating their entire worth by not eating sweets. Only Patrick gave her a quirky, inviting grin, and, just for Luc's ears, a wolf whistle.

Seriously, Luc might kill him someday.

Come here. Look. Look at what I'm doing, right now, crave it, come in reach.

She stood so quietly. In a giant sweatshirt from Harvard that made him want to kill someone. What old boyfriend had given it to her, that she still turned to it whenever she wanted to be wrapped up in warmth? What had she done with Luc's own coat, hung it up amid a mass of garments collected from all the men overwhelmed by the instinct to hide her, protect her, make her theirs?

It was surreal, how steady and quiet Summer Corey was, the beachcomber diva who smiled at men as if she expected their world to turn on it. As simple and still as a ray of light that had slipped through a high window by mistake. He might as well have been some shriveled pale bean sprout left in a closet as an experiment, finally given sunlight. He could feel himself expanding, leaves unfurling, as she watched him.

Was she going to stand there until he went insane? Her presence prickled over his skin, no matter how fast he moved, no matter how lithe and strong and in control he showed his body to be.

Crack. Look at what I'm making. Come over here and I'll put it in your mouth. You don't even have to beg. You just have to crack. Not me for you. You for me.

He could hold her in his hands and put all her pieces back together again. His palms itched to take that raw perfect essence of her and stroke her into one pure expression of ecstasy.

Allez, soleil. Crack. Or, merde, at least come here.

"What is she doing?" he murmured to Patrick when he

ducked into the refrigerator for a second to try to cool himself off. "Why doesn't she . . ." Walk up and run her finger straight down his body to his dick, or whatever she was likely to do next. She was driving him so crazy, he couldn't tell.

A curious glint in Patrick's blue eyes as he reached for some cream. "Did it ever occur to you that she might be shy?"

The woman who walked up to men and ripped their souls right out of their bodies for her casual amusement? "No. It didn't occur to me. She has a *Penthouse* spread about her, *merde.*" More an article, really, about how all the men she touched turned to gold, but they'd included some maddening photos. *He* could tell they were touched up and that a body double had been used, but it made him writhe with fury to think of other men looking at them. He should sure as hell not have looked her up on Google.

Patrick sighed and shook his head. "You know, Luc, for someone so creative, you have an incredible lack of imagination when it comes to other people. Do you think it comes from self-absorption?"

"What the hell are you even talking about, Patrick? You only ever see me with people who work for me. What am I supposed to be imagining about them?"

Patrick gave him a deeply annoyed look and left the refrigerator. Meaning Luc had to go back out, too, because he would be damned if he'd let Summer's eyes rest with such absorption on Patrick instead of him.

He couldn't claim she was disturbing him, Summer thought. Or being a spoiled brat. She knew how not to disturb driven, focused men. If you tucked yourself far away from everything amazing and were really quiet, they didn't mind.

Of course, she couldn't stop her thoughts: *Stop working and look at me. I'm so cold in this city, and you . . . are so dark and hot.*

Why did he have to be so beautiful? That gold-bronze skin, the forged, perfect face and fine, sensual mouth, the black eyes that saw everything, even—with occasional brief indifference—her. His grace and control coiled need in her, tighter and tighter, until it wanted to burst out of her like a spring.

Damn it, that was the last time she went celibate for three years. Time to move on to the Aladdin's Cave pantry or the Coudrerie or some other, safer distraction. She took a breath and started to force herself away from the wall.

"Luc." Alain Roussel came through the door, followed by a small woman in a turquoise wool coat, her curly brown hair stuffed into a clip that couldn't contain it, a camera clicking already. "*Pardon.* Ellie Layne is here. Remember, you said she could come get some pictures of you putting together a dessert for her blog?"

Luc glanced up and smiled.

Something punched through Summer's middle and left her floundering at the huge hole left behind. He could *smile*? That sensual mouth curling, his eyes full of passion and a brilliant, glowing warmth. The camera flashed.

He had *that* in him? But never once an inkling of it for her?

She had *told* him she had been traveling and seasick for four days before she'd insulted him with that tip. How unforgiving and perfectionistic was he? And what had Ellie Layne done that was so perfect?

"Ellie," Luc said. He sounded amused. *Friendly.* For crying out loud, he could be friendly? "How are you?" Luc came around the counter to give the blogger a kiss on each cheek. "You're going to ruin your nice coat."

Oh, come on, Summer thought, outraged. It was *tur-quoise*. In Paris. In the winter.

"Here." He hadn't even acknowledged Summer's presence for an hour, but he took Ellie's coat off for her and tucked it up safe in his glass-walled office. And came back with a chef's jacket for her to wear, probably one of his own, while he himself had changed into that stylish white shirt he wore for the cameras. The one that made him look so freaking hot.

Ellie, meanwhile, was burbling. So much happiness sparkled off her in all directions, Summer was surprised it didn't sizzle when it hit the counters. "I can't believe— *your* kitchens—*thank you*, Monsieur Le—I mean, Luc." She clasped her hands over her camera and caught herself mid-bounce on her toes, trying to contain herself.

"Tell Simon thanks for the sculptures at New Year's," Luc said, *indulgently*. He didn't have an indulgent bone in his body. Not that he had shown to Summer, anyway. "They were superb."

"I know." Ellie beamed. "He's incredible."

"Yes, we did gather you thought so," Luc said urbanely, with the tiniest suppressed twitch of his lips. "Hot, too."

Ellie blushed, and then her eyes went starry. "You read my blog?"

"The posts about Simon get circulated sometimes," Luc said apologetically. "He's so private. You really couldn't have happened to a person who deserved it more."

"You know, I can tell the world you're hot, too," Ellie warned, in what was apparently the best threat little Miss Bouncy could come up with.

Summer caught the hem of her sweatshirt and pulled it straight over her head. Luc's eyes locked on her torso. A white silk camisole just this side of transparent flowed gently around her hips, over the clinging low-cut line of aged jeans. Her bared shoulders prickled with the need for warm hands to caress them, and the line of the silk floated gently low on her breasts, slowly shivering to rest after her movement.

Ellie Layne glanced around to follow Luc's focus, gave Summer the friendliest, most open smile she had ever received from a woman on first glance in her life, and turned back to Luc.

Who dropped Summer from his attention again in Ellie's favor. "Yes, but then, just think how upset Simon would be. If you told people I'm hot."

Was he flirting with her? That sounded like flirting to Summer. Wasn't that a wedding ring on her finger?

Summer slipped her thumbs into her pockets, the aggressive V of her hands drawing the eye to her pelvis. Luc's gaze flicked to the low waist of her jeans, then lifted to her face in a long, straight study, his expression impossible to read.

Ellie's phone burped in her pocket. She snuck a peek at it, grinned, blushed, and turned the sound off.

"Simon?" Luc, amused, refocused on Ellie. He wasn't all cool and unreadable with *her*. He didn't mind *her* interrupting his concentration.

It's really all right, a voice whispered through her. Luc's voice, after she had shattered his dessert, his hand held out to her, his eyes intent, coaxing, just before she'd fled. She stirred, confused. Had he really not minded, that she'd disturbed his concentration? *You're perfect.*

He shouldn't say that to her. It was unfair when she wanted so badly to hear it.

"He likes to keep in touch." Flustered, Ellie covered the screen of her phone as she slipped it back into her pocket.

"I bet he doesn't keep in quite as good touch when she's visiting the ones who are sixty," a warm voice said in Summer's ear, and she looked up to find that golden surfer-chef winking down at her, his eyes vivid blue. "Do you think that was a pornographic message?"

After Ellie's, his was the warmest look she had received since she got to this ghastly city, and Summer's face relaxed in response, tilting up to him.

"Patrick, would you mind walking through the steps in the *baba au rhum* with Sarah?" Luc's coolest voice intervened. "I wanted her to learn how to make it."

Patrick grinned as if he had just won multiple victories in one casual move, winked at Summer, and in a lazy, un-hurried motion somehow managed to be over at a counter helping a tense black-haired young woman before Summer could blink.

"So what can I help you with, Ellie?" Luc asked, still indulgent, affectionate, amused. *Affectionate.*

When Summer was doing her best to survive on four years of stored-up affection for the three months she had to spend in this emotional wasteland.

"Oh, *anything,*" Ellie said delightedly. "Just do whatever you do! Just to *be* here and observe, that's all I want. You don't mind if I take pictures? I won't get in the way?"

"My kitchens are your kitchens." Luc smiled. How many women did his damn kitchens belong to? Summer bit her lip on the rash urge to tell Ellie the Ecstatic that, in fact, they were *Summer's* kitchens and she wasn't welcome.

She'd bet that would get Luc's attention, all right. She imagined every light in the place going out in his sudden black rage. And then she imagined how perfectly con-trolled he would be as he prowled through that blackness after her, and a hungry shiver ran through her.

"Here." Luc patted the counter *right next to him.* When Summer had been standing on the other side of the room, pressed up just beside the door, for an *hour.* "I'm working on a new dessert," he told Ellie.

The woman nearly had a heart attack from pure joy. "Oh! Oh, and I get to *watch?* And put it on my blog before you even send it out to the restaurant? Oh my God."

"*Don't* call him that," Patrick slipped in irrepressibly, and Summer choked on a giggle. "He's going to start making us kneel and pray to him every morning when we come in, if people keep this shit up."

"You waste enough time already without the excuse of a daily prayer," Luc said dryly. Summer's suppressed giggle had drawn his eyes to her again.

Their gazes held, and darkness washed over her. Like a shelter, like a gift. Slowly her hands slipped up from the cocky sexual position at her hips to curve over her own arms, caressing that darkness to her. As if she had been floating, some tiny spark, on the winds for ages, at last to be caught in one hard palm, the other closing over to form a shell of darkness. For a moment she felt utterly protected and at peace and warm, nestled between two careful, powerful hands. *Wait, how had that happened? Summer, never put yourself in the hands of a man who thinks you're worthless. It's a good way to get crushed.*

"For this one, I wanted to start with darkness," Luc said. *Yes, darkness. Sweet, strong darkness.*

"Craggy. Intense." He pulled another of the molds of dark chocolate over to him. Oh. He wasn't even talking to her. He was showing Her Perkiness what he had been working on. "Inside it, there's something softer, sweeter, but still dark." He flipped it over to show Ellie the sealed base. "Layers of ganache and a soft *coulis* of caramel, infused with just the right amount of elder at the top, then thyme, then cinnamon, then curry, then pure dark Venezuelan cacao, so that as you eat it, it's as if you're sinking deeper and deeper into the earth."

Summer rubbed her arms to the rhythm of his words. She felt like a child, lying alone in her bed, watching some

94 · *Laura Florand*

other child be rocked to a sweet lullaby, just close enough that she could hear it, too.

Luc gave that intense, intimate smile straight into Ellie's camera. "I start with that," he said as Ellie filmed, placing the craggy molded chocolate on the center of its pure-black plate, a square plate, severe, barely curved at the edges. "And then—gold falls."

Lips pursed as he blew a finger's touch of gold powder over his creation. Arousal sparkled all over Summer's skin, as if the gold fairy dust had been breathed over her and now held her in a net of desire. Longing ached deep in her.

He glanced up from the chocolate rocklike formation, on which the gold dust glimmered like hidden treasure. His eyes flicked over her. Thoughtful, intent. He could have been a painter, eyeing his subject. He reached for something over a hot burner, pouring it out on marble, molten and glowing gold, then picking it up as it started to cool. Was that half-molten sugar he was pulling so deftly between his hands? Summer's fingertips flinched into her arms. Didn't that *hurt*?

Could she kiss it and make it better?

Stop it, Summer.

He formed the sugar into a jagged ray, balanced on the chocolate abyss so that the ray penetrated into its heart, cradled by its crags.

"I think I'll call it First Light."

Ellie made a delighted sound, clicking away excitedly as she worked her way around the dessert.

Summer had known cruelty by dessert all her child-hood, had sat through endless hours of stifling dinners while all around her at other tables people exclaimed at the gorgeous delicacies that finished their meals, knowing all the time, with every single dessert her eyes ever tracked as it passed her table en route to some other man or woman or delighted child, that always, always, she would do something that would mean that dessert was denied her.

She had never known the true extent that cruelty could reach, until she watched Luc Leroi invent just such a dessert, pour his soul into it, and hand it to another woman with that vivid, passionate look.

She didn't realize she had come forward until the counter dug into her hips. And she stopped, afraid and furious with herself. She had stripped to her camisole and left herself naked amid all these jacketed people. And now she had let him see how much it mattered, the game he played with her.

She dug into her pockets with her hands, the only things she could still hide.

Luc slid something in front of her, but she couldn't look away from his face. His dark eyes were almost . . . gentle. Something in them like that sound in his voice when he had said, so calmly, *You're perfect,* and slipped his coat around her.

Summer, back off now. He'll catch you. And he hasn't even tried. You'll twist in hell the whole rest of your life and never make it back out into the sun.

"*Soleil,*" he said, "sun, sunlight," probably toying with other names for his new dessert. The forged, elegant lines of his face held a hint of softness. She struggled not to touch those lines. Not to beg him to hold her carefully in strong hands. *I'm really lonely. Would you mind, just for a minute?*

"It's for you." He nudged something closer to her.

Summer glanced down at last and nearly jumped out of her skin. The beautiful chocolate-and-gold First Light sat only inches from her. "No!" She fell back a step, flinging up her hands. "Oh, *no.* Don't you *dare*—you made it for her, you made it right in front of her, don't you *dare* pull it away from her and give it to me."

All the tempered beauty of Luc's face turned severe. "I beg your pardon?" he breathed. The whole kitchen had stilled. Beyond him, even the nice surfer-chef looked appalled.

"How could you be so *cruel*? She's . . ." God, if ever there was anyone more vibrant, more enthusiastic, more heart laid out open in love for something, it was that bouncy Ellie Layne. Summer took a deep breath and caught herself, too much already revealed. Lightly, quite firmly, she shook her head at him and lifted a playful but arrogant finger. His eyes glittered so black they cut. "No. No toying with our guests, Monsieur. In fact—" she turned and gave Ellie a warm smile, holding out her hand. "I'm Summer Corey. It's such a pleasure to have you here in our kitchens." She winked. "I *insist* that they spoil you rotten. Anything you want to taste on our menus, you have only to ask."

Ellie bounced on her toes. Summer gave them all a blinding smile and swept out.

CHAPTER 9

Petrified silence filled the kitchens. *"Putain de merde,"* Patrick said finally, the only one who had the nerve to draw a breath. "Luc—"

"If you'll excuse me," Luc said precisely to Ellie. "Just one moment."

He strode through the door by which Summer had disappeared.

"Oh my God," Alain Roussel muttered. "She's only been here ten days, and already he's going to quit."

When Summer stepped out of the elevator, Luc leaned negligently against the opposite wall. As if he had risen straight out of the depths by an act of magic, not beaten her via the stairs. He wasn't even out of breath. In his styled white shirt he could have been a man who had been waiting half an hour for his date.

Except that when his eyes met hers all the light went out of the hall, and she wanted to press herself against him and see if that would dissipate his anger. *I'm sorry, what did I do? I didn't mean to . . .* Revulsion swelled up in her, pure hatred of him. She was *never* excusing herself against unreasoning anger again. He could take his fucking desserts and stuff them up his *ass.* He was not holding those over her.

"Summer Corey," he said, so easily, so coolly, that her own name flicked across her body and raised a welt. "Might I have a word?"

Sullenness stirred harder, just at the tone. She tilted her head and smiled at him, up and under. "I prefer actions."

"Doubtless." His contempt burned all over her skin—nothing in her worth anything to anyone. "But I believe I'll confine myself to conversation."

He took her card out of her hand and opened her hotel room door. One of those elegant powerful hands of his flicked out, as if he couldn't soil his hand by taking her elbow.

Summer grew more and more mutinous as his anger and his control over it reduced her to nothing. "That's what you say now," she murmured provocatively as she passed him.

He snapped the door closed. In the entryway of the suite, the Eiffel Tower reached her already. At least the winter daylight subdued her, Summer thought hostilely. *Made La Tour looks like an old, gray woman, past anything but her own delusions.*

"Don't you ever"—the whip of Luc's tone yanked her around to face him—"come into my kitchens again and tell me to *feed someone*."

She caught herself backing up a step and braced her feet apart, thumbs at the waist of her jeans. "You were *cruel* to her. Making that in front of her and then offering it to some other woman."

"I offered it *to you*." His eyes glittered as he looked at her, building pressure on her to say something.

"And I appreciated that. But you know I don't really eat sweets, and you made it *right in front of her*. And she clearly *loves* these things."

Whatever he had wanted her to say, it wasn't that. Dark anger surged, held in some iron grip she couldn't begin to fathom. He took one step forward and placed a hand over her head, backing her against the wall. She felt the tautness in his muscles all through her body until she hardly dared breathe for the way each breath grew shakier, more full of wanting. She was so screwed up. "Trust me, in *my* kitchens, Ellie is *not going to starve.*"

Why, because he liked *her*?

She slid her body against the wall to escape before she plastered herself against him, which was how screwed up she was. His other arm came up to block her. "But you pulled it right out from in front of her—"

"*I'm going to make her another one.* Do you think I need *you* to tell me how to treat someone in my kitchens?"

What was wrong with her? Her hands fisted slowly by her sides.

"To insist that *I* spoil her? That's all I ever do, is spoil people beyond their wildest dreams, every waking moment of my day."

She rubbed the wall with her fists, utterly confused by this description of himself. And terrified by her crazy leap of hope. He *wanted* people to be spoiled?

"She's here all day. Simon asked me to let her come, because that's what he lives for, to fill her little bucket up with joy, and I'm doing it, because I love how happy it makes her. *She* knows how lucky she is."

Why was Ellie Layne "enough" for him, damn it? Why did he love making *her* happy?

"Well," Summer tried, flippantly. "With you attentive to her every wish? Who wouldn't?"

God, his look cut her to pieces. She wanted to bury herself against his chest to hide from it. Get close enough that he couldn't cut her without cutting himself. "You. You know, your father's right about you. You really are a clueless, spoiled brat. Stay the hell out of my kitchens, Summer Corey."

He walked out.

It was a long time before Summer peeled herself off the wall and walked to the cold window, looking out at the Tower. Even worn and waned by the gray day, that tower didn't yield. Not ever.

She was crying. Shaking with it. Her forehead pressed against the glass, as the tears streamed hopelessly.

Where's her nanny? Mai, you get her. She's acting like a clueless, spoiled brat. Can't she understand that I'm busy with something important? Some fit she had pitched to try to get attention. *You're acting like a spoiled brat. Quit fidgeting at the table and let us talk.*

You're nothing but a spoiled brat. All the things we give you, and you can't stand it that I can't give you more attention. Don't you understand that children somewhere else in the world might starve based on what decision I make? She had probably been five, but they blurred together after a while, the claims of her spoiled brat-ness. She might have been four or six or seven.

Spoiled bitch. I'm sure her daddy gets her anything she wants. Boarding school, a thirteen-year-old who had barely ever socialized with anyone her own age, who had only ever been trained to impress adults with her smile and clothes and manners, thrown in at the deep end with a horde of other exiled teenagers, most of whom were older, none of whom could ever be as rich as she.

She scrubbed her face very hard, scrubbed every last tear away. The bastard. Shoulders straightening, she drew one of those deep breaths that let everyone and everything float away from her, left her light as silk in the wind.

Two more tears welled up in her eyes. She made no attempt to fight them, just stood there as they rolled down her cheeks. Slowly they dried, leaving nothing behind.

She grabbed her phone. "I hate you!" she hissed fiercely to her father. "I. Hate. You."

"Summer, did you call me out of a meeting to tell me that?" Sam Corey asked, exasperated. "I thought it was something important about the hotel. And you can't talk to me that way," he added as an afterthought. "I'm your father. I swear, your nanny spoiled you rotten."

"I was *happy*! I'm your *daughter.*"

"Yes, I know you're my daughter. And believe me, it's not every girl whose father can buy her favorite hotel when he's trying to drag her out of her dumps. Four years on some godforsaken island. Your mother nearly had a fit at how much you had let yourself go."

"When I told you about the problems when they lost communications for days, couldn't you have just invested? Just because I'm your daughter, and you could afford it, and it was a good thing to do? Did you have to force me away from there to pay some kind of price for it? Does everything have to be a bargain with you?"

"You know, you have quite the idea of yourself, if you think three months of your life is worth more than a satellite. Which, by the way, you could afford yourself if you'd been paying attention to your investments instead of lazing around in a damn hammock for the past four years. God almighty, we spoiled you. But you can't always get something for nothing, Summer."

A sharp pain lanced through her arm. Her fingernails, gouging into her own skin. God, she hadn't done that since she was a teenager and her boarding school had intervened with counseling. The counselor had thought she was a spoiled brat, too, unable to appreciate what a wonderful life she had and desperate for attention. She locked the guilty hand around the window frame and stared out at that impervious, merciless Eiffel Tower.

Why was she always the "nothing" in the equation?

Her eyes filled with tears again.

"Just give this a try, for God's sake." Her father's exasperated voice. "You know you would be good at it. You would probably be amazing at it. My God, do you remember how you used to analyze P/E ratios when you were five years old? My friends couldn't get over that. *You* could be my heir if you would put your mind to it, and I wouldn't have to worry about a damn son-in-law."

Yes, she had been quite the hit at dinner tables with that one. Her father would turn to her with a grin, in the midst of his discussions with other businessmen, saying, "Well, let's see what Summer thinks." And she would say solemnly, "But what's its P/E ratio, Daddy?"

She still usually, by the end of the infinite meal, had managed to lose her right to dessert, though.

She laughed a little, bitterly, and more tears got shaken onto her cheeks. Didn't it figure that, within a week back in Paris, she had managed to get herself exiled from the one place here where she was almost happy, the very core of that magic where those desserts were formed?

The one place where . . . she had still been alone, yes. But everything else had just drained away as she watched him. His face so intense, beautiful things flaming from his hands like some magician's trick everywhere he turned.

Yes, she had been spoiled, to not be able to stand his preferring Ellie Layne to her. But she still didn't understand entirely what she had done any more than she had understood half the time at those dinner tables as a child, when she reached down under the table for something dropped while fidgeting and stayed bent too long staring at the forest of legs and fancy shoes, wishing she could play under there, and her father snapped that since she couldn't behave, she wasn't getting dessert.

It was true she had been spoiled. She had wanted his attention on her and not on some bouncy, perky woman he seemed to *like*. But she had tried to be nice to her, despite that. To protect her from that manipulation, to tell her that no one in Summer's hotel was going to torture her by making magic in front of her eyes and then denying her a taste.

She could never do anything right here, and the layers of misery, past and present, piled up like stones on her chest, until she was buried under a cairn of them, her last breath being crushed out of her.

"And it's not my favorite hotel!" she shouted suddenly at her father. "I HATE HOTELS!" She threw the phone, as hard as she could, at the Eiffel Tower. It bounced off the window and fell, unharmed, protected in its little case.

He didn't bother to call back.

CHAPTER 10

Within minutes of Ellie Layne Casset's departure late that afternoon, Patrick found an excuse to start plating one of the chocolate desserts beside Luc. "So did you leave her alive? Or did you flay her, you bastard?"

Luc fisted his hand around three circles of gold sugar and shattered them into bits. Damn it. He shook out his hand, scattering the fragments. "Are you protecting *her* from *me*?"

He shouldn't have used her father's insult against her. Since when did he stoop to imitating anyone, let alone someone so lacking in creativity?

Patrick lifted his fingers in indication of something about the size of an atom. "But she's so wittle bitty. And did you catch those big blue eyes on her?"

Yes. Still and blank, as he swept out . . .

"Stop protecting her, Patrick." It drove him wild with rage, the thought of *Patrick* stepping in to shield her. From him.

"Did you make her cry?" Patrick asked severely. "You're good at that."

"What?"

"All our girl *commis* and interns, before they quit. And me, every night on my pillow. Sarah, has His Godhood made you cry?"

The slender, dark-haired intern paused in the act of reaching across an open flame for a pan, that eternal crease of hers tightening between her eyebrows.

Patrick reached out and caught her arm, raising it higher above the burner. "Careful." He beseeched Luc for sympathy. "It's terrible. I'm so hot women are always burning themselves when they're around me. Not enough contrast with actual flames."

Sarah Lin's mouth tightened, and she grabbed the pan and disappeared again. Patrick didn't appear to notice.

"No, I did not make her cry," Luc snapped. "You're confusing her with someone who cares."

Patrick's lips twisted oddly. "I wonder why I might do that."

Luc rolled his shoulders. What a fucking awful day. Even Ellie's incessant bubbliness hadn't managed to make it better, and he usually liked Ellie quite a bit. In fact, he remembered feeling mildly jealous of Simon's catch. Today she had given him a migraine.

Shit. Was it possible he had really hurt Summer? And worse, had he *wanted* to?

Damn it, his shoulders felt knotted tight enough to snap. He could really use a swim.

Summer cut through water that yielded far too easily compared to ocean waves.

The hotel pool was a thing of beauty, a serpentine river whose brick edges curved around a small island in the middle, full of ferns and wide-leafed plants. More green things grew under gentle lights in banks around the room. Soft night-lights glowed under the water and from discreet points along the walls.

Summer swam around it like a hamster in a wheel. Used to swimming out to the reef on a daily basis so she could walk along it looking for shells, or swimming the half mile out to the neighboring atoll for fun, the compact little pool left her . . . frantic.

But she came here, every quiet, lonely night when it would be high noon on the other side of the world. Slipping into the monotony of it, no waves, no fish to nibble at her toes, no dolphins to arc up to the surface of the water in amused curiosity, no small harmless sharks to provide an illogical kick of adrenaline.

She could forget, let her mind go blank, sink Letheward. The river of oblivion.

Spoiled brat.

Yes, oblivion would be nice. Sleep, no dreams. It was one in the morning. The pool was closed, but if the spoiled brat owner wanted to drown herself, who was going to stop her? In fact, several charities and universities would be delighted. She couldn't say she had her father's dedication, but she had done a few clever things with the million dollars he had given her as "seed money" when she was eighteen. Turned out she had an amazing knack for dating future enormous successes and being the first person to invest in their dreams. Must be her taste for insanely obsessive, focused, ambitious workaholics. It never worked out well for the relationship, but her portfolio was doing great. *Penthouse* had even done an article on it once. "What do all these hotshots have in common? They once dated Summer Corey." She had refused to pose, but they had managed to get some sexpot shots off paparazzi and touch them up.

She tucked her head in and something touched her ankle. She gasped in water, surfacing.

Hands caught her hips and set her, coughing, against the edge. Luc Leroi. The strange lights of the nighttime pool played with the water gliding over his gold shoulders. He stood on the bottom of the pool that her toes couldn't reach, and her elbows braced on the edge put them almost exactly even. A strange sense of power surged through her. She was so used to looking up at men that to be on a level made her feel . . . towering. Invincible.

Exposed. To a man wearing nothing but a slick-fitting black swim short, his body on offer to her. Her gaze drifted before she could help it, over taut abs and strong, supple shoulders, long, defined arm muscles, a core constantly in use, a body that never stopped bending, lifting, stretching, controlling. Gold seemed to spread through her palms, a heat she wanted to stroke all over him.

"Pardon," Luc said. "I was signaling to pass."

Right. The touch of an ankle, pool rules. How hard had he pushed himself to overtake her? Even with all that compact power in his shoulders . . .

Don't pay attention to his bare shoulders, Summer. Or to the rise and fall of his chest. Or to the fact that his hands still held her hips. *Considering how spoiled you are, you have to have enough sense of self-preservation to get out of here with your soul.* But she pulled her cap off, ponytail dropping down to cling to the nape of her neck. Nobody looked good in a swimming cap.

"I'm sorry if I scared you." He seemed to pick his words with great care, his eyes watchful. "You don't notice much when you swim, do you?"

She shrugged, not smiling. How long had he stood there, watching her circle with those steady, impervious eyes of his?

Her body began to tickle all over in perverse pleasure at her vulnerability. *He's not supposed to be your toy, Summer. Remember? His emotions are too much more important than yours.*

Water trickled off his hair and slid down his forehead. He didn't release her hips to brush it off.

Her fingers ached as she watched the drop travel, curling into her palms as it neared his eyes. It caught on his eyebrow. Her own forehead crinkled, her thumb rubbing against her own hand.

"Or any other time," he said.

She had watched him for an hour. What did he think she hadn't seen? "We spoiled brats, we aren't famous for our powers of observation."

His hands flexed into her hips, sending heat lancing through her. "I would apologize for that, if I could make the apology sincere."

Her head went up. "Yes, and I would eat you, if I could stand to put you in my mouth," she said deliberately.

His hands spasmed on her hips.

"Eat your desserts, I mean." She smiled insincerely.

His eyes held hers, a black gloss. Incredulous, hard, searching. "You have a very . . . dirty . . . mouth," he said slowly, as if she was a riddle.

Oh, no, you're not going to figure me out. You've made it clear what you think of me, and you're not getting anywhere near anything that matters.

"No," she said with another wide smile that could leave him no idea how angry she was, and ran the tip of her tongue over her lips again, carefully, before giving a delicate, hungry nibble to her lower lip. "No, I promise, my mouth is perfectly . . . clean."

A tremor flickered over his skin.

She slipped off the support of the edge, pulling her body against his to stay afloat. He jerked when her body pressed against him. "Sum—"

She kissed him. Her mouth open on his . . . heat and warmth, his mouth so *sweet*. Opening to her instantly, taking her into his mouth, letting himself deep into hers. So hard and so hot. Her body slid wet against his as she tried to pull herself even more deeply into that dark intensity of him, and—

A hard hand closed around her chin and separated them,

wrenching her away from the mouth that was still shaped around hers. *"Qu'est-ce que tu fous?"* he asked crudely. "What the hell are you doing?" Crude, abruptly intimate, rough.

Great. Rough, intense sex with a stranger, breaking all barriers into vulgar intimacy. No hearts involved. That would be *perfect*. She surged up against him again, rubbing her hips against his while he forced her chin away from his mouth.

His hips arched into hers, his breath hoarse. His other hand wedged its way to her midsection and forced her back against the wall, away from him. "Do you even remember my name?"

What? Why the hell did he have to bring names into it? "I could just call you 'Gorgeous.'" Something safe like that. Yeah, and he could call her *spoiled brat*.

So much anger flared in his eyes. How powerless *was* she, if he could still control his temper?

She twisted her head quickly, catching his hard thumb in her teeth and suckling it. Breathing hard, face set, he pulled his hand away.

"Luc." She peeked enough to catch the flicker in his eyes as the word hit him. Now as long as she didn't let it hit *her*. "Luc," she whispered again and closed her eyes against any indication of his feelings. She couldn't do this if he was a person. She wanted temporary oblivion, a tiny dip in enticing darkness to get her through these three months here. Then she would go back to the place where she was whole and happy and not leave part of herself behind again with someone who thought she was insignificant.

She found his hand again and curled her tongue around his thumb.

He wrenched it out of her mouth and caught her chin, turning her face back toward his.

She kept her eyes shut. The chlorine overwhelmed his scent, aiding her quest for anonymity. She could forget how delicious he smelled, outside this pool. Like the world had blended its spices on his skin.

"Open your eyes, Summer."

She squeezed them tighter, drawing her leg up his thigh while the hot pressure of his hand against her belly kept her at bay. *Don't be ridiculous. You know you want this, nameless sex with a rich blond brat in a pool, come on, you don't need me to look at you. Let's just get this over with, all right? Lower that pressure. Just a few inches more . . .*

"*Putain.*" He picked her up to set her on the edge of the pool, and she opened her eyes enough to see a black fury.

"I've got higher standards than this," he said flatly.

Twisting, he dove into the water, not resurfacing until he was at the far turn around the little island, leaving her sitting there as if he had just sliced her belly open.

Gutted her like a fish, and left her flopping out of the water.

CHAPTER 11

Higher standards.

Higher standards.

The words expanded and contracted like a fever dream as she walked through the hotel with Alain Roussel, learning its workings. As she looked at financial reports and drew doodles in their margins of waves against beaches and coconut palms. In her room, under the lofty light of the Eiffel Tower, she put more photos of her island life on her big-screen television and tried to stare at them, at all the people who loved her and whom she loved in gratitude for it, until the words went away. But they came back, filling her like a balloon about to pop.

If only that *pop* would ever come. The need for a pin was driving her insane.

Higher standards.

Like she was a burger and fries, offered to his superior palate.

She wondered if he could keep the sneer on his face while he was burying himself deep in her against a shower wall—

What the hell was wrong with her? She sank forward, in that same shower, scrubbing her face hard with her hands.

★ ★ ★

"Did you get any sleep last night? Or are you just sick?"

Luc, noting *gold powder* on the whiteboard, gave Patrick a dark look. "I'm not sick."

Patrick grinned. "No, of course not. Not *you*. It's against your principles."

"Well, it is." He hadn't gotten sick in ten years. It would have outraged him to sneeze on one of his creations.

"Mine, too, *mon cher,* except in ski season. Then I'm always too sick to work for a good two weeks."

"I've noticed," Luc said dryly.

"Oh, come on, I go after Valentine's, it's our slow period. You should come this year, instead of going off to Costa Rica like last year. Volcanoes." Patrick made an exaggerated *pffing* noise of contempt. "Fantasize about exploding much, do you?"

"Go away, Patrick. Do I look like I want to talk to you?"

"Well, *no,* actually." Patrick folded his arms in delight and leaned on the opposite side of the marble counter as if it was a damn bar and Luc was about to mix him a drink. "That's what's so fun. It's usually not this easy to annoy you. So what's with the red around your eyes? Are you overdosing on energy pills? I always thought that energy of yours was unnatural."

Luc gave him a disgusted look. Patrick had as much energy as he did, he just managed to hide it somehow. Maybe Luc should try to learn the trick of that lazy façade. He would bet island sunshine there would *love* a lazy surfer boy.

His eyebrows plummeted as he remembered her face relaxing, turning up to Patrick's the day before. Maybe he should send Patrick off on his ski trip early, a nice long one. When she finally focused, he didn't want it to be on the *wrong person.*

"Ooh. This *is* easy. Look at your eyebrows, all scrunched

so cute like that. A little accusation of drug abuse has already gotten a rise out of you?"

"Weren't you supposed to be working on those Phénix?"

"Oh, sure, sure, sure." Patrick picked up some utensils and started tossing things around. He had a way of working as if he was throwing on clothes un-ironed while half-asleep, but Luc had stopped flinching long since, and only occasionally double-checked it. That double-checking was an unwarranted compulsion that was one of the reasons Patrick would eventually leave to start his own place. "But if it's not drugs, and you're not sick, that leaves . . . " Patrick froze. "You're not allergic to something, are you?"

"Of course I am not," Luc said, irritated.

"Mon cher." Patrick reached out and squeezed his shoulder, across the counter, as if he had had a near brush with death. A top chef wanted *nothing* excluded from his artist's palette. "So glad for you. Then that leaves sleep. Or lack of it." He grinned. "Is she cute?"

"Patrick." She was so far beyond cute. Except when he had caught her tossing stuffed animals with small children. That had been surreally adorable. Surreal? *But she must do that kind of thing all the time, teaching small children. It's the sexy, elusive image of her* here *that is surreal.*

"What am I saying, of course she's cute. To attract His Majesty's attention? She has to be. Are you going to produce gorgeous children?"

"Pa-trick." The word "children" punched through his stomach and left a hole in his insides, his soul a damn American doughnut. *Merde,* this was bad. *She had wanted him to take her against the wall of a hotel pool while she kept her eyes closed so she didn't have to know who it was.*

But . . . she had watched him for an *hour.* As if she couldn't look away. How could she pretend not to know who he was? And how had his life turned so upside down that he had had to refuse wild, kinkily semipublic sex with a beautiful blonde who was offering herself up in a pool to him? No man should ever have to do that in life.

And then be teased by his sous-chef about the cute woman he had spent the night with.

He probably should have leaped at his chance.

But she had his heart stuck to her damned fingers. And she dismissed everything he made for her as easily as breathing. It made him *wild* with rage. It woke that child in him, who so many times had wanted to leap at the beautiful, indifferent Métro commuters and claw at her and *force* her to look at his pitiful dancing. And that child made him writhe.

"She's not a beautiful blonde by any chance?" Patrick asked innocently.

"Patrick. Why don't you go skiing now? Didn't you always tell me the powder was better in January and you only sacrificed yourself for me? The guilt is killing me. Go. And stay away a *long time*. I'll handle Valentine's without you."

"Aww . . ." Patrick blew him a kiss. Luc nearly leaped across the counter and strangled the man. "That's so sweet of you, chef. But I know you're just deluding yourself about managing without me. Plus, my reservations start February 16."

Luc looked at the total catastrophe of the dessert he was trying to invent. He had been working on the thing off and on, in between rushes, all day. The warm suggestion of some delicious ripe fruit just out of reach was working out, but the other element he was working on, this idea of something stretching toward that fruit without ever being able to reach it—it was all just an awkward, over-forced mess. "You know, it wouldn't be any great loss to me to upend this over your head."

"Seriously?" Patrick straightened as if touched by a live

wire. "We can have a *food fight?* I've *always* wanted to do that here."

Just for a second, the idea was glorious. The taut, tense kitchens erupting into battle, releasing . . . all kinds of frustrations. Luc grinned despite himself. "Don't tempt me. We've got a new owner. I wouldn't want to leave the wrong impression."

"Too late," Patrick said sympathetically, reaching out to pat him on the shoulder. "I hear she doesn't like sweets."

CHAPTER 12

"**I** don't." Summer smiled, her heels clicking coldly against marble when she crossed her ankles. "I just . . . really don't like them. I'll be happy with fruit, if you have it."

The waiter's face tightened. He probably had higher standards than her, too. "You owe it to yourself to try him, mademoiselle."

She had tried to try him. A blind taste test, even. Apparently Luc didn't let just any amateur put her mouth around him. And that aroused her because . . . because the contempt and indifference left a hard edge to the sex that would let her enjoy herself and waltz right back out of here just as soon as her cage was sprung. That must be the reason.

"I'll tell you what," she said. "Find me a nice, fresh, ripe mango, the most perfect, straight-off-the-tree juicy mango. That's the kind of dessert I like." And Luc couldn't make it for her. Her friendly smile allowed no leeway at all. "Otherwise, I'm good."

With a look of grave disapproval, the waiter left, dragging his feet as if he was going off to face the Lord of Hell with the news that he had failed to bring back any more souls.

Oh, come on, surely Luc didn't care *that* much. He wouldn't condemn the waiter to the seventh level of hell for his crime as messenger or anything. After all, you had to tolerate the behavior of a spoiled brat. Who owned your hotel. Even if you had higher standards.

"You must be driving Luc right up the wall," Jaime said, horrified.

"Not noticeably," Summer said shortly.

"Well, of course not *noticeably*. The guy would appear to be in elegant control if he was at the bottom of an eight-story building that had collapsed on him in an earthquake. He's going to get an ulcer from that kind of thing. He needs to throw pots at people's heads once in a while." A quick grin flitted across Jaime's face. "Or have a mad love affair or something."

"I'm not really interested in finding ways to relieve His Majesty's stress."

Damn it, Summer, she thought furiously, at a sudden desire to stroke the stress off those shoulders, to take him away on a yacht, to push him back in a hammock and set it swinging. *You need therapy.*

Jaime, meanwhile, lifted a hand to catch a laugh back, blue eyes sparkling.

"What?" Summer asked, irritated.

Jaime fought her giggles, waving a hand. "No, no, I just—you and Luc's stress—you—" She burst out laughing. "Well . . . who knows, in the end you might be good for it."

Why the hell had Jaime wanted to have lunch with her? Why had Summer agreed? Other than the fact that she had been desperate for most of her life to find a woman who actually liked her, of course. Still—had she thought this was going to help in some way, sitting across from the freckled heroine-next-door who took *her* spoiled childhood and went out and saved the world with it?

Why did Summer have to be on a remote Pacific island to blossom into happiness?

"Do you know him so well?" she asked, despite herself.

"Well." Jaime looked doubtful. "Dominique actually likes him, and even more unusual, he seems to like Dominique. I'm not saying you could tell they like each other if you saw them together, but they have a certain rapport, let's say."

Summer raised her eyebrows, remembering Dominique Richard's obstreperousness at the gala. The fact that Luc could put up with him said a lot about Luc.

It also said a lot about Summer. A man who could stand Dominique Richard thought she was beneath his standards. "It doesn't worry you to be engaged to a man who fights with everybody?"

"Only his rivals," Jaime said, amused. "We have a good therapist."

Summer managed to restrain herself from pouncing on the therapist's name and number like a starved cat. "You seem pretty happy."

Jaime just smiled. Discreetly. No reason at all for Summer's own heart to curdle with jealousy.

"So Luc likes Dominique."

"I think so," Jaime said. "You know, for someone who's so photogenic, he's very hard to read. I mean, the media just *eats* him up, with all that intense, restrained passion he shows for the camera. But other than the fact that he believes utterly and passionately in his work, it's very hard to tell what he's thinking. Kind of like you, in fact."

"What?"

"Oh, come *on,* Summer. It's not humanly possible that you like everyone as much as you seem to."

"Why not?" Summer asked, offended. She was nice to *everybody,* almost all the time, and the only things people ever remembered were her slipups, her moments of tiredness or frustration or accidental arrogance, as proof that the rest of the time couldn't have been sincere.

"You smile at everyone as if we're God's gift to you, but you hide on tiny Pacific islands as far away as you can for four years?"

Summer twisted her glass. "You know, there's not really any big secret. No one criticizes me on the island. *They* all think I'm God's gift to *them*. Exactly what I live for, to be surrounded by adoration."

Jaime looked at her for a long moment and then shook her head. Abruptly she dug into the worn, hand-woven purse that was so out of place in this elegant room. "Here." On the back of her card, she wrote a name, number, and the word "self-esteem" underlined twice, and slid it across to Summer. "He's a really good therapist."

It was one thing to be trying to figure out a way to ask for the man's name, and another to have it volunteered. "You know, there's really nothing wrong with me that being back in the tropics won't cure."

"Speaking of the tropics, I wanted to pick your brain about something."

Summer went blank. Jaime was just not the type to ask for fashion tips, which was about all people turned to her for here. And she had plenty of her own money, and her own powerful father. Not to mention power in her own right, something Summer had never quite managed to want for herself, like she was supposed to.

"You know how I've been working to reform cacao farm labor practices?"

"Yes," Summer said uneasily. Saving thousands and thousands while Summer holed up on her island and gave little kids stickers when they wrote their alphabet correctly. She was two years older than Jaime, too. Giving out those stickers had felt . . . really good and important while she was doing it, though. Before she came back here.

"Most of the kids on those farms have never even tasted chocolate. I've been toying with an idea to create a scholarship-apprentice program to bring teenagers to Paris for anything from a one-month exposure to a full chocolatier apprenticeship. Cade and I have enough connections between us to get things started—and you could talk Luc into it."

Jaime had a serious misunderstanding of Summer's power over Luc Leroi.

"Once we have Luc, we'll have the whole network of chefs who have worked with him. That man just breeds top-quality chefs. People kill to get hired into his kitchens. So I think we could pull it together on our end. But is this project just one that sounds good on paper? What might the actual effect on the kids be? Does it just make people long for things they can't have or create injustice? I mean, is this a good idea, or just well intentioned?"

"I have some of the same concerns," Summer said slowly, feeling as if she had slipped down the rabbit hole. A serious discussion with someone of such extensive accomplishments? As if her own experience could have value beyond that little island? "When I think about improving communications with the rest of the world, or bringing back too many wonderful things from Paris to make my kids dream of places far away. But my kids' situation is a little different. Most of them are happy and indulged and have plenty to eat. And that might not be true for them anywhere else."

"And obviously, in the case of cacao farms, establishing legitimate labor practices is the first priority," Jaime said. "But countries like Côte d'Ivoire and Ghana will never achieve economic stability until value can be added to their products in-country—gourmet chocolate bars manufactured there, for example. We're working with Dad to open a factory in Ghana, which is a start. But since I started dating Dominique, I've been thinking about building local, artisan knowledge as well. Changing the world dynamic."

Summer smiled wryly. Jaime was always wanting to change the world dynamic. Summer, on the other hand, was trying to be brave enough to let her tiny piece of the world be washed out from under her feet. Her kids, given good communications with the outside world and opportunities, would go out into that world and not come back to stay on a tiny island. She had a vision of herself growing old and wizened and white-haired, wandering among coconut palms all alone . . .

She got a grip on herself. "I like your idea of having different lengths for their stays. That way a child who finds Paris just too harsh wouldn't be stuck. But I don't know the cultures you're dealing with, and remember that on my island, nature provides plenty of food, and when nature fails, government subsistence programs provide. In a country where people can starve, how much pressure would there be from family for the kid to succeed and change the whole family's fortunes, no matter how much the kid might long to come home?"

"Yes," Jaime said thoughtfully. "Although is there really a choice between a Paris apprenticeship and going home if it means people in your family will starve? I suspect you're being too softhearted." She smiled at Summer, though, as if she liked that about her.

"Or don't have a realistic view of the world," Summer said wryly. As her father often pointed out. "I—"

The waiter slid Jaime's flaming Phénix in front of her and in front of Summer—

The rich orange-gold flesh of a mango, sliced in perfect mouth-size slivers, arranged like a flower on the center of a pale blue plate. Summer stared, feeling as if someone had reached in and closed his fist around her heart.

Why the hell would he *do* that, if he didn't even think she was worth fantasy-sex in a pool?

"Ohh." As her Phénix flames died, Jaime leaned across the table. "Did he make a sun for you? In case you are missing the tropics? How *sweet.*"

A sun, yes, not a flower. A sun in the middle of winter.

"No, really, Summer. If you knew how proud Luc is. That is one of the sweetest things I've ever seen. I mean, not sweet, because you don't like sweets, but . . . you see what I mean?"

It was an irresistible gift of happiness. She hated him for doing this to her so easily when he despised her so much, but she missed her island *so much.* Just one bite . . .

It melted unbearably sweet and sun-filled on her tongue, wafting her to a beach whose volcanic sand scratched against her bare thighs, the salt coating her from the sea, children laughing as they hunted crayfish in the creek.

She shivered at the lusciousness of it, blinking quickly not to cry.

Fortunately, Jaime was digging into her Phénix, making little exclamations of delight. Summer's eyes had time to dry before she looked back up with a quick smile. "Thanks for talking it out with me. See, that's what's nice. When I say 'marginalized cultures,' you see individual people. And you're not sitting there with an agenda, trying to say the right thing to get me to support your nonprofit."

Summer laughed. "No agendas on me." The lack made her father want to beat his head against a wall.

"You're so real," Jaime said affectionately.

Summer couldn't decide which stunned her more, the tone or the words. "Me?"

"I've seen you sitting down on the ground with those kids, so patient. It's amazing. You've always been a little bit that way, the patient little sweetheart to all your ambitious obsessive boyfriends, but when you settled into teaching, it was like you shrugged all the glitz and expectations off you and finally became entirely—true. Just you. No global impact required. I can barely imagine it."

It was the first time anyone had described Summer as "teaching" and not "escaping to a South Pacific island." Jaime seemed to *admire* her.

Shaken, she focused on her mango, but instead of helping pull her together, its essence of the tropics seemed to reach inside her and catch that golden glow she carried, catch it in someone else's hand.

The hand of a man who had higher standards.

Her mouth hardened. This man had too much power over her. If she wanted to get herself back intact to her island, that place where she loved herself and, apparently, someone like Jaime could respect her, too, it was time for drastic measures.

Time to break those three years of celibacy for a nice little bout of distraction. And not with him.

Luc rode on it, all day, the fact that she had eaten that mango. How had that juice felt, as it burst on her tongue, as it had trickled down her throat, what had her eyes looked like as she swallowed . . . had she been happy? Had she smiled for him, a real smile, of delighted pleasure? *I'm sorry I was so—abrupt—last night. But look. I can give you what you want. I can see the part of you that matters. Let me have the part of you that matters.* He plotted more desserts that took off from that piece of fruit, that led her further and further into him until she was utterly caught, like gold in a cage of dark—

"You know, it's a good thing she doesn't like sweets," Patrick said thoughtfully.

"Why?" Luc asked crisply. The dinner rush was nearly over, and Summer had not even made an appearance in the restaurant to be tempted further. Did he have to be so desperately satisfied that she had eaten a piece of fruit he had peeled and cut? "Too small?" She swam a lot, but her metabolism couldn't be anything like his.

"Also." Patrick nodded thoughtfully. "But mostly, I just don't think she'll find that many sweethearts in Grégoire's Hell Bar. Not with what I just saw her go in there wearing."

CHAPTER 13

The hotel's sculpted, blue-tinted glass bar made the place look like the land of the dead. Its descent into hell was even scheduled. In a few minutes, at eleven, the bar turned red as electric rock started blaring.

Luc spotted Summer instantly. Against the unworldly blue, she glowed like natural light in a zombie room, her pale gold dress blending with her golden skin: shoulders bare except for a knotted strip of silk, vaguely Grecian in its loose caressing of her body, neckline draping. A dress that begged for touch.

Just in case he had wanted to take the night before personally.

She leaned back against the bar, one leg swinging gently, a drink in her hand, truly beautiful, that golden beach-comber in her skin and coloring combined with the ethe-real goddess structure of her bones, delicate and defined and somehow strong at the same time. Her body curved deliciously, so small you knew you could manipulate it any way you wanted if she yielded it to you.

The man on the stool beside her leaned toward her, say-ing something, and Luc stepped away from the door. Her gaze flickered toward his movement, and she stilled.

She didn't smile.

Well. Hate was better than indifference, right?

He took a step toward her, and she turned her smile on

the man on the stool. A man who had black hair, damn it all. Could there be anything more annoying than to be her type? He crossed the room.

In a flirtatious testing—*are you willing to let me put my mouth on you?*—the man brought her glass to his lips. As he lowered it, Luc took it calmly from him and slid it across the bar. Grégoire, who had not become head barman here by being oblivious, disposed of the glass immediately and brought out a fresh one.

"Luc Leroi." Luc extended a hand to the man.

The man tried to squeeze it too hard, American businessman style, but Luc had hands like a pianist whose piano keys often weighed forty pounds, and he just let the force bounce off him, not even worth a brief handshake pissing contest.

"Summer." Because the other man was clearly American, Luc thought, *What the hell, I'm not French for nothing,* took Summer's hand, and kissed it.

It jerked minutely in his.

That tiny jerk vibrated through him, a soft chime that would not stop. His hand caressed hers involuntarily in reward as he lowered it.

"Summer . . . Corey?" the other man said, his eyes sparkling with even more interest, and Summer gave Luc a disgusted look.

"I need to talk to you." Luc pulled her off the stool, with a cool glance for the businessman. "You'll excuse us. It's business."

"Business?" Summer's startled credulity made him feel guilty.

"Well . . . not exactly," he admitted, as he slipped them into the Terrace des Fortunées, a vast room completely abandoned at this hour. Through the wall of glass windows, the empty white square of the courtyard ice rink glowed coldly, drizzle freezing to its surface.

Summer faced him with arms folded, pulling the silk of her dress across her breasts. She looked so delectable and golden, in the darkness lit only by the soft courtyard lights, that he kept thinking she would wink out if he didn't close himself around her to protect her from the draft. His whole body ached with the need to protect her. To take her. "Then what, exactly, did you want to talk about?" she said coldly. "I was busy."

He slipped his hands in his pockets to make them behave. "That. What you were busy doing."

Her smile mocked him. He wanted to wind back time, to the moment he had first seen her, to that vulnerable, love-filled person he had believed her to be. He wanted to erase the mistake he had made, when pride drove him out that door and left her lying there. Where might they be now, if he had made love to her until her body was warm and trusting? With his heart in her trash or her heart in his hands?

"What I said, about higher standards—"

"Fuck you," she interrupted.

He rocked back on his heels. "I beg your par—"

"You should. You're boring me." She turned, brushing her dress as if crumbs of him were stuck to it.

He grabbed her arm, and she went still, staring down at his hand, gold against gold. "No," he said softly, on a note of realization. "No, I'm not."

She pulled on her elbow, barely.

Instead of tightening his hold, he moved his thumb. Just lightly, grazing up and down. She took a soft, quick breath. He stroked again, exploring his power, watching her breasts rise and fall under the drape of her golden dress, watching her eyes. "Did you like the mango, Summer?" he asked softly.

Brilliant lagoon-blue eyes flicked to his, and then she angled her face away.

"Did I pick out a good one? Ripe and rich, soft, condensing sunshine into its juice? Did I bring you what you wanted?"

"I don't want you to use *tu* with me," she said, hard and flat, cutting across the spell he was trying to weave.

He took a breath at the slap of it. For a moment, he could only stare at her.

"We aren't on familiar terms," she said coldly. "And I don't want us to be."

Sometimes it was terrible to have so much self-control. For example, he could not wrap both hands around her arms in white-hot anger and squeeze his overly *familiar* imprint on her. "My thumb in your mouth is a familiar term."

Now she did pull her arm free. Just as well. It was all he could do not to crush it in his grip.

"Yes, but I believe we established that my blow jobs weren't up to your standards, so let's stick with *vous.*"

The words ripped at him. They were so ugly. And she stood there in that golden dress, so lovely, and . . . like a tiger, ready to rend her cage.

A cage? What the hell? He shook his head, hard. "Summer. I didn't mean—"

"Jesus, you are boring," she said and strode toward the door.

He thrust it closed with the flat of his palm over her head. She turned in the shelter of his body. Or the cage of it. And stilled, taking a slow breath in exact time with his as he filled himself with the scent of her. Coconut and wistful, determined sunshine.

Her eyes dilated as her head fell back and she stared at him, tongue touching her lips. His body hardened as arousal drove him to crush her back against the door.

Exactly as she wanted. Exactly as she had dressed tonight to go into the bar and let any man do.

"Don't you want to know what I meant, about standards?" he asked tightly. The urge to let himself be *just any man* was terrible, crushing his body between desire and his own adamant resistance to it.

"No," she said. "I don't. You'll forgive me for not talking this out with you, but I have a lot on my mind."

Soleil. I can help take care of all those things on your mind. I can make you forget them.

But . . . arrogant perfectionist, he refused to do it. And he blamed himself, looking down at her smallness trapped by his strength. He actually felt guilty for refusing to let her use him as her blind release and then drop him.

An arrogant, masochistic perfectionist. But then, he always had been. Was famous for it, even.

If he touched her, she would do something. Suck his thumb into her mouth, *putain,* and crack him like a sugar sculpture in the last few minutes before the contest bell rang, years of merciless work shattering to pieces. He had seen it happen so many times, to so many men, that shattering just before someone could have won the prize.

So he put his other hand on the door, framing her. "Summer, I'm trying to tell you that I would like—"

Rage pushed Summer off the door. An impossible force in her, a cyclone spinning her in a gilt trap of formality and tension. All she wanted was his heat, his darkness. And His Superior Majesty despised her for that. *He'd left her alone* because he was too damn good for her. And now he wanted to crack her open to him? Spill everything that mattered inside her out for him, so he could paw through it because he was in the mood? *Fuck* him.

"Do you know what I would like?" she asked brutally. "You're gorgeous. You're all passion, locked up so tight you would never deign to release it on someone like me. And you despise me. And I would like you to fuck me up against the wall until I can't think anymore, until I *absolutely cannot think,* and then I want to pick myself up off the floor and *go teach kids on my island,* and lie on the beach and watch the waves roll in. That's *all* I want from *you.*"

A moment's impossible silence while, from far away through the rage, her words started to echo back to her. Merciless black eyes bored into her, that long matte body rigidly still. "Off the floor," he said precisely.

The first hint of a flush started to rise. Oh, God, when her anger receded out of her, this was going to be *awful.*

"After the bout of . . . fucking . . . I would leave you on the floor."

She stared at him. Red swept in, embarrassment and more fury. "Just get the hell out of here!"

He gently pulled the door open, shifting her weight like a windshield wiper shifted rain. Slipping through, he closed it precisely and quietly behind him. Its hard support pulled away from her back, leaving her standing with nothing, there in the abandoned room.

Slowly, her rage drained away. She brought her fists up to her temples and sank back against the door. Oh, Christ. Oh, Christ. What had she just said?

CHAPTER 14

She was huddled in writing shame on the floor of her room, her bed between her and the Eiffel Tower, when one of the bellmen knocked at her door with a long, narrow package, neatly tied with a bow. Inside, she found what must be some kind of kitchen implement, long, thick, bulbous, very smooth wood, and beside it, a little beautiful glass jar of flavored oil. The writing on the card included was angular, neat, clear: "In case this may be of service. L.L."

It was such a relief to have the rage come back. She swept into the kitchens on it, a force so powerful it could take care of anything and everything in her path. It took her right up to Luc, still in street clothes, glaring at some dessert he was making, as the others cleaned up around him. He turned and watched her approach, black eyes completely unimpressed, but that didn't stop her. "You're *fired*. Get out."

His eyebrows rose faintly. *"Bonne chance,"* he said and turned back to the insanely complex and delicate war of light and dark he was concocting on a plate.

At the far end of the pastry kitchen, some *assistant* in white hissed something panicked to someone she couldn't see and another left at a run. Hugo Faure came charging around the corner, grabbing her. "*Non, non, non,* mademoiselle. Luc—ignore her."

"I was," Luc said briefly, stretching hot golden sugar in his bare fingers with no sign that it burned.

"Mademoiselle, please to come talk with me." Hugo Faure was dragging her away by the arm.

Alain Roussel appeared suddenly, running at the same speed. He grabbed her other arm. "Mademoiselle. I was looking for you. Something urgent. Luc, *s'il vous plaît*—" The director made a frantic cutting motion at him, slicing away anything she might have said.

Luc shrugged one shoulder minutely, not enough to affect the precision of his work as he stretched that gleaming gold sugar so fine, so breakable.

She tried not to look back at him as they dragged her away, but at the entrance she couldn't help one glance. He focused as if she didn't even exist.

And she hated him so much, if her arms hadn't been held, she could have grabbed up that heavy pot there and—

Alain and Hugo dragged her out of sight, closeting her in someone's office.

"Are you *mad?*" Hugo exploded. "Do you know how hard he was to get in the first place? Are you trying to knock one of the stars off of *my* restaurant?"

Summer grabbed up random papers on the desk and ripped them across. Some part of her was scared by her own rage. It was too like her father's. Not violent with body, but violent with words, destructive, and occasionally breaking things. She had thought she had learned a better way—for four years she had been so calm and easygoing—but it was only because nothing had ever gotten to her enough.

"Mademoiselle, with the greatest respect in the world, *non.*" Alain Roussel said it flatly, as if *he* owned the damn hotel. Did everyone here believe himself above her? "Luc may not be fired. I won't fire him, Hugo won't, our accountant will keep paying his salary and give him a raise to make up for the annoyance. *Non.*"

"*Et non et non!*" Hugo raged. "How dare you—just some spoiled *brat*—to come into my restaurant and try to—"

"Hugo," Alain interrupted firmly, his absolute calm cutting across the other man's fury. "Please. I'll speak to Mademoiselle Corey."

"No one needs to speak to me." Summer squeezed her hands around the edge of the desk to choke herself. "I've got it. I've got it."

Stick it out. No firing Luc. No *talking* to Luc. Pace her room, pace the hotel, pace Paris even, swim around that damn pool, stare at the cold rain. Try not to go out with any of her father's candidates, even to save herself from loneliness. Get her father's investment in satellite communications and get out of here, back to the sun.

Three months. Even she was not too spoiled for that.

"But need I remind you," she said icily to both of them. "That *you* do not own this hotel. And I'll fire *whomever* I please."

Hugo drew himself up. "Me, for example?" he said, so much more icily that her own attempt looked like a balmy spring breeze.

Alain grabbed her and put his hand over her mouth. "Hugo. Please. Mademoiselle Corey—please."

Hugo spun on his heel and strode out, his body one giant, dangerous *humph*.

Alain let her go. "Mademoiselle. Take some deep breaths."

"*I've got it.* And I can fire you, too."

"Yes," he said soothingly. "And bulldoze the hotel while you're at it. There's always some trouble transitioning for a new owner."

"What part of 'ownership' do you not understand?"

"Mademoiselle. Are you sure this is what your father would want? For you to destroy one of the best hotels in the world? You do understand that more people than you are affected by your decisions."

Her father had forced her off her island to make himself happy, and now he was in Poland, or maybe it was Croatia, and his only texts had been to tell her to quit pissing Luc off. He could take his hotel and—

She took a hard breath, finally, as Alain had recommended.

"Or is that what you want?" Alain asked delicately. "Are there—some issues there?"

"*No.* No issues. Luc, he—" She broke off, unable to tell what he had done. Any part of it. Especially her role in it.

"I'll talk to him," Alain promised soothingly. Why the hell couldn't she have been attracted to *him*? She needed someone soothing right now. Not some snooty bastard who thought being her lover was beneath him. "I'll ask him to stay away from you."

She would give something to see the expression on that gorgeous, perfect, controlled face when Alain asked him to stay away from her.

He would probably respect the warning, too. All too readily.

God, spring seemed so very far away.

CHAPTER 15

"**S**TOP FIRING LUC LEROI!" her father roared through the phone first thing next morning. "Are you insane? How spoiled are you? Hugo Faure's retiring next year. Leroi's reputation and talent will be all that carries the place until the new chef can earn respect. What do you think is going to happen to the hotel if the restaurant loses three stars at once next time the Michelin comes out?"

"He asked for it," Summer said, rather cheered. Nice to know her father was suffering, too. "I guess I rub him the wrong way." Or didn't rub him at all. By his preference.

"He's a *chef*! He's one of the best in the world! Of course he's arrogant and touchy! Go soothe his temperamental, perfectionistic soul, like you're so good at, and quit fooling around."

"Well, you know, Dad, I've been *trying* to do that, but he says he has higher standards than me."

There was a long, icy silence. "What? What did you just say?"

She was regretting it already. Maybe she needed to borrow some of Luc's control. Her whole soul curled in longing at the thought of him sharing some of his control with her. Wrapping it around her like a cape to tuck her in, against his body. "I guess I'm not his type."

"He said he has—*higher* standards than—Mai, I'm trying to talk." Her father's voice grew muffled. "I don't give a damn if she *was* wearing that sweatshirt when he said it. It's"—his voice came back to the phone—"I'm going to kill him. And you, meanwhile, can you *go out with Saul Jenson*? I know for a fact he's asked you three times since you got there, because I told him to. *He* knows how to analyze a company, and I think he might be a decent guy to boot."

"Quit pimping me," Summer said indignantly. "Or give me a commission if you do. How about a day off my sentence for each man I go out with?"

"I'm not *pimping you!*" her father roared so loud she had to pull the phone away from her ear.

"I don't know what else you would call it. And you leave Luc Leroi alone."

"Well, I have to, now that I think about it," her father grumbled. "It's not going to stop you being spoiled for me to interfere, and he's one of the most famous pastry chefs in the world and the camera loves him. You don't mess with things like that. You just concentrate on being glad you have the money to afford them. Or, in your case, that your father can afford to *give you the hotel* where he works. Can't you be grateful?"

Summer looked from the Eiffel Tower to her photos. On the screen, a group ran an outrigger canoe into the water, Summer's blond head gleaming among all the dark ones, almost lost in the shot because she was smaller than the rest and half-swallowed by a wave. "I guess not, Dad. Now if you had been willing to invest in Pacific Islands communications without forcing me into exile, then I might have been able to drum up an iota or two of gratitude."

"You have a really screwed-up idea of what 'exile' is, if

you think a remote island isn't and Paris is. It's only three months, Summer."

"Yeah, barely enough time for you and Mom to squeeze in a visit."

"I *know,*" her father said, missing the irony. "See why I want you to move back to civilization now? Listen, could you at least try? Give the three months a sincere effort. Come on, honey, I need to start forming an heir for all this. What do you want, for it all to disintegrate when I'm gone?"

"Paris, honey," her mom's voice said from farther away. "We could hardly pick a more beautiful spot."

"Maybe not," Summer said. "But *I* could."

"What, are you still here?" Patrick grinned, pinning another photo to the board. Luc and Summer in the bar the night before, with the caption, *Will the King Lose His Throne?* "I heard you got fired."

"Fuck off, Patrick." Luc slammed a block of chocolate against the counter, breaking it into smaller chunks inside the solid bag that protected it. Could he make that chocolate into a spear that would plunge through that smile of hers, impale her to the wall, make her—wait, that was all she wanted from him, wasn't it? To be impaled to a wall. Arousal gripped him. A wild desire to just *do it.* Do her. But if she gave him that vague smile afterward, he would—

"I was making plans! My name on the menus, everyone talking about *me* as if I were a god . . ."

"Patrick, don't make me fire *you.*"

Patrick straightened from his favorite pour-me-a-drink position on the counter. "Would you?" His eyes brightened with hope.

Luc's heart squeezed so hard he had to slam the chocolate a few more times. *Putain,* was Patrick that close to making up his mind to set out on his own? Begging to be kicked out of the nest? The best and brightest always left him, damn it. He had *raised* Patrick, from the time the younger man was a screwed-up fifteen-year-old apprentice and Luc a nineteen-year-old sous-chef. "No. You know I never let anyone escape alive. Especially if there's a chance of tormenting them forever, in payment for their disrespect."

"I'm *not* alive!" Patrick protested. "Look. See this finger? That's bone sticking through it."

"You can't work yourself to the bone sleeping on top of my counter, Patrick. Besides, I'm sure I could find some good use for your immortal soul, if I do kill you with overwork. Go do some, so I can."

"Kill me with overwork?" Patrick moseyed over to his current task. "Or yourself?"

"It's a contest," Luc said. "Go lose it."

But by the time they left the kitchens at three, it was Luc who had most clearly tried to lose it. Perfectly controlled, unfaltering, with a wildness beating inside him like an impossible drum, trying to break through his skin. *Let me out. This is not working.*

No. Everything beautiful comes through control. Control. Keep your control.

"I kind of missed Sunshine today, didn't you?" Patrick fell cheerfully into step beside him as he headed out. "I wish she would stop by and fire you again. Have you tried making her a peanut-butter-and-jelly sandwich? Something she might like?"

Luc's teeth ground. "Patrick. I'm going for a walk. I need to get out of this hotel for a while. Meaning, you need to walk the other way."

"But you would miss me," Patrick said soulfully as they made their way to the lobby.

Luc heaved a breath.

Patrick grinned.

And cooperatively checked when Luc did, at the sight of Summer Corey.

She stood in the lobby facing a man who looked too old for her, but the man clearly didn't agree. In a tailored suit that suggested a great deal of money, the man leaned toward her possessively, and Summer tilted her head back to keep his face in clear view, small and golden and . . . it was probably his damn over-romantic imagination that made him see a deer cornered by a wolf. The hotel's top-of-the-line security had been tripled since Summer arrived. She didn't have to put up with anything she didn't want to.

Patrick flicked a glance at him. Anger held Luc rigid, unable to think past it.

And Patrick strolled forward, bent down, and kissed Summer Corey straight on her stunned mouth. *"Ma chère,"* he drawled, draping an arm around her shoulders and pulling her against his side before Luc could lunge for him and rip his head off.

Rage roared up, a thunder.

Summer sank against Patrick in relief, her smile warming into something personal just for him.

"Who *is* this, darling? Keeping you entertained again while you wait for me? *Mais je vous remercie, monsieur."* Patrick waved a vague, royal, dismissive hand, a king gracefully thanking a courtier for playing lutes for his mistress while he was dealing with some national emergency.

"Who are you?" Aggression came off the man in civilized waves.

Putain, first Patrick had kissed her, claimed her, and now he was going to get to fight for her, too?

"One of my chefs," Summer said easily, setting Luc's teeth. Patrick was *his* chef. His sous-chef. *She* only got to own . . . him.

He started forward, much too late to do anything but kill everybody.

"Summer?" a calm, strong female voice asked.

And Summer looked around and literally threw herself into the other woman's arms. "Cade!"

Cade Corey Marquis rocked under the impact of Summer's body, hugging her awkwardly. The older man frowned, taking a step back, as if this slim, brown-haired woman, so much smaller than he was, made him wary.

"Cade Corey." Summer relaxed the hug but held on to one of Cade's arms, articulating her cousin's name very clearly and firmly. "Could I talk to you?"

"Of course," Cade said, sweeping Summer out of there while the older man turned on his heel and disappeared out of the hotel as fast as he could. Cade might as well have been carrying her off on a white steed. Luc hadn't even gotten to be the fucking dragon in the scenario.

He walked, his head one giant echoing beat, beside Patrick, trying to make it out of the hotel before he broke.

"What the hell is wrong with you?" Patrick asked without preamble as soon as they were through the doors.

"Does your mouth feel good from that kiss?"

Patrick grinned. *"Putain, ouais."*

"Allow me to correct that," Luc said and hit him full on it.

Patrick staggered back hard against the stone façade of the hotel. "Shit, this is so much better than a food fight." He grinned and dove for Luc full-body.

CHAPTER 16

"I had no idea we were that close," Cade said as she stepped into Summer's suite. "But I'm delighted to see you, too, cousin."

Summer crossed to her television and turned on the scrolling photos of the island immediately and then stood there in front of them a moment, taking a deep breath. She felt violently sick. She felt so grateful to Patrick she could kiss him again. And the thought of Luc gazing at her with that flat contempt stirred so much misery in her she could have been fifteen again.

A photo passed of Summer dressed in a pareo, wearing a crown of flowers and a lei of them draped around her neck, the sun just setting behind her, her face lit with laughter. "Oh my God, that's fantastic," Cade said. "Summer. If you're so happy there, what did you come back here for?"

"A deal with Dad. We need another satellite over that region. Sometimes the islands lose communications for days. If someone gets injured or sick, there's no way to get medical attention in time. I only have to last three months."

"I knew he had gotten a lever on you. You know, my father placed a lot of importance on having an heir, too, but he eventually got over it, when he realized I wanted something else. When I could *tell* him I wanted something else."

"I've told him," Summer said dryly. "I said it very loud and clear, I went and said it in his ear. He said if I wanted to be useless the rest of my life, I could at least marry someone worthwhile."

Cade winced and gave her an apologetic look, guilty about never having heard her own worth dismissed in her entire life. "I know about jumping through hoops. Although most of mine were ones I set for myself, I have to admit. So why were you so happy to see me? Don't tell me getting kissed by that golden god there was a hardship. I know he's not your usual type, but you have to admit he's cute. And brave, given the look in Luc Leroi's eyes."

Summer shrugged uneasily.

Which made Cade's gaze uncomfortably penetrating. "Who was that older man?"

"Somebody I knew in boarding school," Summer said briefly. "I'll tell hotel security not to let him in again. Don't worry about him. He just had to try to revive an old flame. He's not dangerous."

A tiny silence. "In boarding school? He looked to be a good twenty years older than you, Summer."

Summer clenched her jaw and watched the island photos scroll. Oh, that was a nice one. Summer seated on the ground while a group of girl children made a rather hilariously sweet tangle of flowers in her hair, trying to practice their hairdressing and flower-weaving skills.

"Do you want me to make him uncomfortable? Or I'm sure if we mentioned it to your father—"

"No!" Summer said sharply, nausea rising up in her so violently it was all she could do to keep breathing evenly, to keep smiling. "It's fine, Cade. Not my father."

An assessing little silence. "You've got my number, don't you? In case you change your mind later? Because if that man is as power-hungry as he looked, I'm pretty sure it wouldn't take me much effort to make him sorry he bothered you."

"Just let it *go*, Cade. Can we talk about something else?"

"All right, fine," Cade said after another long moment. "I wanted to talk to you about this idea of Jaime's."

Oh, thank God. A topic Summer actually felt good about. "The idea of bringing teens here to apprentice?"

Cade nodded. "You could be really helpful."

First Jaime and now Cade. Two of the most amazing women she knew thought Summer's experience was valuable. *Yes, those smiling faces on my kids, the way their eyes light when they understand something for the first time, the way I learned to be part of a culture not my own, with no crutches anywhere, only me . . . those are valuable!*

"If we go through with it, could you help us figure out best practices with these kids? Jaime said teenagers always have to leave your island if they want to continue schooling, that you're the only reason they can stay as long as they do, so you have to have seen this."

"It's a small island, Cade. Only one of my kids has graduated since I got there."

"And how is he doing?"

"Great. He went to the University of Hawaii on a . . . scholarship."

Cade sent her a knowing glance. Summer shrugged. She still had her doubts about her Pacific Islanders Scholarship Foundation—should she *really* be facilitating those teenagers' steps out into the brutal wide world?—but then again . . . Tehau's eyes had gleamed so very bright with pride and dreams. Other kids, whom she didn't know, must have the same dreams, and her old boyfriends' various stocks were doing outrageously well, so the scholarship fund had been easy enough to start. Kind of funny, when she thought about it. The way she would invest in start-up after start-up in college, because some boyfriend looked at her with pride and dreams in his eyes, and she couldn't resist. And then the boyfriend poured himself into the dream she had enabled and forgot all about her.

And now she was a teacher, giving kids the same ability—to pursue their dreams and forget all about her. That was what teachers did, wasn't it? Helped build someone and then faded out of that person's mind and world as they went on to bigger and better things.

How ironic, and how strange, that she was now pouring herself into a job where no matter how much she felt loved, she would end up, once again, forgettable. And she had never even realized it before.

"So do you think it's a good idea?" Cade asked.

"Good lord, Cade, I don't *know*. You never know all the consequences of trying to help someone. Some of those teenagers would leap at the chance. But yes, some of them might also lose touch with their family and cultural roots; yes, some people might get hurt. Isn't that the way dreams work?"

"Will you consider helping?"

"With money? I would probably be willing to back anything you or Jaime decided to do."

Cade's lips quirked. "Thanks. That's quite a tribute, coming from *Penthouse*'s most famous indicator of a man's future success."

"What can I say?" Summer shrugged as if it didn't hurt one damned bit. "I'm gifted at picking men who can pour all of themselves into their work."

"But I meant help in a more hands-on way. It would be nice to have someone who is not always looking at the big picture. Who can care for individual people. Sit down and talk with these kids. Make sure they're doing all right."

Summer got terrifying visions of teenagers traumatized by childhood exploitation and uprooting, compared to her happy, sunny kids, and took a step back. "I don't know if I can handle that kind of thing, Cade. You need professionals."

"I thought you were a professional," Cade said mildly.

"With training! Specialized training!" Not someone who had developed all her teaching skills through trial and error and extensive website research after stepping off a boat. Cade Corey actually thought of Summer as a professional? A little warmth spread through her. "And I've already got a job, actually."

Cade, who had trained her whole life to take over a multibillion-dollar corporation and only recently thrown that all over a windmill, surprised her by not mocking her job. She smiled. "If ever you decide to relocate, I wouldn't underestimate what you can handle, Summer."

Yeah, but Cade could run the world if she felt like it. Summer felt physical revulsion at the thought of running the world. She tried to think what advice she could offer someone like Cade, and even what she came up with was counter to all the Corey sisters' will to change seven billion people at once. "Start small. With people you know would be good chefs to these kids. Sylvain, I assume?" Summer had barely met Sylvain. "Dominique?" Hadn't Jaime said he was aggressive and always spoiling for a fight? "Luc." Her voice firmed. Yes, he despised her, but she had seen him in his kitchens, the patience and discipline, the way his temper never flared. Except with her, of course. It was too bad he didn't have a soft side to him. But still . . . "Luc would do great."

Cade's blue eyes gleamed. "I can't help noticing Luc is a slightly different take from the men in your *Penthouse* spread."

"I did not pose for th—"

"Does he have some bigger dream he's pursuing that I don't know about, and that you're about to help him fulfill? Bigger than being one of the top chefs in the world? Or as you get older, have you decided to start dating men who have already succeeded in life, rather than ones waiting for your start-up skills?"

"I'm not dating Luc," Summer said between her teeth.

"Oh, right. He probably wouldn't let that golden chef kiss you if you were."

"Exactly." She didn't know why she had imagined, that first instant she saw Luc in the lobby, that he would rescue her again, sweep her out of it as he had that first night. You only got that spoiled-brat luck once, she supposed.

Cade nodded, a glint in her eye. That woman needed a better outlet for her urges to run the world. "You know what? Why don't you come to dinner tonight? You can bring Luc."

"We're not a couple, Cade."

"Great, it can be like some dating game show, where we can watch the two of you circle around each other while we say things to stir up trouble. Sylvain will love it. It would be like having Luc as his own personal voodoo doll. Come on."

"No! Cade!" Luc would be Sylvain's voodoo doll? With *her* as the pin? Was the woman used to running one of the world's largest corporations just an emotional *idiot,* or what kind of vulnerability was Cade seeing that Summer didn't?

Cade laughed. "All right, fine, you can come stag. Which is a hilarious thing to say in conjunction with the name Summer Corey, but if that's the way you want it. I'll see if Jamie is free, too, if you like. It will do you good to get out of this hotel."

God, yes. Especially after that brush in the lobby with the nadir of her past. Summer nearly hugged her third cousin in gratitude.

★　★　★

"That was so much fun," Patrick said cheerfully half an hour later, as the two men sat with their legs dangling over the Seine. Freezing. The doormen had had to throw water over them to break it up. The scandal would last years, or at least Luc's role in it would. Nobody expected Patrick to behave. "We should have fights like that more often."

"If you kiss her again, you won't survive the next one."

"Now, see, Luc, I don't know how you could expect a man to know that. You need to work on that impervious manner of yours a little more. Like, work on shaking it up. There she is, facing some creepy asshole who clearly wants to eat her alive, *dying* for Prince Charming to come and save her, and what were you going to do? Leave her to him? What the hell is wrong with you? Don't you like being Prince Charming?" Patrick rubbed his lips in a way that made Luc's knuckles itch. Apparently you had to really pound a man to drive away the memory of Summer's mouth. "It's not like it was torture."

"Cade Marquis was her Prince Charming, Patrick. Not you." But just for a moment, her face had lit for Patrick. Rage slammed inside him again.

Patrick shrugged. "I just kiss 'em, I don't keep them forever after."

It was amazing how hard it was not to pound Patrick's mouth over and over and over, to a bloody pulp, until all possible memory of Summer's lips was erased from it. "Go kiss someone you would mind losing, why don't you?"

Patrick's eyes flickered and he looked away. Before them, a barge passed slowly, a little blue car chained to the roof. The Seine rocked gently in its wake, tossing an old shoe about wistfully in its brown wintry waters. It wasn't raining, but low gray clouds weighed down the day, pushing people to retreat to where it was cozy and warm. Their wet hair was that close to turning into icicles.

"Creepy asshole?" Luc said.

"Well, he was a lot older than her, and she clearly was doing her best to protect herself from *something* about him with that flimsy smile thing she does. Are you just willfully unperceptive where she's concerned, or still that damn mad because she asked you to carry her bags? Why can't you see that yourself?"

Luc's eyebrows drew together. He stared after the barge, profoundly disturbed at the thought that Summer might have needed him and his tangle of pride and hunger had left her unprotected. "Do you really think she's shy?" he asked after a while.

Patrick smacked his forehead into the palm of his hand. "Luc. She's desperately shy."

"But she's got a *Penthouse* spr—"

"If you mention that word one more time, I'm going to go look at all the photos, and then think how mad at me you'll be."

Yes, anger kicked him just at the thought. "They used a body dou—"

"I've got a good imagination."

Luc set his teeth.

"Luc. I know you never gave up on me, but sometimes it's a lot harder not to give up on you and wring your damn neck than you think."

What was that supposed to mean? "You're just jealous." He knew it could be a little wearing on other people, his insistence on being perfect absolutely all the time. But . . . it worked. By trying hard enough, he *could* be perfect.

"Yeah, that has to be it," Patrick said dryly.

Neither man said anything for a long while. They just sat there and froze. "I suppose I'm going to have to give you a raise," Luc sighed eventually.

"Oh, sure," Patrick said. "I mean, I'm precious. And giving me the chance to hit you once in a while only goes so far as a bonus. Although, *putain,* you have *no* idea how many times I've wanted to haul off and punch you. If I kiss Summer Corey again, do I get to hit you some more?"

Involuntarily, Luc's fist clenched. Damn it, where was his *control?*

"I *do,*" Patrick said, delighted. "Well, *merde,* Luc. This could be a real stress reliever for me."

Luc half turned on him, rage surging back.

Patrick's eyes glinted. He scrubbed his hand elaborately over his bruised mouth. "Look. I'm wiping it off, see? It's all gone. I can't even remember what she tasted like."

So Luc hit him again.

It was better than losing his control with Summer, after all.

"You are in serious shit," Patrick said after that bout. "You nearly got us arrested that time. You're giving me moral qualms, *mec,* it's like shooting a sitting duck. Plus, you've got to think of your hands: neither one of us is going to be able to do anything decent tomorrow, with our hands all bruised, and we've got a banquet of five hundred. I'll tell you what: I think she's a pretty little sweetheart, and if she needs someone to snatch her up, I'm more than happy to do it. But since you've got it so desperately bad . . . *go after her yourself, merde,* and I won't."

"I am," Luc said between gritted teeth. "Unlike you, I want her to know my name first."

Patrick gave that some thought and finally shook his head. "Well, that's fucking fastidious. But isn't that just like you?"

Luc sliced him with a look.

Patrick shrugged. "I would wish you luck but I'm not sure you deserve it. Must be your humble sous-chef here isn't understanding your technique. You might need to demonstrate it more clearly."

Luc shook his head, massaging his nape with one bruised hand. "She doesn't like sweets," he muttered.

An eyebrow went up, and then Patrick's white grin flashed. "I can't claim to have ever tried you personally, Luc, but I bet you don't taste sweet."

CHAPTER 17

"No fucking way." Luc glared at the damn spreadsheet on his screen, which never, ever wanted to add up in a way that made sense. But it had already been such a bad day, why the fuck not do accounts to top it off? *I failed her, didn't I? There in the lobby. I never fail at anything, but I think I keep failing her.* "Go to hell, Sylvain."

Over the phone, Sylvain's voice was rich as chocolate with amusement. "I told Cade you would say that. Here's another idea: you can come over for dinner by yourself. We'll invite Summer another time."

"And just happen to get the dates crossed? I'm busy, Sylvain."

"Fine, but dinner is a time-honored custom for getting to know a woman. As opposed to, say, dragging her off into an elevator or beating up on an employee in such an obscure way she doesn't even realize it's over her."

"She had a *Penthouse* spread, Sylvain. If she doesn't know it was over her, she's being deliberately obtuse." Shy was one thing, but she knew damn well what she was doing when she breathed into his ear that she could get her mouth around *almost* anything.

"Ha!" Sylvain's chocolate voice got richer with gloating. "I told Cade I'd get it out of you. So it was over Summer."

"The next time we're at a *Championnat,* Sylvain, I'm going to crush your pathetic chocolates into the ground." Luc hung up. And accidentally took the call from Dominique coming in at the same time.

"Luc. What the fuck? Are you having some kind of psychotic breakdown?"

"Dom. Have I ever shown any urge to talk about my mental health with you before?"

"You attacked one of your employees!"

"It was *Patrick,* for God's sake."

"Patrick! Luc." Dom's voice turned severe. "You know he hero-worships you."

"It wasn't—" Luc broke off, torn between guilt and reason. Yes, Patrick did hero-worship him, in his very complicated way, but *no,* Patrick was not some vulnerable dependent he had just abused. "He *kissed*—" Luc stopped, cursing himself.

"Fuck. Luc. This wasn't over that spoiled blonde, was it? She got to *you*?"

Did people think he was not human or something? Every other man in the world could salivate after her, but he was supposed to be immune? When she was running those careless fingers right through his soul like it was her dog's fur?

From inhuman because he was some kind of animal beneath them all, begging in the Métro, to inhuman because he had perfect deity status . . . how had he missed out on the chance to be *real* in the transition? He didn't want to only be alive through what he made anymore. He wanted to pour himself into that little, beautiful body and—

"What is she doing to you?" Dom asked, appalled.

"Absolutely nothing," Luc snapped.

"*Putain.* Seems as if it would have been better to ruin your reputation and draw every restaurant critic out there down on your doors, looking for flaws, over *something.*"

Dom was so annoyingly right sometimes. Luc hung up on him for it, glared at his fucking accounts, and then called Sylvain back. *I can get you right, soleil. I can get you . . . exactly . . . perfect.*

It was raining again, heavily, as if to make up for the dry day when Summer hurried into the town car under the umbrella a doorman held for her. Cold drops spattered through her sexy filigree hose, making her flinch and shiver as she slid into her seat. She probably should be wearing jeans to have dinner with Cade and Jaime when the only other men around belonged to her cousins. She was so bad about this stuff. She just could not, in such intimidating company, release the one value that this elegant, ambitious world had always acknowledged in her: that of being able to draw all eyes in a room. *Look at me, see my pretty dress, don't I look pretty?*

She sighed, closing her eyes, and leaned forward to tell the driver to wait while she ran back and changed into jeans. No point alienating the only two women in Paris willing to allow her near their husbands.

The door opened before she could speak, and a long, lean body slid in, matte-skinned, dark-haired, bringing with him a whisper of vanilla and—nutmeg?—and something crisp. *Cade,* she thought viciously as he relaxed back into his corner. Cade Corey was playing boarding school games. The car pulled away before she could regroup, into the strobe-play of dark and light in the wet streets. Water pounded on the roof and blurred the lights running like a string of diamonds up the Champs-Elysées.

"I'm not interested," Luc said. His body blended into the leather seats, darkness on darkness, black coat, black hair, black eyes.

Her teeth snapped together, grinding in a way they hadn't in years of Pacific peace. "Yes, all right, I got that."

"Not in the way you wanted," he said, as pure and indifferent to her as the glossy night-black Seine rippling through the sheets of rain as they crossed over the Pont Alexandre III, lamps glowing.

She stared at the string of wavering glowing bridges stretching all the way to a blurred and feeble Notre Dame, wondering how much it was possible to loathe someone. *Damn you, Cade, did you actually mean well?* Or was it just a boarding-school trick to bring the spoiled blond bitch down?

"On a longer acquaintance, perhaps in different circumstances and an established relationship, if it's something that turns you on . . ." He made a little moue, an opening of his hands and shrug of his elegant shoulders. "I wouldn't necessarily be averse."

"To a yacht?" Summer asked dryly.

He held her eyes, his jet-black like the Seine, jewel-lights dancing in them from every car and lamp they passed. "To a wall," he said very gently.

She flushed beet red, tearing her eyes away from his.

"But I don't leave women on the floor," he mentioned, as the car slowed for the narrower streets in the Sixth Arrondissement. "Disturbing indication of your sense of self-worth as that idea may be." The car drew to a halt. "Or perhaps of my worth." He flicked his fingers as if ridding them of an unpleasant texture as the driver opened Summer's door.

She scrambled out under the great golf umbrella that the driver held for her. Luc slid across the seat and rose behind her, his body pressing full-length to hers as he took the umbrella. "We'll call the hotel when we're ready," he told the other man, negotiating Summer's body forward in tandem with his so they could keep the driver covered while he slipped back into his seat.

He did that so easily, controlled her whole body. And

she liked it so much. She fought not to lay her head back against his shoulder and yield herself to him.

The rain closed them in an intimate bubble, giving her an excuse to stay close. She turned to look up at him—and gasped. One hand flew to her mouth and the other to stop just short of his cheek, for the first time clearly visible in the rain-dimmed circle of light that reached them from an old street lamp. "What *happened* to you? Are you all right?"

A long, thin cut over one cheekbone, and a fresh rain-gray bruise swelling all around it that promised to be a mottled blue and yellow before it was done.

His eyebrows went up. "You don't know?"

"*No.* I—was it an accident? Why didn't anyone tell me?"

"That's a good question." He turned his head just enough to bump his cheek against her fingertips, and something shivered across his face. Pain, probably. She snatched her hand back. "*Merde,*" he said softly. "You're completely isolated here, aren't you?"

She flinched back from him. The umbrella followed her, with no comment from him as the rain began to spatter his back. She clenched her fists and forced herself close to him again. "Nobody gossips to me about you, no," she muttered. "If that's what you're worried about."

He gazed down at her unreadably for a long moment. "I think that might actually put me at a disadvantage." A smile ghosted unexpectedly across his face. "I can't get them to shut up about you."

Yes. He was surrounded by people who knew him and liked him, or at least respected him and needed his fame and skill. She owned the damn place, and that meant nothing whatsoever, compared to him. Why should it? She hadn't done anything to earn it.

They headed down the pedestrian street, Luc's body brushing hers in constant friction. He turned them into the alcove of Sylvain's apartment building, a green door turned almost black in the rain-drenched night, and reached past her face to enter the code.

The rain sheeted down around them, darkening the street, glistening in the storefront lights, a soft and beautiful sound. For one intimate moment, she could almost imagine winter in Paris being beautiful. An excuse to spend cozy hours curled up with someone, in a little world of two. The nasty weather a gift to lovers who needed each other's shelter.

This was the part where he should kiss her. Where they should sway together under the falling rain and . . .

"Are you ready to up your stakes in this game?" His steady, quiet voice blended with the night. "Put in something more valuable than a yacht?"

Game. She could barely hold herself off him, her need for him was so great, and he wanted her to put everything valuable about her into the pot for some damn game. Wasn't that just like an ambitious man? "You would rather have a Bugatti?"

The door clicked. He pushed it open, his eyes narrowing. And then that imperviousness of his broke suddenly, laughter glimmering in his eyes, an affectionate warmth that wrapped around her shoulders like a warm blanket after a chill. "I'll tell you what. You can give me a Bugatti for my thirty-fifth birthday. Far be it from me to throw a car like that back in your teeth."

She turned back in the stairwell, confused. "Are you about to turn thirty-five?" She had pegged him for a few years younger.

"My birthday's December 21. You missed it this year, which is too bad, it was a big one. Thirty. The perfect opportunity to give a man extravagant presents. Although, of course, I couldn't have accepted it on such short acquaintance."

Her eyebrows snapped together, a rare frown. "I'm not going to be here in five years." God, no. The only worse thing she could imagine than spending another five years in Paris dependent on her parents for love and attention would be to spend five years here dependent on *him*.

A muscle tightened in his jaw. But he gave her that still-surprising smile of his, so contained and so packed with brilliance it wrenched her heart out of her body, and gestured her to precede him up the stairs. "The trick, now, is going to be figuring out what to get *you*."

Laughing warmth embraced them as they stepped into Sylvain and Cade's apartment. The place was so . . . homey. Great casement windows must let in beautiful light in the right weather, but now just emphasized how sheltered they were from the rain that poured down outside them. A colorful rug filled most of the hardwood floor. A comfortable couch faced a discreet flat-panel television. The coffee table had been raised and unfolded in some clever European way to spread itself out into a dining table that was already set.

Fascinating. Summer would never have guessed that Cade, too, longed for a place that was real and home. Her bitter thoughts about Cade faded. Her cousin might think setting her up was funny, but it was clear by the mischievous warmth in her greeting that she didn't mean harm.

"Luc." Sylvain clasped his hand, grinning. "You're looking like hell. Tell me again how you got in a fight?"

"A *fight*?" Summer jumped, bumping into Luc, who had to steady her. She gripped his coat sleeve. "Someone *attacked* you? Where was hotel security? Is it because you're out in the streets getting home so late? I can have a car take you." Wait, no, he hadn't been bruised earlier that day. It couldn't have been an attack on the way home the night before.

Sylvain choked and slanted Luc a glance full of mirth as he bent to kiss her cheeks. "She's worried about you, your majesty."

"I noticed," Luc told him. "Why don't you shut up?"

Summer flushed. "Sorry," she said stiffly. "I should have known your godhood didn't need any mere mortal's concern."

Luc's eyebrows shot up. "Did you just call *yourself* a mere mortal? You're exactly as human as I am, Summer Corey." An odd expression crossed his face. "Exactly."

"That would be not at all," Summer retorted.

"She's got you there," Sylvain said and drew Summer into the kitchen to greet Jaime and Dominique. When Jaime's fiancé bent for *bises,* Summer pressed herself back against Luc's side. Big, rough, aggressive, and not very discreet about how little he thought of her, Dominique woke the wrong memories.

Luc glanced down at her in surprise, then, to her shock, curved one arm around her waist. Summer's whole body gave a little gasp of relief and pleasure. *Thank you for not leaving me alone. For once.*

His arm tightened to bring her to face him. His other hand lifted, but he stopped it just short of touching her face. The way he held it, half-curved just shy of her cheek, reminded her oddly of the way she had held her palm over that basket of *financiers* that had greeted her the first morning in that cold hotel, soaking up their warmth.

Oh, she realized for the first time, a sweet, confusing grasp around her insides. *He sent that basket to me. It had to have been him. After he walked out on me, left me freezing there . . . he sent that basket of warm gold for me to have as the first thing when I woke up.*

"And I need the concern very much," he said quietly. "You don't think I'm human *at all?*"

"Oh, come on, give her a break." Sylvain picked up a knife and went back to dicing mushrooms. "Who does?"

Luc gave the chocolatier a steady, dangerous look. "Why, thank you, Sylvain," he said silkily. "I had no idea you were one of my worshipers."

Sylvain's white grin flashed. *Touché.* "Luc, just because we think you're inhuman doesn't mean we think you're a *god.* Can't you think of any other inhuman things? A statue, a robot, a monster, a demon—"

"The Lord of Hell," Summer muttered.

"That's a good one," Sylvain agreed. "Fits him perfectly."

"And what would be *hell?*" Luc asked Summer between his teeth.

"The hotel." She waved a hand. "Paris."

Everyone stopped serving drinks and prepping food to stare at her, dumbfounded. *"Paris?"*

Yeah, that was right. Only a spoiled brat could be unhappy here. This place always took precedence over her own emotions. She pulled back into herself, which ironically meant closer to Luc, still seeking him like shelter. "All right, fine. You can be the Goblin-King instead."

"The *what?*"

"You know." She twined her hands through the air, trying to imitate his when he worked. "Weaving wonders to lure mortals to their doom."

A tiny beat's silence. "To their doom?"

"Like in *Labyrinth,*" Jaime explained helpfully and grinned. "He's better looking than David Bowie, though. You have to admit. Maybe he should be a Fairy King, at least."

Dominique Richard stiffened at the compliment to the other man's looks, but Jaime tucked her hand in one of his big, scarred ones and smiled up at him, refusing to take back her comment even while she reassured him, and his hard mouth softened.

"I was thinking of his kitchens as the hell, myself," Sylvain said cheerfully. "I hear he's a merciless taskmaster."

"Like you aren't," Cade retorted.

"Only when you want me to be," he told her outrageously, and Cade laughed and pretended to pinch him. Summer felt so jealous of happy couples she could have clawed something.

"Did anyone ever mention to you that Summer spent her teenage years in a Paris boarding school?" Jaime asked Luc, suddenly serious, holding his eyes. "What was that like, Summer? Hell, by any chance?"

Why would Jaime bring that up in front of Luc? Like he needed to know how she had spent five years rejected and despised by every single person who walked the earth? His opinion of her didn't need any reinforcement.

"Oh, a dream come true," Summer said lightly. "But I'm on to other dreams now." She forced herself away from Luc to explore the little living room and the rainy view, trying not to let the Corey sisters' happiness get to her. It was better than spending an evening alone looking at the Eiffel Tower, right? Or going out with the first man who looked at her twice, as her father put it. Just so she wouldn't be alone.

Luc joined her at the window, curling her fingers around a wineglass. With everyone else in the kitchen and the rain sheeting just the other side of the cold window, the moment married too strongly with the one under the umbrella, at the door below. As if they had shifted to that cozy place they were meant to be together. Her heart tightened. She would have given anything, just then, to never have offered him a yacht. To have walked up to him that first moment in the hotel, laid her head on his shoulder . . . and been welcomed. Sometimes she wondered whether everything about their relationship could have been different if she had had enough trust in her first instinct to do just that.

It hurt too much to think about. "Did you take care of that?" she asked of the cut on his cheek.

His hand lingered on hers around the wineglass. "Would you bandage my wounds, Summer? Actually care if I got hurt?"

What kind of horrible person did he *see* when he looked at her? "Yes, but only because I need psychotherapy," she snapped.

"For anger management?" he asked helpfully.

"For being attracted to you!"

A tiny pause, while her words echoed back to her. She winced, eyes squeezing shut.

"You might think about the anger management," said the man sporting multiple bruises, his voice almost a caress. She peeked at him. He was looking at her as if she had suddenly dropped all her clothes and stood there naked. And as if this time, he liked the view. "You say the most fascinating things when you lose your temper. "

She flushed, setting her teeth, and whispered: "That whole thing about . . . the wall, I was just trying to be offensive! I don't actually want you to—" She broke off, in despairing rage at herself.

"Of course not," Luc said soothingly, and she almost relaxed. Did he really understand? Maybe forgive a little? "Not right now. But it's interesting to note that when you are in a real rage, you think that's how you would want to be dealt with."

"Fuck you," she said bitterly.

His eyebrows rose. "Is that just an example of your foul mouth or another Freudian slip?"

She turned away.

"I started it." His voice curled around her and held her still. "So it's all my fault."

"You started a fight?" Luc? "Was it some kind of long-range plan, or did you actually lose control?"

His eyebrows crinkled. "You have a very odd idea of me, Summer."

Right. Just because he didn't lose control with her didn't mean some other person might not be worth it.

Her nostrils stung unexpectedly, and she fought it back. She wasn't crying again for him. But she asked despite herself: "What was the fight *about*? Did a critic insult one of your desserts?"

That cut lower lip tightened in a way that had to hurt. He didn't relax it to relieve the pain, though. "You don't know *anything* about me, do you?"

"No more than you know about me," she said flatly and started to turn again.

He braced his arm against the window frame, blocking her in. Holding them in a tiny cave of dark glass, rain, and him. From the kitchen, warmth and laughter washed over them, in little ripples. He leaned in on her. His black-silk voice caressed her, arousing her and opening her to him before she even absorbed what he said, so that the words hit straight into her sex. "Do you know that I could strip you naked in less than a second? Do you know how fast I could touch every part of your body? And how long I could keep doing it? You've seen what I can do with my hands, haven't you?"

Her nipples peaked. Her sex softened helplessly against her panties. Oh, God. She had always known that with the slightest effort he would catch her.

He leaned closer. His voice seemed to reach right down between her legs and rub her to his tune. "You may not want desserts, but I could make you one of mine," he breathed.

And while her body was still jolting with the aroused, helpless understanding that until now, he had not even bothered to toy with her, Dominique and Jaime spilled out of the kitchen, carrying plates, and he straightened away.

Oh, yes, *that* sent her running, Luc thought. She didn't know what the hell to do when he took the sexual-aggressor role from her, did she?

Except scurry to tuck herself between her cousins in the kitchen. That was almost hilarious, that she thought she could hide from *him* in a kitchen. It was also endearing and sweet, and he was sick and tired of resisting his protective instincts. Because if Patrick was right, and she really did need him . . . God, but he wanted to be her hero.

"Mind if I take over?" he asked Sylvain. Sylvain gave a slow grin and handed him the knife.

"Not at all."

Such a small apartment kitchen, and maybe Summer did not understand. She seemed to have lived much of her life far away from people. Seen by a camera lens but not close up. He, on the other hand, had almost never had a private moment: busking in crowded Métros all day; sleeping in the street; sharing bedrooms after his foster father took him because Bernard always took too many kids, unable to turn them away; working his way up through packed, intense kitchens.

He didn't have any problem negotiating that workspace to brush against her, over and over, every single time he reached for something. A tickle of his arm against the nape of her neck. A brush of his thigh against her butt. A breath against the top of her head.

Summer's hands grew clumsier and clumsier on the asparagus she was trying to snap, piece by slow piece. The urge to protect her grew stronger and stronger, protect her with himself, the danger. Damn it, how might their world have been different if, that first night, he had tucked himself in that comforter with her, given her his body heat, stroked that beautiful hair back from her face, and made her happy?

He nudged Cade out of his way—because Sylvain was far more secure than Dominique, who might ruin the whole evening if Luc dared nudge Jaime—and took the counter space beside Summer. Rolling up his sleeves, he picked up a knife—and barely avoided cutting Summer's finger off when she grabbed his wrist.

"*Merde,* Summer, do you know how sharp Sylvain keeps these knives? *Shit.*" Hair rose all over his body.

Summer flushed as everyone looked at them.

"*Dis, donc.*" Dominique raised his eyebrows. "When you don't even shout at your interns."

"Sarah doesn't do stupid things like that!" Luc snapped, and Summer's flush deepened.

"*Allez,*" said Sylvain, the only one who could see Summer's face fully from the other side of the counter. "Luc."

Luc sent him a vicious look, fighting his fury at another man intervening to protect Summer from him. Cade glanced between Sylvain and Summer, her expression shifting from surprise to a noticeable chill.

Annoyance and shocked pity hit him at the same time. *That* was why Summer had clung to his side when they got here, broadcasting *boyfriend* signals. If she didn't have a boyfriend, she didn't have *anything.* She was just too luminously gorgeous. Men pursued her, and women hated her, and there was no one she could relax with and confide in. She had to show up with a boyfriend just to appease other women's wariness enough to get within speaking distance of their husbands. Cade was supremely self-confident, her and Sylvain's relationship was so happy it made Luc's teeth hurt, and yet one involuntary kindness toward Summer on Sylvain's part and Cade was already prepared to defend her territory.

That was how alone she was. And he had left her to it. When she had walked straight up to him, so afraid of that loneliness that she had offered him a multimillion-dollar bribe to save her.

What a fucking fool he had been.

He took a long breath and touched the back of Summer's hand. "You scared me," he said quietly. "I'm sorry."

Summer's lashes lifted. For a second, he thought her eyes shimmered with something other than a smile.

"I'm sorry if I've hurt you," he said slowly.

What if, all this time, under that easy, flippant dismissal against which he beat himself, she was exactly as vulnerable and sweet and warm as he had believed her to be, that first minute he saw her? When she was so tired that all her defenses were down.

"Oh, don't worry about *me*." She backed away from her asparagus, task half-finished, wiggling those fingers around which she wrapped him so carelessly. "See? All intact. I was actually wondering about *you*."

He slipped his hands into his pockets, against the surge of emotion in him, the burn on the back of one protesting. "I'm strong. Don't worry about me."

Her mouth set, stubborn. "Have you at least taken care of it?"

I'm trying, Luc wanted to shout. "Taken care of—what?"

"That!" Summer gestured toward his pocketed hand, annoyed. "It looks bad! It could probably get infected. And your knuckles are all skinned and swollen. What *have* you been doing to yourself?"

"At a guess, beating the crap out of someone," Dominique said very dryly.

Luc shot him a look. "Honors were even. Shut up, Dom." Spoiled bastard. Jaime probably lavished sympathy on him every time he stubbed his toe.

"And getting very clumsy in the kitchens. For some strange reason." Sylvain sounded unbearably amused, but not unsympathetic. "Hot caramel? Sugar work?"

"A *commis* knocked the handle of a spoon, and the caramel landed on my hand." Luc started to shrug, thought better of it, and tried to look bravely suffering instead. He knew, by the expressions on the other chefs' faces, that he was doing a shit-hell job of it, but he was pretty sure he could get better with practice. For the right incentive.

"We've got some bandages in the bathroom," said Cade, who was an *angel,* even if an amused one. Thank God Sylvain had married her.

Luc tried impatient indifference, the kind of thing that might convince a woman who liked to take care of small children that he sure as hell wasn't going to take care of *himself.* "It's fine." He reached for the knife again.

Summer's hand closing around his wrist shocked all through him. The clumsy play had actually worked? Never, not once in his entire life, had anyone showed pity for his wounds. "Come here," she said sternly.

Luc's body felt too hot, as he followed that bright head down the unlit hall, as she spread the antibiotic ointment over the splotch of the burn on the back of his hand. Sugar burns, the most frequent risk in a pastry kitchen, were nasty, the 320-degree caramel sticking to skin, hard to get off quickly even immersed in water. And ointment was the wrong treatment, but he let her do it anyway, bracing his hand against the sink, so close to her in the small bathroom he could smell her hair.

"Coconut," he murmured. "And tiare."

Summer's fingers trembled a little as she tried to open the bright blue chef's bandage.

An image of a little blond girl in a beautiful, empty hotel room, cooing over her stuffed animals and bandaging
their make-believe wounds in the absence of anyone else
to pour love out onto, flashed through his mind and
wrung his heart in passing.

*Fuck, yes, I changed my mind, I'll be your toy. Take all that
care and lavish it on me.*

Except he could barely absorb the tiny bit she was giving him right now.

"It's the perfect scent for you." He lifted one thick
strand of gold hair, breathing it in.

She looked up fast and bumped back into the sink.
"What are you doing?"

He decided to go with honesty, mostly because protecting himself was just not working. "Trying a new technique."

Her eyes flared in panic. She stared up at him like he
was about to kill her for dinner.

"If you have a dream in your head, but every time you
try to realize it you end up with a bloody mess, you have
to try something different." His mouth curved wryly.
"Plus, two of the least qualified men in the world to give
me advice on dealing with women have both recommended I adjust my technique, so obviously . . ." He gave
a humorous shrug.

Summer let go of his hand—*merde*—and clutched the
sink behind her. "That's not fair."

"I don't actually know how to *play* with other people,
so you'll forgive me for not knowing what *fair* is." He
touched that vulnerable lower lip of hers, just with his
thumb. It trembled open for him. "I'm sorry it's taken me
so long to adjust my technique. I don't have as much experience with this kind of thing as you do."

Summer went white. And then flushed deep red. And
then smiled her heart out. "Oh, don't worry, I'm sure

when you've practiced as much on women as I have on men, you'll be marvelous."

And she was gone, back to the refuge of the others, leaving her smile behind her like a damned Cheshire cat.

The others were setting dishes on the table when they got back to the living room, Luc still cursing himself. He didn't understand, when he was so elegant and controlled in everything he did, how he could keep bludgeoning her with thoughtlessness. He had only been trying, very cautiously, to let her know something about himself. Maybe that old wild child in him was determined to ruin his life.

He hated every other man who had touched her with a profound loathing. But he was used to trying over and over again to get something right. He couldn't judge her for it. In fact, he couldn't even wrap his mind around her courage, that she had thrown her heart out there again and again, that she had kept trying. How could she bear it? When he even thought of loving *her* and losing he—

Shock roared up in him. A clawing fear. He wanted to lock himself in his closet, curled over the box of childhood treasures he had managed to keep, and pretend that nothing precious could be torn from him ever again.

Putain, he realized, staring at the back of her golden head as he tried to force his soul out of its fetal ball. That was why she was so afraid of him. Of anything but sex. Because he might matter.

"Mom always said you were the sweet one," Cade told her cousin, eyeing his bandage ruefully.

Summer's step hitched.

"The angel-child," Jaime laughed, rolling her eyes. "I remember."

"She used to talk about Summer in the car with dad whenever we were on the way home from their place,"

Cade told Luc. " 'The *sweetest* little girl, I could *smack* Sam and Mai.' "

Summer stiffened.

"We were a little bit jealous," Cade said, "since I was always getting in trouble for being too bossy, and Jaime for doing things like pitching an unholy fit on the lawn to save an anthill."

"You *were* too bossy," Jaime pointed out.

"The damn ants bit me all over!"

"You should have paid more attention to where you were stepping!"

Cade laughed. "But anyway. In contrast, you definitely stood out. 'Such a loving little girl, it breaks my heart.' I think Mom wanted to adopt you."

Summer threw Luc a sudden look, as if he was still holding that big umbrella and she was getting drenched. He took a step toward her and she slipped over by Jaime and Dominique. *Putain.* So now Luc was worse than Dominique?

"Dad, too," Jaime said dryly. "Neither one of *us* could analyze P/E ratios as a dinner-table trick when we were five years old. That trick used to piss Mom off, too, though."

"I could do it by the time I was seven!" Cade said defensively. Jaime rolled her eyes.

Luc tried to remember exactly what a P/E ratio was. Something to do with stocks, because his broker mentioned it on the rare occasions Luc actually let the man talk to him. *Summer* could recite that kind of thing when she was five years old? "Is that what you did over dessert?" That could explain a lot.

Pure, vivid hatred in those blue eyes. And a smile. "No, over desserts I was bored, mostly. I'm not much into sweets."

Sylvain and Dominique both gave Luc looks of such appalled pity, he wanted to hit someone. Again.

"Mom would have lost it if she had seen you in college, in the tabloids all the time, going through all those boyfriends," Cade said, and Sylvain winced suddenly, shot a glance at Luc, and closed his hand around Cade's arm.

His juggernaut of a wife, of course, plowed right on. "She probably would have staged an intervention. Kidnapped you and submitted you to endless talkings-to." Cade's expression grew wistful at the mention of things her mother had never lived to see. Then her eyes crinkled, rueful and sympathetic. "Carried you off to a remote island, perhaps, until you learned how to pick a man who would take care of you."

Summer closed her eyes.

"So, Dom," Luc said. "This bloggers' award for Best Éclairs in Paris. Did you bribe the judges, or do you think they just couldn't afford mine? Why weren't you on the list, Sylvain? Still haven't learned how to make an actual pastry?"

You had to hand it to the solidarity that developed when men survived working in brutal kitchens together. They would seek out any excuse to vent that old urge to kill each other—and they could always do it as a team.

And Luc, after years of heading the most brutal kitchens of any of them—those of a top hotel's Michelin three-star restaurant—had little trouble directing a simple conversation to keep it off Summer for the rest of the evening, especially when he let them rib him instead.

As the evening stretched, the men kept talking shop, since their careers consumed their lives, and the women, denied Summer's childhood as a subject, talked . . . saving the world. Once she forgot herself, Summer's questions about cocoa institutions and economic policy, government levies, taxes, tribal influences on politics in cocoa-producing West Africa, and smallholder farmers shaped the whole conversation. She didn't know anything about any of it, and yet she knew exactly what to ask, as if each question and each answer was part of a complex five-dimensional puzzle she was putting together for Cade and Jaime. Once the Corey sisters got over their surprised appreciation, their discussions grew both more excited and more focused, the sky their limit as they plotted the reformation of cocoa production. It hadn't been just money that she gave all those boyfriends-on-the-way-up, had it? Did any of her exes even realize how much she had focused their dreams?

The warm, happy female voices glittered over his skin. The only consistent female in his youth had been his foster mother, Pascale Durand, her rigid, unsmiling, relentless efforts to shape his savage childhood into something acceptable to her had pushed her to the margins of his life while Bernard Durand had quickly formed the center. She had been a dry well where the love Luc had so desperately sought was concerned, while from Bernard Durand he could, when he was merciless enough with himself and perfect enough, at least milk pride. After he left his foster home, starred kitchens were a brutal and often sexist world very few women survived in. Until his colleagues started establishing their family lives and inviting people over for dinner, he hadn't really witnessed, close up, the way men and women could unwind and relax with each other, the warmth and love that could buoy up a whole room.

Had Summer? he wondered suddenly. With her father who spoke to her as if a beautiful smiling daughter was some ghastly disappointment, with parents who after four years of rare contact had only paused at the hotel for a few hours before dashing off again to more important things?

Under that smile, was she as clumsy and terrified and tempted by all this as he was?

★   ★   ★

It would rain forever, shutting them in a car, in a room, under a comforter, buried in each other's warmth . . .

Summer pressed her head against the glass, focusing on the empty streets as the car slipped away from Sylvain's apartment. *Stupid. You could have asked for another car to carry Luc straight home.*

"So you were a sweetheart as a child?" Luc's voice was gentle and warm, washing over her like the dark rain. It made her want to slip off all her clothes and bathe in it. But then, she had always wanted to bathe in him. He just hadn't thought she had enough to offer in return.

"So they say," she said to the dark streets.

" 'They'?"

"My nanny, and apparently Julie Corey. My mother, too, I guess."

In the reflection in the glass, she saw Luc turn his hands palms up, studying them. "I wonder if you were sensitive. And fragile. And easily hurt." His dark-lullaby voice had an odd note. As if he was trying, with great care, to wrap his mind around a beautiful alien species.

Even the Eiffel Tower was extinguished by the rain at this hour, an almost invisible shadow. She fought not to look at him as they crossed the Pont Alexandre III. "I'm quite strong, actually."

"You must be incredibly strong," he agreed, stunning her into glancing at him. One finger traced around the bright blue bandage she had put on his hand. "But it's a different strength than mine, and I may have . . . misunderstood you. I'm sorry if I've hurt you, Summer."

Her heart began to beat very fast. She waggled her fingers at him, staring back out the window, vague and dismissive: Who, *you*? Hurt *me*?

The touch of his hands shocked through her, closing around her hips. Lifting her, he brought her astride him, manipulating her body as easily as if it was . . . nothing. "You have no idea how poorly I respond to dismissal," he said, slipping his hands under her coat, stroking them up her ribs to cup her breasts. She gasped on a wave of eroticism. They were in the back of a car, and he had just taken her body as if he had the right. And she wanted to whimper and rub herself against him, beg him to use her however he wanted.

How she hated herself.

"You probably had a lot of toys growing up, didn't you?" He cupped her breasts completely, caressing them, supple, clever fingers learning from every expression that shocked across her face. Her body sighed forward and those same hands braced her off him. *"I didn't."* His fierce voice closed around her like handcuffs on her wrists. "I had almost no toys, and I've kept every single one I ever had." His thumbs pressed in a deep circle into her nipples, sending her arching in complete submission. *"Forever."*

He set her back in her seat. She stared at him, uncomprehending. Something savage washed across his face, and then his hands flicked out, lightning fast, and buttoned her coat just before her door opened.

Summer looked up at the doorman holding an umbrella for her and then back at Luc, blind. He was already sliding out of his side of the car. She fumbled to her feet, shaking, as she darted a glance at Luc across the car roof.

He braced one forearm on it as the rain pounded him. "Think you can handle that?" he asked evenly.

Summer's heart tightened until she thought something would snap. She lifted her chin. "In exactly seventy-seven days, I will have earned my father's investment in Pacific Island communications and will be going home to my island and my kids. *My* job. So you tell me how that works out with being your forever toy, to you."

His face tightened under a wash of cold rain.

A wave of impotent rage pushed her forward, past the edge of the umbrella, rain streaming down her own face. "And I, too, have a heart that can be broken. I'm sorry, I must have thought you knew."

CHAPTER 18

I, *too, have a heart* . . . Luc shoved his hands through his hair, staring at the Eiffel Tower through his apartment window. Did she really think he did not know that? Or had so many people forgotten her heart that every single thing he did with her had been seen through that fear? *How badly did your heart get hurt before you would prefer to be fucked and left on the floor rather than risk it again?*

How could anyone live with her heart so unprotected, nothing between it and the people who would eat it for dinner but a shimmering smile?

He finally left his apartment well after midnight and walked Paris, crossing luminous bridges over the Seine, glistening with the recent rain, strolling past the Tuileries as far as the Louvre, then crossing the Pont des Arts. He loved walking this city, each step a reaffirmation of his victory over it. He had started out as the lowliest and most despised and forgotten of children in it, and now he owned Paris. Everyone flocked to him.

He had beaten his own life, beyond recognition. And he didn't know why, in reaction to Summer, the very person he had to be so perfect to reach, that old life had come back out of its coma, ready for another round.

From the Pont des Arts he strolled back along the Left

Bank as far as the Eiffel Tower, walking down the long Champ de Mars. In the playgrounds there the hand-cranked carousel was closed, night stealing the colors from all its pretty ponies. He had never once ridden on that carousel as a child—no money—and now he was too big.

Summer Corey would have ridden it as many times as she wanted, a happy little girl, trying to catch rings on her wand as the carousel went round and round and her pink pony went up and down. He hoped she had laughed and laughed, in pealing delight.

If he ever had his own child, he was going to be the worst father ever. Unwilling to deny her one single thing. But so driven to be in control. *Putain,* what if she didn't like sweets, like her mother, and left him no way to express *anything* for her?

What the hell had he just thought? He pushed the idea from his mind before he got vertigo, gazing at the night-shadowed playground.

Once, when he was nine or so—young enough to still be with his father—he had played for much of a morning with a little blond girl here. He still remembered it. In fact, he still had the little jeweled flower bracelet she had given him in a cardboard box of similarly rare precious toys in his closet. He hadn't been lying about keeping his toys forever.

But he let everything else go. Just like his mother, really, who had let *him* go, the person who—surely? Her own child?—should have been most precious to her. Even his father had let him go, although not before he had tried to keep a ten-year, desperate clutch on his son that had taught a harsh lesson to both of them. It was a clutch that had left Luc nothing to hold onto but a little girl's flower bracelet and that had left his father, in the end, with nothing.

For the twenty years since Luc had been torn from his father's grasp, Luc had taken raw ingredients, shaped them into something incredibly beautiful, tiny magical drops of his heart, and let them be taken from his hands and carried away to be eaten.

He never even tried to hold on to his sous-chefs, into whom he poured so much training. When they were ready he loaned them the money to get started and sent them off to soar.

He hadn't been able to keep that little girl, either. Only the two of them in the playground, on that winter day when everyone else their age was in school. Two more disparate creatures could hardly exist, she a magic princess child, five or six, all golden, her features almost ethereal, such a pretty little girl, so untouched by time that she could have stepped out of fairyland into the tense world of Paris.

She had looked at him as if he had hung the moon. In his worn, poor clothes, with his tense, rough manners, and his sullen knowledge that everyone looked down at him. Or didn't see him at all.

The little magic princess, who was so tiny and charming and beautiful she made all those elegant snobs on the Métro look like peasants, had followed him all over the play equipment while he showed off for her, and she tried to do what he did, and he jumped down from the bars to stand under her and tell her to be careful.

He had wanted her to be his little sister so he could keep her and her utter adoration all for himself, so he had made up a fairy tale where he was her dark knight, and she was his princess, and he used to play it sometimes in his head, long after his father had come to get him and her nanny had taken her away. In fact, when Bernard fostered him, he used to think of that little girl as he added this little touch or that little flourish to a pastry that would make her clap her hands in delight and look at him as if he was her world.

Even at the age of ten, he had known that the only way that little girl would need his protection was if he dragged her out of her bright, happy life into his own dark world. Even at the age of ten, a part of him had not cared, as long as he had that adoration for his very own. As long as she looked at him as if he hung the stars.

"You're not quitting?" Patrick asked the next morning, after multiple attempts to tease Luc resulted in no response at all, nor movement, Luc standing deep in thought, hands pressed on marble. "For real this time? You seem . . . very quiet."

"I'm thinking," Luc said. In the mirrored surface of a glossy, heart-shaped chocolate tarte his face looked honed, determined—born out of chaos, ready for a war of the gods. "And no. I'm not quitting." He trailed four rose petals across the tarte and changed his voice to carry through the kitchen. "Everyone listen up. We're doing a new menu tonight."

Summer was going to ask Patrick about the fight—after all, he was always nice to her—but as soon as she saw him in the hall, half the question was answered. "Wait." She stopped dead in front of him. "It was with *you*?"

Patrick tried to grin, but his mouth had taken several punches. The corners of his eyes crinkled, though. "Don't blame yourself. I've been trying to provoke him into a fight for years."

"Blame myself?"

"Oops. I've said too much." Patrick covered his mouth with one extravagant hand, its knuckles swollen.

"Wait. *Now* can I fire him? He can't fight with his *employees*." And it would save her from—she wasn't sure anymore what it would save her from. Her heart tangled so badly when she thought of him that it was all she could do not to throw herself at him and ask him to save her from the mass of dark vines.

Except she had thrown herself at him and asked him to save her before.

Patrick laughed. "Mademoiselle Corey, I understand the desire to strangle Luc, but you probably shouldn't keep sublimating it into an urge to fire him. I mean, you could take me as your head *chef pâtissier,* but I think I would rather strike out on my own. Get my own stars. I'm not that interested in stealing someone else's. Besides, I like the bastard."

"Why?" Summer asked incredulously.

"His perfectionism, his passion for his work, his imagination, his patience—even though it makes me want to hit him sometimes—his self-control (which makes me want to hit him *all* the time), his discipline, his sense of humor, and his *joie de vivre.* Also, you know, there aren't many chefs who are willing to let you learn every damn thing you can from them and then back you when you go off to become their rival. Or take a screwed-up fifteen-year-old under their wing and become a lodestone he can still rely on twelve years later. Don't tell him I said any of this, will you?"

"We're not on friendly gossip terms," Summer said very dryly.

"Well, no, clearly, but there's always pillow talk."

Summer gaped at him, as if that lazy, easygoing surfer had reached out and wrapped a fist around one of her internal organs. And then squeezed.

All while hanging out waiting for the next wave.

"His *joie de vivre?*" She ignored the pillow talk reference as best she could. "Are we talking about the same man?"

"No, but that's because he hasn't been himself since you showed up. Oops, there you go, I said too much again." Patrick pretended to bow and headed on. Almost at the corner, he paused and turned back. "He looks just as bad as me, by the way, he's just hiding most of it. I went for the ribs. I don't know how you might compare—maybe you could get his shirt off?"

He strolled around the corner, laughing.

CHAPTER 19

Summer's kids had timed a video conference when both sides of the world would be awake, 7:30, and for once they were getting enough bandwidth to make it happen. Their grins kept freezing in the slow, choppy connection. Whenever the image froze she would hear the audio of the youngest kids complaining she wasn't moving, why not? And in the background, explaining, was her substitute, Kelly—an ambitious new graduate in her father's employ, who had leaped at the opportunity to help Sam Corey out by spending three months in the islands.

They were showing her presents they had made her and were going to send her on the next boat. "Since we know you must be missing us!" They had been for their annual shell-collecting trip on the nearby, unpopulated island where a certain tiny orange snail crawled rampant, and had finished the painstaking process of cleaning them and threading them, ten long strands for her. Several other batches of ten already hung in her little house on the island.

One of the older boys had carved a dugout canoe, having learned the technique from his father, who sent them to be sold at the market on the main island a week's boat trip away. "To travel back," he said. His younger brother beamed proudly as he showed her the little tiki he had carved to take care of her.

"I love it!" Summer exclaimed, and there was a knock on the door.

God, she hated hotels, the way no space was really your own. "Come on in!" she called.

No card key slid in the lock. Another knock.

"Come *in*!" she called more loudly.

Another knock. Oh, for crying out loud. She took advantage of another freeze in the transmission to dart to the door. "I really don't want—" She broke off as the crack revealed the knocker.

"It's not housekeeping," Luc said acerbically.

"What do *you* want?" she demanded rudely.

He gave her a long, steady look that made her throat itch. Like a premonition of hands closing around it. "You," he said, and she started visibly, hand finding the edge of the table on which her laptop sat.

Black eyes followed the stretch of her arm, the grip of her fingers. She flushed and released it, then remembered her schoolkids.

The transmission seemed to be irreparably frozen. She wasn't even getting audio on her end, and Kelly was typing in the chat window to let her know.

"Can you still hear *me*?" she asked.

Yes, but not getting through.

"Let's try again tomorrow. That's so sweet. *Moi, aussi, je vous aime.*"

She shut the laptop just as Luc shifted to try to glimpse the screen. His lips pressed together.

"You love someone?" he asked blandly, as if no one could possibly have suspected her of being capable of loving.

"Why else do you think I'm in such a hurry to get back to the islands?"

He shrugged. "Better weather, less work."

Probably a lot more work, actually. Her kids' schooling was a lot less ambitious than her boarding school curriculum, but she did try to make sure they had a well-rounded education. And Alain so did not need her interference. "That, too. But I've got someone worth going back for."

"Does he know the kind of things you say to other men when you're mad?"

Her lips pressed hard together. "Tell me what you need and get out."

"Odd that you would use *vous* with someone you love."

"I talk to all three of them at once. I thought I mentioned we were very laid-back in the islands."

Luc smiled just a little. "Since you were actually talking to your schoolkids, that's quite nasty, what you're trying to make it come across as."

Summer flushed and curled her hand into a fist to keep from grabbing the laptop and breaking it over his head.

"Do you talk to them often?"

She shrugged sullenly. Usually the satellite connection wasn't enough, and she had to get through another Paris day without the crutch of a handful of small island children.

"*Do* you have an island lover, Summer?"

Not in three years. "Is that any business of yours?" she asked him hostilely.

A tiny flexing of his jaw. "Apparently I think so. Or I wouldn't have asked."

"Why don't you tell me what you want?" If he said *you* again . . .

But he had stopped, his attention caught by the photos sliding across her giant television screen.

Lush green mountains plummeted into an azure bay, a photo that unknotted every muscle in her shoulders whenever she saw it, tension flowing out of the nape of her neck as the beauty of it sighed through her. It slid away, replaced by one of Summer sitting on the sand, legs folded, a tanned, raggedy mess of badly cut hair and uncared-for skin, and the Capri-length cut-offs that didn't even show off her legs properly but were as short as island mores allowed. She had black-haired kids piled all over her, one climbing up her back like a monkey, face peeking just by her ear, one toppled in her lap even though he was too big to fit in it, a couple of the older ones pressed on either side, grinning faces against her shoulders. Shy, serious Vanina was making bunny ears above her head, looking thoroughly pleased with herself.

Luc made a soft sound. She glanced at him, her own grin at the photo fading. He looked dazed, a little blank, as if someone had hit him over the head.

A new photo slid into place. A little out of focus, because she had been letting Ari, one of her six-year-olds, use the camera. Summer, hanging like a pig for roasting from a wooden pole being carried by two men. They had all gone to Nuku Hiva for the Heiva festivities midsummer—pretty much the entire island had gone, all together on the deck of a cargo boat—and the men had just finished taking second place in the race with the poles laden with bananas over their shoulders. They had started joking about whether Summer weighed more than the bananas, which, of course, had quickly degenerated into jokes about whether she weighed more than a trussed pig as they pretended to carry her off to be roasted. Then one of the men, a little drunk by then, had made a joke about peeling the banana and eating it, and Summer had laughed and dropped off the pole to go do something else. She had been two years celibate by that time and kind of liked the idea of being peeled and eaten by someone, but her whole balance on that island depended on the missionary morals self-portrayal.

The photo slid, and she winced. That stupid expression on her face, frozen by the camera just at the wrong second, but she had kept it because it was the one that had captured Moea's upside-down grin, as he hung from a branch, offering her a mango.

The next one . . . oh, for crying out loud. The proper way to climb a coconut tree was not to wrap one's legs around it but to press the soles of the feet to the trunk on either side, pushing up with a frog-like motion. This series captured multiple ludicrous moments as Summer tried to learn the technique, various islanders laughing uproariously in the background.

She looked as awkward and ridiculous as it was possible for someone to look. Normally this series made her laugh her head off, but—

She grabbed the remote and turned the screen off before Perfectionism Personified, who doubtless hadn't had an awkward moment since he was thirteen, could see any more of the show.

He looked as if he was trying to suppress physical pain.

Didn't that just figure? One day, he would probably marry some picture-perfect woman he could hang up on the wall in his apartment, instead of having to deal with any flaws.

Eyes of pitch cut toward her. "What the hell was that?"

"Oh, get over yourself," Summer said, stiffening. Did he think the whole world was supposed to be perfect all the time, just in case he was watching?

A flicker of confusion in his eyes, but it didn't knock him off target. "What the hell were you doing on that island?"

"Teaching school." She shrugged. "I'm not saying I could handle it in an urban high school, but on a tiny island in the Pacific, it turns out to be the perfect job for me. Everyone loves me."

"You were *smiling*." That tiny muscle flexed in his jaw,

probably his equivalent of pure rage. "Like you were *happy.*"

"Sorry. I didn't realize my being happy would ruin your day."

"Who the hell was taking those pictures?" He shifted, his body suddenly dominating hers. His eyes glittered. "Damn it, you do. Have an island lover."

"I haven't had a boyfriend in three years!" she yelled, and he jerked as if, for once, *she* had whipped him. "And it's not your business."

"Yes," he said flatly. "It is. Trust me, if I was constantly coming on to *you*, you would have the right to know if I had a girlfriend."

She whitened. "I'm sorry, grabbing a woman in a car and telling her you want her for your toy doesn't count as a come-on?"

He ignored that. "That damn smile you do here doesn't mean *anything*, does it?"

"I'm just trying to be nice. What am I supposed to do, scowl at everybody?" Which people would have criticized, too. Nobody had ever been happy with her here. Rich and blond and none of it to her credit, she had been born to be the world's scapegoat.

"I don't want you to be nice to me," Luc said.

"Yes, you mentioned." She put her desk between them.

"When? Do you define blow jobs as being nice?" Luc asked incredulously.

She flushed crimson. "I never actually—"

He made a slicing motion of his hand. "I'm sorry," he said abruptly. "I'm sorry. Let's not bring that up again."

She took a deep breath at the apology. Her mouth softened, tremulous, that close to burying her head against his chest and crying. The urge scared her to death. She did not want to be fragile, and definitely not around him.

"Summer." His voice changed, dark-night gentle. Dark

knight. "I didn't mean what you chose to think, about the toy, you know. Why do you always hear the wrong part of what I'm trying to say?"

"Look, I'm busy," she said roughly. "Just tell me what you want."

He watched her a long moment before he allowed her change of subject. "Let me show you the kind of thing that has been spreading through the media." The headlines came up as soon as he typed the hotel's name into her computer, images of her and him, titles like: "Is the Leucé falling apart?" "Irreparable Differences?" "New Directions for Luc Leroi?"

"It's an uproar, Summer. Bloggers and critics are slipping in from everywhere, trying to be the one to catch the story, or the first to predict the loss of a star. There's a writer from *Le Figaro* here tonight. Supposedly in secret, but we've got good connections. I want you to act like you like me." Black eyes rested on her. "Like you wouldn't dream of being parted from me."

"I'm trying!" Alain had already talked to her about it once. In public, she smiled around him until even her face hurt.

That muscle in his jaw ticced. "Like you really like me. Not like some socialite raised to heap extravagant praise on the woman she's about to stab in the back."

She folded her arms. What the hell did he know about the social survival skills necessary in an elite boarding school full of pampered but poorly raised girls? Walk a mile in her high heels and then maybe he would have an excuse to mock how she balanced in them. Or he might even understand why she preferred going barefoot. "What else do you want me to do? Kiss your feet in full view of the dining room?"

"No. Relax and put some sincerity into it. As if you genuinely like me."

"I'm doing the best I can!"

That made his jaw tighten until she thought he might crack something. "Maybe your acting ability isn't up to such a challenge. Maybe you should try genuinely liking me instead."

She gaped at him. "How in the world am I supposed to manage that?"

That perfect face of his hardened. Obsidian eyes flicked, unsettlingly, over her body and to the wall behind her. "Quite." He turned and left.

CHAPTER 20

So she tried.
   To make up for her temper and her screwups.
   She really tried.
   A little midnight-blue dress, silky and dark to bring out her eyes and set off her hair, one part naughty suggestion and two parts elegantly flirty. Skin fresh from the spa, impossibly tall, strappy sandals that would bring her up to his shoulder. She looked like someone a supreme perfectionist could stand to be seen in company with. Which she should, given how much she had had to practice at that role all her life.
   She stood a moment in the entrance to the dining area, wondering who the critic was. She hadn't been able to catch one of the staff to give her a clue—probably just as well. Her acting would seem more sincere if it wasn't aimed toward one person.
   You like Luc, she told herself, trying to get into her role.
   You like him.
   You like him.
   How does it feel to like him? Muscles in her neck slowly unwound, sending a little shiver down her spine, as if ice had melted. As if something fighting too hard, for too long, had finally been allowed to give up. She wanted to turn on her heel and hide back in her room.

But it was too late. She had offered herself on the altar of the hotel's success; she had to carry through.

You like him. Oohs and aahs as a waiter reached a table. The Aladdin's Cave, little footprints sneaking across jewel-flecked sand to where the sesame seed lay. Exclamations of delight and wonder as someone hesitated a long time before the beauty of the creation, turning it every which way to examine it, before finally dipping a spoon into it to find out what such beauty tasted like.

And then more aahs. Eyes closed in exquisite pleasure.

Tropical fruit bloomed in a small crystal vase, papayas and mangoes and pineapple arching out of it in a stylized exuberance of hibiscus, bougainvillea, birds of paradise. A single white tiare flower made of sugar, just like the flowers that grew on a bush beside her little hut by the beach, graced the yellows and golds of the mixture on one side.

Three golden orbits of a star around a dark, proud mountain. Pomegranates spilled like blood across new-fallen snow. Gold light falling into a rugged, dark abyss, melting a pool of liquid chocolate where it fell. The red-white *Pomme d'Amour* gleaming its dangerous challenge.

They were all for her.

Every single one, something he had made for her.

In this very same room where she used to sit as a child, watching every table fill with desserts she would never get to taste.

She turned her head to let her gaze linger on the dessert at the last table—a playful collection of those handcrafted chocolate-marshmallow teddy bears that she had seen in the playroom, now dancing around a mass of golden curlicues—and nearly ran into Luc.

He steadied her with a hand around her arm, and she looked up past that familiar open-throated white shirt, immersed in the pretense that she liked him.

His black eyes seemed very dark, gazing down at her. That was silly, they were always dark. His fingers held her arm gently, and his chest rose and fell, once, on a deep breath.

"Hello," he said and bent.

She stared up at him, caught by that supple, always-controlled mouth as it descended.

He closed his hand around her chin and turned her head just enough to kiss first one cheek, then the other. The brush of his lips teased mere millimeters away from the corners of hers.

They had never exchanged *bises* before. What did cheek kisses even mean, in their situation? Her fingers touched the corner of her lips as his exceptionally controlled fingers slid slowly from her chin.

"Summer." He tucked her hand into his arm. "Come have dinner with me."

Right, to show their solidarity to the critic. Her stomach shimmered with a thousand little fairy wings as she walked beside him, her fingers curling into the silk-wool blend of his coat.

The maître d' sat them at a tiny table for two tucked under an enormous bouquet-tree of roses, in the corner of the glass windows that revealed the night-lit streets of Paris. And yes, the damn Eiffel Tower, glowing in the dark, a backdrop to Luc's head.

"Where's the critic?" she murmured as she sat, to keep herself focused. The maître d' glanced at Luc in surprise, and Luc took one of her hands across the table and pinched the knuckle gently, making a little *no-no* gesture with one finger over the back of her hand.

"Don't worry about it." He shook his head slightly at the maître d' as he left. "You're doing beautifully."

Of course she was doing beautifully. She always did. It

was just . . . people seemed to think that was something wrong with her.

"The first time I sat down at a table like this, I was probably three years old," she said wryly. Some of her earliest memories were of not getting one of those desserts, in fact. Her training in how to do beautifully had been merciless. "It might even have been in this same room, although it's been remodeled."

Luc laughed ruefully. He seemed to have forgotten that his fingers still curved over the back of her hand. Relaxing from the pinch, they began to trace over her knuckles as if his hands didn't know how to be still, caressing the soft skin and tendons. "The first time I sat down to a three-hour dinner in a three-star restaurant, I was twenty-five. That table over there. I had been making the desserts that went on tables like this for years by then. They were courting me to come here, and I saw what Hugo Faure could do, and what this place could be, and I agreed."

"And we're so lucky to have you," Summer said, a little loudly.

He pressed his nail into the back of her knuckle and stroked over it again immediately, chasing away the reprimand. "Summer, don't worry any more about what the critic might think. Just relax. Be yourself."

Relax. Be herself. The temptation of it. Relax into him, let him wrap darkness around her and hold her there, the way she had always craved. Just keep her safe a little, until she could get back to the sun.

"Trust me," he murmured, fingers stroking the back of her hand.

There was a reason she wasn't supposed to do that, and it didn't have anything to do with him. But it blurred, under those skilled fingers. They found every part of her hand, so idly, so absently, forgotten by him. The exquisitely sensitive flesh between thumb and index finger. The just-short-of-ticklish spot at the base of each finger.

The Eiffel Tower behind him started to sparkle like stars in his black hair, and she forgot even how much she hated that tower.

Luc said something to a waiter, dictating how he wanted the dinner to go, orders so natural, so rhythmic, with no need for any menu, that despite her complex rebellion against someone else dictating her choices, they rocked her like a boat in a sheltered sea. He queried her with his eyebrows and a little smile, and she nodded, ready to do anything for that little smile. His fingers had never stopped stroking her hand the whole time. Nor had he ever once looked at her hand as if he knew what his fingers were doing.

"So how did you end up on an island of under three hundred people teaching school?" he asked, just like every man she had sat down to dinner with since she got here. That, too, lulled her. Made her feel as if she knew what she was doing.

"I jumped ship." She smiled, still remembering the joy of it.

A querying eyebrow. The bruise on his cheek looked worse today, blue and yellow.

"Some of us had rented a yacht, for a postgraduation cruise. And I got off when we stopped to swim in a lagoon and decided not to get back on."

Those fingers stilled on the back of her hand. He looked at her very steadily, under utter control. "You left your boyfriend at the time without a second thought."

She supposed it was normal he assumed she had a boyfriend on a postgraduation cruise. She nodded.

An odd expression on Luc's face. For the first time he looked down at his fingers lying over the back of her hand.

"That must have thrilled him," he said, low, a strange tension in his voice.

"He recovered. He's got a promising career in Hollywood now, in fact. I wouldn't have suited him."

"Don't you mean he wouldn't have suited you?"

"Also." Very few men seemed to suit her fixation with ambitious oblivious workaholics and her pathological need for attention and desire to play in the sand. None, in fact.

"You never regretted it?"

"Just once." She shrugged, and then grinned. "Tropical island paradise. Even I'm not too spoiled for that."

"Tropical island paradise. Without electricity. Or luxury. Or variety." Luc was watching her intently.

"I didn't say it would suit *you*," she said a little sullenly. That dream of getting him to run away with her on a yacht was so long dead by now. Or it should have been.

His face tightened.

"And the electricity only goes out some of the time," she muttered.

"So when was that once you regretted it?" That sudden, contained grin of his, that intense look full of warmth and passion all pent up, that hit her so hard. "A bad sunburn?"

He was *teasing* her. "Umm . . . no." She took a strong swallow of her wine and closed her eyes a moment on its dulcet gold, her stomach churning at the real reason for that one regret. She opened them to find Luc still watching her intently. "You know, you have stars in your hair," she said, and then flushed.

He touched his hair, confused, and then glanced behind him at the sparkling Eiffel Tower. With a laugh he turned back to her, his eyes very intrigued. Warm and dark. "You have the sun in yours. But all the time. Mine will go out in a minute." He cocked his head, his smile deepening to show a heretofore unguessed-at crease in each cheek. Just a bit too restrained to be a proper dimple, which was like him. "These stars will," he clarified, with amused arrogance.

She smiled, but she felt a little anxious. "I can't really affect your star count, can I? You're amazing."

His eyes caught hers. He sat up slowly straighter. "You mean that."

Well, of course she meant it. "I had been in the Pacific for four years. I just really didn't know who you were at first."

"But then why—" He caught himself and shook his head. "Thank you," he said simply.

The waiter brought two white . . . plates didn't seem the right word, since they were barely two inches wide and a foot long. Three tiny mouthfuls occupied each one: a delicate flat white spoon with a gleaming mint-colored jewel; a slender stick that speared two little orange-dusted, savory marshmallows; and an eggshell-size white cup of soup over which balanced a puff of something on a mahogany spoon.

"Hugo's newest *amuse-bouche*." Luc smiled. "I was working with him on it. I invented something like this for one of my plates." He indicated the mint-colored teardrop. "It's the thinnest capsule of gelatin that holds it together, and then . . ." He broke off. "You'll see. He wanted to do the same thing in a savory dish. And then these." He pointed to the orange-dusted marshmallows. "I've dropped this particular dessert for now, the one where I did two little handmade *fraises*—a little play with the *Fraises Tagada* candy that most people loved as children here. But Hugo was always intrigued by the idea of doing a similar texture and look, but with something savory. The sugar is usually key in a marshmallow, so we tossed ideas back and forth for several days before we came up with this. Try it." He sat back. "Taste. Feel what happens with the textures."

It was already so simple—the white on white, the small mouthfuls—and so elaborate and so completely beautiful. It reminded her, incongruously, of a Polynesian weaving of flowers, the sweet-scented white on green, simple in look and not that easy to do, rich with its own nature. She glanced up at him, wanting to show such a lei to him, to watch his creativity play with it, to see what dessert he came up with based on it, then caught herself and shut the thought down. *That's not going to happen, Summer.*

He'll never give up Paris for you.

A chef like him can't give up Paris. It would mean giving up everything he is.

He picked up his own teardrop-bearing spoon and lifted it to his mouth, raising his eyebrows at her expectantly until she lifted hers, so that they slid the spoons between their lips at the exact same time.

Liquid burst into her mouth, cool and green, some bubble of spring. She smiled over it, laying the spoon down. He nodded to the middle element of the long, narrow plate, the marshmallow creation. Two transparently thin rectangles framed it below, and he indicated them first. "The switch in textures," he said. "It's the essence here."

Crackling on her teeth, a savory, nutty flavor on her tongue. Then the gentle, dusted warmth of the little bits at the end of the stick, which made her smile, they were so surprisingly like and not like a marshmallow. And then the savoriness of the light puff on the wooden spoon, and the reassurance of the smooth, pea-based puree.

Luc watched her as she ate it. She, who had eaten so many of these things, so many elegant dinners, handling herself among the most mercilessly elegant company, began to feel self-conscious. "Do you have fun?" she asked suddenly. "When you guys come up with something like this?" Obsessive-compulsive perfectionists at play.

Luc studied his little wooden spoon, twirling it in the

fingers that had played with her knuckles. She kept feeling that touch, ghostlike, with every deft movement of the spoon. "Y-yes," he said, with some reservations. He smiled ruefully. "Patrick is infinitely good for me, in terms of lightening me up."

"The same Patrick you had a fight with?" His hands today showed no signs of swelling, but the burn was a red, blistered mark on the back of his hand. "No one ever told me why that happened."

An odd little smile. "I'll tell you tomorrow."

Yeah, right. What *had* the fight been about, that no one would say?

"Patrick said you had a sense of humor and *joie de vivre*." She couldn't keep the question out of her voice.

His eyes narrowed. "When have you been discussing me with Patrick?"

"I asked him what the fight was about," she said impatiently. "When I saw he was the other side of it. He wouldn't tell me." Oh, yeah, and he had told her not to mention his comments about the *joie de vivre*, too. Oops. "You really have *joie de vivre*?"

A waiter brought a basket of breads, half a dozen shapes fresh from the hotel bakery. Luc gave her one, warm and faintly grained under her hand. "Summer, where do you think these desserts around you come from? Some arid, dry hole inside me? I don't understand you sometimes. It's almost as if you literally cannot see them."

She blinked warily. "I'd forgotten you thought you understood me most of the time."

"No, I don't think that." He broke off a bite of his own bread, smeared it with a tiny touch of fresh-made butter, and proffered it to her. "But I do think I look at you, I look at you every second you're anywhere I can see, and for whatever reason, you're afraid to look at me."

So of course she looked at him. Behind his head, the

Eiffel's sparkling subsided and the stars in his black hair went out. The stars in his hair had been cute, sweet, luring her in. Now without them, all blackness, he was irresistible.

That wasn't true, though, what he had said. She had stood in his kitchens for an hour once, watching him, and he had never looked at her.

He turned her hand over, his fingers stroking her pulse. "Why are *you* afraid of *me*? That's the real question."

She tried to pull her hand away. He gave it a warning squeeze. Oh, right, the critic. Damn it, she couldn't do this. She was sinking down into darkness, and she wasn't going to get back out.

"If it's because I hurt you, again, I'm sorry." The subtle rub of his fingers at the most sensitive point of her wrist triggered every other erogenous zone in her body. "I didn't realize I could."

Couldn't they show the critic she respected him without *touching* so much? Wrestling her hand away would look bad. And the shimmers that ran through her body from her wrist stole all her muscles.

She bent her head, her eyes closing just one second to shut herself in complete darkness. She wanted so badly to be spoiled by him.

"*Have* I hurt you, Summer?" he asked very softly. His hand curved completely over hers and held it there, in its own little cave. What she would give, to be in a cave of him. What if she would give up herself?

"I think this might be a bad idea." She forced her eyes open and looked at him. "I think my own idea about what kind of contact we should have was better."

A bitter flash in his eyes, quickly veiled. "Thank you for doing it. I don't think you have any idea of the damage a bad spate of rumors can cause. I really appreciate your willingness to . . . pretend."

Meaning she couldn't just leave the table to save herself. She looked down at his hand on hers again, doomed.

"So what made you regret that decision to stay on an island, only once?" His voice lightened to teasing again, but the choice of subject felt—like a little curlicue of sugar that might grace one of his desserts—anything but careless or casual. "Did you fall out of a coconut palm? Break your arm?" He ran his hand all the way up the length of her forearm and back, turning it, checking for scars.

Summer stared at her forearm as if she could see the whole path of his fingers glowing against her skin. She shook her head mutely.

"Cut your foot on coral? Get bitten by a shark?"

"The sharks are actually too little to—"

He shook her arm gently. "I know. Did I ever mention my mother was Tahitian? There were a couple of years there, when I was a lot younger, when I would read up about the islands and pretend I might go there."

He might as well have told her that he had dreamed about going to live on Pluto. Actually, that sounded much more plausible for him. Dark, remote.

"Why didn't you?" She had seen his salary. He could certainly afford to travel.

One shoulder lifted and dropped. "I was busy."

Of course. Too busy, achieving too many wonderful things, for a vacation.

"And my mother ran back home to Tahiti a few months after I was born rather than tough it out in Paris with me, so I admit my attitude toward the islands was . . . complex," he said after a moment, his voice neutral.

Shock ran through her. He had just stripped something out of his soul and was offering it to her, which must have hurt like hell, and yet she couldn't tell it from his controlled face. Summer talked about the Paris weather with more passion. "Why didn't she take you with her?"

That control of his set a little harder. "I have no idea."
He released her hand and picked up his silver fork as the
waiter slid sea urchin shells in front of them, filled with
some kind of mousse. "I thought you must like seafood.
It's one of Hugo's best dishes."

"*I'd* take you with me," Summer said involuntarily. A
dark-haired intense little boy for her son. Maybe she could
get him to hang upside down grinning from a mango tree.
A dark-haired intense adult for her lover. Maybe she could
get him to rock in a hammock and smile at her. She
couldn't imagine leaving either child or man behind.

His fork halted. He set it down beside his plate, food
untouched. Something grew in him as he looked at her,
pressing out against his shell, like a boiler about to explode.
Wild and very, very dark. "My God," he said, very low.
"That's why it was a yacht."

She flushed crimson and looked down at her plate. "No
good roads for a Bugatti there," she mumbled, trying her
best to make it flippant and funny.

Across from her, absolute stillness. She couldn't look at
him, still blushing. "Excuse me." He came suddenly to his
feet. "I have to check on something in the kitchens. I'll be
right back."

Colleagues and employees filled the corridors. Luc's office was half-walled with glass. Nowhere could a man lose
control in private, and it had never been a problem before.
He had never lost control.

He finally locked himself in the bathroom and stood
with his hands gripping the sink, which had the disadvantage of putting him face-to-face with a mirror. He pressed
the top of his head against it instead of facing that wildness
in his eyes, and stared instead down at his hands, gripping
the edge of the sink. Strong hands. Powerful hands. Hands
that could control *anything,* that could do *anything.*

Bronze hands, because of his mother.

I'd take you with me.

Everything in him fought to roar out of him and grab her, in uncontrollable starvation.

All this time he had been offended, believing himself worth more than a yacht. When she had curled her head into his shoulder the first night she saw him and tried to take him with her. To *live* with her on that island.

One woman, who should have loved him, had left him for life in the sun when she barely knew him.

One woman had tried to take him with her into her sunlight the first minute she saw him.

It didn't mean anything, of course. She had been punch-drunk with fatigue, as she said. And probably would have ditched him a month later for someone else she gave another yacht to.

It didn't mean anything. She would still choose the sun over him, if he didn't go with her.

It didn't mean anything.

It meant everything.

He couldn't go, of course. Twenty years of passionate intensity to be the very best, to rule over his world, couldn't be put on an island of three hundred people. He would probably recarve the island into its ideal form, spoonful by spoonful.

But . . . she had extended the offer.

Now he just had to find a counteroffer that would beat life on a tropical island. When all he had done to create value in his life—his desserts, what he could make—was exactly the thing she had always refused to touch.

CHAPTER 21

Summer had eaten so many elegant meals, and yet none more charged than this one. It was fraught with pleasure, the tension of it pulling everything tight, so that when he lifted a spoon to his mouth and nudged her, with supple eyebrows, she felt as if the string that pulled her spoon up to his bidding was actually passing through her heart so tightly it might snap.

Guided through every bite by a man who had helped create the symphony of tastes she was experiencing. Who knew intimately every flavor and texture in her mouth.

By the end of the dinner she was braced against the coming dessert like a small child with her heels dug into the ground, watching the Hoover Dam above her break, but Luc cast a thoughtful glance over her face. And then smiled at her and stood again. "Give me a minute."

Summer wanted to get up and run. As the minute stretched to five, she bowed her head, rubbing the prickling nape of her neck. *Maybe he changed his mind. Maybe he decided I didn't deserve one of his desserts.*

Oh, damn it, Summer, grow up, get over yourself.

At the next table the waiter was describing Luc Leroi's special Heart of Winter dessert menu in passionate terms. "Just launched tonight, *messieurs, mesdames, une surprise,* unannounced, you will be among the first ever to taste these . . ."

A teddy bear arrived before her, dancing, twirling on a long wooden stick in callused, clever fingers. She started to look up at Luc, but her eyes got caught on the little bear, so cute, so funny that her braced heart softened and her face broke into a smile.

Fresh-made marshmallow dipped in chocolate, the bear's face picked out in whimsical colorful touches, a red scarf around his throat, little yellow buttons down his front. One of the marshmallow-bear lollipops off the Goldilocks-themed kids' delight of a dessert that she had spotted earlier. Those marshmallow bears that he had once offered to her on a tray, sprawled among all the secret candies of her childhood.

Tears backed up in her so suddenly they clogged her heart, which started pounding frantically to drive them through. It was so innocent, and so cute, an exquisite version of the bonbons she used to see in *boulangerie* windows in Paris, tugging on her nanny's hand when they were out for walks, until Liz smiled and bought her a tiny bag of them.

The secret little treasure that no one had ever tried to withhold from her.

"Not too much?" came Luc's gentlest, darkest voice, as he sat across from her again. He was smiling, but again the darkness in his eyes shut out everything else in the room, until the only light left was her. Leaving her, therefore, brilliantly exposed.

She bit her lip.

A tiny flex of his eyebrows. "Still too much?"

She twisted the little bear in her fingers.

"Or there's this, if you prefer," Luc said, and a waiter slid a pure white plate in front of her. The dark chocolate sphere that she had shattered once before, revisited, the bars of it strong this time but wide, so there was plenty of room for the golden heart to look out. To escape. The heart itself, the size of her fist, sat supported on another cradle of darkness, gently curved. Snow-frozen mousse entirely covered with gold leaf, it gleamed in the light from the chandeliers. "I think I finally got it right."

Her heart burst. She covered her face with her hands. The bear, forgotten in her fingers, caught in her hair, and Luc removed it deftly, tugging the strands. "Summer."

She pulled her hands apart just enough to stare at him between them, hiding her face from the rest of the room. Her lower lip trembled uncontrollably.

"Summer." He leaned across the table, and his hands came up to frame her own, adding their larger shield to her face. "What do you think I'm trying to do to you?"

"I don't know. I've never—it's like I could have any dessert in this room I wanted. It's like they were all made for me."

"You could," Luc said. "They were. I made a special dessert menu, so that everything, at every table, was designed for you."

Heart of Winter. With everywhere, a ray of sun.

"Summer. Why does that make you want to cry?"

She struggled to breathe evenly. Summer Corey did not cry in public. She only smiled. "This is—I've never seen anything so beautiful in my *whole life.*" *All those things held out of my reach because I wasn't good enough—none of them were as beautiful as this.*

His face suffused with something. An energy seemed to push against his skin, making him bigger, until his soul filled the room, leaking through cracks in that iron control. "Thank you," he said, stifled.

"How could you do something like this for me?"

He looked at her as if nothing about her made sense. "Summer. How is it even possible that no man has ever truly spoiled you?"

That made her eyes sting again. Her skin shivered with the need to be spoiled, to be cherished. She stared down at the dessert.

Luc's chest rose and fell in light, shallow pants. "Summer. Are you going to eat it?"

She picked up her spoon, shaking all over. Afraid to touch it, because it was so beautiful, and she might never see something like it again. She gestured at the top half of the sphere with its carved bars. "Is that to close back over people who get lured inside?" she whispered. "And capture them so they can never get out?"

Luc's will pressed at her, eager, barely held back. "Go all the way through, Summer. In one fell swoop. No half measures."

It took courage to press her spoon down, down, cutting through gold, into more gold, a gently yellow frozen mousse, and then—darkness spilled out like a shock. Molten dark chocolate, gushing over her spoon like blood from a deep wound. Luc made a tiny sound, as if he had just been stabbed. She looked at him.

"It's all right." He waved her focus back to his dessert, although he had a hand pressed to his chest.

She drew the bite at last to her tongue, the spoon trembling, her lips trying to press closed in resistance at the very last second, so that she smeared her own lips. But it was in, inside her mouth, and everything about her liquefied. Cold and sweet, hot and melting, luscious and intense. Luc made a hungry sound.

The taste of it broke her. A lifetime of resistance. She dug into it again, greedy as a child, and when she got two bites down, three, and still he had not jerked it away from her, her face grew slowly radiant. He had given this to her. As if he found her worth every good thing he could imagine.

All the tastes she had dreamed of as a child, watching others savor their treasures—it was better than anything she had ever imagined.

His eyes were very dark, and there was a flush under that matte skin by the time she finished every bite. He made a muted sound when she licked the last of the chocolate off the tip of her finger, as if he had been punched.

Reaching across the table, he stroked his thumb deeply across her mouth, then slipped that thumb to his own lips and sucked it clean. "Summer. You don't want coffee, do you?"

She shook her head mutely.

He took her hand and pulled her up. "Then come here."

CHAPTER 22

Summer's breath grew shorter and shorter as he led her up to her room, a scary sensation that she was falling a very long way and had no idea how to stop it. He took her card key, and she turned, caught between him and the door as he slid it into the lock. He was studying her, an unfamiliar curve to his mouth. Just at the corners, a softening or a tenderness. It faded to absolute seriousness.

This time she remembered about the *bises,* when he bent his head. She angled her cheek for the first kiss.

His fingers closed around her chin again. A soft stroke of his thumb along her jaw as he turned her head back and pressed that kiss straight on her mouth.

She gasped, and he took advantage of the parting of her lips instantly, rubbing them softer and more open with his, tasting her with his tongue as if they had kissed a hundred times, as if he owned her mouth.

Summer made a little, desperate sound and clutched at the door. It swung away from her, and her hands slid off its smooth surface without purchase, like the frantic heroine sliding off the edge of the cliff, plunging to her death, no superhero to swoop in and catch her mid-fall. But instead of saying one word, just one single no, she let her head fall back.

Let him have her mouth. As if he owned it.

Heat and desire thundered through her so suddenly she felt dizzy.

He took his time. As if he could savor that kiss forever. Touching her with only two points of his body, that hand on her chin. And his mouth.

His mouth.

How could any man do that with his mouth? As if there was no flavor of her that he meant to leave unsavored. Focused on every texture, every taste.

She kissed him back hard suddenly, half-biting at his mouth.

"Shh." He closed his mouth against the bite and shook his head so that his lips brushed softly back and forth against hers. "Shh, Summer, it's all right."

No, it *wasn't*. How could he, how *dared* he, say that? It wasn't all right, it could never be all right. She felt close to weeping with how wrong it was, and yet she couldn't make herself tell him no.

She took a frantic breath, and again he took the access offered, and more. His fingers caressed very, very gently, as if he was tracing something fragile, along her cheekbone, circled with the most delicate touch imaginable over her temple, and then threaded into her hair.

How could he kiss her as if he would own her forever and touch her as if nothing more fragile or more ephemeral existed?

Don't do this, don't do this to me, she wanted to beg him. *Not this incredible beautiful thing. You're going to hurt me.* But she couldn't bring herself to say a word.

"Shh," he said, as if he was trying to soothe someone coming out of a nightmare, make her see there was nothing to be afraid of. Such a lie. "Shh, shh. Summer. *Ne t'inquiète pas.*"

His fingers circled warm and sure over the nape of her

neck. And still he kissed her, gently and mercilessly, as if no end could ever be found to his patience and persistence and care. *Don't worry?* How could he say that to her?

The barest brush of fingertips up and down her nape. He was winning over her mouth. Her trembling tension could not hold. He was stealing all the fight in her, all the bite, all the urgency, slowly reducing her to his rhythm, a leisurely subject of his tasting. "There. There, there. You like that, don't you?"

She did. Every brush of his fingers left a fine trembling all through her, waves on waves of it, taking over her whole body. *Her whole being.* And all it took, from him, was that barest flick.

He drew a long breath that seemed to pull the air through her mouth right out of her soul and lifted his head just enough to look down at her. The thumb of his other hand came to replace his mouth, rubbing back and forth across her lips, endlessly, sometimes barely grazing, sometimes dragging, as if he could never get enough of that texture. He eased her farther into her room.

Her hands climbed over his arms, pulling herself up into him. She couldn't hold herself back. Just the same as at the pool, only worse, much worse.

He was dragging her down into a vortex, bright light into a swirl of darkness. *"Soleil,"* he whispered. *"Mon soleil."*

No, I don't belong to you. I don't. I'm not yours. But he was kissing her as if she should belong to him. Everything could be right in her life if she did.

The silk of his hair against her fingers made her shiver. The muscles of his shoulders made her hungry for more hardness. As Luc kissed her, easing her through the room, the Eiffel Tower started to sparkle again, a dancing glitter all over the shadowy room. *No, go away,* Summer thought to the Tower. *I don't want you here.* But if *la Dame de Fer* was anything, it was odiously persistent.

The slowest of slow dances, through those sparkles. He lifted her suddenly, bringing her thighs around his hips, so that he could rub his mouth down her jaw to her throat. Her head fell so far back the arch of her own body in yielding was half pain.

He slid her down his thigh, finding her zip. The silk of her dress bunched up her body with her downward glide, then, when he pulled his own body back, slid off her to the floor, leaving her in bra and panties and sandals, one toe covered in a pile of blue silk.

She felt a carved surface against her spine, wood against one shoulder, cold glass against another, and opened her eyes. Sparkles danced over his face as if he had been transformed into some creature from another world. The tower must form the backdrop to her body.

"Oh, no," she said. "No, not here."

"You're so beautiful," he whispered, trailing his hands from her bare shoulders down over her lace-veiled breasts, like a blind person learning her by feel. But he saw everything, the way her breath hitched and her bottom rubbed involuntarily against the frame. "You're perfect here. Just perfect."

"But—" The sense of that so-hated symbol at her naked back was . . .

"I love the way you look against that glow," he whispered. "Everything sparkling around you. God, Summer." His hands cupped her breasts. "You're *so beautiful.*"

"I know," she said uneasily. "But—"

"No," he interrupted. "You have no idea what I'm talking about. You always think you do, but you don't. *Belle comme le jour.*"

"Look, you're not the first man to tell me I'm beautiful." She forced impatience, trying to find an edge to cling to in this sweet swirl of darkness. Why did she want to drown herself in it? Why did she feel she would come out of it shinier, truer, more whole?

"Oh, Summer." Luc stopped her by running one hand from her breast, straight and sure and hard down her body, to cup her sex as if he knew exactly where she wanted his hand to be. She gasped and arched into him— oh, yes, he knew *exactly*—and forgot thought. "That was so exactly the wrong thing to say. What am I going to do with you?"

His thumb moved as if he knew precisely what he wanted to do with her. She gasped again as she slid off the frame so that she was entirely against the glass.

The cold of it shocked her shoulder blades. He pressed until her bottom settled against the glass as well, her sex sandwiched between cold and heat.

"God, I need you." His thumb moved again, and she twisted frantically between the glass, with the cursed iron form that looked down on her, and the clever heat of his hand. "You have no idea how much. I can make you need me as much."

He needed *her*?

"I can make you feel how perfect you are. *Soleil,* don't you feel perfect now?" His eyes, glowing the copper color of the tower, ran over her body like a hot touch. She felt naked in her midnight-blue lace bra, the tiny matching thong under which his hand so easily slipped, and sandals.

"Don't you?" His thumb insisted, as her body went helpless to it and her mind struggled. *Not here, not so completely, not so easily, not . . .*

Black eyes gleamed hot copper as she came. He held her only with the hand against her sex as she shattered uncontrollably, her bare arms pressed helpless for purchase against the glass. "*God,* so beautiful," he whispered hoarsely.

She fell forward against him as the convulsions peaked and slowly released her. "I'm not—I'm not—oh, God." She shuddered against his chest as he forced the peaks to keep coming, forced the words to break into nothing.

He pulled her against him as snugly as if he was soothing her after a nightmare, but this was something more dangerous than a nightmare, a whirl of chaos that might re-form her. Tension rippled through his muscles.

"Oh, yes, you are." He turned her against his body, pulling her back against his chest. His arms shook with hardness restrained. "Look. Summer, look at you."

He walked them backward just enough that she could see herself in the glass, reflected like a whisper against the Tour Eiffel. Behind her loomed his harder, bigger form, more difficult to see, the black of his hair blending with the glass, the shape of him coming out of darkness to grab her from behind. He was completely clothed.

"Watch," he breathed. "See what I see."

Her eyes met her own in the glass, begging her not to lose herself, this self held slender and fragile and naked for her own display in his arms. And then his two fingers slipped deeply inside her, possessing her as his thumb moved again over flesh already so sensitive that she shattered for him again unbearably. Her eyes closed, the Eiffel playing over her face until she couldn't tell anymore where the sparkles inside her ended and the tower began.

As she sank out of it at last, her weight heavy against the brace of his body, her breasts crushed against his arm, half sobbing in pleasure and despair, the Eiffel Tower, too, stopped glittering.

Oh, God. The sparkle only lasted ten minutes. He had made her come twice in less than ten minutes.

"Do you feel perfect yet?" he asked the nape of her neck, her body bowed over his arm.

All of her was flowing out, like a receding sea, as the waves eased, fell back. Flowing into him. Leaving her quiet, and weak, and oddly at peace.

"Not yet, *soleil?*" He lifted her in his arms, like a rescued princess. *Which was entirely false.* She had rescued herself, years ago. He was carrying her off *from herself.*

The room felt gentler, somehow, without the sparkles. As if Summer had just been offered as a sacrifice to the Tower, there against the window, and so the Iron Lady was appeased.

Luc lowered her onto the opulent bed, nestling her among pillows. "I half imagined you sleeping in a sheet hung hammock style between two chairs."

"Did you really?" she asked, because she couldn't stop that hunger to know that she had been in his thoughts, however indifferent he had seemed. He was stroking back the hair that had gotten tangled over her face, shifting into gentle, long caresses of her body that settled her more deeply into silk and softness and pillows. It would be a lie to say she had never felt such a hard hunger in a man's body before, but she had never felt such hard hunger combined with such gentleness and control; she had never had such tension held back while her own was released by him, over and over. "Imagine me?"

"Not usually here." Something grim invaded his tone. "Usually in sand and sun and sea and very, very far away." He lowered his head and kissed her again, and anyone would have thought it was a first kiss, that he was starting the seduction from scratch, his mouth was so thorough, claiming hers, so tender.

It made no sense, that tenderness matched with the hunger that shivered over his skin, drawing his muscles taut. But she responded to it with craving, dying for tenderness for so long she could gorge herself sick on it.

Her arms stroked up and down his silk-smooth back under his shirt. She fought his clothes off, running her hands over the lean hard strength of his chest.

He stilled for her touch, muscles rigid. It delighted her to please him, to have him focus so intensely on her slightest movement.

"You're so beautiful," he whispered again. "Summer, how can you not know?"

"I *do* know," she said, a little aggravated. It was bigheaded of her, perhaps, but she could hardly be ignorant of the effect her looks had on men. Men had been falling for her all her life. It was her own fault, really, that she only fell in return for the ones for whom beauty was never enough.

She pushed that thought away. Right now his body was too wonderful under her hands. She had forgotten to fight the hook. Now she only wanted to plunge in deeper.

Have him plunge in deeper.

Why wouldn't he plunge in deeper?

She pulled herself up to press kisses over one strong shoulder, all the kisses in her, a soft, hot rain, over muscle and bone, the join of his neck, the hollow of his throat.

"*Soleil.*" He wrapped one arm around her, holding her tight up against him, while the other arm held up their combined weight. "That's what's so strange. You don't even understand what I'm talking about." He sank down onto her, slowly, the control of that one arm never faltering, until they were lost in pillows and silk, his body the only hard thing to hold on to.

She kept kissing him, everywhere, stroking him while he stroked her. A great feast of each other. She wanted to layer him in sunshine thick as honey, to coat herself all over him. Wild urges shimmered through her, to tell him she loved him, to beg him again to run away with her, and she buried them all in kisses. Kisses carried no failure. Did they?

He, too, seemed to want to dip her entirely in him. As each tried to kiss right down to the other's toes, they ended up lower and lower on the bed, until they were about to fall off the bottom. Luc laughed and hauled her back up the bed again, dragging her body the length of the silk, and they started over.

I love you. It almost slipped out again, as she laughed with him, breathless at how wonderful his body felt. It seemed to fit just right, to say it.

She kissed it to the muscles of his biceps instead.

"Summer—" He slipped his thigh between hers to press hard against her sex as he explored her breasts. "God, it's not fair."

What wasn't fair? That he could shatter her over and over and still not break? No, damn it, it wasn't. She had wanted some power here.

But when she slid her hands down to his sex he caught her wrists and drew them to his mouth, kissing them over and over until he laid them gently on a pillow and held them there. "You do like this," he whispered. "You need this." The way his gaze ran down her body made her feel so small and exposed and his. And utterly and profoundly beautiful. Not intellectually aware she was beautiful, but from deep within her all the way to the last layer of her skin, *actually beautiful.*

"I can make you—you can learn to need me," he breathed, and suckled her breast deeply into his mouth at the same time as his hand slipped where his thigh had been.

This time, when she shattered, he took everything out of her. He wouldn't let her come down, his hand rocking her gently, keeping the convulsions coming until she was wiped out.

She curled away from him at last, crossing her thigh over to dislodge his hand, since he still held her wrists. "Too much," she murmured. "I can't anymore."

And he laughed, caressing the most loving kisses all along the line of her throat. "You can if I want you to."

CHAPTER 23

C*ontrol.* Wildness beat in Luc, maddened. *Control.*
Of all the raw elements he had ever touched—only
the purest, only the finest—she was the most beautiful.
The most exquisite. *And look how she responds to my hands.*
Arching, stretching, glowing, as he took that luminous
beauty of hers and let it bloom into something no one
could even imagine. No one could resist.

She's so . . . sweet. As long as I keep control, she's all mine.

Apparently she could. Do whatever he wanted her to.
But after the fourth time, Summer pulled pillows over her
sex and face, as limp and exhausted as a pretty piece of silk,
littering the street at the end of a long, wild Carnival. All
around her his strength and darkness, and he could do
what he wanted with it. Nothing she could do could break
him. But he made her beautiful. Ragged beyond coher-
ence.

And helpless. Completely without power.

"Mmm," she mumbled when he nudged her yet again.
Her sense of beauty was receding, growing impotent and
hopeless, battered against iron control. And she didn't
know what else she had. Certainly not the strength to pull
a comforter over her and hide. He had taken even that.
"I'm going to sleep."

He pulled the pillow off her face and gave her an indignant look. "I beg your pardon?"

It took her a second. Then she laughed, relief and pleasure penetrating her exhaustion. "Oops. I forgot." She sleepily stroked that beautiful tight ass of his, calling up her warm, inviting smile. "Go ahead." She might not have another orgasm in her, but she would be more than happy to take him inside her while he let himself go. It might even make right that something that had been shifting wrong ever since her first orgasm, when she had reached for him, and instead of coming to her, he had set about giving her another one.

But he stiffened, staring at her smile.

"Oh, no," he said low, hard. "Oh, no, by God, I won't."

What? Something painful shafted through her, worry solidifying, throwing everything out of kilter. She was just his thing to manipulate. He would not lose his control to her.

She found her thighs squeezing tight together, trying desperately to get that barn door shut after the horse was stolen. Four times.

"Not that damned polite, pat-me-on-the-head smile for *this, too.*"

What was wrong with her smile? It disappeared. Was it not up to his standards?

He stared at her, his muscles tightening and tightening until they propelled him off the bed. *"Putain de merde."*

He stood with his back to her, rage compacted in his body, in that fist by his side. But how was it her fault? He had been the one who kept taking control of her, not letting her wrap around him as she had been so eager to do, holding her down as he shattered her one more time.

"Blame yourself," she said sharply. *Never accept it, when they reduce you. Never.*

He turned his head enough that she could see the tense, perfect line of his jaw. The backlighting from the window veiled him in a blur of shadow. "I do."

What? Somehow that didn't seem right, either. Was she so much an object to be handled that she didn't even have a role in the postmortem accusations?

"I clearly—mishandled things," he said, right on cue. "I was aiming for something a little different."

The pain of that curled through her. She didn't see it coming and was surprised when she tried to breathe and discovered her lungs crushed so she couldn't. *Mishandled things. Aiming for something else.*

"Well. You let me know what thing you want me to be, and I'll see if I can live up to your expectations next time."

He half turned, sharply. "*What* are you talking about?"

"What are *you* talking about? In fact, why are you still talking? Aren't we done yet?"

His nostrils flared. Both fists clenched as he turned fully to face her. A dangerous, naked, aroused man, muscles straining for action, an atavistic wildness just lunging to get out.

She stared back at him with no fear whatsoever. If he fell on her savagely, it might just set things right. She might even discover more energy left than she thought.

He took a hard breath and jerked his pants on over his naked butt. She winced a little when he zipped them so savagely, but *of course* he kept in perfect control even then and didn't do himself an injury. "You're right. I'm not in a good state for this."

She stared at him in shock. She didn't know why. Anyone would think she had enough experience of men to predict his ability to walk out in a huff over his sexual fantasy not going exactly as planned. Over her being, somehow—not good enough.

He abruptly leaned over her, caught her chin, and kissed her hard on her open mouth. He was still pulling his shirt on as he stepped into the hall.

Leaving her body empty, and in a vulgarly specific spot, her skin growing cold, and hatred growing. Into something powerful enough to save even her.

The bastard. To have turned all his patience and control on her, to break her down infinitely until every bit of love and joy and desire slipped out of her and clung to his skin, and not ever once break open himself. Give her some of him back.

When she had told him, no blunter way possible, that the absolute limit of what she wanted from him was to be fucked against the wall and left on the floor.

The unutterable bastard.

CHAPTER 24

L uc wanted to *howl*.
He knew he had screwed up. The icy shower beat it into his brain. To have her all his, so utterly and completely and helplessly his, over and over his, and to end it in a *fight*?

Arousal had been some dark monster grown five times the size of his body, ready to burst out of his elegant skin and leave it in peeling shreds for all to see. But he had been controlling it still. Somehow, holding on to one last little shred of control and about to let it break, thank God at last—until the slap of that smile. That same damn smile she had thrown blindly over him the very first night, wrenching out his heart and giving him fifty euros in return.

That warm, sleepy smile, arms sliding over his back, saying, Come down here, I may be exhausted but you are welcome here.

"My God, I've never seen anything like it." Patrick whipped a plate away from him and gave the destroyed flourishes of the Victoire a disgusted look. "You're starting to break things just by looking at them. You don't have any of those film crews coming today by any chance so they can see who the real star of the kitchens is?"

He gave up on righting Luc's mess as he spoke, pulling a new one together to replace it and sliding it through the pass to the waiter.

Luc snarled.

"I don't even want to know how you got yourself into this state after what *I* saw of how things were going last night. Whatever it is, I'm quite sure it's all your fault."

Luc's snarl turned murderous.

"I hear the hotel's got a gym," Patrick said. "I sometimes use it instead of hitting *you* over the head."

But on the way up for one quick, homicidal bout of pounding a punching bag or straining against some insane amount of weights, he ran into Summer.

In coat and scarf and looking as if *she'd* slept like an angel.

Which she probably had. *An angel exhausted with pleasure, curled up among her pillows, unable to keep her eyes open.*

"Summer," he said with deep relief. It would probably have been better if he had run into her *after* the gym, but still.

She pulled her gloves on, giving him a vague, cheerful smile.

Putain, he was going to *kill* somebody. Himself. Her. *Death by shrapnel; he exploded. We never knew he had all that stuff in him.*

He bent down to kiss that cheerful smile right off her face, to make her look at him.

She turned her head away so that his lips slid over her cheek.

His hand spasmed with such a need to yank her head back around and *force* her mouth to take his that he had to take a step back, locking his hands under his elbows.

"I'm sorry, I'm running late," she said lightly, as if she made absolutely no distinction between a kiss, a conversation in the hallway, or another bout of sex; she was equally apologetic for having better things to do than all of them. "Let's catch up later."

Oh, yes, he was going to kill someone. Her.

"After all, I don't want him to ditch me." An amused shrug.

He stared at her, eyes burning. "You don't want *who* to ditch you?"

"My therapist, of course," she said with a little what-a-silly-you-are laugh.

His nostrils flared. Hidden under his elbows, his knuckles dug into his muscles. "You're really going to see a therapist to learn how to stop being attracted to me?"

"Obviously," Summer said with a wink, "I need some help."

His jaw clenched. He stepped very carefully aside to let her pass, because he could not trust himself to do anything else.

And then he went to the damn gym.

It did help. It helped to work himself into pure, livid exhaustion, until he was drenched in sweat and hanging on the bag to recover.

A little.

It made a space in his aroused, wild, frustrated mind for her face framed by his hands, her lips trembling uncontrollably and her blue eyes brilliant with tears she was trying not to let fall. Because he had made a whole room full of desserts for her, offering her everything that was most beautiful about himself.

It made space for him to remember that.

He took deep breaths, hanging on the bag. Pressing his face against the leather, letting his pulse return to normal.

Oh, shit. Had he made her cry?

The amount of times Summer pulled her phone out that day and nearly told her father she quit went beyond counting. She walked instead on foot along the Seine all the way over to the Gibert Jeune on the opposite bank, down near Notre Dame. It was the most beautiful walk in

Paris, and she tried to tolerate it. Bridges strung over the stygian waters like bracelets of old bone over a long, brown arm leached of life. Far in the distance, Notre-Dame fought the gray sky, proposing itself as salvation, fooling many a traveler into thinking it was just a few steps farther, *press on, don't give up and sink down into the Métro.* Behind her, the Wicked Stepmother Eiffel loomed in inexorable pursuit.

Summer knew the distance between the menace and refuge very well. Her boarding school had sat only a block from the tower, and God knew she had fled that as often as she could. Notre-Dame had been a good place for a teenager to sit and bury her face in her hands and slowly dissolve into tears of self-loathing and despair, while the rose window and the vast murmuring space kept alive a fragile, stubborn desire to love herself, despite the fact that everyone else hated her so much and even her parents had thrown her away.

She walked toward Notre-Dame automatically now, in her high-heeled little boots, consciously torturing feet used to flip-flops. Paris's beauty and glamour had always trumped every emotion Summer could ever have. No one could be lonely here. No girl who had been given Paris should want still *more* proof of love and affection. Not unless she was really spoiled.

But Summer would exchange this, the most beautiful and most heartbreaking walk in the world, for a stroll down a beach in the moonlight, with the Southern Cross low on the horizon, any day of the week.

A cold wind ate at her cheeks, and a few hardy men tried to harass her, but she barely noticed them. Her feet cramped by the time she reached the Boulevard St. Michel. The façade of Notre-Dame had had a good cleaning since she was last in Paris, and it glowed against the grayness, stubbornly pale and perfect. She stared at it, across the water, and the memory of all those times she had wept in it as a teenager rose up and choked her heart. She would not go back there. She would *not* be that girl again.

She pivoted, crossing the street, which put her right under the glorious fountain of the warrior angel Michael, crushing the devil beneath his foot and challenging the masses of Boulevard St. Michel to do the same. Paris was persistent that way, forcing its superior beauty on you every way you turned.

As a little girl she had thought the bronze was a strong, proud woman, defeating some merciless, sneering man with a curvaceous sword and graceful dance move. *Take that,* the woman had seemed to say, with her upraised victorious arm, her lovely face untroubled by all she rose above and defeated, her wings so ready to lift her and let her soar away. Liz, for all her passion for Paris history and love of sharing it with her charge, had never once corrected her. It had been later, at boarding school, that someone in her art class laughed at her and told her what she should have realized all along. It was the Archangel Michael. Not a woman triumphant but the angel who had cast Eve out of Paradise for being so stupid as to eat something lusciously tempting.

She stood a long time looking up at the proud half smile on the elegant face. It could have been a woman. She tried to imagine Luc as the devil, looking up with craven rage at the angel triumphing over him, but it was impossible. Some man took advantage of her absorption to try to slip his arm around her waist, and his face instantly replaced the craven fallen devil's. Damn.

She shrugged the man off with difficulty and went into the bookstore, buying big piles of books for her kids that she hauled back in bags so heavy they cut into her arms and left no ability to reach for a phone and cop out of her kids' future because a man had given her four orgasms in one night and she couldn't handle it.

On her bedside table sat a bouquet of two dozen chocolate marshmallow teddy bears on long lollipop sticks.

She was not entirely sure what was a more evil thing for a man to do, give her four orgasms without *ever losing control* or give her a bouquet of teddy bears as a thank-you gift for them when he knew that cracked her heart wide open.

She flung herself back out of the room before she could eat one and ran into a hard, supple wall. A gasp of scent— oh, God, he smelled so *good* today, some tiny, teasing spice she wanted to trace all through the citrus and caramel and chocolate on his skin, until she could figure out what it was.

What if she learned him so well, she would know everything he had worked on that day just by burying her face into his throat when he came home at night and taking a deep breath?

Shit, stop, Summer, stop! You're not doing that, forming your life in this miserable place around a man who might notice you briefly at midnight yet never find you worth opening his heart to.

"Summer." Luc's velvet night voice closed over her, and agile, perfect hands caught her before she could fling herself back into her room and slam the door.

"Oh, dear, not you again." A playful, mocking tone that suggested *he* wasn't worth more of *her.* She winked at him ruefully. "To be honest, I've had about as much of you as I can take today. It was fun, though." She lifted a hand to pat his cheek.

He caught it easily, as if it was nothing to him, to catch it, to run his thumb over her pulse and send it skittering, all while pulling her hand away from his face, not letting her touch *him*. "Summer."

She gave him a bored half smile, her eyebrows faintly lifted. He stood so close she could have leaned right into him. And been his damn puppet again. His little doll he played with. It made her want to cry to think of the night in those terms. But what else had it been?

"Summer." His fingers stroked her wrist so gently as he drew it down by her side. Her heart pounded with the longing to hide herself against him, but she just couldn't. You couldn't hide yourself against someone who would manipulate your soul out of your body while staying in perfect control. "I'm sorry if I screwed up. Sorrier than you can guess, I suspect. I went too far. Apparently. And I was almost insane with frustration right there at the end; I had to leave."

Yes, of course. Leave rather than crack. Wasn't it so lucky one of them had that option.

"Summer, you know, when I'm working with . . . raw materials"—he stroked his hands up her arms, with familiar gentleness, as if he had the right to take control over everything around him and turn it into what he wanted—"I often have to try more than once, to get it to turn out just right."

Anger spiked. Was he going to practice on her until he got her just right?

He leaned over her, hands sure, arousing, as they caressed her arms. His breath warmed her lips. "Summer. Let's try again."

She jerked against him and he blinked, focusing on her anger with difficulty through a haze of other expectations. "So sorry you couldn't make me perfect the first try."

His hands slipped over her body in surprise as she ducked free, and he caught her arm. His gaze searched her as if her failure to understand made no sense. "Summer," he said softly. "I wasn't trying to make you perfect for me. I was trying to be perfect for you."

She frowned at him, uncomprehending. "But you already are perfect."

"I have to work at it, all the time. You just are."

What? "You can't possibly really believe that."

"Then why do I say it, Summer? What do you think I want out of you, that would make me lie to you?"

Not her money, not her father's power, clearly not just sex. Oh, God, this scared her so much. What if he really wanted all of her? What if she was just a bite he could so easily swallow whole and forget as he went on with the hearty, full meal of the rest of his life? She couldn't stand it again. She wanted so desperately to disappear from this spot in his hold and reappear on her safe, sunny island that she was shaking, on the edge of tears. "You said I was a spoiled brat."

"You asked me to fuck you against a wall." His fingers slipped under her coat so that they curved just below her throat like a Roman collar. "I believe, as far as insults are concerned, you hold the honors."

She gave him a bitter look. "Instead of which, we had to do it your way."

His hand tensed. "I beg your pardon?" His eyes locked with hers. And filled with stunned incredulity. "Are you *complaining* about last night?"

"Isn't that what you were apologizing for?"

"I was apologizing for losing my temper and walking out that way. I don't see how *you* could possibly complain about—" He broke off, his face growing paler and paler, his body tighter and tighter. "Go ahead, Summer," he said finally, his lips barely moving. "Tell me how you could complain about last night."

"Well." She fell back instantly on her best defense, lightness, and shrugged. "I *am* spoiled."

A muscle ticced in his jaw. His hand flexed on her collarbone. He nudged her backward into her suite, black eyes boring into her as the door swung shut behind them. "You know, sometimes, it's harder to resist your so charming invitation than you might think."

"Oh my God!" she exclaimed excitedly. "I gave you a teensy bit of trouble resisting something? Are you *sure*?"

That hand on her collarbone pushed her with slow, steady pressure against the wall. Not rough. But inexorable. Luc never miscalculated how much power he needed to put into his hands. And yet for all his control, there was something violent in the long, tense lines of him that seeped out of that bronze skin and held her still. Her body was melting for him already, in recognition and readiness.

"I told you," he said, a little grimly, "I wouldn't be averse."

Excitement shot through her like relief, sucking up all other energy, focusing it on pleasure. On him.

"You're not going to get away from me." His hand flexed against her collarbone, holding her prisoner, while the other hand arrowed to her sex. "And by God, I'm going to give you what you want."

His fingers slid under her panties and parted the crease of her, that fast, the switch to intimacy too radical, the effect on her too hot. "Stop," she whispered.

He checked, his gaze stripping her face, and the lips of her sex curled around his fingers and clung, out of her control. Why was *she* the one who always lost control? And to think people had warned her against treating *him* like a toy. Because of all those dark emotions of his that were much too valuable to be spent on someone like her.

"You might need a safe word," he told her grimly.

Her mouth twisted as his hand cupped her sex more fully. *"Je t'aime?"* she suggested ironically.

His whole body jolted, the heel of his palm grinding against her clitoris and her pubic bone. His eyes flew to hers.

Under that black gaze, the pressure of his hand already driving her frantic, she faltered. "That's—that's the safe word." Wasn't that *obvious?* How could he think anything else?

His hand flexed involuntarily over her sex, and pleasure released through her like juice squeezed from a lime. He braced an arm over her head, the eyes just inches from hers a black gloss of fury. "You're going to pay for that."

His hand moved again, and she shivered, dampening his palm, helpless to him. Oh, she knew he was going to make her pay. She just didn't entirely understand her crime. She put her chin up, her mouth cynical. "You're going to leave me like this?"

His thumb took a leisurely path up the folds of her sex, as if he had all the time in the world to explore her any way he wanted, and found her clitoris. He rolled it very, very gently, the most delicate of movements. Heat flushed her. She pressed her hands against the wall, trying to find some purchase as she lost all strength, but could not let herself cling to him.

"No." He wound her hair around his wrist, pulling her head back. "I just want one price. You're going to look at me while I make you come. If you close your eyes, you don't get anything until you open them."

She bucked against him frantically. He held her mercilessly. "What about you?" she cried, desperate and wounded and furious. "When do *you* lose control?"

"I don't. And you're not going to make me," he promised her.

"That's not *fair.*"

"Then use your safe word."

She bit her lip. Their eyes locked. The moment stretched, a silent battle, until he bent down and took her lip away from her teeth and bit it for her.

Then she fought him for control, because she couldn't use that safe word. She yanked at his pants and forced her hands in, trying to get to him before he got to her. He grabbed one of her wrists and pulled it over her head, but she managed to keep the other one free. He couldn't get it, without releasing the other maddening hand on her sex, and that one he wouldn't let go. He was ruthless with it, lethal, driving her even as she twisted and bucked away from her own orgasm.

She came helplessly, sobbing, her hand a vise around his sex, squeezing with every last desperate bit of strength in her as she fell into him.

He was breathing harshly, like some great beast in a wild fight. "Stop it." He released her sex at last to pull her hand away from his penis. She held on as tight as she could, so that he had to drag her hand off him, and he shuddered violently, his head arching back.

"I hate you," she panted at him.

"No, you don't." He ripped her panties down. She was still wearing her damn winter coat and soaked with sweat. "Summer, don't say that."

"I *hate* you."

"Don't—" He was shaking all over, great spasms of his muscles. He yanked her hips in suddenly against his. "Shut *up.*" He kissed her deep, a complete invasion, so that she couldn't talk. She shoved his pants off his hips.

His muscles jerked under her hands as if he was being wrenched apart, and he bit at her mouth. She arched up against him in a sudden glimpse of a long-despaired of victory, twisting her hips against his.

His fingers spasmed into her bottom, so hard they hurt.

And then in one hard thrust, he was inside her. He gasped, wrenching his mouth from hers and staring down at her.

"Oh." Her head fell back. Oh, that felt so *good*. So right. She could stay this way, pinned by him, forever.

"Oh, God," they both said at the same time, in two languages. But *she* sounded as if everything had just been made right with her world. He sounded as if his was being destroyed.

He dragged his hands up her body and wrapped one in her hair, letting her own strength—and the wall—hold her up. She wrapped her thighs around him, dragging her hands over his chest, yanking at buttons stitched far too strongly for her to break.

"You're so beautiful," he said desperately, ramming her back against the wall.

"Oh, God, so are you. You feel so good." So perfect at last, to have him inside her and all around her and hers. Losing himself to her as she lost herself to him. "I love it."

Wait, did that make her sound like a slut? The spoiled woman who loved *it,* who couldn't get enough of sex? "I love you," she corrected herself. Not just anybody. Him, inside her. He was perfect.

His body bucked so hard and deep it hurt, and then froze there. She took deep breaths, adjusting to him so deep. *So good, so good, so good.* He could move again anytime. Her eyes fluttered open to find him watching her, utterly still. What . . . ? Oh, that stupid safe word. "I didn't mean that." She petted his arms. That damn shirt was driving her crazy. "Don't stop."

His eyes flared. "Didn't *mean* it?"

"Don't *stop.*" She dragged harder on his arms. "It just slipped out. Sorry. I don't know what comes over me sometimes."

A hand slid into her hair, close to the roots, locking her head back against the wall. His eyes searched her face, supple eyebrows curled together, as if he could strip her soul out of her and shake it up to inspect like so much dirty laundry.

She tried again to hide her face in his body and met the imprisonment of his hand, holding her stripped and exposed like that. Her face crumpled in distress, and she twisted her head as far as she could to the side, tearing at her hair.

His hold loosened, letting her hide.

"Don't stop," she begged, petting hard through his shirt, trying to fit between the infuriating buttons. "I love i— yo—I l—don't stop."

That was okay to say, wasn't it? Don't stop?

It must have been. Because he thrust so hard into her she gasped for breath and couldn't talk anymore. And then all that blackness in him came out, and he completely lost control.

She wrapped her arms around him, holding on for dear life, as he took her like a raging thing, let loose and starving. Devouring her, thrust by thrust, until he shattered inside her. Burying his face in her hair as if she was the only thing that could hold him together.

Luc felt as if he had broken himself into a thousand pieces. It scared the hell out of him. He didn't know what he might *do* without all those iron bands of control. The essence of him might keep floating out to the edge of the universe.

Little atoms of him, millions of light-years away from each other in a vast void, lost and panicked.

Little atoms of him, curious and intrigued, calling, *Hey, look what's way out here! I think I might be at the edge of the universe.*

Does anyone else want to come out here with me and make a star?

He hardly dared look at Summer, he who had insisted she look at him. She was limp in her winter coat, damp with sweat, probably feeling battered. He forced himself at last to meet her eyes, feeling sullen and clumsy and like he wanted to kick some tin can across the Métro. Feeling wild still, with no idea in hell how he was going to get himself back in that iron shell.

She was gazing at him steadily, her eyes wondering, absorbed.

She was seeing him, all right.

Damn it, couldn't she have looked at him when he was at his best? All the rest of the damn moments of his life?

"Don't say you hate me. Summer." His voice was rough. Had he shouted? Surely not. Probably just growled and panted himself hoarse. "Don't say that."

"Well, I *did* hate you." She petted his shoulders. He needed to get his damn shirt off.

He needed to get her coat off before she got heatstroke. *Bordel.* "Don't say you love me, either. That . . . isn't kind."

Her face went blank. Then her eyebrows flicked together and she searched his face. It wasn't a good moment for her to be searching his face. For one of the first times in his adult life, he wasn't sure what someone else might see.

"This is what you wanted?"

She made a wobbly motion of her shoulders, not entirely sure. There was a hint of a smile on her face, but her eyes were somber.

"Did I hurt you?"

"No." A flicker of something in her eyes. "I'm strong. Don't worry about me."

He pushed her coat off her shoulders before she died of the heat, then her sweater. The camisole under that was drenched. *Putain,* he was a savage.

But she had *wanted* him to be a savage. And it touched something profoundly triumphant and hungry in him to have her so slick with sweat and vulnerable to him. To be peeling away her layers, to see how much smaller she seemed without them. *Merde,* he *was* a bastard. She was so small now, between the wall and him, without her winter clothes. Small and golden.

He traced the marks of a bathing suit strap, the paleness of her breasts and belly. The bikini image slipped—with some regret—from his mind to be replaced by that demure Speedo in which she swam like a dolphin in the hotel pool. A dolphin trapped in SeaWorld.

She was utterly beautiful. And she was in his arms. Now that he had her attention, maybe he could remind her how very, very good he could be when he was in control.

The effort to regain control felt like batting his hands at all those atoms fleeing free across the universe. He caught some of them, but the rest of them just floated away from the currents his hands made. Some of them were laughing. Some of them glowed as if they streamed from a supernova.

He picked her up like a baby. "Oh, and I don't leave women on the floor when I'm done with them."

He headed toward her bed, with its welcome of soft comforter and pillows.

She turned her head away from him. Something he had said had just hurt her. "You leave them on a bed?" she said mockingly.

He lowered her gently among the pillows and slid his hand into her hair. "When I'm done."

CHAPTER 25

He left her in the morning, having slept from midnight to daybreak with one arm firmly around her waist, her body pulled snug against his, his face pillowed on her hair. He left her with her hair stroked back from her face and tucked behind one ear, and a kiss planted just beside that ear, the gesture slipping hazily into her sleep. Until she half wasn't sure if she had dreamed it, later. He pulled the comforter up around her to replace the warmth of his body, tucked it in over her shoulders, and slipped away softly, barely shifting the mattress, almost soundless in the suite. She fell into deeper sleep again and woke with the marks of him all over her body—the flush from his jaw and the ache of her muscles.

The mattress shifted and her eyes startled open. Luc settled on his side with his head propped on his hand, studying her. His face, when her eyes first fluttered open, was unguarded. Shields came up quickly, but not as many, perhaps, as there once had been. "*Pardon*. Did I wake you?"

She was completely naked, and the comforter had slipped. She flushed. Why was he always the one in control? Just for one brief moment the night before, he hadn't been in control. "I thought you'd gone to work."

"I went to get things set up. Noé can handle things for a couple of hours. He's second sous, and it's good for him to get out from under me and Patrick." He picked up a thick strand of her hair, playing with it with complete attention. "Go ahead and sleep."

She did try, unnerved at the possibility that if she didn't, he might take it into his head to show her how utterly lost she was in him again. But she couldn't manage to. Not with those eyes on her, the eyes that looked at an utterly perfect—to her—dessert and said, "Who did this *merde?*" and tossed it in the trash, doing it over better. She had never been enough even for her own parents, and they were nowhere near the perfectionists that he was.

She opened her eyes and found him, just as she feared, watching her as if he could see every eyelash that might not be perfectly aligned. He curved his hand around her cheek, a thumb tracing over her eyebrow. Probably straightening out sleep-ruffled hairs that had started to drive him crazy. "I hit Patrick because he kissed you, and I didn't like it," he said. "I shouldn't have, but . . ." He shrugged. Good lord, *Luc* of all people was flushing.

He might as well have just told her he was the Incredible Hulk. "*You* hit an *employee* over something that stupid? He was just being nice."

His mouth compressed. "Funny how you can turn your cheek to *me* when I bend to kiss you."

"You're not nice," Summer pointed out. Though she still remembered that coat sliding around her shoulders, that quiet voice telling her "You're perfect," the way he had wrapped her in the comforter before he left her.

His jaw set. "I'm not careless. It's inconceivable that I would walk up to a woman I barely give a damn about and kiss her, to be nice or for any other reason."

Her fingers uncurled. She started to reach out to him. To tuck those fingers against a man who was never, ever careless.

"And I don't ever want to hear the word 'love' come

out of your mouth again unless you mean it." His voice was calm, but it was inexorable.

"But—" Her eyes flickered over that unyielding bronze face and shut tight. Why did he think she couldn't mean it? It was true that she had said it before to men, although he only knew that by assumption. Once again, she had met a low expectation. Did nothing she said have any value, and was it always her fault?

"Are you planning more visits to your therapist?" he asked with a pretense of idleness.

"Definitely." She rolled onto her back and stared at the luxurious dusky gray and rose. She hadn't actually been to see Jaime's therapist yet, but that was because she was a damn fool. "Yes, definitely." Slipping out of bed, she found her bathrobe and the remote control and set the images of her islands scrolling again. Her own therapy. The one that had worked.

"Why?" He stood, an elegant and imperturbable contrast to her sleep-disheveled vulnerability. "What's so wrong with being attracted to me? You were the one who started this, Summer."

"I didn't really know you at the time," she said wryly.

A shadow passed over his face. She saw it hit and was stunned. Something she said had *hurt* him? What had happened to that invulnerable iron shield of his?

"No offense meant," she said quickly, anxious.

He turned and walked to the window, giving her only his back against the morning sky. A clear cold sky, for once, with only a few long pale wisps of cloud behind the Eiffel Tower. They had turned no lights on in the room, and he stood in silhouette. Unreadable, one way or the other.

She had bruises on her butt that were going to show the shape of his fingers. Now how, exactly, should she read *them*?

"I'm not staying. I'm leaving in the spring. Ten weeks."

He slipped his hands into his pockets.

"I don't want to get too"—*heartbroken*—"involved." *I don't want to be here twenty years from now, trying to get you to look away from a window at me. Telling me not to tell you I love you because it can't possibly have any value, coming from me.*

He turned suddenly. "What was your one regret?"

"What?"

He crossed to her, taking her hands before she could think to hide them in her bathrobe pockets. The man moved *fast*. "You said you regretted your choice of the islands just once. Why? What was the once?"

"Oh, I don't—" She pulled on her wrists, angling her body away. His grip tightened, flexing easily with her movement. "That's not—let's talk about something else."

"We can talk about something else next, certainly," he said. "Why don't we talk about this right now?"

It was that steady, night-velvet voice of his. Her wriggling wrists slowly subsided, her heart easing gradually into a deep, quiet rhythm. She closed her eyes, wanting to lay her face against his chest and let all her muscles go. His scents warmed her self-imposed darkness: him, a fresh shower, and aromas twining through from his trip to the kitchens that morning. Grapefruit, and something nutty, and something buttery gold.

"It was all my own fault," she said roughly, quickly.

His fingers flexed around her wrists. She peeked up at him, but he just watched her, saying nothing. She inched closer to him.

There was no way she could tell him about this without him thinking what a spoiled brat she was. "Just some guy I kind of—dumped—got . . . upset." She pulled very hard on her wrists, trying to catch him by surprise.

It didn't work. Tension flared through him. "What does that mean?"

She looked anywhere but him. It was so *cruel* of him to hold her wrists like that so she couldn't get away. "We had been . . . dating . . . for a few months when I fell for this other guy and—I was stupid, okay? It was just—he was all aggressive and macho, and I fell for *that,* especially since Tane was *so* laid-back that it was starting to drive me crazy, even though I loved it at first. But then, Puni kept leaving flowers on my picnic table and making me *laugh,* and—I don't know." She was trying not to cry again over this raw, ugly thing that had happened.

A tiny silence. "Are there two men or three men in this story?" he asked.

She gazed at the floor.

"Three," he said. "In four years. All right, you're a bit hard to hold, but I knew that already. I hardly think it's your fault that you're beautiful. There's always another man around ready to grab you if the first one isn't perfect. *Putain,* so would I be. Why are you this embarrassed?"

"In one year," she told the floor. "It was a small island. After that, I had to move to a different island, and I stopped dating."

Again the silence. "You had to change islands? Was the man who got upset the local chief or something?"

"No, but I mean—I didn't really realize the kind of impact my, my—sex life—could have on such a small community." In other words, she had been spoiled and oblivious. He probably didn't have any trouble recognizing her mark on this tale. "I had screwed a lot of things up, and—" She shrugged uneasily.

Still more silence. "When you say he got 'upset' . . . what did he do?'

Summer started to cry. She threw herself away from him, all her weight yanking on her wrists, and he caught her and pulled her back into him hard. "Oh, fuck," he whispered, holding her very tight. "What *did* he do?"

It calmed her almost instantly, the tightness of that hold. She could press her face into his chest, and this time she didn't have to pretend her own darkness, this time she could have his. She scrubbed her face against him, trying to bury herself deeper. He curved a hand around her head, and she hiccupped and stopped crying, every muscle in her body relaxing. This felt so good. So exactly what she had been seeking, all her life. Just this moment, making everything about her okay, for the rest of her life. "Nothing," she whispered against his chest, and he took a gasp of breath. "Nothing. He just kind of—lost it, and he—grabbed me, but then—someone else heard, and—it was okay. I know I shouldn't have—I just—everybody *loved* me, and they didn't even know about my father's money, and I just—I shouldn't have been so—spoiled."

He petted her back in steady strokes. She lay against him until, under that stroking, she saw nothing at all. No images of accusation and raging hurt and hard hands ripping at her, no thud as her body hit the sand. Just steady, enveloping darkness, and the scents of citrus and something warm and dark. Oh, she could stay here forever.

"I didn't mean to be," she said despairingly into his chest. It felt easier to say this, when she could only see and smell him. "Tane was so cute, and he kept playing songs for me, and it was the first night I was there"—the hand stroking her checked just the tiniest bit, but then continued—"and I was so *happy*. But then, he was *so* laid-back, I mean his house was filthy, and he just lay around smoking marijuana, and he drove me *crazy*. And we had only been dating for a couple of months, and *he* didn't seem to care, and Nato was all aggressive and macho, and he just *went after me,* and—I don't know. Everyone was so exotic, and *I* was so exotic to them, and I guess nobody seemed real to me yet. It was like I was living in a story. It was easy to just fall for him instead and not think about the effect. But then—he was so bossy, and jealous, and he thought I should be cleaning his house but then he would get so mad at me about how I didn't do it right, and—then he moved into *my* house, while I was at the school. And I just wanted to get away from him, and Puni was so funny, and he was always leaving me flowers, and . . . I don't know. I didn't really understand I wasn't the only main character in this story." She went ahead and said it for him: "Spoiled."

He said nothing for a while. He had stopped the long, steady strokes, but one hand still rubbed gently on the small of her back. "You were—how old? Twenty-one? Twenty-two? Fresh out of Harvard, via a yacht cruise?"

She gazed downward somewhere in the vicinity of his navel, her eyes barely open against his chest. His voice was so quiet, so calm.

"How does getting summa cum laude at a place like Harvard work?" He sounded neutral, a researcher gathering information. "From here, we have the vague impression that it's the top university in the world, but very expensive. Is the summa cum laude something your father bought for you?"

Everybody always thought that. "I worked for it. I worked all night on presentations, I locked myself in the library and studied for exams, I wrote papers until eight in the morning. Then fell asleep on top of one and had my grade docked for turning it in at 9:30 instead of 9:00."

"No favoritism?"

Sometimes she wanted so desperately to be back on that island where no one cared, she thought she would crack into a million pieces just so she could be more easily shipped there. "I think the professors who were impressed by my father, and maybe graded more lightly, were balanced out by the ones who graded harder because they thought I was spoiled, or because they were trying so hard *not* to grade too easily that they went in the other direction. I worked. I met with professors when I got bad grades on exams and tried to figure out a way to do better. But—you know, they *are* good at long-range planning, at Harvard. How much, behind the scenes, might have been influenced by the hope of having one alumna and her father leave with extremely good impressions of the school . . . I can't know that." Ever. Never, in any situation she had found for herself, except teaching school on that island, could she know for sure how much was to her credit. "And they give some kind of cum laude to half their graduating class, so . . . I don't know. I did work for it, but it doesn't mean anything."

Her father hadn't thought it meant much. And he was one of the few people who knew for sure that he hadn't openly bought it.

Luc cupped her face in both hands and studied her a long moment. "You know how you are spoiled, Summer? If I talked to myself the way you do to yourself, I would be sleeping under a bridge. It's quite a luxury, to be able to spend your life beating yourself up and still sleep in a suite like this. Quit."

Quit sleeping in luxury suites or beating herself up? She took a deep breath, and let it out slowly. "I've been trying," she murmured. Trying both. "I don't really have this trouble on the island." Neither luxury suites, nor a vulnerable opinion of herself. Or maybe on the island her self-esteem was vulnerable, but no one was attacking it.

His eyebrows flicked together. His hands tightened on her cheeks. "You're happy there."

Her smile bloomed. "Very happy."

His face tightened. "You worked very hard, and earned something very difficult that you decided didn't have any value, and went on a cruise, and jumped off on a remote island. And acted like a girl let out of a convent at Carnival, although I really don't think you're the first college student to have three affairs in a year, Summer. And after a year away, a violent attack, and the ruins of your easy paradise, you still chose to go to another island rather than come home. While you stopped dating entirely. For three years. And then walked in here and straight up to me."

"You know, I was really just trying to get someone to show me to my room," Summer mentioned, aggravated.

A sharp smile, the edge of his teeth showing. "There were three actual bellmen standing in that lobby, Summer. With uniforms on and everything. I can promise you at least two of them would have jumped at the offer of a yacht."

"Oh?" She tried to look interested. "Which ones?"

He just looked at her a long moment. "You know, Summer, one advantage I have over you is that every damn thing I've accomplished in my life, I know exactly who accomplished it. I have no doubts about myself whatsoever. So you might not want to test me so much. I'll pass."

She gathered her bathrobe around herself and gazed at him in utter awe and envy of that confidence, that complete conviction. Wishing that confidence was wrapped around her in place of the bathrobe.

He stroked a lock of messy hair back, drawing it through his fingers and playing with its texture. Holding her entire being with just that gentle tug and shift against her scalp.

"Tell me something, Summer," he said very quietly. "Why are you so afraid I'll catch you? No one else ever has."

He had no idea how hard she fought not to give herself entirely up to him. "I don't know." *I've just known from the first you could. I want you to hold me. And never let me go.*

But I want to be able to go. Before I get crushed. It's so miserable here. She didn't make sense.

To want something so much and to be so desperately afraid of it.

She grinned. "Maybe because no one else was nearly as gorgeous?" Or as strong. Or as steady and controlled. Or as full of that pent-up passion that she longed to free. "Anyway, I'm out of here in April, so I'm just exaggerating about being trapped."

She was lying even worse than usual, that was what she was doing.

That flicker in his face again. What had happened to his iron armor? That was the second time she had landed a blow. "We'll see," he said.

"What?"

"How much you're exaggerating. Although I would prefer some other word than 'trapped.' " He tucked the hair behind her ear. " 'Held,' maybe?"

A spark blown in the wind, caught in two strong hands that closed over it like a warm cave.

There was a knock on the door, and Luc's hands flew faster than sight, closing her bathrobe, flicking tangles out of her hair, before room service brought in a selection of *viennoiseries.*

"Are you sure they're going to survive without you?" she asked after the man pushing the cart left. She felt self-conscious, sitting on the edge of the bed, breaking a roll so that golden flecks spilled onto her bathrobe and the scent teased warmth around her.

"I think over the past five years here, I've earned the right to come in late one morning." But tension built in him, under that cool ease, like a coiled spring. He tried not to pace, but that energy didn't know what to do with itself. "I need to set up a schedule that will free up some of my evenings. Now. Starting this week. It will be good for the sous-chefs to have full responsibility more often, and probably good for me to not be looking over their shoulders, although"—He winced a little at some image of possible results, closed his eyes, and took a deep breath. "It will be good for everyone. I'm even thinking about working with Hugo and Alain to close the restaurant Sunday and Monday. None of the other three-star restaurants stay open seven days a week."

Really? He would do that for her? When she would never in her life have dared to ask? Hope sparked, all unexpected. "I can give people raises to compensate for the increased responsibility or the shift in hours, if that helps. Or work out a way to compensate for any loss in revenues."

His jaw tightened. "Summer. I don't care if your father gives you the entire world wrapped in a bow. I do not need *you* to intervene in my kitchens. I don't need you to help me accomplish anything in my life."

It hurt so much, it was so utterly true, that she couldn't do anything but hold the bathrobe together at her throat while behind its plush white all her insides plunged in dizzy, sick freefall.

"I probably really should go." He shifted to thread his fingers into her messy hair and kiss her. He cocked his head when he lifted it, searching her face. She didn't know why. Her lips had responded to his. A perfectly proper kiss. He must have decided it was one, too, or if it wasn't, that it didn't matter as much as getting to work. He stroked her hair back from her face, curved his hand around the nape of her neck, and gave it a little squeeze.

At the door, he stopped just long enough to look back at her and hold her eyes. She was still managing a light smile, which made his eyes search hers again, but her smile didn't falter. "By the way, Summer," he said, "in case you didn't realize—your taste in men has improved."

CHAPTER 26

Luc leaned over the big calendar on his desk, erasing and writing things in. Damn it, why the fuck did the president have to eat here so much? Luc would have to be on that night. Next Friday, he was taking Patrick and Noé out to Valrhona to help develop a special Leucé chocolate, so that day was shot. Here—Patrick was just going to have to handle that banquet. It was good preparation for his own place, being in charge at the big events.

"So can we take my car?" Patrick asked, stepping cheerfully into the office. "To Valrhona?"

Luc gave him a wary look. He had never ridden passenger with Patrick before, and God only knew what Patrick might do. "I was thinking I would drive."

"You're *always* thinking you would drive. Everything. Seriously, you have to learn to *let go.*" Patrick moseyed over to Luc's desk and set one hand on top of the calendar before Luc thought to flip the page. Patrick's glance only flickered down to it—by rights, not even long enough to read it all—but his face suddenly split into a grin, and he looked closer. Then looked back up at Luc, the grin half-fading into something . . . practically misty-eyed. "Luc. This is adorable."

"Patrick, will you get the fuck out of my—"

"Has she *seen* this? I'm getting all mushy just looking at

it." Patrick tapped a finger on one of the many slots where something had been erased or put in brackets and words like, "S.—theater?" "S.—skating?" had been added. And then there were all the slots were Luc had determined he should be able to take the afternoon break instead of working through it and had just written, "3–5: Summer."

Luc set his jaw and rode out the flush as best he could. It had been easier to keep himself from flushing a few days ago, before Summer shattered his control. The damn control just hadn't been working right since.

Patrick frowned, studying the calendar further. "You know, Luc, I might want to have a love life, too. Do you have to put me on *all* the evening slots you're going to the theater? Make Noé do some of them. He loves being out of our shadow."

" 'Our'?"

Patrick grinned. "Well, it's true that I cast more of a radiant glow, but for some reason, not everyone wants to bask in my reflected glory. Besides, if I'm on all the nights, and you're mostly days, I'll never see you again." He looked utterly woebegone. "Not to mention, I'm not sure how many fine crumbs you might grind our intern into if I'm not there to protect her. Why don't you switch her to nights with me?"

Ah. Luc glanced through the glass walls at Sarah carrying a giant mixing bowl that looked bigger than she was, face flushed with the strain and jaw set in absolute determination not to ask for help. He slid a glance at Patrick, who rested against the desk with his back to that view, possibly on purpose in order to keep himself from slipping over to help her, but it was always hard to tell with Patrick. It would ruin ten years of working Patrick past his screwed-up childhood if Luc kept Sarah out of his reach. But Patrick wasn't a boy who could barely shave anymore, and Luc wasn't sure what that made of him, the chef, to sacrifice their intern's right to an un-harassed work zone to keep Patrick happy. It would help if he had any idea what Sarah thought about Patrick, but Sarah would hardly confide in him. An odd thought crossed his mind, Summer slipping into their kitchen life with a smile, helping negotiate these workplace romance issues. Maybe if she was very clearly attached to the chef, which would give her a natural role as queen here and make her less of a threat to other women . . .

Alain Roussel pushed the door to the office open, glanced at Patrick, and hesitated as he looked at Luc.

"Oh, don't mind me." Patrick folded his arms like a man in for the long haul. "You can say anything in front of me."

Alain looked at Luc again, waiting. Luc flicked open a hand. "Go ahead." Patrick settled more deeply into his position, looking pleased with himself.

Alain took a deep breath. "We're to close the restaurant Sundays and Mondays, starting three months from now, as soon as current reservations run out."

Luc gaped at him. Patrick's arms fell from his chest. "I beg your pardon?"

"She's the owner, Luc. I couldn't argue her out of it. Actually, she wanted it to start next week, and I argued how much damage that would do to our reputation to cancel so many reservations. So she thinks she's compromising. She was very—did you two get in another fight or something?"

"No." She had seemed just a little—odd when he kissed her that morning, but . . . wait, what the hell business was this of Alain's? Luc gave the director a cool look.

Alain glared at him despairingly. "Did you *have* to crack? I never expected any control out of her, but *you*."

"It gives a man a whole new perspective on life, doesn't it?" Patrick said cheerfully.

"I'll talk to her." It confused Luc no end to not feel angry. The thought of taking two days off a week to enjoy her made him feel as if, for the first time in his life, he could lay his head down on his desk and just—let all the tension drain out of his muscles. His desk, *putain, non,* that would be a waste. How about two soft breasts . . .

"No, you won't," Alain said bitterly, and Luc was already so deep into the fantasy that he narrowed his eyes dangerously at having someone try to interfere in it.

"Talk to her. She's gone out for a run."

A run? Summer swam for exercise. And hated winter. "In the rain?"

Summer ran until she couldn't run anymore. She came in streaming, her face coated with rain under the baseball cap with which she had tried to keep it out, running clothes plastered to her body, limping on calves already tightening up.

Luc appeared before she had even gotten through the lobby, sugar on his hands and a red streak down his cheek. He stilled a half-second at the first sight of her, and then came forward fast. Under that controlled, superb flow to his movements, wildness simmered very close to the surface.

"What the hell is the matter with you?" He swung her up into his arms, which earned them a few flashes of cameras, and hauled her off to the elevator, where she writhed her way out of his hold, hunching her shoulders as cold water dripped down them.

"I can't swim far enough in that fucking pool."

He punched the button for her floor. "How far did you run?"

"From here to Notre Dame and back? Probably about twelve kilometers." God knew, she had walked the distance enough in her time. She brushed past him as the elevator doors opened, limping despite herself.

He came after her. "How far do you usually run?"

"I don't. But I've got great cardiovascular."

"So your lungs could handle it way past what your legs should have." He marched her straight into her bathroom, opening the faucets full blast, stripping them so fast with those flying, deft hands, she barely had time for an exhausted blink. He picked her up and he sat down in the great pool of a tub, with her in his lap, hot water foaming around their legs as the level rose. She shivered violently at the warmth.

He drew one of her legs up, massaging the foot and calf with clever, strong fingers. "Trying to get away?" His voice was—angry. Arousal grew in him, pressing into her naked butt, the water foaming furiously around their thighs. Outside, city lights fought the growing dimness. Oh, God. Not only was she naked to that snooty city, but the way he held her leg up to massage it meant that her sex was spread wide, too. The water burbling against it.

"Yes," she said, and tried to escape, which made her slip off his lap and fall backward into the water.

He hauled her out by her leg and laid her across his lap, resting her head against the side of the tub. "Summer. You're not going to get away from me, so stop it."

His fingers dug so cleverly into her overused muscles. Climbing up her calf. Easing tendons around her knee. Digging into her lower thigh. She gasped and shivered, and water burbled more intimately against her sex, proving the lips of it had parted.

From this angle, Luc's face looked severe. Beautiful. It always hit her like a ton of bricks, those honed, high masculine cheekbones, that sense of a stripped-down, lean, dangerous beauty burned clean of everything but its hardest core.

"You have a nerve." She wriggled against him, and his arousal grew harder, his face more dangerous, and his hands climbed higher up her thigh, digging in relentlessly. "You can shut me out of your mind without any effort at all, but I'm supposed to decide this is worth something? Worth what? *Me?*"

"Yes," he said flatly. "Exactly. You're supposed to decide I'm worth you."

That stopped her dead. She stared at him, a whole rush of things inside her that made her want to reach up and latch on to his shoulders to hold herself steady. The water foamed to her waist, hiding his hand as it traced calmly— and thoroughly—over her wet, open sex on his way to her other thigh. She shivered convulsively, glaring at the city stretched out before her.

So many boyfriends, why did *he* feel like the first man who could reach in and actually take her? *Your taste in men has improved.* Yeah, improved to the point of being suicidal. Way to go.

"Not a yacht. Not a smile. Not the change from your wallet. You."

"Is this revenge?" she asked, confused. "You're still trying to punish me for that first night? Because that's cruel, even for you, to want all my life as forfeit."

"Even for me?"

She tried to hide her face in the water. He braced her up out of it with an arm. "I don't know why I said that."

"Cruel?"

"You're right," she said rapidly. "Let's have this conversation tomorrow, when we're both fresher. I'm not making any sense." She started to duck out of his arm.

It wrapped around her and held her hard. "Let's have it tonight."

All through her, muscles eased, not just from his fingers but from the fact that he had locked her unyieldingly against his body.

"I've never shut you out of my mind, Summer. Let's

start with that. And you have no idea how much effort I've put into trying to do so."

She twisted into his shoulder, sinking into him. It took so little. Just his hold. Just his reassurance. And everything in her yielded to him. Why was she so damn weak? Why had she *always* been that weak, that hungry for any scrap of love?

One arm held her. The other drew her leg up, massaging her other calf. The position held her sex wide and not quite touching his arousal, water rocking gently between them. "Now maybe you can tell me what I've been doing that feels so cruel to you."

She shook her head against his chest. She didn't want to reinforce what a spoiled brat she was, that he was cruel because she wasn't the center of his existence and because he was so utterly exquisite a trap for her.

"Summer. I can learn to make things exactly right. But you have to tell me what I'm doing wrong, first. I have no idea how I'm being cruel."

Her eyebrows creased against his wet skin. "*Exactly* right?"

Muscles shifted against her face with his shrug. "At a minimum."

"You don't have to be exactly right."

"I already said that was just a starting point." He shifted her until she was astride him, his hands massaging deeply into her butt, so taut from the run. She shivered uncontrollably at the release, her sex rocking and rubbing against his with every press of his fingers. His eyes glittered, his need unmistakable.

Why did he *do* that? Refuse to let himself go? "I like you the way you are," she protested.

He made a skeptical sound. Did he need reassurance? Everything in her bloomed with delight at the possibility of giving him something he needed.

Abruptly she slid forward over him, taking him deep in her slick, welcoming body. He made a hard sound. She shivered with rightness, everything settling into its place. "I love this," she murmured.

She felt him stiffen at the "I love" and hurried the "this" out, before he could reprimand her. That was okay, wasn't it? To love *this*.

It seemed to be, because his body curved around hers. "Do you, *soleil?*"

She nodded, her cheek rubbing against him.

"Is it perfect?" he whispered.

The acquiescence of her cheek against silk skin and muscle shivered pleasure and relief all through her. "More."

He rocked her hips very, very gently, very, very slowly, back and forth on him, so that the water twisted and poured around him, and he drew her almost, almost off him, bereft, and then oh-so-slowly pressed her back until she had every last bit of him. And then he held her there, grinding her harder, watching her squirm and twist and clutch for what she wanted and he controlled. "Tell me one cruel thing I did today."

This. But her body clutched around him so frantically, and her back arched so that her nipples thrust wet and taut into the air, and it wasn't cruel. She loved it utterly.

"Tell me, Summer." He pulled her slowly off him again.

She writhed at the threat of separation. "Just the truth," she gasped.

He rewarded her by letting her rock halfway back on him. She whimpered a little, astonished that she felt secure enough to let him see her beg. "Which would be?"

She tried to turn her face away, and he leaned forward suddenly and caught it, kissing her and kissing her while her body was held mercilessly, half-impaled, nowhere near full enough.

How could he *do* that? How could he have that much control? And—the thought teased at her deliciously—how and when could she break it again?

"Tell me, Summer." He left her mouth gasping for him the way her body kept clutching for more, kissed his way over her chin and down her throat.

"That—you don't need me to—" With each word he slid her just a tiny bit farther back onto his erection. When she stopped speaking, he stopped moving. "Accomplish anything." Again she tried to twist her face away. He let her, but only to bite the strained muscle of her shoulder. "It's okay," she whispered to that merciless city sparkling in a half circle around her. "You don't."

"Summer." His hands left her butt, left that ruthless control of himself and her, and slid up to frame her face. "How could you think I don't need you?"

She settled onto him with a rush of relief, gasping with it, her body clutching him frantically. "Look at us right now," she said hopelessly.

"Summer." His own head arched back, and his hips shifted against her, the movement making her whole body ripple. His thumbs traced her cheekbones blindly. "I don't need you to accomplish things. That's true."

She tried to turn away. Again he held her. Body gentle but inexorable, supple but iron-firm.

"I need you for something else," he said, very low.

She stopped breathing. Opening her eyes, she found him watching her with absorption, as if against all that 180-degree view of the City of Lights, she was the brightest and most beautiful thing he saw. She might as well have been dipped, whole-souled, into a healing balm. That look made something wounded and hiding want to creep out into his hands.

"You don't even need me *right now,*" she said desperately. "You're just—playing."

His eyes flared with astonishment, and then a sudden profound understanding—not of her but of himself. His hands curved around her breasts, and he rubbed wet thumbs over her nipples, making her twist helplessly, thrusting her hips against his in a way that only built her pleasure, pushed the need higher and higher, without satisfying it. Only his hands could satisfy it, and only if he chose. "I am playing," he agreed softly. "I like to play with you. I like to see what I can do with you. I like to make you utterly mine and utterly in the control of *my* hands. You may be able to shatter my control, and I may . . . *love* it, but yes, I'll take it back the next time." His voice went very deep, fierce, yanked out from somewhere deep in him. *"I like it."*

She began to shake, so aroused by the words that she couldn't find that spot where she should protest them. Was she that beautiful to him? Every way he shaped her?

He plucked her suddenly off him, over her wrench of protest, and turned her so that she sat with her back against his chest, facing the whole spread of the city below. "Oh, no, not—" She tried to twist back into him. He was supposed to *hide* her from that city, in her bathroom fantasy.

"Shh." He hooked her legs on the outside of his and spread his, holding hers tight with his hands until she stopped fighting and acquiesced to the way he spread her so wide, squirming with hunger and vulnerability. "I like this, Summer," he whispered into her ear, a dark voice from behind, and his hand scooped between her legs, delving into her sex in a way that made her jump, her bottom writhing against him. "I like it, and I *need it*. I need you helpless in my hands. You have no idea how beautiful this is." His other hand played with her breasts, squeezing them gently, rubbing the sensitive nipples so delicately. "It's worth any amount of control to have it." One long finger slipped deep inside her and twisted, supple and teasing, while she gasped on a rising crescendo. "Beg me a little, Summer?"

"I love you," she said, and his finger spasmed inside her. She moaned.

"And you say I'm cruel," he muttered. "What a cruel beggar you are. Don't say that. Say please."

"Please, I love you," she said helplessly, her body straining toward him, toward release, toward his every touch. "Please. I love you, I love you—"

He wrapped one hand over her mouth and plucked her clitoris like the string of a guitar, over and over, a tiny, rapid, merciless rhythm until she lost all the words his palm extinguished and twisted and twisted against that hard hold and arched entirely off him with a scream muffled by his palm, her body shaking and shaking, emptying her soul into his hands.

He turned her abruptly and shoved them all the way to the opposite end of the great tub and thrust straight into her, driving her back against the wall. She gasped at the force of it. "You're so beautiful." Water streamed off him, that lean body of his all wild, taut muscle, his face burned clean of anything but passion.

He kept saying that as if she really *was.* She slipped her hands up those slick shoulders. "Let go," she whispered. "Lose control."

His body shook in hard, long spasms that drove him deeper into her. "Hold me while I do," he whispered. "Hold me together. Don't let me go."

So she wrapped her arms around him as hard as she could and held on.

And he let all the wildness out.

The city looked so different, from a big fluffy towel, lying on her side with him behind her, gently stroking up her belly and breasts, between the folds of the towel. He had fed her a banana and hot chocolate from his kitchens, which had tasted heavenly after the run, a lovely, luscious darkness, barely sweetened, her secret childhood pleasure all grown up. Now they lay quietly, Summer thinking oddly that the city in fact looked very beautiful, sparkling like that. The Eiffel Tower, curtained by the rain that had started mid-run, looked a little dreamy, a little wistful. As if she wouldn't mind bending her proud head and cuddling up for the night, too. Summer actually felt a little sorry for her.

"Hugo has hit the roof about you closing the restaurant two days without his permission," Luc mentioned idly.

She had done it with stubborn determination to be angry and not hurt. She didn't look at him. "Not you?"

He shrugged, his body shifting against her back. "I kind of liked it. You asserting yourself in my life." Humor slipped into his voice, like that secret smile. "I'm far too good at exerting control for you to need to make it easy for me."

His hand kept caressing her idly, no sign of temper in him, and she lay quietly, soaking up the sweet reassurance.

"Besides, Hugo is just annoyed at the way you handled his ego. He has a family and he already takes two days off a week, except when it's absolutely impossible. I'm the one who's never been able to . . . let go. Excessive arrogant determination to be in control *might* be one of my character traits."

Might. She laughed. "You can't even call it a flaw?"

"It's not a flaw." But his lips pressed a smile into the nape of her neck. "If it was a flaw, I would correct it."

She laughed, and the urge to tell him she loved him swelled up again. She caught it, afraid to ruin the moment, but the need to suppress herself stirred up unhappiness. "So I'm your lesson in how to let things go?"

His arm hardened around her. "No. I don't need any more lessons in how to let things go, thank you. But two days off might help me hold onto . . . something else I want in my life."

Summer stared at the Eiffel Tower, her heart beginning to beat too fast. "It doesn't start for three months. Alain pitched a fit at the idea of cancelling reservations."

"I know." His fingers stroked gently up and down her breastbone, brushing the sides of her breasts in passing. "Spring can be really beautiful in Paris, Summer. Especially if you have someone to see it with."

She had seen spring in Paris many times before. But she couldn't help wondering what that season for lovers was like for people who felt loved. Her chest tightened, her eyes stinging.

Wait. *A whole restaurant filled with delights for her, a gold heart melting at her touch, pouring out its dark insides . . .*

Her eyes stung harder, but her chest oddly relaxed for a breath that seemed to fill her whole body.

"Do I hurt you?" Luc asked, very low. "When I lose control?"

She caught his gently stroking hand and snuggled it to her, shaking her head. "I like it. It's as if I matter."

"As if you matter?"

She linked her fingers stubbornly with his.

"Summer, when I don't lose control, I do it to value *you*. And to value myself."

Everything that's beautiful comes from control. She rolled over. "Who are you quoting?"

"It's something my foster father taught me. You use all your control to value the product with which you're working, and to value what you yourself can do with it."

She stiffened in outrage. "I'm not your *product*."

"No, I didn't mean—" He broke off. "But *this* is my

product, Summer. This." His hand encompassed her and him together. "Whatever I can make of it for you."

Annoyance built. "Do I have any role in it at all?"

"It *is* your role. You're everything."

"I just get to be?"

An odd little shrug. "You're already perfect."

So many things about this pissed her off, it was crazy that the "already" should be the last straw. As if he wasn't. Lying there all forged and beautiful, with that indefatigable gymnast's body. "Luc, you do not think I'm perfect. You think I'm spoiled and arrogant and annoying and—"

"Hiding. I do not, by any stretch, think you are arrogant, Summer. Maybe that first night, when you were throwing money at me, but even that . . . isn't that funny? Even that was a sign of how very little you value *yourself.*"

"I actually like myself quite a lot," she said wryly. "On the other side of the world from here."

His face tightened. For all the grace with which he could move, he carried more tension in him than any man she had ever known.

She pulled at his shoulders as if to tug him down on top of her, and when he yielded his weight she slipped away through the pillows and twisted to land on top of him. He tensed, bracing his torso off the bed. "Relax. You know, you don't have to be perfect all the time."

He made an incredulous noise, as if she had just said he didn't have to breathe all the time. So much tension surged through him that when she touched one finger to his nape, he made a sound as if she had plucked a note.

"Give in a little. I'm not helping you do push-ups. Let me be in control."

He allowed his lower body to sink down, torso still braced. "Summer, I don't think this is a good idea. What are you do—" A little gasp as her fingers curved around his shoulders and dug into those taut muscles that ran into his neck. "Oh. *Oh.*" He sank into the pillows. "Summer." He buried his face suddenly in one arm.

That bunched his shoulder up, and she dragged at that bent arm until he finally relented and let her pull it to his side. He pulled a pillow over his face to replace it. "I don't promise my massage will be as good as yours. I'm making this up as I go along." She traced the line of his muscles, learning how they fit together. If she pressed here, would that release tension? A muffled sound came from under the pillow. "So let me know if I hurt you."

"You won't hurt me," said the pillow. "It's not possible."

"Yes, that's what I thought," Summer muttered, pushing deep with the heels of her palms, grinding them slowly into his muscles like a pestle into a mortar.

"Summer. *Putain.*" His body shivered, arched, subsided. She lifted her hands. "Too much?"

"*No.* Don't stop. *Soleil.* Your hands. I'm being kneaded by sunshine."

Deeply pleased at the fancy, she took a minute to savor the smooth skin of his back before she began to apply pressure again, starting gently and working deeper. "I don't really know what I'm doing."

"Don't stop practicing," he murmured. "Bernard used to have us do things ten thousand times if we needed to, until we got them right. If we flinched away from something, like peeling the hot paraffin off hot pans, he would grab our hands and force them full-palm down onto the heat, to teach us to be tougher. Am I burning your hands? Because I feel that hot, right now. Like melting wax."

Hot paraffin off hot pans? One hand slipped down his arm, to make slow circles in his loosely upturned palm. Her eyes stung, crybaby that she was. She wanted to kiss his palms, far too late to heal those wounds. "Bernard, your foster father?" He had mentioned, also, a mother who had disappeared. Little pieces of him, here and there, that came together.

"Mmm." His voice burred. "Don't stop. Practice on me ten thousand times."

Her nails pressed a tiny threat into his muscles. "Until I'm perfect?"

"Summer, your every single touch is perfect." He moved the pillow just enough to show her that secret smile of his. "When *I* do something perfect, I don't get to stop. In fact, it's almost a guarantee I'll have to do it ten thousand more times, sometimes in one weekend."

She leaned her weight into him, trying to make an impact on those muscles. He was so taut. "Do you like that?"

He shuddered, lashes heavy on his cheeks. Dark, straight lashes, growing heavier as the massage continued, as he stopped wincing and arching to every pressure and his muscles unwound, until he was all yielding, and her hands could skate gently over his back. He seemed asleep, not what she had had in mind when she started, but maybe it was another way of losing control.

Happiness grew in her. She stroked that smooth back a long time, enjoying the ease she had brought to it, until she finally slid off him with a peek at his face. Yes, asleep, his body heavy. She slipped down to press a little kiss into his lax palm.

There. Her secret wish to make those old wounds better. She slid back up to tuck herself beside him.

His arm wrapped around her and pulled her under him. He threw a leg over her, holding her in place as he braced himself above her in the dark room. "It was to teach us we could handle things that hot," he told her softly. "The paraffin felt like it burned us, but it didn't really. That was his point."

Her own fingers curled instinctively to protect her palms against such a lesson.

"You have a very powerful maternal instinct, don't you?" he murmured.

She did? Summer Corey? That was the first time any man had ever popped *that* one out at her. "I wasn't really planning to lull you to sleep," she denied.

"I'm not asleep." His mouth closed over hers, kissing with everything in him, his eyes closing in pleasure, as if she was a symphony of flavors. And his chef's palate couldn't get enough of them. "I'm lost."

She lost herself in the kiss, cradled under his body. She forgot that she had wanted to be in control. She only wanted to be lost in him.

He was lost?

His hands threaded her hair back from her face, so gently he could have been handling spiderwebs he didn't want to break. "I could kiss you until there's nothing left of you," he whispered.

Where the words should have woken that visceral fear of being reduced to nothing in someone else's life, instead an image grew of herself: golden, strong, glowing in his arms like a precious star. "No, you can't."

His thumb traced over her lips. "Don't underestimate how long I can kiss you."

A soft smile, almost as contained as one of his, full of an astonishing amount of confidence. "Don't underestimate how long I can last."

CHAPTER 27

Summer came awake to a sense of tension. Luc stood with a remote control in hand, watching her island photos scroll across the screen. Deep green cliffs falling into brilliant seas, close-ups of old hands weaving tiare flowers, Summer coming up out of the sea with a small group of islanders after rising to the challenge of a swim around the entire island. Summer laughing. Other people laughing. He watched all of them, a tautness growing in his shoulders that made her hands itch to massage them again.

He turned it off as the photos began to repeat and went into the next room, rummaging in the suite's little kitchen before coming back to the picture window. He looked utterly beautiful and stark and poetic, framed against the extinguished Eiffel Tower. His city.

Her muscles ached, from running and from other activities her body had grown unaccustomed to. She pulled a pillow to fill the empty space he had left in her arms and he looked back at her.

A half smile, his face a little strained, as he shifted restlessly, pacing the room with his hands in his pockets. A caged tiger, long used to its confines. "I don't suppose you have any food here, do you?"

She blinked. The tiger wasn't seeking freedom, just

hungry? "I could order room service." The hotel offered it twenty-four hours a day. Sometimes she thought if she saw one more excessively perfect, complex dish, she would throw it against the wall.

He made a face. "I guess that will have to do. Unless you want to go out and see if we can find *un Grec* or *un McDo* still open."

"A *McDonald's*?" *Him?*

"Fries." Craving filled his face. "With lots of salt."

"I'm sure the hotel bistro does something with fries—"

An impatient movement cut her off. "I don't *want* hand-cut, perfectly cooked fries. I don't want something so special you have to pay attention to every bite of it. Potato chips. Potato chips would be good. Do you have any Coke?"

She gaped at him.

His eyes gleamed, as his tongue touched his upper lip. "You know what would be good? *Du lait concent résucré.* I could eat a whole can about now."

A slow delight grew in her face. "You're *kidding* me." The haughty three-starred finest pastry chef in the world liked *junk food*? Mass-produced, chemical-stuffed, schoolboy treats? *McDonald's*?

He shifted, flushing a little. "I don't eat the whole day, all right? Nobody does. There's too much adrenaline; we're working too fast. Sometimes we have a tasting session when we're developing a new concept. Or a quick lunch at the hotel cafeteria. But a lot of times, people can't calm down enough even then to eat properly."

"So you come home and start stuffing yourself with junk food as soon as you relax enough," Summer realized. "Because you've burned through thousands of calories."

His flush deepened even as he tried to look as if this was perfectly acceptable behavior.

The man who created the most beautiful, magical culinary treasures in the world . . . ate crap.

"Why don't you bring home some of your ice cream, which you insist on throwing away when you don't use it the same day? Or the macarons or cakes that don't get eaten?" Something of *quality*, for God's sake. It was like he was some abused animal, spending its life eating refuse while it gave its body up to the rest of the world for nice, juicy steaks.

"I don't *want* it. I spend all day working with that stuff. I want something I don't have to *think* about. Salt, fat, sugar." His eyes glittered at each word. The man was literally starving, she realized. Right this minute. If he spent all day working at the speeds she had seen without eating, he was burning up his own muscle mass at this point. "I just want to *eat*. I'm too tired for a transcendental experience." He laughed, his face softening. "Besides you, of course, *soleil.*"

She was so crazily in love with him. And he would probably gag her if she tried to say so. Her heart plunged at the realization of exactly how much he mattered to her. Nothing good—for her—could come of this.

"I'll tell you what." She ignored that plunging sensation, helpless before the urge to take better care of him than he was taking of himself. "You stay here. I'll handle this."

There was definitely something Ali Baba about being in the darkened *Économat* alone in the middle of the night, shifting its great rolling shelves like clothes on a rack, revealing sodas, chips, Vegemite, pickled herring. Limping on stiffening calves, she grabbed cereal and dried pasta, then raided the kitchens.

Luc was lying on the art deco couch when she got back, one arm over his eyes, appearing asleep except for the fact that he was gnawing on one of his own knuckles.

He shifted his arm enough to look at her, eyes glittering with the reflected copper light.

She went into her little kitchen area, and he unfolded his lean form from the couch with as much grace as if he hadn't been using his body at top speed for twenty hours and followed her. "Sit down," she told him firmly.

He took a bar stool, leaning on the black granite counter, gazing at her as if she was a unicorn come out of the woods.

"Here." She showed him the selection of sugarcoated cereals and one healthy whole-grain variety, which he ignored, eyes brightening at one studded with marshmallows. She laughed and poured it. "Want some extra sugar on top of that?"

"Yes," he said defensively, trying to pretend he wasn't embarrassed.

"We're going to have to work on your eating habits." But she added a spoonful of sugar and slid the bowl across to him. His hand seized hers before it could withdraw.

She glanced at him. He was looking down, and under her gaze actually brought his other hand up to shield his face. The hand that held hers squeezed very hard, before he released it to take his spoon.

"Start on that." She pulled out a pot and filled it with water.

His gaze flew up from his cereal. The spoon froze in his mouth.

She set the pot on the stove and added some salt. He slowly swallowed his first mouthful, his spoon hovering in the air.

She pulled out a skillet and diced a thick slice of pancetta into little *lardons*. Luc placed both hands flat on the granite, still as a statue. Once his chest moved hard, as if he had finally remembered to breathe.

She started to flush. "It's pretty basic. I had a friend in

college who thought I needed to at least master how to boil pasta and toss cheese on it. And a neighbor on the island started teaching me when she realized I was mostly living off yogurt, mangoes, and crackers."

Yep, here she was boiling pasta for a man who could create the seven wonders of the world if you handed him some sugar. But what was she supposed to do? Let him keep surviving off chips and candy?

"You're *cooking* for me," Luc breathed, as if he was afraid he would shatter the moment, if he spoke too loudly.

Her flush deepened. "I'm not sure it qualifies as what you consider cooking."

"My God, Summer." He dragged his hands roughly over his face and then slid them up to knot them in his hair. His knuckles slowly whitened.

She pushed at the sizzling lardons with a wooden spoon, not taking her eyes off his hidden face.

"*Putain,* you're going to break me," he whispered harshly. "Like a raw egg."

He pushed away from the bar, crossing the suite to stand at the Eiffel Tower window, forearm pressed against its glass as he stared out.

She lowered the heat under the *lardons* and followed him. "Are you all right?"

His face was scarily bleak. "You have *no idea* what's going to be left of me when you leave."

She flinched back, hitting the cold glass. What a horrible subject to bring up.

"It's been fourteen years since anyone has cooked for me. I mean, they have. Top chefs in restaurants trying to impress me or convince me I should come be their *chef-pâtissier*. But to *feed* me . . . just . . . *for me,* not to feed their own ego . . . just—to whip me up some pasta because I'm *hungry* and you think I would like it." He closed his hand around her upper arm, too hard.

She blushed crimson. "I'm just going to stir some *crème fraîche* into it." Maybe he was assuming something of a much higher quality than he was going to get. "It's nothing."

"I know what you're going to do. I'm salivating just thinking about it. It's not nothing, *soleil*. It's . . . you have no idea."

CHAPTER 28

Snow. Polynesian vanilla snow. Ebony. Great dark chocolate standing stones fallen into each other over the ages, a gate to lure her into another world. Blood. Four pomegranate seeds, trailing to the ebony gate. Adrenaline punched through Luc as he placed the last one. He had to get what he felt for her out, through this one controlled outlet, he had to—

A can slid in front of him. He looked up in shock. Summer. His concentration on her had been so deep, he hadn't even realized she was there.

She was already slipping away from him. Panic surged, the need to catch her, all those emotions that he had to control. "Summer." He kept his voice firm, and it caught her as if he had thrown a net over her, an ability that made him hot all over.

"Drink it." She nodded at the can.

He looked down at it. A sports drink. The kind of thing marathon runners drank to replenish their electrolytes. Oh, God. Emotion swelled through him until it threatened to explode him again. The atoms of him that she had already shattered all over the universe swirled giddily, not unhappy, but entirely unnerved to find themselves still so loose and free and glowing.

"I was thinking of you," he said, and she flushed a little with pleasure and took a step back toward him, but shook her head at the same time.

"You didn't even know I was here."

His heart began to thump so hard it hurt itself against his iron shell. "This is for you." He turned the newly invented Blanche-Neige toward her. *Don't refuse it. Eat those pomegranate seeds. Don't smile, don't smile, don't smile.*

She looked down at it. Just for a second she was braced— and then her face softened suddenly. Wondering. She slipped back to him, one of her fingers creeping toward the snow. "You were concentrating on me?"

He slid a spoon into her hand. "Do you want to see what you taste like? In my—" It wasn't his head and he couldn't say "heart." It was as if his foster parents reached a great fist inside him and strangled the ability to speak. *Just look at it. Eat it. Eat what I can't say. It's all there. Everything. You already ate my heart.*

"This is—me?" Her fingers closed slowly around the spoon, her face so full of disbelieving delight that he couldn't clarify for her, tell her that no, it was him. The cold, and the dark gates of hell, and the flaring desperate red pomegranate seeds to trap her.

"Taste it," he whispered. "Then you'll see." His hand guided her spoon so that it dug through the vanilla snow and scooped up a pomegranate seed at the same time. "Taste it," he said again, and guided the chilled spoon to her mouth. "It's not very sweet."

Get addicted. Until she didn't know how she had ever spent her life without the sweet taste of him on her tongue. Until she wouldn't be able to go a day without him.

An intense joy shot through him when she parted her lips and let him slide the spoon into her mouth. He watched the flakes of cold hit her tongue, the tiny tart touch of pomegranate, the whisper of sweetness, sugar queen snow. She made a soft, wondering sound. "You made it for *me?*"

Why did this always surprise her? "Entirely for you."

Something flushed across her face, like the brink of tears. "Thank you."

She ate it all up, pomegranate seeds and all. His body grew hungrier with her every bite, until he finally took a sip of the sports drink and nearly gagged. He didn't because—well, she was watching him as if he had hung the moon, and he had exceptional self-control.

"It tastes like crap," he muttered to Patrick in the refrigerator, because he had to complain about something to suppress himself. He was almost ready to dance a jig. And he *never* danced; he hadn't danced a step since the social service system had pulled him from the Métro.

"Fuck you," Patrick said jealously. "No one's bringing *me* sports drinks."

Luc shrugged, trying not to pick up bottles of cream and start juggling them. Something his father had just realized he would be good at when Luc had been taken from him. Luc had been pretty excited about it—juggling took up room, and you couldn't do it down in the depths of the Métro, and while you were doing it, someone else had to hold out the hat—but they had never really gotten a chance to take that particular show to the quays of the Seine.

"And you are such a narcissist," Patrick told him. "Are you going to make her watch you all day?"

"She seems to like it," Luc said defensively. When he had patted a spot right by him at the counter, she had looked so happy. And now he got to feed her little tidbits of things, and she seemed to grow even happier with each one she ate. So did he.

"That's because I keep making sure she can get a good view of me," Patrick said pityingly, but Luc only laughed out loud. Sarah Lin, coming into the refrigerator, stopped dead.

Still grinning, he breezed back to Summer . . . and stopped, shoulders stiffening. One hand slipped into his pocket, his grin vanishing. With the other, he gripped Bernard Durand's hand briefly. "Monsieur."

Summer, who had just been saying something to his foster father with a smile, glanced up at him searchingly, then slipped her hand down into his pocket with his. It was the oddest sensation he had ever felt in his life. It threw him completely, that warmth tucking into his self-control.

After an instinctual jerk that almost flung it out, he suddenly twisted his hand and linked his fingers too tightly with hers. "Summer, my foster father, Bernard Durand. Monsieur, this is—my—Summer Corey."

"So Luc learned under you?" Summer said to Bernard, with a friendly ease that made it clear how much more training in the social graces she had had than either of the two men. "You trained him how to do these amazing things?"

Bernard's chest puffed subtly. Amazing. Summer could affect even him. "Just the basics, with me," he admitted. "Just how to do everything *exactly right*. He was the one who went on to get hired by the top Paris kitchens, and then—" The older man gestured to their surroundings, that pride pressing against his containment in the way that was a balm to Luc's soul.

"Exactly right?" Summer shot a glance at Luc. "Ten thousand times, until they were perfect?"

"Well. Getting them perfect wasn't an excuse to stop," Bernard corrected. "It doesn't work that way."

"Clearly." Summer transferred that smile of hers back to

Luc, and the difference hit him hard in the stomach. *Putain,* it wasn't the same smile at all. When had it changed? Her eyes *lit* for him.

"How old was he when you started training him?" he heard Summer asking and stiffened a little.

"Well, you can't officially apprentice anyone until they're fifteen," his foster father hedged. "But he would do some things from the time he was ten." Some things a couple of hours a day, usually at four in the morning. One of the many things he owed to his foster father was a sense of how much he could work, without faltering and without complaint.

"After school?" Summer asked, and he remembered her discussing cocoa labor practices with her cousins, always knowing what question to ask, what little crack to push at until she got to the truth. The ability she must have learned from her father, the most successful investor in the world—now applied to his life.

Fuck, that couldn't be good.

"Or before." Bernard shrugged. "We start early in the *boulangerie.*"

Summer was getting such a look in her eyes. She was going to kiss his palm to heal his wounds again any second. An itch spread from his hand all the way through his body for that kiss. *Bordel,* he was going to be running up to her every time he skinned his knee in the park at this rate. Something that had always tightened his throat into sullen pain when he had seen other kids do it, when he was little. No maternal instinct at all?

That first impression he had had of her—when her sunshine fell on his world and melted it, and him, at her feet—hadn't been wrong, after all, had it? It had always been exactly right.

"I wanted to talk to you." Bernard interrupted his thoughts.

"I know," Luc said guiltily. "I need to come see everyone."

Bernard slipped his hands in his pockets, a gesture Luc had learned from him. "Something else." He indicated Luc's office with his chin.

Luc felt an inexplicable need to drag Summer with him, but Bernard clearly wanted privacy. "Excuse me a minute." He tucked her hair behind her ear, rubbing his thumb along that beautiful cheekbone of hers.

"So," he heard Patrick say cheerfully as the office door closed behind them, "had any good kisses lately?"

He propped himself on the edge of his desk, where he could keep an eye on Patrick, and glanced at Bernard, expecting a request to help a new foster boy having trouble.

Bernard kept his hands firmly in his pockets, hesitating. "Your father's been by again," he finally said bluntly.

It took a minute to sink in. "My—father?" Luc's heart seized. He couldn't even think or feel, just fall, in some long starry arc. "Wait—*again*?"

"He used to come by sometimes when you were a boy. Cause trouble trying to get you back. I had to call the police on him several times. Then he finally stopped for a long time. But he showed up again last week, wanting me to tell him where you are. I wouldn't, but he's back again, and . . . I guess he's right about the fact that you're thirty now, and can make your own decisions. Of course, he thought you were twenty-eight," Bernard added contemptuously.

It was harder to keep track of time than Bernard realized, when you lived off what you could carry. That had been one of the many things Luc had had to learn very quickly, when Bernard took him in—the extreme importance of impossibly precise units of time, down to seconds.

"And anyone would think he could find out where you are. It's not as if you've changed your name."

And it was harder to think of Google or checking the three-star restaurants of Paris, when you were playing an accordion for food in the Métro. Was his father still doing that?

"Do you want me to tell him where you are?"

Luc's heart began to beat very fast. Until he couldn't breathe to keep up with it, and he pressed his hand against the calendar with Summer's name all over it. "No," he said. Not now, not now. He was *happy*. "No. No. *Again?* He came by a lot?"

"Sometimes." Bernard looked judgmental. "They put him in jail a couple of times, for threatening violence to get at you, and that slowed him down."

Luc put a hand over his heart to cover it, trying to hold it together. Oh, God, why had Summer shattered that iron shield of his?

"He was a terrible father to you, Luc."

"I *know.*" His heart hurt so badly he hoped someone was ready to call 112. "I know he was, all right? I was there." But Marko had *hugged* him. Not infrequently, either, even if hugs did alternate with cuffs. And he had kept him, when his own mother had abandoned him, and he had, apparently, tried and tried to get him back. And sent him forth to humiliate himself in the Métro and blamed him when he failed and . . . Luc's insides were such a mess, he couldn't stand this.

He looked through the glass at Summer. Her eyebrows were knit delicately as she watched him. When his eyes caught hers, she moved abruptly to his office door.

"Don't tell him," Luc said very quickly just before she opened it.

Summer looked from Luc to Bernard, hesitated, and then very quietly slipped up beside Luc. Her gaze caught on the calendar, full of her name on his schedule, and she stilled a second, her arm halfway around his waist. Then she let it slide on home and squeezed him hard. The simple, consoling touch was like a chime on a tuning fork, vibrating through his body in perfect harmony. "Are you all right?" she whispered to Luc.

His arm tightened too hard around her. "Yes. I am now."

CHAPTER 29

On the counter sat mango juice. No Coke. Quick sugar but better for him. Next to it lay bags of sweet potato and beet chips. And she was making him a steak with Roquefort sauce.

If those little hands of hers squeezed his heart much tighter, he might break down and cry.

Don't leave me. It was all he could do not to clamp his hands around the far edge of her counter, press his face into the cold granite, and beg. *Don't leave me for your island and your sunshine. I need your sunshine here. I'll do anything. I'll take care of you. Let me take care of you. I want to be the person you can turn your face up to as if I was your hero.*

His father hadn't just left him? His father had come back and fought for him?

"Why do you hate Paris so much?" he asked.

She tried to peek under the edge of the steak to see whether it was seared without disturbing the marks from the grill pan. Hugo would have a heart attack and die at the way she was handling that steak, but Luc kept his mouth shut. She was doing this for him, which meant there was nothing she could do wrong.

"Well . . . it's really cold." She shrugged. "And rainy."

"The better to cuddle up under the covers with someone." He slid off his stool, despite the fourteen hours on his feet that day, and circled the counter to wrap his arms around her from behind, just the way he had wanted to that second evening when he had offered her his coat instead. "Are you cold, *soleil*?" What a scared idiot he had been that night, to only offer his coat.

She shivered into his heat and flipped the steak. The scent of it made his teeth itch to bite something. Her shoulder there. Kiss her all over while the glorious thing cooked.

"I'm always cold here," she said.

"Except now?" He let his breath heat the nape of her neck.

She shivered again, deliciously, and pressed still more snugly into him. "Not now."

"You don't think you could acclimate?" Soft as a secret into her ear, his teeth tingling to bite into that little lobe, the slope of her bare shoulder . . .

Her adamant headshake nearly hit his nose. "I hate it here."

He stroked her arms, fighting the venom in her tone. "Purely hate?" More than a place she had nearly been raped? He had grown up in Paris's streets and tunnels, and he *loved* the damn city, loved making it worship him. How bad could her luxury boarding school have been?

She transferred his steak to a plate, endearingly awkward compared to the professionals he was used to, and slid it across the counter to the spot where he had been sitting. Its scent was driving his starving body mad, but he kept hold of her. She bent her head very low. "It's so lonely."

He drew her around the counter to the stool beside him, pulling it so close their knees bumped. "It might not be so lonely, if you have someone to"—*love you*—"hold you."

Another quick little look. He cut his first bite of steak

and proffered it to her lips, giving no indication of what it cost him not to snatch it for himself.

As she licked the sauce off her lips, he took the next bite—a big one—and nearly writhed into the bliss of it. God, that tasted so good.

"That's what I used to think," she said. "But somehow it never worked out that way. Not for long."

He so did not want to torture himself by thinking about her ex-boyfriends again. But he made himself ask: "What do you think went wrong?"

Analyze the attempt to create something beautiful and impossible. See how it had failed. Don't fail.

A little shrug. "I think it probably just doesn't work out when you put yourself with someone just because you're lonely."

"So what about this particular someone you've put yourself with because you're lonely? Are you going to give me a chance to work out?"

Her eyes lifted to his, very wide. She didn't answer.

"How did it not work out? Somebody let you go when you needed him?"

She bent her head. "I think I might be very needy."

He dipped his sweet potato chips into the Roquefort sauce in utter gluttony. "So what do you need?" He proffered the sauce-laden chip to her lips.

"A crazy, incompatible thing, probably. But I'm going to get over it."

"Why don't you tell me what it is, before you decide whether you need to get over it or not?"

"I—" She shook her head. "No, it's too crazy."

"You know, when I come up with ideas, I don't admit anything is too crazy or impossible."

She hesitated, looking at him with so much—that was longing, wasn't it? He was starting to understand what he needed from her—her sunlight and her vulnerability, and something much much bigger that he still could only say with desserts. But what did she need from him?

"This is the most delicious meal anyone has ever made for me in my life," he murmured to her, twining the compliment gently around her, watching the giddy power of his voice over her. "Your pasta yesterday is the only thing that can compete with it. *Thank you.*"

She blushed with delight. For someone who should be used to compliments, it was amazingly easy to make her feel special. Was that one of the things she needed?

"So what's this crazy, impossible thing you need, Summer?" *You don't think things are possible, but I think everything is. And I'll do whatever I have to, to keep this.*

"Oh, just—" She made a sudden movement to slip away, but he had his thigh on one side of her stool, blocking her in. She shook her head despairingly and stared at the black granite counter. "Apparently I want an intensely ambitious, passionate workaholic who gives life everything in him. And I want him to choose *me* as more important than any of that."

He stroked his hand over that irresistible hair and let the heat of his palm rest on the strained muscles of her neck. "How would he show you that you were more important?"

A little silence, and then that rueful, self-deprecating shrug. "Give me all his attention."

"And how would you know you had that? How would you know that your ambitious, passionate workaholic always had some part of him thinking about you?"

She snuck a glance at him.

"Would he take all that passion and drive and discipline and make the very best thing his life could produce, and give it to you? And when you ignored that, would he try to do something even better? And would he keep doing that, no matter how insanely busy he was, *every damn day, twice a day?*"

Her eyes widened, locked on his.

"And when you rejected, over and over again, the best thing he could possibly be, would he change for you and try instead to make what you wanted, no matter how humble he had to be to do it?"

She had the bluest damn eyes. They clung to his; her lips were parted.

He sat back. "I'm just asking, Summer. How would you know?"

"I—I was just thinking he would give me hugs and like to have me around."

He hadn't had a hug since he was fostered. Maybe what felt like an incredible glory of physical affection to him wasn't nearly enough for her. He stroked his hand from the nape of her neck to her far shoulder and let his arm wrap around her. Carefully. Not at all sure he was doing this thing called "affection" right. But liking it. Oh, yeah, he could do this one hell of a lot more, if she liked it, too. God, he would have to get used to it, though. There were moments when it made him feel like he was about to pass out.

"And I'm not staying here," she said very rapidly to the counter. "I'm not, I'm not, I'm not, I'm not."

On the plus side, she did have to say it five times. Like maybe the trap of him was closing around her. He grimaced at the image. "What's the hold your father has over you, to keep you here?"

"They need another satellite out there. He said if I would give running this hotel a try for three months, he would invest. I've been doing my best not to really run it—it's not like Alain needs my interference—but I have to stay here." She darted him a glance. "I know it seems spoiled not to want a luxury hotel as a Christmas present, but . . . I really hate hotels."

He *loved* this hotel. He loved everything about it. The gold and the marble, the chandeliers, the precise perfect elegance everywhere you looked, the rich and hungry people who flocked here for him, just for him. The absolute distance from anything resembling a dirty packed Métro car full of people who ignored him as he poured his heart out.

He squeezed her nape gently. "Well, let's get the hell out of it, then."

CHAPTER 30

They walked down the Champs-Elysées in the middle of the night. Street lamps glittered like a stairway to heaven, curving up the slope of the Champs to the lofty glowing Arc de Triomphe. The car lights sparkled off the wet pavement in jagged dances, and Luc laughed, swinging her hand like a young man out on his first date.

His happiness fascinated Summer. She found herself relaxing into it until she was starting to laugh, too, for no reason, just because they were walking so firmly on the eggshells of her past.

"Look at this view." He gestured from the Arc de Triomphe all down the wide bejeweled boulevard to the Place de la Concorde with its piercing proud Obélisque. "Summer, *look* at it. Is this not the most beautiful city to be king of in the world?"

He was like her mother, of all people. Mai's joy in this city was so triumphant that she could not conceive of any other way to feel about it. Where had her mother come from, she wondered suddenly, that she was so thrilled to play at princess? That she thought her daughter would rather be a princess than have a family life? Mai had never talked much about her childhood.

"It's freezing," Summer murmured, ruefully.

He pulled her into the panels of his coat and kissed her until she was warm again, laughing triumphantly when he lifted his head. He seemed ten years younger, but in a surprised and delighted way, as if he did not recognize from his own youth how young he felt now.

He led her to the Trocadéro, where they stood on the esplanade above the great fountain, turned off for the winter. Across the river, the Eiffel Tower glowed her heart out, and Luc leaned against the esplanade and stared at it, exhilarated.

"Sorry," he said a little sheepishly when he realized Summer was watching him. "I don't get out much. I love this city."

She wanted to beat her head against something. "Of course you would," she muttered. That damn *smug* Eiffel Tower. *Look, here's another person I can make love me better than he loves you.*

Not that he had ever said he loved her, of course.

Unless you counted an entire restaurant full of desserts, designed for her, as a declaration.

She looked up at the exuberance in the normally taut profile, with the Eiffel Tower as his backdrop. Her head tilted. "You know, it does almost look beautiful this way."

"Almost?" He sent a wry glance from the Eiffel Tower to her, then turned his back on the tower completely, sitting against the wall of the esplanade and pulling her between his legs. "I have less than three months to show you how beautiful this city is, don't I?"

He didn't seem to find it an overwhelming challenge. With Paris in his pocket, what man wouldn't be cocky? He didn't understand. No one ever did understand how she could hate Paris.

He didn't seem to be paying that much attention to Paris itself anymore, though, his thumbs tracing over her cheekbones and his fingers drawing through wings of her hair, in that musing absorption into which he sometimes fell, looking at her.

"I love you," Summer said quietly. *Yeah, take that to the belly, Eiffel. You thought I would be afraid to say it so close to you, didn't you?*

Luc's hands jerked in her hair, stinging, his face blanking as if he had been hit by a shock wave.

"No one has ever told you that, have they?" she realized, her hands rising to find his. He called his foster father *monsieur*, after all. And his mother had abandoned him.

His fingers moved uneasily in hers, as if he might be thinking of wrenching his hands away. "Twice," he admitted. "Girls in high school." His mouth curved reluctantly, an uncomfortable wryness. "It didn't work out for them. They had no idea how desperate and clingy it would make me."

Twice. He was thirty years old. She stepped into him, pressing herself against his chest and wrapping her arms around him, under his coat, holding on as tight as she could. She didn't say anything. She didn't know what else to offer.

"And people say it all the time," he added awkwardly, "when they eat one of my desserts. 'I love this man, isn't he amazing?' "

Her arms tightened around him. She pressed a kiss through his shirt.

His hand stroked her hair. "You've heard it a lot, haven't you?" he asked, low.

She nodded against his chest. "All the time. My mom loves to say it, and my dad doesn't really say it to me—he's not that demonstrative—but he certainly tells other people he loves me."

A very long silence. "The mother and father who spent one evening in your company, in public, before going off to do something else, after you had been self-exiled in the islands for four years?"

Summer said nothing, but she pressed herself a little tighter against his chest. His arms circled around her, the hold changing so she couldn't tell anymore if it was for him or for her.

"And you've said it a lot, haven't you?" he said very softly, as if he didn't want to but he just had to know.

She bent her head, defeated. Yes. She had many, many times thrown herself into loving someone. She had failed herself that way, and apparently him, too. Although every time, right there at the beginning, it had never felt like failure. It had always felt like hope.

She turned away from him, but he stood and shifted, not loosening his arms, so that she ended up standing with her back to his chest, his arms still wrapped around her, both of them gazing at the Eiffel Tower. *Oh, you damn bitch, I could beat you down with a sledgehammer.*

Except, of course, even without the police to stop her, Summer could batter those iron girders until her arms fell off and not even make a dent.

The Eiffel went out as she glared at it, totally black, and Summer's jaw dropped in shock and an odd terrified hope. And then, of course, the stupid taunting sparkling started, all over the blacked-out Eiffel, its last little act of gloating for the night. "I suppose you've never said it," she said stiffly.

"Oh, I've said it." A twisted, old darkness in his voice, turned against himself. "When I was trying to explain to those two high school girlfriends why they couldn't ditch me." A vision, suddenly, of an intense sixteen-year-old, wilder, more ragged, no polish on him yet, begging, "But I love you!" Her hands flew up to close around his arms, her heart wringing. "I like to think I've learned better than that these days."

She squeezed his forearms, wishing one of those girls had picked up the heart thrown to them, so that he wouldn't have been hurt, wouldn't have learned to make so many walls. Except then, of course, he wouldn't be here with her. She petted his arms uselessly, a lousy balm for those old wounds.

"Summer, look at me," Luc said.

She didn't want to, but, as always, his voice had that power over her, and it turned her around. That god's forged face of his was very serious. "I love you, too," he said quietly. Her heart gave one great leap of hope and fear, and his hands came up to frame her face. *A spark, sheltered between two curved hands.* "I suspect, unfortunately, in a very different way than you love me."

She stood caught, unable to say a word. "I love you" and "in a better way than you can ever love me." Between the sweetness and the cruelty of it, those two curved hands had just clapped together and ground her into nothing.

Why was she always the nothing in the equation?

The night air against the parts of her he didn't touch felt very cold. She couldn't stand the thought of stepping away from his warmth into it. And *Oh, God. I don't want to be the third girl to throw his heart back at him.*

But . . . if his heart had so much worth to him, and hers had none . . . Her whole body felt clogged with tears, right up to her stinging nose. But her mouth firmed. Her chin went up just a little. "Enough to come back with me to the islands?"

Something shook across his face. He stared down at her. "Summer. I can't be nothing again."

She gathered all her will, all that precious still-fragile belief in herself. And she closed her hands around his wrists and pulled his hands from her face. "Neither can I."

CHAPTER 31

Luc was very quiet as he led them down the slope from the Trocadéro, heading not back to the hotel but toward the Seine and the bridge across to the Tour. If she ended up in some romantic embrace under seven thousand tons of iron, she was definitely shooting that tower a bird.

A pair of inline skaters barreled past them down the slope along side the fountain and the Jardins du Trocadéro, calling out to each other in laughing alarm at their speed. Luc pulled her safely out of their way, and his arm stayed tightened around her. "Summer. I'm very bad at this. I always did have to practice ten thousand times to get things right, and this—the practice runs just hurt too much. Don't listen to me, when I say something wrong. *Look* at what I make for you. *Taste* it. You will *never* be *nothing* to me."

Sometimes she thought if she could sit him down in a hammock on her island, come home to him from a day of coaxing rambunctious kids to focus on subtraction, even she could handle this. "You have to believe in me," she realized suddenly, out loud. "I can't believe in you, if you don't believe in me. It would be suicidal." *I'm just not that strong, yet. To keep believing in myself when the person I love doesn't.*

Silence. He couldn't say that he believed in her. But af-

ter a long moment, he lifted a hand to tuck one strand of
hair behind her ear, and his thumb stroked her cheek before it fell. He took her hand again, and they walked on
without saying a word, Luc so deep in thought that he
never even glanced up at the Eiffel Tower as they passed
under its dark feet. Summer tucked her free hand at the
small of her back and shot La Tour a bird on principle.

He drew her into the night-dark *allée* that ran between
ranks of trees beside the Champ de Mars, and she squeezed
her eyes shut against fate. "Never tell me you live around
here?"

He hesitated. "Why not?"

"Oh, just"—she shook her head—"I went to school
here."

Another step. "There's a wealthy girls' school right
down the block from me," he admitted reluctantly.

"The Olympe?"

He nodded, and Summer's soul winced into a fetal ball.
She cast frantically around for some happy memory of this
beautiful city, the city that always made it inexcusable for
her to be unhappy, and managed to call up a smile. "My
nanny used to take me to play here a lot when I was little.
You know that little carousel and the playground by it?"

"I—do know it, yes." It was too dark under the trees
to read his always-difficult-to-read face, but his voice
sounded odd.

"I had the most desperate crush on a boy I met there
once." She laughed a little. "He was dark-haired, too, now
that I think about it. Maybe he started the trend." She
shook her head, with affectionate reminiscence. "I thought
he was so awesome. He could do *everything* on the playground. And he was so patient. After he finished showing
off for me, he picked me up and helped me reach the bars.
And he even played knight and princess with me."

Luc had gone peculiarly still.

"I used to fantasize about him for ages. We would run off to an island and live off moonlight and flowers, that kind of thing. I suppose you can tell I didn't have a lot of friends."

Luc was just one black shadow in the darkness.

"I used to make Liz take me back here every day when we were in Paris, and I would drag out my playtime for hours, hoping to see him. But he never came." And then the boarding school, so near that playground, had wiped the memory out for the longest time.

"He was probably playing a tambourine in the Métro passing under your feet," Luc said suddenly, his voice rough, strange. As if years of elegance had slid off it. "He would have liked to come." His hand flexed on hers. "You would have had to eat the moonlight, though, if he made it for you."

"In the *Métro*?" Her hand sought his face like a blind woman trying to recognize an old lover.

The elegant, sensual mouth twisted against her palm. "Have you ever been in it?"

"I took it sometimes when I was in school here. When I was sneaking out. I—remember." Startling and exciting, the sense of doing something a little dangerous, the self-denigrating awareness that most people did it every day. The noise, the crowds, the—people begging for change. Sometimes with an accordion, sometimes a baby. "Luc. Why did you say that? Why would he have been in the Métro?"

He didn't answer, his hands in his pockets, his shoulders very straight. He had the most beautiful clean-cut shoulders. She traced his eyebrows. The boy had blurred so long ago in her brain, her own personal knight, with those dark, insistent, demanding eyes, holding hers . . .

"Luc?"

So very straight, those shoulders. Sheathed in a black

cashmere Dior coat like . . . hand-tailored armor for a dark knight to forge his way up into the world. "Possibly because he had a Gypsy father who hadn't found any better way to make his life than to busk there. And his mother had opted for the sun and sea and flowers instead. Not that she would probably have done better than my father, if she had stayed here. Disappearing on a newborn doesn't suggest great force of character."

Her hands closed around his convulsively, in another stupid, vain wish to squeeze healing into all those old wounds. She drew his hands up to her face, tracing those long, masculine fingers, the fine dark hair, the incredible tensile strength of them. *A boy swinging from the bars like a monkey, his grip strong. Then him lifting her up to try to help her reach them . . .*

She curved his hands around her cheeks and held them there with both of hers. She did not know what to offer him against this, other than her insufficient self. Shit, no wonder he had always had higher standards than her. "I thought you were fostered. By a very strict, workaholic perfectionist."

"When I was ten. The police picked us up in the Métro during school hours. My father . . . wasn't judged fit to keep me."

"You didn't go to school?"

He stiffened and tried to pull his hands away, at an angle toward his pockets. "Not until I was ten. I was never very good at school."

She turned her cheek more deeply into one palm, nestling into the scent and texture. His hands checked in their flight. "I didn't go to school until I was thirteen." She kissed the base of his palm. "And I was very bad at it, too. I know it's not the same thing."

Her experience never had quite the same value as anyone else's. The money and the looks took it over. Only the media had ever felt different about that, which might have explained why she had encouraged the paparazzi so much back in the old days. Until she had stumbled onto all the hate groups on the Internet and realized the huge dark ugly underside of that media love.

Anyway, it was true, you could hardly compare a luxurious education by a nanny to growing up in the Métro, busking for a living.

"You were summa cum laude at Harvard, Summer." Luc sounded pissed off. "And you told me your father didn't buy that. Don't put yourself down for me."

"I was bad in a different way." Summer bit her lip to keep her cheek nestled in his hand. This wasn't about her, and she didn't need to turn away in hurt because her way didn't matter. "I always had trouble making real friends." She had spent her entire teenage years one raw mess, in fact. Having never, before the age of thirteen, spent any significant time with anyone but the nanny who adored her and was paid to do so. And then hitting full throttle, in the midst of an excruciating sense of abandonment and loneliness, the fact that most girls her age instinctively and viciously hated her.

During college she started to pull herself together, but it probably hadn't been in the best way, patching herself up with boyfriends and media attention and an intense determination to excel at something that might get her father to think she was worth his time.

The Métro. Her hand flexed involuntarily on Luc's, still held to her cheek. "Did you have a place to *stay*? And food?"

"Sometimes." His voice was neutral.

"Luc." Her hand seized his very tightly.

His other arm wrapped around her and pulled her in

close. "Not maternal at all, are you?" he whispered to her hair.

She didn't know why he kept saying that, when she felt so small and utterly protected in his hold. Not exactly childlike, because the moment was packed with far too much sensuality, but . . . as if she could yield all her vulnerability to him. And it would be okay. Those hands would stay cupped and careful and not crush her absently. A strange stupid conviction, given how absently they had just crushed her up there on the Esplanade.

She certainly didn't feel like his *mother.* She just wanted to take better care of him. She kept thinking no one else ever had. Not even himself. He had never learned to buy that sweatshirt of his own to sink into when he needed a refuge.

"You have no idea how much good this does me," Luc breathed.

To hold her? Really? How? Wasn't she the one being needy?

"It's cold, and I'm getting sick of the damn Eiffel Tower looming over me," Luc murmured. His breath warmed her head. "Come to my apartment, Summer."

The idea seized at her nerves, like a test she could fail. But it filled her with longing, too. She glanced up at him, the great night-black leg of the Tour looming beyond him, as he led her away. "You don't like the Eiffel Tower?"

"She's kind of smug, don't you think? Like she knows she is the most important thing in the world, and there's nothing anyone else can do to beat her mark on it." Luc gave that iron tower a long, cool look. Clearly begging to differ.

Even though *his* mark on the world was made with things that got eaten in minutes, shattered at the wrong touch, or melted if no one served them in time.

"I love you," Summer said quietly and very firmly, tightening her hand on his.

His head angled sharply back toward her, Eiffel Tower forgotten. "Yes, come tell me about that, Summer. Come tell me all . . . about . . . that."

CHAPTER 32

Luc had a brief qualm when he let her into his apartment, because despite the prime location and stately old Haussmanian building, with its staircase carpeted with red velvet, the apartment itself was like the bags of potato chips at the end of the day. It was neat enough, because his foster mother had been relentless in her training of a wild child picked up out of the Métro, and because he had never gotten into the habit of accumulating many things, but he just spent so little time or attention on it.

But Summer's face lit even more than when she had walked into Sylvain and Cade's. She didn't have much more experience of cozy, warm homes than he did, did she? Except on her island, he thought with a chill, and pushed the thought away.

She slid out of her boots and let him take her coat, but slipped away from him before he could turn her against the door and kiss her, examining the place.

"It could look like a showplace," he mentioned, in case that mattered to her. "I've talked to Louis Dutran about it—I suppose you probably don't know his name, either. He's an exceptional architect and interior designer. He did the Leucé rooms in our remodel. He's got some ideas for it, I just haven't gotten around to thinking about them."

"You want to make your apartment look like a hotel?" Summer went to the window, hiding her face from him.

"I want to make it look like whatever would make you happy," he said firmly.

Her eyes caught his for one bright moment, and then she looked back out the window. "You can see the Eiffel Tower," she said reproachfully.

The window looked across one of the *allées* and over the Champ de Mars. On the fourteenth of July the entire kitchen staff packed his apartment to see the fireworks. He had paid a lot extra for that view. "I usually consider her a tribute to my accomplishments," he admitted.

Summer laughed, her face lighting with admiration. Oh, God, that was perfect. He could spend the rest of his life wallowing in that happy delight in him. "I really might be a narcissist," he mentioned reluctantly.

"No, you're not," she said, amused, and it was the first time he had understood that someone really could speak *caressingly*. Her voice stroked his entire body. She glanced back at the Eiffel Tower and shook her head. "I wish I had your confidence."

"You can have it," he said quietly. He didn't want her to be weaker or smaller than she could be. But he utterly loved the thought of holding her safe in his hands. Yes, she could have his confidence to wrap around her. He was pretty sure that was what he had built that confidence to do. Maybe it would even wear off on her over time.

She gave him one of those long looks of hers, as if he had said something that had almost caught her—what, damn it? What else could he say that would help spring that trap?—and then looked back out the window, but in the opposite direction from the Tower. Her temple rested against the glass.

His gut tightened as he realized what she saw. The corner of that boarding school, just visible. He could imagine her there now. See past the sexy silky glamour to a little girl so desperate to pour love out that she latched on to a boy in the park. She had never learned to build an armor of iron. And so she just flickered and slipped through the years of bruising as best she could, a candle flame beaten by the wind. Until she got herself to those islands, a sheltered place where she could finally let the full glow of her expand until it lit everyone around her. He had seen that glow in her photos. He just didn't yet know how to take her off her island, drag her into the place she considered such a hell, and still keep that glow for him.

The hell of Paris. She really was kind of spoiled.

He stepped to her, wrapping his arms around her from behind. *You're not alone here anymore.*

And, the thought rushed through him at the feel of her body in his arms, *neither am I.*

Her head rested back against his shoulder, but her gaze was still focused down the street. "You must get a lot of panties with cell phone numbers thrown at you from the Olympe's dorm windows," she said wryly, her voice light.

He laughed, but his fingers rubbed at the tension he felt in her ribs, her stomach pulled tight against a blow. "I don't walk that way on a regular schedule anymore. It's embarrassing."

"You've never been tempted to pick a pair up?" she asked dryly.

"The panties of a fifteen-year-old girl who's desperate for romance? Summer. I didn't live here when I was a teenager."

Her stomach was trembling a little, under his arm. But in the window he could see the ghostly reflection of that light smile. "Not your style now?"

"Summer!" He would have been angry, except that smile of hers in the window was so silky and light, and the muscles of her stomach were so tense. "Somebody picked yours up, didn't he?" he realized slowly. "Some thirty-year-old disgusting enough to take a lonely teenager up on an offer like that."

"They weren't panties, it was a photo and a love letter," she said stiffly. "He was quite cute."

"Black-haired, I suppose," he said with resignation. *I had the most desperate crush on a dark-haired boy I met here. I used to fantasize about him for ages.* Him.

God. Had she been looking for him all this time?

She shrugged against him.

"How old was he?"

Her stomach flinched. And he never would have known, if he wasn't holding her. "My dad said he was thirty-four," she said carelessly.

Ah. So her father had found out about it. Why did he know already that couldn't have been good? "How old were you?"

"Fifteen," she said and flushed, lifting her chin proudly.

"Barely," he guessed, stroking her hair. "You were fif-teen, barely." He was surprised she had lasted that long. Hadn't she started boarding school at thirteen? Meaning she had spent two years without love before she cracked?

"It wasn't—" She stopped. "He didn't—that is." She turned her head away from the boarding school, but that meant she faced the Eiffel Tower. She looked away from it, and her gaze crossed his in the mirror. She closed hers finally as the only escape and bent her head. "He never went past panties." Her face flushed deep red.

Luc felt sick. Some pedophilic *asshole* teaching her all the pleasures of her young body, all so gallantly. He could imagine her, all full of hope, learning her first orgasm at some bastard's clever hands, feeling so loved for the first time in her life. "What did your father do?"

"Oh, Vincent was really going out with me as a lever

against Dad, you know. That was why he was so careful not to go . . . too far." Her throat was clogging. Luc tightened his arms on her, rocking her minutely. "So Dad gave him what he wanted, and let me see it, you know, let me see him choose money and power over me, and then he destroyed him, of course." She had cleared the clog from her throat, speaking so lightly. He might have been fooled, if he hadn't had his hand on her belly to feel the shudders . . .

"What did your father do to you?"

"Nothing," she said, surprised. "I mean, yelled at me, of course." Her belly trembled violently under his hand. "Told me I was a little wh-whor—" And suddenly she was sobbing, a violent convulsion of her body, so much worse than when she'd told him about the assault. He wouldn't have thought anything could make Summer ugly, but these sobs did, crumpling her around his arm until he had to sink down to the floor with her. "A little wh-whor— and he was the only thing that got me through the *day,* the only reason I could *survive,* knowing I would see him again, that he lo—I thought he lov—" And she stopped trying to talk, curled so tightly into herself it was like she was trying to crush herself out of existence, and all he could do was hold that ball of her in his lap and curse her father and all bastards in a low, harsh rhythm, rocking her.

God, this is how miserable she was. This is how she sobbed, night after night, under the Eiffel Tower she hates so much. No one held her after that. They dusted her off their hands back into that boarding school and left her completely alone. She must have sobbed like this, in secret in her room, for months. Maybe years.

This is what I have to beat, to hold her here.

"God *damn* it," he muttered. "I was nineteen years old. I was at my first job, right across the river. I even walked over here sometimes. *Putain de bordel de merde de . . .* Why couldn't we have met then?" He might not have known how to stroke her just right through her panties back then—he probably would have dated her for a year before he even tried, she was fifteen fucking years old, after all. Even for a nineteen-year-old that was young. Besides, a passionate romantic took a while to work up the nerve to touch his princess.

But he would have been sincere. He would have been crazy in love with her, willing to do anything for her. They would have escaped to all the romantic spots in Paris, they would have been two almost normal, blissfully happy teenagers in love.

"You think you could have stood up to my father when you were nineteen?" Summer mumbled into his shoulder. Progress. At first she had been crumpled completely into herself.

"What could he have done to me? Tried to get me fired? If you think I'm arrogant when someone interferes in my kitchens, you should have seen the chef I worked for then. He would have eviscerated your father. And I might mean that literally. Knife skills."

That convulsive tightness was easing slowly out of the ball he held in his arms. Her sobs were gentling, as if they had been some old ugly disease she had just had to get out. Not gone now, but not as ragged. "He probably would have offered you money. And then told me when you accepted it."

"Summer. I'm not a practical person." He had a vision of him throwing her father's money back in his face, an impassioned teenager fighting to keep his golden princess. This was, in its way, an inane conversation, and a cruel one, a taunting counter-reality that should have been. But it seemed to be doing her good, to imagine it.

"You must have been a wild-eyed romantic at nineteen," she agreed softly, loosening further, enough that her hands could creep around his waist and clutch. "My God, you still are. You just know one way to show it."

"I'm working on the other ways. Summer, I love you." He took a hard breath. It still felt like ripping his chest open. You would think filling that whole restaurant with desserts would have been more than enough self-exposure. But no. She needed something hard.

"More than I can ever love you, right." She started to shift off his lap.

He held her. "I never said more. Just differently." Harder. More permanent. An iron that couldn't be shattered, not even by her.

Except it felt like atoms of light filling the whole universe.

He sighed and petted her hair. "You love so easily." She could not possibly feel for him as much as he felt for her. No one ever had.

She flinched and crumpled.

No. He realized. *No, not easily. It takes all her courage. You* knew *this already. Why do you keep forgetting it?*

Because he wanted to stay in control. He wanted to be the one whose word *love* meant something. Because they had met again twenty years too late, and now he was a fucking coward. He was afraid of what would happen if he let himself go into those slender hands. He was afraid he would believe in her. And then she wouldn't know what to do with him. And she would let him go.

"Summer. If anything, you love more." More than this massive dark thing that pressed outward against his breastbone, striving to explode him, to bury itself in her, to bury her in him until he crushed everything there was of her in his need to make sure she was his?

"Better, anyway," he said quietly, stroking her.

She looked up at him at that.

"I'll practice," he said, although it took all his much more meager courage. "What—what I feel will look better, more—palatable, over time."

Her eyebrows knitted.

He lowered his forehead to hers and admitted self-mockingly, "It's the most awkward, unwieldy, primitive raw ingredient I've ever worked with."

"Luc." She curled into him fully now, a warmer softer cuddle than the wretched sobbing ball. It made him feel as if he could breathe again, past her own hurt squeezing his lungs. *"Palatable?"* One of her hands petted his cheek. "I like the primitive, unwieldy. Real."

Maybe, but that didn't mean he couldn't make it better. Into something she could never give up. He forced himself to give her one of her own smiles, glimmering, teasing. "Just wait until you see how good it can get, *soleil.*" He would take her to all those crazy romantic spots they should have seen as teenagers sneaking out, making out, in palpitations just to be able to hold each other's hands. He would show her the sudden magic moments of winter. The first signs of a Paris spring. He had ten weeks.

Ten weeks to make her love her own personal hell and the man who wanted to trap her in it just because he so adamantly needed to rule over it.

CHAPTER 33

It was a satisfying feeling to bring Summer back to the hotel in the morning completely debauched, her lips full and bruised, her eyes blinking deep, heavy blinks, her body so full of the memory of him, he liked to imagine it still shivering and clutching, wondering how he could possibly not still be inside her.

Damn idiot. If he had done it the night they met, her first experience of Paris after four years might have been *happy.*

Her hair was just a little too perfect for the look, because he had fixed it for her when she couldn't get her hands to do much more than rest on the nape of her neck, caressing herself lazily where his teeth had grazed. He reached out now and twitched a strand free, so that it hung by her face in just a suggestion of someone who had been completely undone. That was better.

She slanted him the best she could do at a warning glance from those heavy eyes. He smiled at her ruefully. "I might be a little . . . compulsive."

"I'm not a thing."

"I know." He twitched the strand of hair so that it lay just so over her shoulder. "But I love playing with you anyway." She blossomed in his hands. Glowed and came and clung to him and loved him. His whole world went right when she pressed her hands into his bare shoulders, laughing above him, her gold hair spilling down toward him like a stairway into heaven.

"If you've got higher standards than her, get your hands the fuck off her," a hard voice said, and Summer jerked violently, that glow in her dimming low.

"Dad?" She turned to face the couple crossing the chessboard marble of the lobby.

"Surprise, honey!" Her twin mother swept her away from Luke into an eager embrace. "I missed you! Did you get that picture I texted of Prince Frederic? He's getting cuter all the time, don't you think? I wish you had come to his sister's engagement party; your father even likes him."

"I didn't know my sentence allowed for furloughs to parties in Poland," Summer said dryly, and her father gave a huff of impatience.

"Your sentence. Three months in Paris in one of the finest hotels in the world. Honestly, Summer, if you're going to keep talking like that, I don't know why we even bothered to stop by."

Luc watched Summer go mute, as every need to express resentment, fear, unhappiness was silenced by the threat that if she did, they would walk out and leave her with no one at all.

He wrapped one arm around her shoulders and pulled her into his side. "You always shut your daughter up like that?"

Her father frowned at him. "Mind your own business."

Luc raised his eyebrows with hauteur. "I honestly spend as little time on business as I can. It's boring. But I'll mind my own more important things, certainly."

Summer stared up at him as if he had just done something heroic, but he had no idea what. Tell her father what a bastard he was? Honestly, it was pure pleasure.

Sam Corey glared. "Summer, are you dating someone who thinks *business* is *boring*? Why do you *do* this to me?"

"Maybe she's not doing anything to you. Maybe she's living her life, and I make her happy," Luc told him coolly.

Her father turned on Summer. "What the hell is going on here? I thought you told me he had higher standards than you."

"Your daughter misinterpreted something I said rather radically. And you should stay out of it."

"*I* think he's cute," Mai Corey told her husband, her eyes sparkling. "Come here, honey." She looped her arm around her daughter's waist, drawing her toward the elevator. "Let me show you this dress I got you in Warsaw. *So* pretty. I got you a size up from me, too, just in case, with all that island living and Monsieur Leroi here, but I can send that one back if the smaller size still fits."

Luc stared after them with incredulous fury as Mai Corey pinched her daughter's waist and swept them into the elevator. Summer, looking as if she had been dashed with a bucket of ice water, glanced back at him and her father, her brow furrowing anxiously as the elevator doors closed.

Luc pivoted. Sam Corey met his look with one of his own, one that probably cowed men he had power over. "What are you doing with my daughter?" he said again.

"Ah, when you told her to kiss up to me and keep me happy, you didn't mean that literally? I did wonder about a man who didn't give a fuck how his own daughter felt, as long as she made everyone else happy."

The other man's mouth compressed. "I never told her to kiss *up* to anyone. She's *my* daughter. What are you doing with your hands on her?"

"You probably don't want to know what my hands did with your daughter," Luc said cruelly.

Sam Corey stiffened with incredulous rage. Ah, was it

easy to get him to lose control? Was that one of the reasons Summer liked Luc's control so much? Luc gave him an urbane smile. "I'm just guessing. I've never had a daughter myself."

"You fucking bastard," Sam Corey said softly, incredulously. "It's true what they say about arrogant chefs, isn't it?"

Luc shrugged.

Sam Corey pushed open the nearest conference room door. The Marie Antoinette room, all gold and soft blue, featuring a painting of a woman soon to have her head sliced off. With a grunt, he gestured Luc inside.

Luc raised his eyebrows.

"If you're waiting for me to say please, of your courtesy, you're going to wait a long time," Sam Corey growled.

Luc held his eyes for a long, steady moment.

"You rather we have our first proper talk at dinner, in front of Summer?"

Luc inclined his head slightly and stepped through the door.

"You look beautiful, honey." Mai Corey pressed her cheek beside Summer's to give her a quick hug that posed them side by side in the mirror in Summer's suite. Her mother's eyes sparkled with pleasure at the reflection of them as twins. "Just like a princess."

"Did you grow up really poor, Maman?" Summer asked suddenly.

Her mother stiffened. "What makes you ask that? Was it something I did?"

Summer shook her head. "You're always elegant and perfect. I just wondered if you did. And had a really rich fantasy life about becoming a princess one day."

Mai Corey's mouth softened, and she stroked her daughter's cheek. "You're my princess, sweetheart. I want everyone to see how perfect you are." She tucked the strand of hair Luc had loosened back up into Summer's chignon.

"And you always wanted to go to boarding school in Paris, didn't you?" Summer said softly. "Like Madeline."

Mai Corey laughed. "I told you that when you went for your interview. Although it was kind of a farce, that acceptance interview, when your father could have bought and sold the place a hundred times over. But I wanted you to be accepted on your own merit. Paris boarding school! *How* I used to dream of that when I was little."

"That's right." Summer had done great at that interview, to please her parents, even though she had spent considerable time after the interview throwing up in a nearby bathroom. "I guess I just didn't really—think about it, then." It hadn't occurred to her that the interview was a farce, either. She was only thirteen.

Her mother gave her a little hug, still sideways, facing the mirror. "Sweetie, you don't know how happy it's always made me, to be able to give my daughter all these things. I just—wish you *wanted* them more, honey. I've never understood what you do want."

Summer hesitated and gave her a shy smile through the mirror, unable to say it face-to-face. "You know, my favorite times growing up were when you used to play Beauty and the Beast with me in hotels like this. You know how we would pretend wherever Dad was working was the West Wing, and all the staff were the magic hands opening the doors?"

"Oh." Relieved delight filled her mother's face, and she squeezed Summer again. She, too, still spoke through the mirror. "Really? Well, that's all right, then."

Summer nodded, even though those times had been so very sporadic.

"My parents were awful," her mother confessed to her. "If it hadn't been for my grandmother, I don't know what would have happened to me. I tried to do better. Wasn't Liz wonderful? I must have interviewed five hundred people to find such a good person to take care of you."

Summer was silent for a second, before she gave her mother's waist a little squeeze. Really, it was always true, that Summer was just too spoiled to understand how good she had it.

"We still look like twins," her mother said with intense satisfaction. Her fingers stroked, light and sweet, over the corners of Summer's eyes, finding them via the mirror, still without looking into Summer's actual face. "Although I wish you would take better care of your skin, honey. The spa here can do microderm abrasion, or if you need a little more, I know someone in Paris who's really good."

"I'm twenty-six years old, Mom. Maman."

"I know, honey." Her mother's fingers stroked so gently, a maternal healing touch. "That's what worries me about these. You're so young to have lines already."

"They're from laughing."

"And being out in the sun too much while you do." Her mother patted her shoulder with affectionate reproach. "Try holding it back to a softer smile when you can, sweetheart. It will help."

Sam Corey slammed the door of the Marie Antoinette room shut. Luc suspected it was Sam Corey's favorite conference room in the hotel, one where he could imagine everyone else losing their heads to him.

"What are you doing with my daughter?" the older man snapped.

Luc smiled sweetly. "Whatever I want."

A fist thumped hard on the carved gold door. "God-damnit, man."

"You know, if you didn't want your daughter to fall in with so many wrong men, you probably should have spent more time with her, teaching her how to recognize the right ones." He noted that on his very short list of rules on how to bring his vision of a happy, black-haired, delicate-featured little girl to successful fruition . . . way down through to when *she* got married and lived happily ever after and had kids and . . . whoa. He pulled himself back from a dizzying brink.

"Has she been complaining about how little time I spent with her *again*?" Sam Corey snapped.

"No. She never complains. I think she might be afraid to."

"And well she should be," Sam Corey said roughly. "There's never been a more privileged child in the whole freaking world."

Luc closed his hands around the edge of a table, leaning back against it, and just looked at the older man. Second note on his short list: *If you give her everything but a belief in herself, you've screwed the fuck up. Also, no matter what trouble your fifteen-year-old daughter gets herself into, never, ever call her a whore.* "Let's talk about something else. Why don't you tell me your daughter's good traits?"

The other man glared at him and shrugged. "She's beautiful, but she knows it. She's got a brain on her like you wouldn't believe—given the way she's wasting it. She could talk P/E ratios when she was five years old—"

Luc supposed it was a better way of being a performing monkey than playing a damn tambourine, but it still made him nauseated every time he heard that.

"—and instead of doing something with it, she's teaching a dozen kids on some godforsaken island."

"Maybe it's not godforsaken," Luc said whimsically.

"Huh?"

"Nothing." He hadn't been in a church since he left his foster father's house, and even back then it had only been for foster-cousin baptisms and first Communions. It was a weird thought to pop into his head. But if he had been one of those little kids or their parents, a bright, loving woman who was happy to do her best for them and didn't think there were "better" things she could do with her life would have seemed like a gift from God to *him*. "Can you say one full sentence about your daughter without taking away the compliment in the second part?"

Sam Corey set his jaw and glared at him.

"Try," Luc said. "Try hard. It will do you good."

"She could be so much better than she is!" Sam Corey burst out. "The *privileges* she had. The opportunities."

"You're right. It's a good thing we're not having this conversation in front of Summer. Back up and try again. You're not convincing me it's a good thing for Summer to have much contact with you, and I might end up having some influence on that."

Sam Corey's jaw locked. His eyes tried to bore through Luc's skull, but that iron only weakened for sunlight.

"*Allez*. Your precious daughter. You want her to go to a man who can take good care of her. Right? Work it from that angle. Tell me something special about her."

Sam Corey strode across the room to the portrait of Marie Antoinette. At first, Luc thought the older man had dismissed him, and maybe that was his intention. But the hard face slowly relaxed, with memories. Her father gave a little laugh, suddenly, and turned. "All right. She always had focus, that girl. I remember how she used to slip into my office and just watch me. She'd watch me for an hour at a time."

"That must have felt nice." Luc could fit a little girl of his up on the counter beside him and delight her whole little world. He had no idea how to do anything else, where little girls were concerned, but he figured he could handle that part. Right, and if a nine-year-old boy helping a little girl climb on the monkey bars could have such an impact, he bet his little black-haired vision would be all over having her own dad do it. Three things on his list, now.

"Yeah. Of course, you had to be careful. Give her any attention, and she'd try to climb in your lap. Clingy, that kid. Real needy."

"Because she wanted to climb into your lap?"

"Yeah." The older man was silent for a moment and then sighed. "I miss it, though, sometimes. Wonder if I shouldn't have taken advantage of it more when I had the chance. I kept trying to make her more independent, but . . . maybe we needed another daughter so we could get the next one right. God knows, Summer went off the deep end later. Still trying to get all the attention, I guess."

Luc just looked at him. "So, the lesson is, if I have a daughter, I'll let her climb in my lap as much as she damned well wants. Thanks for the tip." He would let her mother climb in his lap as much as she wanted, too. His heart clenched at the thought of having them both in his lap at once, Summer holding a black-haired baby, and him holding them both.

Sam Corey sent him a hard look. "You think you can do better?"

"I always think I can do better. And so far, I've always been right."

Sam Corey grunted. "You know, from one arrogant SOB to another, I almost—'like' is not the word."

"Good. I don't want you to like me."

The blue eyes glittered, so much harder than his daughter's, so much tougher. "That's a first. A man who would rather have my daughter like him than me."

That took considerable time for Luc to wrap his mind around. *"Putain,"* he said finally. "That's a *first*? Are you sure? She's beautiful."

"Do you even know what a billion dollars is?"

Luc tried briefly to imagine it and not very hard. He had a lot of other things occupying his head right now. "Not really. I could probably figure out how many zeros are involved if I felt like it, though."

One of the world's richest self-made men gave a crack of incredulous laughter.

Luc shrugged. "That's the thing about zeros. If you don't have any, they're all that matters. But once the string of them gets long enough, they're boring."

"Oh, for God's sake," Sam Corey said. "Why does she *do* this shit to me?"

"I'm seriously the first man who ever thought your daughter was more important than your money? That's insane. And you want her to *marry* someone like that? Why do you hate her so much?"

Sam Corey stiffened. "I don't hate her! What the hell has she been telling you? She's my daughter. I love that girl. That doesn't mean I want her to do any screwed-up thing that crosses her brain, though. And *somebody* has got to take care of this holding company after me, and it sure as hell won't be you."

"That's right, it won't," Luc said, revolted. "Find a fucking CEO or whatever it is in your business."

"Somebody has to keep an eye on the CEO afterward! And it's not going to be a girl who wants to spend her life swinging in a hammock!"

"Then get better board members, *merde*," Luc said, bored. "Surely you don't need me to tell you how to solve your business problems. If you do, may I suggest a serious shake-up in your management team?"

Sam Corey glared at him, livid. "You know, it's not going to work out as well as you think. That girl needs a lot of attention."

"I'm very focused."

"Yeah? And when you've got a crazy day ahead of you,

and so many things to do and decisions to make that you barely have time to breathe, and she's pouting because you won't drop it all for her, what are you going to do?"

"I think that's something for me to talk about with her, not with you. She doesn't pout, by the way. I've never seen it once. I guess you broke her of that a long time ago, made her put on a smile instead."

Sam Corey bared his teeth. "Don't you *tell me* all the things I did wrong with my daughter."

"I'll tell you whatever I want. And unless you want to hire an assassin with all that money of yours, there's not a damn thing you can do to stop me."

Sam grunted. "Don't tempt me."

"You should let her go, you know. Quit trying to butcher her into your idea of perfection just to show her off to the world. Set her free. And by the way, she doesn't laze around in a hammock. She teaches school on a remote island to kids who would otherwise have to be shipped off to boarding school on another island, away from their parents, to get an education. You ever wonder why keeping them with their parents might be so important to her?"

"Boarding school would probably do them a world of good," Sam Corey said roughly. "What's she educating them for? So *they* can grow up and laze in hammocks?"

"You know when I said I didn't want you to like me? I was understating the case. You couldn't insult me worse." Luc strode to the door.

"I don't even know what she sees in you," Sam Corey said, disgusted. "It's not all those pretty desserts of yours, is it? I thought I wore that one out on her when she was a kid. It was about the only way you could get her to behave at the dinner table instead of fidgeting and causing trouble all night, taking away her dessert. But she's got more steel in her than you realize, from the outside. Got to the point where you couldn't hold even that over her head anymore, she refused to care. Of course, by that time, she had learned how to behave herself, so I guess it worked over all."

Luc went stiff with shock and fury. He pivoted, like a whip cracking. "You *bastard*."

The older man's eyebrows went up. "I thought I told you not to tempt me."

"*You* were the one who stole that from me. You fucking *asshole*."

Sam Corey looked supercilious. "For someone who's supposed to be so controlled—"

"I'm controlled. You have no idea how controlled I'm being. You held them over her head, didn't you? You *punished her* for what? Not behaving up to your standards?"

"Well, what the hell did you want me to do instead?" her father asked, exasperated. "Spank her? Let her get away with whatever she wanted? Tell you what, once you've finished raising your own kids, let's have this talk again."

Luc closed his eyes suddenly. "*Putain,*" he murmured. "What a crappy grandfather my kids are going to have."

"Are you *kidding* me?" Sam Corey demanded, outraged. "You're thinking of giving your kids *me* as a grandfather, and you're *complaining*?"

Luc gave him his daughter's very own glimmering smile. "I guess I'm just spoiled."

Sam Corey's mouth shut into a thin line. He glared with a fury he clearly thought Luc should fear. Luc smiled back at him urbanely. *Go ahead, do your worst. You have no power over me.*

The door opened, revealing Summer and her mother, and the quickest dress change Summer might have ever made.

Sam Corey gave Luc a thin, hungry smile. "Summer, you'll be happy to know your latest boyfriend has been arguing your case. It's a stupid man who doesn't take good advice, and he's right. I should set you free. So I'll invest in that satellite, since it means so much to you. You don't have to stay here anymore. Just go on back to where you're happy."

CHAPTER 34

et her free. You should let her go. Neither Luc nor Summer spoke until they were inside Summer's suite. Luc was still ringing with the shock of her father's announcement.

You bastard. The cuddles in the afternoon, the time, the attention, the things she needs—*she hasn't seen I can give them to her yet. I'm still* practicing. *This isn't as good as I can get for her.*

Of course those damned photos were scrolling, picture proof of how much happier Summer could be somewhere else. Summer's gaze fell on them as soon as she stepped past the entry, and her face filled with wistfulness.

Luc wanted to break something, to pound things in impotent rage, the way he had when he had first been wrested from his father. *He had had ten more weeks, damn it!* Ten weeks to show her how magical Paris could be with someone's hand tucked in yours. Ten weeks to let her confidence unfurl, as she worked with her cousins, as she found her own strength here. Ten weeks to get over his mistakes, to show her how perfect he could be once he learned what she needed.

Ten weeks to soak up all that sweetness, to get over the shaky sugar-shock reaction to it that made him so difficult and touchy, to learn to absorb it.

It's Paris, damn it! Not hell! Do you know how hard I worked to make this city love me?

That bastard Sam Corey. Who would sacrifice anything, even his daughter, to prove he could always find a way to have power over someone.

"It's so warm there," Summer said. "And they really do need me." The photo of the kids tumbling over her scrolled across the screen.

They need you? One long, wicked claw raked across him. *How could you? How could you long for that? How could you want it more than you want me?*

And, deep down, a keening, desperate child's cry: *I knew she couldn't love me enough to hold on.*

"Summer. You're not going?"

Summer looked back and forth between him and the photos.

He fought to breathe. He had practiced this for twenty years of his life, having the most beautiful thing in his hands and letting it go. To disappear in a few forkfuls.

But I love you! That desperate plea. *You can't leave me because I love you!* He was supposed to have gotten bigger than that, better than that, more in control.

He had just desperately wanted her to be that one thing he could hold on to.

You should set her free. Why had he ever said that? *Let her go where she's happy. Let her go where she feels needed. Don't drag her into your world just so she has to depend on you. Just so she turns toward you like a flower to the sun because you're the only source of happiness she has.*

Don't do that to her. Be bigger than that.

That sobbing ball of misery he had held in his arms. *Don't force her to face that every second of every day, for you. When she could be* happy.

Even your own father, as bad as he was, knew in the end when to let you go.

"Go." He felt like he was dying. But he didn't think she could tell. No, he still had that much control in him. Not to show his mortal wounds.

Summer looked at him as if he had tossed her a float when she was drowning. "What?"

Or was that look as if he had struck her?

"You need to go back." He—what he needed to do, he still had to figure out. *Wait!* A tiny voice of new knowledge yelled somewhere deep in him, trying to be heard past the belief of two decades. *No, you're wrong about that! Papa didn't just let you go! And what the fuck does it matter what he did? He was screwed up! Figure out what you should do. For her.*

Summer had gone very still. On the screen, a photo scrolled by of her laughing up at some black-haired grinning giant of a man, probably a hundred pounds heavier than Luc and only some of it muscle, but jealousy and hatred hit him anyway. Was it someone like that who would make her happy?

Undemanding, easy. Raised in some happy family and knowing when to hug her, knowing when something he said would hurt her. Not needing to practice.

"You can't stay here," he said and realized it was really true. She couldn't. This place killed her. She had found her own warmth and happiness and *nobody,* not even he, should steal that from her. "I want you to go back to your island."

She rocked a little, as if he had hit her. "But I thought—"

"It's all right, Summer." He could barely speak. He had no breath in him to speak with. But he locked the pain in, used all those years of fighting through humiliation and hunger and longing in the Métro. Locked it hard. So no one could see. "I'm strong. Don't worry about me."

Her tan turned pasty, all light drained from it. Yes, he had torn her. She wouldn't leave him easily. But she would leave him, just the same. "But who will—" She broke off. "Will you *eat?*"

She should just go. Now. He couldn't stand this. "Summer, I can take care of myself." *But I loved being taken care of.*

She looked stunned, confused. She scrubbed a hand over her face, and then folded her arms around herself. "Your—your shoulders get so tight. Don't you nee—"

If she finished that sentence with "need me," he might crack into a million pieces again. And this time, he didn't think bits of him would be floating out happily to the edge of the universe. "The hotel has an excellent spa, Summer."

"Oh." She rocked back. If she mentioned next what he had told her in the bathtub, that he needed her body yielding to his, he would break one of these fucking art deco chairs.

But she didn't. Her face emptied out. The torn look was gone, leaving . . . nothing.

And then she smiled at him. Warm, generous, blind, pat-him-on-the-head. "Oh, all right, then. Well . . . if you ever want a vacation in the tropics, I guess—"

It was the smile that did it. After everything, after he had danced his hardest, poured everything there was of him out for her. Because it shredded him. Because, wild, he wanted to shred her in return. He had to leave before he could. Or maybe because he knew that leaving was the very thing that would hurt her the worst. He turned around and walked out.

To his job.

To the city he had made love him.

To what he could control.

This city doesn't love you, you fool. This city eats you. It's not the same thing.

CHAPTER 35

Summer left the hotel numb. In the early hours of a cold, crisp day, the sun shining down on the seventeenth-century palace façade. She didn't tell her parents what she had decided, and she didn't even tell the hotel director. She could send him a text from the airport. One of the hotel limousines pulled up, a car into whose depths she could sink, no need for any kind of contact, or anything to pull her out of the blank, white pain.

Two of the doormen were herding another man back, glancing at her. Only when she was halfway in the limo did she look back at him, one last second of delay, for Luc to come running out of the hotel and grab her, saying no, he was out of his mind, he did need her, he did.

But Luc was working, and even though the hotel gossip had to have alerted him to her departure, he didn't appear. Summer fought the urge to crumple to her knees, half-hidden by the limousine door, clutching herself. She had to get out of here. To where people couldn't hurt her this much.

The man being herded back by the two doormen met her eyes, briefly, his so dark and glitteringly intense, revealing a stubborn passion in an aged, defiantly un-humble face. Straight shoulders and a bitter blankness to his expression, and a sullen, angry set to his jaw. Worn, worn clothes, worn, old lines around his eyes.

"You could at least tell him," the man said hostilely. "Tell him 'Marko.' At least ask."

Summer straightened slowly and came away from the limousine. "Tell who?"

One of the doormen shifted to put his body between her and "Marko" as if the man was a threat. "It's just one of the gypsies, mademoiselle. Please."

She shifted aside. "Tell who?"

"Monsieur Leroi," the other doorman told her, low, and shook his head.

Summer felt a shock right through her heart, as if that heart was someone else's. She slipped between the doormen up to the dark-eyed man, her hand going out instinctively to his arm. He looked at it as if it was a whip. Those same wary shields, those same intense eyes, only muted. This man had none of the perfection of Luc's shields, of Luc's intensity.

She took a deep breath that cut through her and turned. "Please go tell Monsieur Leroi that I asked if he could—" What could she say that would protect his privacy? That wouldn't headline to the whole hotel that his father was here? But that wouldn't leave him unwarned, either? "Please just tell him what this man asked, that there is a Marko who is here to see him. Monsieur—" She touched the man's arm again, but very lightly, catching herself at the last second. "If you would please wait for him inside."

She led him into one of their smaller conference rooms, saw the man's eyes as he took in its opulence of gold and marble and burnished wood tables. Shock, hunger, envy, greed, resentment . . . hunger. Maybe even a confused, stunned pride.

Her heart hurt her so terribly it could not possibly be hers. Somehow Luc's had gotten into her body in its place.

She was hurting in anticipation for him, so much she could almost forget how easily he had reduced her to— nothing. Nothing he could need.

Luc got there so fast. She met him outside the door to the conference room, and his eyes caught hers, so black they could have been soaking up the last ray of light in the world. She felt nearly extinguished. And yet, as it had in the past, her own sense of herself flickered stronger under that gaze. He was in his chef's clothes, a streak down one cheek, another on the front of his jacket, and even though it was only nine in the morning, he had clearly been working himself into a sweat for hours, the dark hair damp on his temples.

When he saw her, even though he must have expected her after the message, he rocked back on his feet, his face growing even starker.

"I think it might be your father," Summer said, and he grabbed both her shoulders, his hands digging in harder and harder, his eyes closed. She tried not to wince under the pain of the grip, and all at once it relaxed, and he rubbed where his hands had tightened, his eyes still closed tight.

She reached up to cover his hands with hers, and he flinched and yanked them back, eyes opening at last. Her hands fell limply back to her sides. "Are you going to be all right?"

Something whipped across his face and was gone. "I'll be fine," he said, so neutral he might have been sanded into nonexistence. "I'm strong. Don't worry about me."

"No," she agreed, low. "No, of course not."

He looked across the lobby at the great glass doors of the hotel and the limousine. "You were leaving?"

His voice was so even, she felt flogged. She didn't answer.

He took a breath and straightened his shoulders. "Good,"

he said, and her tummy flinched as if he had knifed it. "You should go."

Even with the knife in her stomach, she looked from him to the closed door and what waited for him beyond it. "You don't—you don't nee—"

"No," he said quickly. "I don't need you to deal with my own father, Summer. I'll be fine."

She took a step back. He closed his hand on the door-knob. They stared at each other. And then, in unison, they both turned sharply away. Luc went into the conference room and closed the door. And Summer climbed into her limo and rode away.

CHAPTER 36

Summer sat in the little house and sank into its scents of coconut and sea, and the leis of white star tiare flowers with which the islanders had loaded her neck, and the sound of the geckos running across her ceiling, chattering. All the tension relaxed out of her.

To be back in a place where people needed her. Really needed her. Not just for stupid things that they could replace with restaurants or spas. Everyone here had been thrilled to see her back early. The mountain of leis that had risen to her forehead now draped the length of low concrete that was all that passed for a bedroom wall here. Only her substitute had not been overjoyed to have her stay on the island cut short.

Summer, though, relaxed infinitely as the children piled all over her, full of excited stories of the things they had been doing with "Miss Kelly," what the replacement hadn't known and they had had to teach her, a fun new game Kelly had invented. Maybe it pricked her a little, to realize that if she had stayed away, Kelly could have taken her place permanently and served these children well, too. But the kids hugged her so hard, so glad to have her back. Summer blossomed into their welcome, lighting up as parents kissed her cheeks over and over, as a lei fell over her head, as someone showed up to bring her food. She re-laxed into that need and love for her until, when night fell and everyone was back in their homes, she started to cry.

She could not stop. For days. She walked on the beach, and thought how desperately Luc needed to have some-one take him for a stroll on the sand. And she sobbed.

She gripped a coconut palm, and the palm bark felt nothing like his skin. And thought how Luc needed to do something crazy and ridiculous, like learn to climb a co-conut palm. And she sobbed.

She co-taught with Kelly, and thought she had pulled herself together, happily centered helping her kids again. And then she got home, and no one was lying in the ham-mock to smile at her, and she burst into tears again.

She ate the most delicious mangoes in the world. And thought of a human being so brave he could take raw ingredients—stupid things like sugar and leaves and flour—and create something God would envy. That no man had ever created before. He was like—he was like Ta'aroa, the island god of creation, in his shell in the mid-dle of Nothingness, opening that shell and crying out into the Nothing, forcing beautiful things into existence with his will alone.

Because he—

—needed people. That was the story of Ta'aroa. He had felt so lonely, he had willed the world into existence.

She drew patterns in the sand and thought of Luc mak-ing something so extraordinary, every day even better, that would be eaten in minutes. Everything into which he poured his life was fleeting. For someone else's brief, in-tense pleasure.

Why, he was just a man, she realized. All this time, she had been treating him as if he was inherently above her, as if something deep down gave him that godlike status her father had had when she was a child. But he was just—a man. It was the most extraordinary thing about him.

She stared down at her drawing in the sand—the Eiffel Tower. Deep-drawn and stark, stamping the beach. A big wave hit the reef, and its ripple across the lagoon climbed up past her toes. Leaving behind only a soft, gleaming trace of that tower, a humbled memory of her past.

She gave the ocean a thoughtful look and a high five. And suddenly she laughed, on a surging sense of rightness. *Fuck you,* she thought gaily to the Eiffel Tower. *You're not beating me out of this one.*

And she got up, found Kelly, who was thrilled to stay on, and headed back to Paris.

"It's about time you got back," Patrick said coldly, plates spreading out from his hands like a magician's cards, and Summer stopped short. Every single person on the pastry team was glaring at her, and her first reaction was to curl in on herself, to hide behind an insouciant smile. People *always* hated her in Paris, damn it.

She took a deep breath and forced her chin up. "Where's Luc?"

"What is this, some kind of game to you?" Patrick snapped. "You waltz in and out with those kissy lips whenever you please, and tough *shit* for what it does to the person you're playing with?"

It had taken her seven days to get here. Communications had been out again, and though fortunately no child had been sick and in desperate need of a doctor this time, there had also been no way to call in a seaplane. There were a lot of black moments, when the words "I don't need you, go" rang and rang in her head, in seven days. The stars overhead when she curled up on the deck of the cargo boat in the middle of the South Pacific were an incredible boost to courage, though. But now *Patrick,* the laughing, sweet one, was lashing her.

Summer braced her feet, fisted her hands, and crossed her arms. "You cannot talk to me like that." No smile.

"What, *now* you're going to fire me? *Finally?* What are you trying to do, completely destroy him? Now he *needs* me. I can't walk out on him *now.*"

Summer slapped her hands down on the marble. "Tell me where Luc is before I *smack* you."

"You know, if I ever want financing for my own place, all I have to do is threaten a lawsuit, at this rate. Where the hell do you think he is?"

"At home?" Brooding in his apartment? Unable to force himself to work without her?

"He's halfway across the Pacific. Actually, I hope he's made it to your godforsaken island by now, because otherwise he's been captured by pirates."

Summer's hands fell limp to her sides. She stared at him.

"Summer." The anger faded out of Patrick's voice, and for the first time since she had met him, it went quite serious. "Have you made up your mind this time? You can't leave him again."

"He told me to—"

"He's screwed up! Just because *he* thinks he has made himself absolutely perfect doesn't mean you have to fall for that. You can't always listen to what he says, Summer. Sometimes you have to be stronger than that."

Past Patrick, the intern turned her black head and looked at him, her eyebrows drawing together into a tiny crease.

"But—now what do I do?" Summer opened and closed her hands in restless fists. "Do you think he'll come back when he sees I'm gone? I don't have any way to get in touch with him out there."

"Look, you're the one who decided to isolate yourself on an island with half-assed communications. I guess you can figure out how to deal with that the same way everyone else you knew had to."

CHAPTER 37

Summer's footsteps slowed as she approached her little house. Well, that explained why no one had noticed the seaplane coming in, an oversight unheard of in their remote island life. Everyone on the island was gathered around her picnic table, laughing and talking. In fact, two more picnic tables had been carried in and set up to form one long table. On it were spread several hundred éclair shells, unglazed. Children bounced on their toes around the table, parents trying to keep them from touching.

Luc came out of her house, carrying a red plastic bowl she normally used to serve potato chips at their little school events. He set it on the picnic bench, awkwardly low for chef's work, and filled a pastry bag with the chocolate cream in the bowl. His face revealed his concentration, that purified focus. He could have been in his own three-star kitchen. Except that when little Vanina grabbed at his wrist, he blinked in surprise, looked down, and gave her an astonishingly sweet smile.

Then Vanina spotted Summer and let out a squeal of delight, and all the children dove for her, wrapping their arms around her legs and waist as she tried to hug them all. One of the big fathers nearby tried to catch her shoulder and help her stay upright, but another child hit the increasing mass, and her feet tangled with someone, and she went down onto her butt in the sand, kids piling all over her.

When her face reemerged from the hugs, Luc was squatting on the other side of the kids, watching her gravely. His feet were bare, that white shirt he liked was unbuttoned halfway down his chest, the sleeves rolled up to his biceps, and his Dior jeans were now cutoffs. The whole vision was surreal. "Why didn't you come *back?*" Summer said. "I've been waiting for you for days! Finally, I got hold of Kelly, and she said you looked really good in a hammock and for me to stay the hell in Paris this time!"

"I'm not sure I'm suited to a hammock," Luc said. "Maybe it would feel different with company. I've mostly been walking along the beach and swimming, and your neighbors invited me to a couple of cookouts where your kids did a dance performance for me. They said it was one they choreographed all by themselves as a school project for you, about Ta'aroa, the creator god. And then I decided to test the effects of this much humidity on pastries, and the effects are terrible. But people seem to enjoy them anyway." He stretched his hands across the slowly calming children and picked her straight up with him as he stood, swinging her free as the children laughed and caught at her. "You know my world. I wanted to see yours," he said. And kissed her, fiercely, his hands locking in her hair until the roots stung. "Thank you," he whispered, "for going back for me."

She grabbed on to *his* hair and gripped *it* until it must have stung, kissing him back so hard she almost bit him. "Why did you tell me to go if you didn't want me to go? That hurt!"

"Because I thought I could be a better person than to trap you in your own personal hell, if you wanted so badly to get back to paradise. I was wrong. I'm not that good a person. Twenty damn years of working on it, and I'm still that same desperate kid." He loosed her hair abruptly and dragged her back over to the picnic tables. "I'm sorry, Summer, but it's so fucking hot here it's about to ruin the cream. Oh, *pardon,*" he said absently to the little kids. "I grew up in kitchens, mostly. I have nearly as foul a mouth as your teacher by now."

Summer gave him a reproachful look. "They don't know I have a foul mouth," she muttered. "*I* can pretend."

"Yes, let's talk a little bit more about your ability to pretend once I get these people served. You didn't have to fucking smile at me when you walked out, Summer. Why don't we make a deal that you'll only smile at me from now on if you mean it?"

"Sure, just as soon as we can make a deal that you never hide what you're really feeling, either. I'm not going to start second-guessing when I smile, Luc." Along with everything else she second-guessed. She watched, fascinated, as he picked up the pastry bag again, and realized abruptly that it was a Ziploc bag with a corner cut off as an approximation of a pastry bag. "What did you do for a tip?"

He angled it to show the wood. "Some of the boys carved a few different sizes and shapes for me."

"Me!" Moea shouted happily. "I made that one!"

Summer grinned at the twelve-year-old and gave him a thumbs-up. "Where did you get all the *ingredients*?"

Luc shrugged. "Once I said what I would need, people kept bringing things." He lowered his voice for her ears alone. "The eggs are nice and fresh, heritage local, but please don't get me started on the damn candy bars I had to break up for the chocolate. I think they've been melting and hardening in people's cupboards for years, and they were a very cheap brand to begin with. I even had to melt down Corey Bars, Summer. *Pour l'amour de Dieu.*"

Summer grinned and patted the nape of his neck because she just had to touch him. "Poor baby."

He held up a stoic hand. "It's okay, Summer. You could have warned me, so I could have packed properly, but I'll survive." He squeezed cream stuffing into the éclairs at lightning speed.

The children danced around him excitedly, and adult members of the audience gave impressed murmurs. One of the teenage girls, to whom Summer had lent her camera at her departure, started clicking away. That shot was definitely going into Summer's collection, the elegant, perfect, world-famous *pâtissier* making éclairs for hundreds on picnic tables under the coconut palms.

"I love you," she murmured, uncontrollably.

He stilled a fraction of a second, his eyes closing. "God, I've missed hearing that." His hands flew on. It would have taken Summer hours to try to fill so many éclairs, and there would have been a mess everywhere. It took him a few minutes, and despite his tools, not a blob of cream fell out of place or burst through the shell of an éclair. "I love you, too, Summer," he whispered suddenly, in the midst of it, as if he finally remembered she might need to hear it, too, and gave her a hard, fierce kiss that barely interrupted the flow of his hands.

He apparently already had some of the teenagers apprenticed, because they ran into Summer's house whenever he started to run low on cream in the too-small bowl and brought out a replacement from, she supposed, her refrigerator. The electricity was presumably working. When he was done stuffing, he handed the bowls and what was left in the bag to the kids to eat and disappeared into the house himself, returning with a big pan of chocolate *glaçage*. An expression of acute pain crossed his face as he started to spread the icing on top of the éclairs.

"Are you all right?" Summer asked.

"The surface is *matte*! You can't even see yourself in it. You have *no* proper ingredients or equipment."

"It's still going to be the best thing anyone here ever tasted, you know," she murmured, looking around at the happy faces of the islanders. Nobody like Luc had ever popped into their lives before. And while a couple of them might possibly have been exposed to French pastries on trips to larger islands, most of them could never have had an éclair.

"Thank you," Luc said dryly. "You relieve my mind."

Summer burst out laughing and wrapped her arms around him from behind in a hug that smeared icing all over the edge of the pan. He stopped work just long enough to catch one of her hands from his chest, lift it to his mouth, and kiss the palm very hard.

The delight in the éclairs was so extreme that the children begged him to make another batch right away, begged so hard that he might very well have done so if the ingredients were available. Instead, everyone threw together a great barbecue, shifting the center of operations to the neighbor with the best grilling equipment, a few houses down the beach. It was close to midnight before they could slip away, some of the islanders nudging each other and grinning after them, others—mostly the younger, single ones, including Kelly—looking rather hostile.

The waves washed in, the gentle glow of tropical moonlight tranquilly beautiful. Cool, damp sand shifted, a gentle, reassuring massage into bare toes. "Jeannine said it was the worst mistake I could have made, to tell you I didn't need you," Luc said, almost as quiet as the waves, his hand locked tight around hers. "She said that was probably what you needed more than anything else, someone who needed you and wouldn't let you go."

Like you, Summer thought, looking up at his profile against the Southern Cross and the moonlit sea. *That's what you need most, too.* She had wanted to see him walking on the beach with her forever. Before she even knew him, she had wanted it. "You talked about me to Jeannine?"

"I had to talk to someone, Summer. And I've always wanted a grandmother." Luc fished in his pocket and pulled out a linen square. "She gave me this."

One of his Valentine linens. Unlike Jeannine's, this one was pathetically hemmed, and the black embroidery of his name was a hopeless choppy mess. She had tried to do it right after he told her he kept his toys forever, and she had abandoned it, stained with several drops of her blood, when she had heard him coming.

"I was bored," she said defensively. "I thought maybe I could learn how to embroider."

Luc's thumb traced over the three red drops of blood, scattered across the white linen and his black name, mangled by her unpracticed hand. "It's a better present than a Bugatti," he said quietly, and suddenly turned, crushing it between their palms, kissing her and kissing her. "I need you," he muttered roughly into her mouth. "I need you. All right? God, how I need you." He tumbled them onto the beach, half-sheltered by the outrigger canoe Summer's next-door neighbor kept pulled up there midway between their houses. "And I've always wanted to make love to you in the sand," he whispered fiercely. "And wash you off in the waves afterward."

So he did. They made love with a desperate tenderness, gasping, clutching, stroking, hungry. And much later, Summer dragged him to her hammock and pushed him down on it.

"Your house doesn't even have *walls,*" he muttered,

"and you sleep on a mattress on a concrete floor. Summer, there's so much more to you than you let people in Paris see, and I am *going* to taste every single layer of you."

"I can't believe you let Kelly see you in a hammock before I did. That was *my* dream."

"I've barely spent five minutes in a hammock since I got here, but it's not my fault if Kelly has been spying on me. This place is one giant fishbowl. I never realized that busy Métros and kitchens are actually fairly private places compared to a small island where everyone has plenty of time to investigate everyone else's affairs."

"Five minutes? You need to learn how to relax, Luc."

"Well, come teach me," he said and pulled her down on top of him. "Ah," a sigh as her weight settled on him, and that chronic tension released out of his body like a loosed rubber band. "That does make it much better." He rocked them gently for a while, sinking into the moment. "Isn't it Valentine's Day?"

"I think so." Summer tried to count, making allowances for the international dateline. "Patrick said to tell you that he has taken your extended leave as a sign you wanted him to do his own Valentine's menu."

Luc stiffened. "That's a joke, right?"

Summer hesitated. "It can be a little hard to tell with Patrick, but I don't *think* so. He had his own sketches spread out all around him when he told me. He promised he wouldn't waste Jeannine's linens, though."

"Putain." Luc started to surge off the hammock. Stopped halfway. And sank slowly back down into it, muscles relaxing again as he snuggled Summer back into her spot. "I can't really do anything about it right now, can I? You should have seen what I was going to do at the restaurant on Valentine's Day for you. It would have—" He caught himself, clearly dying to describe it. "I'll have to do

it next year. Or maybe when I propo—" He caught himself again.

"I liked having one of the world's best pastry chefs travel by air and boat to a remote location to make éclairs on a picnic table with hand-carved tips for my entire adopted family," Summer said. "That worked as a Valentine's Day present for me." She thought she was speaking lightly, and then right at the last, her voice choked up suddenly, her nostrils stinging, and she clutched at him.

He squeezed her gently in return. And said, " 'One of'?"

So she laughed, even as the laughter knocked one tear out onto his chest. "I love you," she whispered.

He squeezed her again, his finger drawing great hearts over and over on her back. She wasn't even sure he was aware he was doing it.

"Did you know I've never even had an éclair before?"

"I hate your parents. At least my father couldn't afford them. And much, much better éclairs await you in your future. Summer. These stars are incredible. I lied about the hammock. Around one every night, I've been lying here, looking at those stars and thinking of you. I'm so proud of our three at the Leucé, and you have millions."

"Yes," Summer said wistfully, turning so that she could look up at them, her head resting on his shoulder. She was going to miss those stars.

"You're never alone here, are you?"

She shook her head against his chest. One giant fishbowl. "I can take out a canoe or go for a long hike or swim. I can be alone if I really, really want to."

"Which happens . . . never, at a guess."

"No, once in a while," she protested. "I got used to it, you know. Being alone."

His hands wove through her hair. "It's funny, I was never alone. But I think I got used to it, too."

"Oh, Luc." She pressed a kiss into his bare shoulder.

"I want you to be happy, Summer. I thought I knew how to let things go." His arms tightened around her. "I guess, in the end, I'm still too much like my own father. Do you know he came back year after year to try to make contact with me again? That he got arrested twice? And until a week ago, I thought he just . . . let me go." Tension flexed through his whole body. "I thought maybe that was what you had to do sometimes, for people you loved. Accept that you were bad for them."

She wrapped her arms around him and held on tight. His own arms closed around her convulsively. "I'm so glad you're here," he whispered.

"How did it go? With your—father?"

Luc grabbed fistfuls of her hair and used it to cover his face. "It was horrible. Coming right after you—" He broke off and shook his head. "Do you know how hard I've worked not to get ripped apart that way anymore? It was horrible. And I'm already giving him money, and he's already feeling threatened by my success, I can see it. When I marry you, it's going to explode his head. Unless you can get your father to disown you, maybe. That might help."

Summer blinked at the word "marry," but Luc didn't even seem to realize what he had just said.

"It would have been so much easier to leave him out of my life. But—he did come after me. *Tu sais?* He never forgot me. And I think he's proud of me, too, and just as torn up as I am. And"—could the moonlight off the ocean possibly be catching moisture in his eyes?—"I really needed you after that meeting, Summer. I really. Really. Really. Needed you." His arms squeezed her too tight. "You ate the damn pomegranate seeds. You ate my *heart.* You weren't supposed to still want to go."

"I *didn't* want to go. I was thinking how much I would miss this place and that it was going to be so sad to say good-bye to everyone here. And then you started in about how you didn't *need* me. And what is this about pomegranate seeds? You're not Hades, Luc."

His mouth twisted. "I did try to tell you that."

"I think the Fairy King was closer. But mostly—mostly you're just a man."

One eyebrow went up. His mouth was very bittersweet, wry. "Never say so."

"That's what makes it so incredible. What you do. You're just a man. A human mortal *man*. And you do— what you do."

There was a long silence. *"Merci, soleil,"* he said softly. "After all those people who call me a god, I never realized you could give me a promotion."

Again, a long silence fell, peace stretching, as they unconsciously let the hammock swing to the rhythm of the waves.

"I had an idea," he said. "That isn't a choice between here and Paris. That has more sunshine in it for you."

She traced a hand between the panels of his shirt, left open when he pulled it back on after they got out of the waves. He had such a lean, gorgeous body.

"The south of France. A nice old stone house and a garden. Maybe bordering on a lavender field. Or maybe an old house in one of the old hill towns, with a little courtyard for our garden, so it would be close to the restaurant. We would have to look around, see what house we fall in love with. Maybe you can help me with the business plan, since I've never had to do one, and you're so good at asking all the right questions. One of the first chefs I worked under did that, Gabriel Delange. He was *chef pâtissier* at the Luxe, and the chef there, Pierre Manon, fired him in a fit of jealousy at how much attention he was stealing. So he opened his own place in a little hill town near Grasse. He got his third star three years ago. He did so much for his little town's tourism, they built a fountain to him." Luc gave that tiny, contained grin of his and admitted: "I wouldn't mind having a fountain built to me. And"—his voice got all funny again—"I have a really powerful vision of you with four black-haired kids in lavender fields." He took a deep breath and watched her.

She got all funny. As if her whole being had disappeared into a burst of butterflies, fluttering upward, outward. It felt dizzying and tickling and terrifying and lovely. *"Oh,"* she said very low and hard. A breath. Another breath. Butterflies were dancing in starlight. "Would you be watching us from a wooden swing under a grape arbor?"

Their eyes held, one of those moments when they realized that, despite all the surface differences, their souls were exactly matched. "That's what I imagined at first. Especially if it's been a hard day and I just want to watch you for a while and feel happy. But now I think I'll want to get up and play with the five of you."

"F-four kids?"

A little shrug under her body. "I don't know. That's just how many I see."

Summer's tummy could not whirl more. She squeezed her arms around him again, because she had to squeeze onto something for stability. She could see this, too. It felt so *happy,* as if they could patch together their two love-starved childhoods and make one whole family so full of love it was overflowing.

"You might have to help me. I don't really know how to play, except with food. Do you think you could help me with the restaurant accounting, too? Or at least help find someone good we can pay to do it. I hate to make you, but I do not have a summa cum laude from Harvard in economics, and I loathe doing it."

"This is a really beautiful vision," Summer whispered.

She could barely speak. Butterflies made out of starlight couldn't speak. "One where I'm—an important part of it."

"Oh, *soleil*." His arms tightened hard around her. "To make a happy family? You're *crucial*. You're the one who figured out how to do that, all on your own, while I was just figuring out how to be the most important man in the room. I wonder how many years of living happily ever after in lavender fields we're going to need before we trust each other's role in it. I'll try to trust that you can stay with me, if you can try to trust that I will value you."

"This is good practice," she whispered into his chest. Scent trailed over them, with the breeze—sea and salt, and the gardenia plant growing by her bedroom half-wall.

He curved a hand over her shoulder, seeming entirely content to dust grains of sand off her skin, one by one. "Yes. It is." They swayed for a while in silence. "I know it will be a wrench for you to give this up. I know it will break your heart. I just—do you think it's possible it might break your heart to make it *wider*? So you can move on to your next thing in life? You don't have to abandon this world entirely. I would love to come back here for a month every year on vacation, and you could teach me to relax. But I know you're probably worried about the school year, about who will take as good care of your kids as you."

"I thought I could start up a grant," she said, and his arms flexed around her. "A teaching assistant fellowship for new graduates. You would be surprised how many bright, enthusiastic people in their senior years at top universities dream of just one year of adventure before they continue their competitive lives. And if I word the fellowship right, and make it properly competitive, this is one they could put on their CVs to show future employers how amazing they are."

Luc wrapped her hair around his wrist enough to nudge her head up off his chest. "Summer. How can you see how amazing that would be on someone else's life experience, but not insist people see it as just as amazing when you do it?"

She shrugged, instinctively self-deprecating.

"*Soleil.* I need you more than you can manage to understand yet, but I was right, what I thought that first moment I saw you. You need me, too. I'm not going to put up with you belittling yourself this way, or with anyone else doing it for you."

"You used to do it yourself."

"*One time,* Summer. I had just handed you my heart and watched you pass it on to some other woman because you didn't care for it."

" 'Higher standards?' "

"Oh, for—higher standards than to be your casual pastime, Summer. Not higher standards than *you.* It wouldn't be possible."

Her heart sparked with joy.

"It wouldn't," he repeated, tightening his hold on her waist. Again they rocked in silence for a moment. "So . . . your grant idea suggests . . . you've given this some serious consideration."

She took a tight breath, a band constricting and releasing her heart, in a rhythm past her control, so that she had to grab for air whenever she could. "You don't have to give Paris up for me. As long as we find an apartment with a fireplace, I'll be *fine.*"

That compressed grin of his that she had come to realize meant so much laughter and happiness was welling in him that he didn't know what to do with it. "Summer, sometimes you have to let go of your past."

"I know." She peeked past the edge of the hammock to give the ocean a firm nod. "I'm going to sit on the Champ de Mars and watch fireworks go off all around the Eiffel Tower and thumb my nose. Uh—you'll be sitting with me, right? You don't have to work Bastille Day?"

He laughed, a deep almost sleepy sound. "I mean me. I want to let go of my past. I don't want to spend my life striving not to be that kid in the Métro. I *like* that kid in the Métro. He won a princess, didn't he? And I'm getting attached to the idea of sunshine and lavender and having a garden I can relax in with my family."

Summer's happiness just grew and grew. "If we go to the south of France, maybe we could still take on some of Jaime's and Cade's interns and apprentices."

"What?"

She explained.

"You said I would be good at that?" He searched her face.

She nodded firmly.

"I'm sure I could be persuaded," he said ruefully, stretching her hair out in a pattern along the ropes of the hammock. "If you want me to do it."

"Maybe we could even take one of the kids from here. If there was someone really interested in it. Dying to see the rest of the world. Or maybe they could just come visit."

"I'm going to end up like my foster father," Luc said with an odd smile, alarmed and intrigued. "All those foster kids and apprentices."

Her hands closed over his palms. "Without the hot paraffin."

He shook his head, but his fingers linked with hers and pressed them gently. "Nobody uses hot paraffin anymore anyway, Summer. And my foster mother was . . . very rigid. Not like you at all. You would bring . . . warmth." He cradled her hands against his face, in what seemed retroactive longing to have had that warmth for himself.

"He's a good man, you know," he said softly. "He tried to do his best by us. It's strange to think that you might help me to become an even better one." He said that in a low rush, like a caterpillar claiming to believe in butterflies.

"I love you," she said, and his face split into a smile.

"It just pours out of you, doesn't it?" he said wonderingly. "I should have wrapped myself up with you that first night and never let you go. You might trust me now if I had. What an oversensitive, overcautious, arrogant idiot I was."

Summer nodded.

He laughed and then was serious again. "Do you think you can learn to trust me with yourself, Summer? I know I'm terrible at this so far, but I really do know how to take care of beautiful, precious things. And I love you. I really, truly love you, however bad I am at it, just the way you are."

She could feel herself growing more and more luminous with every word he said. But she repeated firmly, "I'm not a thing. Not for anybody. I think I had to learn that, too."

His fingers, which had started to pick up strands of her hair and weave them again, paused. "Does that mean I don't get to play with you anymore?"

She blushed. "I'm not talking about that at all. Hush."

He laughed a little, low and pleased. She could feel him growing a little aroused against her again, but he didn't seem in any hurry to do anything about it.

She sat up enough to look down at him. "And to answer your question—if you can trust me, I can trust you. If not, it all falls apart."

He looked so perfect lying in that hammock in the moonlight. Exactly as she had imagined him there. Even to the stars in his eyes as he looked up at her. "If what you need to trust is that I will love you, and take care of you, and try not to hurt you, and try to give you what you need, forever, then . . . it would be my very great honor, Summer. But I'm going to need a lot of help."

"I hope so," she said. "Since I'm not planning on being just the object in a couple ever again."

He smiled, his hands stroking gently over her lower back. "All that softness, all that gentleness, all that flippant, beautiful sunshine. I'll need you to give it to me. Just pour it out over me and trust me with it, Summer. I'm worth it. I promise."

"Luc. Of course you are worth it."

His face lit in one of those rare moments when you could see all that brilliance inside him. "See? That's what I need."

She felt . . . soft and light, and utterly beautiful for it, when he talked like that. As if soft and light was an okay way to be. Maybe even an extraordinary way to be.

"I love you," she said solemnly. "I know I've said it too many times before, to other men. I'm sorry. I've always been trying to find someone I can love."

"I know." He kissed her palms, cradling them to her mouth. "I think I've figured that out about you. Don't apologize for yourself to me, Summer. Just—stop. Stop with me. Don't look anymore."

"I did stop. For three years. When I first threw myself at you and you *looked* at me the way you did, I thought I was right back where I left off, when I ran away to the islands. But I think maybe I grew just as much as I thought I had while I was here. That maybe I grew enough to actually go after the right person. As soon as I saw him."

EPILOGUE

Luc paused in the doorway to the garden, resting his shoulder against the jamb, letting the day sigh off him and pleasure fill him. Summer sat on the wooden swing under the arbor, their six-year-old, Océane, in her lap. It must have been one of those moments when the oldest still needed to get her share of mommy lap time, too. Their three-year-old, Lucienne—Lucie—was busy chasing the kitten the girls had begged to adopt a couple of weeks ago, when it showed up mewling on their doorstep. Scents of lavender, rosemary, and thyme were released into the air, as Lucie pursued the kitten through the bank of herbs against the wall, which she wasn't supposed to do, but she was three and the herbs were sturdy, and no one reprimanded her. At first charmed by the kitten's antics, Luc and Summer had soon found themselves taken aback by how much trouble one small kitten could get into, never having had pets growing up themselves. But he supposed they were figuring it out. Océane had promised to take on the responsibility of feeding the kitten and cleaning her litter, and so far was being extremely good about it, barely needing reminding. Luc nurtured the parental hope that giving their children certain chores would somehow keep them from being the most spoiled kids in the world, but he knew—God, how well he and Summer knew—that their kids were truly spoiled, right down deep to the heart spoiled, with that complete, trusting belief that they were utterly, entirely loved.

He was kind of getting spoiled that way, too, though.

Summer was gazing up through the grape leaves at the sky with that expression on her face that meant she had been cuddling Océane for a while now, that dreamy maternal pleasure of a mind half on other things even while her whole heart sank into the pleasure of a small body curled into hers. He loved his own moments like that.

Both girls were black-haired and dark-eyed, with Summer's delicate features, and he knew people accused fathers of being biased, but good God, they were *gorgeous.* Utterly, adorably beautiful. It wrenched his heart out every time he thought about them growing up, going out into the world. Since the French system required school atten dance from age three, Océane was in school already, of course, and Lucie had to start this fall, something he and Summer both had a lot of trouble with. He didn't want to let them leave yet, not even as far as stepping into a classroom. He would still like at least one more, because even though it was not humanly possible to love his little girls more than he did, a part of him longed to give a little black-haired boy all this happiness, too.

Océane spotted him and her face lit. *"Papa!"* She spilled off Summer's lap and ran across to him, and he caught her up and hugged her, fighting as he always did not to hug *too* hard, not to just crush her to him and keep her forever. *Oh, baby, baby, Daddy's going to have a hard time letting you go.*

Hands tugged at his jeans, and he looked down to find Lucie demanding her share. He shifted Océane to one arm so he could pick Lucie up with the other, and the damn kitten jumped at his ankles at the wrong moment, so that he sat down with an *umph* on the grass, both girls tumbling into his lap.

He laughed out loud, something his little girls had taught him that even Summer hadn't been able to do all by herself. She loved it, though. He could always tell by her smile. That real, brilliant, happy smile.

A familiar hand touched his shoulder, and he tilted his head back to catch that smile now, and they were both smiling when she bent her head and kissed him.

Seven years, and that sense of love and security and trust was still something that grew in them, still had to grow a little bit more every day. He liked it, nurturing its slow but steady growth. If it had started out as a small seed, it seemed well on its way to being a very healthy baobab tree one day, and he was happy to nourish it and let it be nourished any way he could.

He had had it easier than Summer, in that growth of belief in them. Not at first. The first year after Océane's birth had been exhausting beyond anything either of them had been prepared for, and he had gone around with a knot in his stomach he could never admit existed, because he *knew* Summer wouldn't run out on him and their child, he *knew* it, he told himself that a million times, but he just couldn't get that knot to loosen. Some of the things he caught himself doing that year were so insane, like pouring himself more and more into proving he could feed them and care for them, feed them better than any man in the world, that Summer didn't have to run away to a better life like his mother did. It was a particularly illogical drive, given that Summer's level of wealth and privilege made the comparison with his own mother's choices ridiculous, but for a while there, he couldn't stop himself.

Océane had never seemed to sleep more than fifteen minutes straight, something that in retrospect might have been connected to the fact that neither of her parents could let her cry for more than two seconds. And Summer's hormones had swung all over the place postpartum.

The doctors had made her supplement Océane's feedings almost right away, claiming she wasn't producing enough milk, and Luc knew better than to mention this out loud, but he still sometimes wondered if it hadn't been her body shutting down in some way in reaction to the intense stress Summer put on herself to be the perfect mother. Or maybe the doctors had been wrong and they should have persevered with the nursing, who knew, but Océane had cried from hunger, and that had been about all either of them could handle before they obeyed the doctors' orders. Luc could not allow his own daughter to go hungry for anything in the world.

Luc had *loved* stretching out on a couch with his little baby nestled against his chest while he fed her a bottle. It had filled him with so much joy that his old iron carapace had shattered forever, and even today he could only occasionally catch a ghost of that iron shield back, when he needed to deal with some problem in the external world. In his happiness, it had taken him a long time to realize that while he was feeding their baby, Summer was crumpled on the edge of the bathtub behind a locked door, silent tears of grief and failure streaming down her cheeks.

Nobody could beat herself up quite as well as Summer did. Especially if her parents had been recently visiting, as they had briefly after Océane's birth. Some vulnerabilities lasted forever, he supposed; he was usually a bit of a mess just after his own father showed up, too.

So he had bought them a wider couch and gotten Summer to stretch out with them, and that had seemed to help everybody, her seeing how happy they were, how happy he was, because he was very happy. He was incredibly happy, while his baby and his wife fell asleep against him, Summer's arm stretched across his chest to curl over him and Océane both.

Lucie had been so much easier, not because she herself

was an easier child—she had quite a temper, to tell the truth, and came up with crazy things to do that had never crossed Océane's mind and so her parents weren't expecting—but because Luc and Summer had relaxed more by then. And that made *everything* easier. Lucie actually slept, for God's sake.

He knew, though, that, despite the relaxation in each other and in their family, despite the growth of that seed that should someday be a great, old baobab tree, that Summer still had to reaffirm to herself sometimes that she was valuable and valued. Sometimes he saw her do it—take a breath, pull into herself, assert a smile.

Whereas he—there had just been this moment. Océane was about two years old and curled up on Summer's chest, asleep with her thumb in her mouth and Summer half-asleep. He had been watching them, a little amused, mostly just relaxed and happy, wondering which one of them was most likely to wake up on him if he tried to carry them each to their beds. And Summer's lashes had lifted, and their eyes had met, and she had smiled at him. It wasn't that the look was any different from a million other moments when their eyes had met and she had smiled. But all of a sudden it hit him so hard that he believed it: *She's happy. She's so incredibly happy. She's as happy as I am. She's never going to leave us. Never. She's mine forever. She's Océane's forever. She loves us.*

And that fear, that knot, that thing low in his belly . . . it was gone.

And that tree just grew and grew. Sometimes he thought of himself as the tree, the strength, and of Summer as the sunshine and water that poured herself out and made it so strong, but sometimes he thought he probably should come up with another analogy.

Still, he liked the way that growing tree sheltered people, too, the foster kids Jaime and his own foster father

Bernard sent them when they were old enough to apprentice. Those kids—when they fully grasped what their new chef's wife was like, it was as if they had died and gone to heaven, and Luc still sometimes looked at them with incredulous jealousy when Summer was wrapping them up in bandages for tiny wounds and in warmth for everything. A lot of them were severely illiterate, and she sat them down and taught them and gave them *stickers.* And pretty pencils. And even store-bought lollipops occasionally, until Luc broke down and started making her those teddy bear marshmallow ones to use instead, while they argued back and forth about whether sweets should be used as rewards. *They're not rewards,* Summer insisted. *They're just . . . because.* And then she kissed him. *Thank you for making them, chéri.*

So . . . he made them. And she gave them out with abandon.

His new restaurant still only had two stars, which he figured it had gotten almost automatically on his name alone. He meant for it to get a third star eventually—he really did—but he just had so many other priorities right now. He went home evenings, for one, or at least most of them. And he let those foster kids get schooling and playtime, and didn't make them practice something ten thousand times, and that meant sometimes a dish reached the tables that was just a hair off perfect.

Weirdly, this had made him immensely popular, and he had found himself centered in some kind of "back to what matters" cooking movement, some strange confluence of fair trade and locavore and who knew what else. It helped that the *chef cuisinier* who had joined him to build the restaurant here had a kind of rough-and-ready deliciousness to his style and liked to go out into fields of apple trees or vines after the harvest had passed and physically glean the food that would go on the tables himself.

It was all very strange and very different from the first thirty years of his life, but God . . . it was good.

It was so very, very good.

"I love you," he mouthed to Summer, as he hugged their kids and the evening sun angled across her hair and made it glow nearly as much as her smile turned down at him.

"I know," she said, resting a hand in his hair and stroking his head. "I think I'm beginning to figure that out."

Acknowledgments

With all my thanks to Laurent Jeannin, chef pâtissier of Epicure, the Michelin three-star restaurant of five-star hotel Le Bristol in Paris, for his infinite generosity, enthusiasm, and patience, in welcoming me behind the scenes in a Michelin three-star restaurant's pastry kitchen. There are only eighty Michelin three-star restaurants in the world, and to be the *chef cuisinier* or the *chef pâtissier* of one is a coveted title, but as if that is not enough, Laurent Jeannin also won the "Pastry Chef of the Year" award in 2011.

My thanks also to Leah Marshall, director of Le Bristol, the Parisian palace hotel that was named in 2008 "best hotel in the world," and to Kevin Chambenoit, *directeur de la restauration,* for permitting and orchestrating the visit, as well—of course!—as to my Paris-loving agent Kimberley Cameron for creating the opportunity.

For some behind-the-scenes glimpses of Laurent Jeannin's amazing work, please visit my website at www.laura florand.com.

WORTH ANOTHER TRIP
TO PARIS

(No, Paris is not paying me a commission. But I'll look into that.)

Of course, *The Chocolate Heart* is all about those rarest of rare jewels, the three-star Michelin restaurants and luxury hotels. Of those, I must particularly note:

Le Bristol, 12 Rue du Faubourg Saint-Honoré75008 Paris. www.lebristol.com

Le Bristol is that rarest of jewels: a Paris "palace" hotel with a Michelin three-star restaurant. And afternoon tea in its Jardin Français—or, in my case, afternoon *chocolat chaud*—is a luxurious, elegant experience. Indulge yourself, even if only once, in this very special treat of supremely fresh *macarons* or a perfection of other pastries as well as an incomparable *chocolat chaud* made by Pastry Chef of the Year (2011) Laurent Jeannin and his incredible team. Most of the research for *The Chocolate Heart* was done behind the scenes here.

Two other palace hotels with Michelin three-star restaurants from which I drew inspiration (from the décor and the chefs) are Le Plaza-Athénée, www. plaza-athenee-paris.com, and the legendary Hôtel de Crillon, www.crillon.com.

But while three-star restaurants and luxury palace hotels might require six-month reservations (not to mention a luxurious

*budget), Paris is full of places that will allow you your own mo-
ment of elegance as you let yourself be tempted by pastries and
chocolates and that magical wonderful gift of Paris called a macaron.*

Jacques Genin, 133, rue de Turenne 75003, jacquesgenin.fr

Personally rated by me as one of the top ten gourmet
experiences in Paris: sitting in this exquisite *salon de chocolat,* drinking *chocolat chaud,* while outside, winter sets in.
Jacques Genin is considered by many to be one of the best
chocolatiers in Paris. The rosebud wall and exposed stone
of Dominique Richard's salon in *The Chocolate Touch* were
inspired by this beautiful spot. It's just off the Place de la
République, so enjoy it before or after your stroll up the
Canal St. Martin, pretending to be Dom and Jaime.

Ladurée, 16, rue Royale—75008 Paris, www.laduree.fr

In *The Chocolate Kiss,* a little bit of Philippe's fifth-
generation *pâtissier* pride, the way he is emblematic of
Paris, and the ornate, fairytale quality of his *salons,* are inspired by Ladurée. Ladurée invented the *macaron* and was
famous for them long before they became the popular delicacy they are today, and sitting in the nineteenth-century
salon of the original store on Rue Royale drinking
Ladurée's rich, dark *chocolat chaud* or savoring any of their
elaborate and exquisite desserts is an experience in itself.
Don't just stand in line to grab a macaron and go—really,
it's worth taking a seat under that painted ceiling. Imagine
yourself an aristocrat from another time . . . Ladurée has
several locations these days in Paris, but if you can, the
original Rue Royale salon is by far the most romantic.

Patrick Roger, 3 place de la Madeleine,www.patrickroger.com

Showman chocolatier Patrick Roger has multiple boutiques now, but his latest high-concept store right near Ladurée is not to be missed for his giant chocolate sculptures in the window. Patrick Roger's chocolate sculpting ability was a little bit of the inspiration for Dominique Richard's sculpting in *The Chocolate Touch*.

Pierre Hermé. *Multiple Paris locations,*www.pierreherme.fr

A true King of Macarons, internationally known. His *Ispahan* was the inspiration for Philippe's rose-heart gift to Magalie in *The Chocolate Kiss* and has, additionally, inspired imitations and variations in pastry shops all over the world. You deserve to try it at least once. Alas, you can't sit down in his boutiques, so plan to wander with your treats to the banks of the Seine or the steps of Saint-Sulpice, depending on your location.

Un Dimanche à Paris, 4-6-8 Cour du Commerce Saint André, 75006 Paris, www.un-dimanche-a-paris.com

This is a concept restaurant/*salon de thé/boutique,* and the concept is chocolate. This is, quite simply, an extremely fun place to be for anyone who likes chocolate or anything else that's delicious. The *chocolat chaud* is, of course, superb, as are most of the pastries, including, of course, their macarons.

And You?

I love to discover new places to indulge. Come share your favorite places for moments of elegance, great *macarons,* luscious *chocolat chaud,* and top-quality artisan chocolate, both in Paris and around the world, on my site: www.lauraflorand.com. Chocolate, I have discovered, knows no frontiers, and chocolate lovers travel everywhere. Or we will, if we're tempted enough.